"I'M NOT TO BE DEPENDED ON," NORA WARNED HIM. "NOT FOR LONG. YOU KNOW WHAT I'M LIKE."

"Yes." He bent his head and rubbed his cheek along her thigh, then looked at the smooth flesh, studying it.

"It would be impossible. You know that."

"Yes." He took her in his arms and drew her to him, kissing her throat, his hand going to the small of her back. Her arms wound around him.

There was nothing hurried or brutal this time. They had worshiped at this shrine before and knew the sweetness of it beforehand, his strength mastering her, and her hunger overpowering him. And lying afterward together, laden with satiety, her breath cool against his neck, and his hands memorizing her. She was his sister, his love, the woman who belonged to him—forever.

Novels by Marvin H. Albert

THE GARGOYLE CONSPIRACY
THE DARK GODDESS
HIDDEN LIVES

HIDDEN LIVES

Marvin H. Albert

A DELL BOOK

Published by
Dell Publishing Co., Inc.
1 Dag Hammarskjold Plaza
New York, New York 10017

For information address
Delacorte Press, New York, New York.

Dell ® TM 681510, Dell Publishing Co., Inc.

ISBN: 0-440-13500-1

Reprinted by arrangement with Delacorte Press

Printed in the United States of America

First Dell printing—May 1982

for Xenia Klar

PROLOGUE

They were known as three men. Each of their lives begins in obscurity and terminates in mystery. What links them is even stranger: they were the same man. Three disconnected parts of one disordered, stubborn and unquenchable life.

Most of those who at first doubted this truth are finally accepting it. The time has come for me to reveal the full story, including those parts that are still painful for me.

About the identity of the first man there was never any doubt. He was the young American artist, Nicholas Grayle, who vanished in 1928, leaving behind thirteen full-scale paintings which came to be considered among the best work of the period. It was common belief that he must have died a short time later, or he would have been found. This was not questioned until almost two decades later, when a great number of previously unknown paintings were discovered, bearing Grayle's signature.

The second was a Foreign Legionnaire of unknown origin, calling himself Ishmael Moser, who deserted the Legion to join a Berber rebellion the French forces were trying to crush.

The third man, a scarred, solitary figure who appeared in the south of France in the year before World War II, carried credentials naming him as Jean Hugonnet, a retired French businessman from North Africa.

The task of unraveling the thread that led from Jean Hugonnet back to Ishmael Moser, and finally to Nicholas Grayle, fell to me because I was the only one left who was aware of it. I had known him better than anyone else still living. Certainly I had known him longer; from his first life to his third.

The emergence of these new works of his, and the shock waves they have caused in the art world, prove one thing I always felt about him. He was a lucky man; and even the gods, it has been said, have little power against a man with luck. But of my other feelings about the man himself, I am less certain. Did I love or hate him? Envy him? Perhaps even fear him? I still cannot be sure.

He never looked like anybody's conception of an artist. There is that description of him in the late twenties, by the woman whose Paris gallery had handled the early Grayles: "The hands of a blacksmith, the build of a stevedore, the head of a moody peasant, and the mind of an inspired savage." But there was much more to him than that: even to what he looked like.

There are two photographs of him now on my desk.

The first is from a slim book published recently, called *Nora Cesari: Photo-Journalism's Forgotten Artist*. It is a picture she took during a visit to the village of Eze with Nicholas Grayle. There he is, as I remember him from those early years: that tall, hard, lean figure; those heavy, sloping shoulders and wide-boned, almost ugly face; the big hands and powerful nose; the direct, probing gaze; that sensual and stubborn mouth.

In Nora's picture he is wearing a white shirt and trousers, and a carelessly cocked straw hat. He stands against an old, dark stone wall that contrasts sharply with his youth, yet reasserts the solid strength of his figure. Nora caught that precarious mixture of relentless drives in his face. It is a face that had already explored and tasted life, and found it terrible, awe-inspiring and delicious.

He is laughing, and the laughter at first seems directed into the lens of her camera—at us. But it is directed higher: at Nora Cesari. Laughter at pleasure remembered, pleasure anticipated. A healthy, joyous picture.

The other photograph of him on my desk is on the front page of a French newspaper published in 1928. It shows Grayle being taken from the courthouse to a police van after the verdict had been pronounced in his trial for murder. His wrists are manacled, and he is flanked by uniformed police.

Again, he is looking toward the photographer. An unbending stare; the expression thoughtful, a bit curious. He seems to be studying a wall that needs to be broken through.

There is another photograph on that front page, beside his: of Nora Cesari, her features contorted with rage. She is the one who looks like a killer.

Part 1:
NICHOLAS GRAYLE

"We judge an artist by his
highest moments, a criminal
by his lowest."
                    —Shaw

"The Saviour himself says: He
that is far from me is far
from the kingdom; He that is near
me is near the fire."
                    —Origen

1

She was making her way down the porous, sharp-edged rocks of a cut in the sea cliffs, between Morgat and Cape Chèvre, when she saw him for the first time. That was in the summer of 1926.

One of the fogs which frequented the broken coastline of Brittany had pulled the ocean horizon in close to land that day: a heavily moving wall of whiteness that obliterated water and sky beyond. On either side of her the cliffs reaching into the Atlantic were battered by waves surging out of this whiteness. But within the narrow inlet there was a short curve of sheltered beach. It was there he was standing, below her on this beach: his legs planted apart as though prepared to absorb some unexpected movement under them, hands locked behind him. He was watching the ocean and fog.

She hesitated, looking down at his solitary figure. This tucked-away spot was usually deserted. Finally, she resumed making her way down. When she reached the bottom, not far from him, she removed her shoes and stockings, her bare feet sinking into the cold mixture of sand and mud as she started toward the other side of the beach. She glimpsed his profile in passing, and what she saw there was unexpected: a brooding concentration of brutal force, yet so precisely controlled that the dominant quality was one of unusual quietness. The impression stayed with her as she moved on, her footsteps soundless under the noise of the surf.

Grayle turned his head to glance after her. Then he looked back at the ocean reaching out into the fog. It was two years since he had arrived in Europe, almost a year that he had lived in Paris. Twenty-five years since his mother had left him with her sister, when he was three, and sailed away to France. And come here, somewhere close to this spot where he stood now, to drown herself.

This was, he thought as he stood there against the strengthening wind, a perfect spot for the bitch to do it. A haunted, unnatural place. It was not the sea and fog. Grayle had spent too much time on merchant ships to regard these dangers as unnatural. But this place was a gatherer of unrealities; and had been, long before his mother had added hers to it.

Behind him was a land where great stone megaliths, set in their positions by the Celts three thousand years earlier, remained, still summoning the forces of their earth spirits. Where Merlin was supposed even now to continue his magical captivity under the enchantment of Viviane, snared in the spells he had taught her.

And out there where Grayle was looking, hidden within the fog, lay the barren island of Sein, to which the Druids of the mainland had rowed across the Bay of the Dead to bury the bodies of their priests. And the mythic, walled city of Ys, engulfed forever beneath the waves when the Devil, disguised as a handsome youth, seduced the king's daughter into unlocking the sea gates.

All those legends—and the woman who had given him birth swimming out to join them.

Grayle turned his head and looked again toward the girl at the other end of the beach. She was crouched there, curiously examining a broken shell she'd picked out of the wet sand. He smiled suddenly. A hard, broad smile that bared his teeth. *There* was the kind of woman who meant something: a woman with the tangy ferment of purpose and desire.

The dead woman was—dead.

For a moment his mind slipped away and he was back in his room on Rue Mouffetard, looking at all the sketches he'd tacked to the walls for the painting waiting to be born; sketches he kept shifting around in an effort to find out what the painting was going to be about.

It was then that he laughed, and felt the laughter, and

knew he was going to be just fine. There was nothing for him here. Finding that out was worth the trip he had made.

He climbed between the scarred cliffs and began his return hike along the path at the top. It ran through wind-scoured rocks and harsh, gnarled bushes. This stretch of Breton coast was one he didn't like. A shipwrecker coast. He walked steadily, his stride eating the miles before he came to the solitary house he'd passed on his way out.

It was protected by gnarled pines from the sea winds, and surrounded by a wall made of the same rough stone as the house. Grayle stopped and looked at it again. He didn't know what he had to say to the man who lived inside it; what he cared to hear from him. But curiosity initiated by the two paintings he'd chanced to see on Rue de Seine had caused him to come out here in the first place; and that curiosity was still in him.

There was a low wooden door set in the wall, its dark red paint weathered by the salt air. The top of it was on a level with his chest, and he could see inside. One end of the low house was set against the wall, and at the other end an additional room had been attached at a right angle, forming a semienclosed terrace with a small garden dominated by a stunted oak. The old man sat in a wicker chair before a round iron table beside this oak, his gaze fixed on a spreading vine growing up the inner wall. He was wrapped in a coat too large for him, and wore a wool cap and thick, knitted scarf.

Grayle rang a small bronze bell beside the red door. The old man turned his head and looked in Grayle's direction, but did not get up. After a moment a slim, gray-haired woman emerged from the house and came briskly toward Grayle. She was small and somewhere in her fifties, with lively green eyes in a prematurely wrinkled face. Opening the door, she held it with one hand as she looked at him.

"Good day?" Her voice was deep and perky, her smile full of charm, but her gaze assessed him candidly, noting the worn condition of his clothes.

Grayle was disconcerted to find himself taking an instant liking to her. A woman who had aged without losing her firm hold on youth. "Is this the house of Claude Cesari?" He pronounced the words carefully; he'd gained a wide French vocabulary with surprising ease, but his grammar was still haphazard and he knew his accent to be rough.

"Yes, I am Madame Cesari," she told him, and dropped her hold on the opened door. "You have come about buying the house?" She'd caught his accent; Americans could dress atrociously and still have money.

"No, I saw two of Cesari's old paintings in Paris and was interested. The gallery owner told me he had more here."

"Ah, I understand." Cesari's wife had an accent of her own: Scandinavian, Grayle decided. "You are interested in buying some of Claude's pictures?"

"I'd like to look at them," Grayle hedged.

"Of course, come inside." She led the way across the garden terrace to the old man. "Claude, here is an American who has come all the way out here to see about buying some of your pictures." Her voice was louder and deliberately distinct.

The man in the wicker chair looked up at Grayle and managed an unsure smile. He appeared to be in his eighties, a large man whose flesh had wasted from his frame. The heavy bones of the hands lying on the iron table stood out sharply in the loosened skin. His cheeks had sunk in deeply, the mouth was collapsed, the eyes vague in their focus. Grayle could detect no resemblance in the features, but he hadn't expected any; he knew he took after his mother's family.

Claude Cesari said, "Good day," in a trembly voice, and continued to look at Grayle with that uncertain stare.

It required an effort for Grayle to conceal the sharp sense of shock. All he'd really wanted here, he'd told himself before coming, was to see what the man looked like, to know he really existed. He'd imagined him for so long, in so many ways. But never like this.

"Please," Claude Cesari's wife said to Grayle, "come in." He followed her into a large room that served as kitchen, dining and living quarters. There was a large framed painting on one wall: a self-portrait of Claude Cesari when he was perhaps thirty. A sensitive, handsome face, quietly sure of itself. Dark wavy hair and dark brooding eyes. A firm, sensual mouth. Behind him was a stormy sea, and the rocks of this coast, rising in tormented shapes into a dark-clouded sky.

"He was so beautiful," Madame Cesari said, looking at the portrait with him. Her voice was proud, and wistful. She made a soft sound like a sigh, gazing at the painting. "He is not what he was, you know. Inside his head, I mean. Sometimes it frightens me; he has become so dependent. He was so much older than me, and he spoiled me too long; made a child of me. It is hard, having to decide everything now, to tell him what to do." She turned from the portrait. "Would you like a coffee? Or I could make some tea?"

"No, thank you." Grayle found himself fighting something akin to claustrophobia. "I'm sorry, but I don't have much time."

"Of course . . ." She led the way toward the added room which formed a right angle to the main house. "This is his studio," she said as they entered it.

The room was large, with a single big window letting in a lot of light. Claude Cesari's paintings were all around it, some framed and hung, others on the floor leaning against the walls. On a large oval straw rug an armchair faced an easel holding a stretched canvas.

"He still works?" Grayle asked.

"Oh, yes. Almost every day. Sometimes for an hour. When he paints, his hand is what it was. So strange—that, he does not forget." She motioned at the walls, the paintings: "Please . . ."

Grayle strolled around the studio slowly, studying the works of Claude Cesari. Some were impressionist landscapes. More were like the two he'd seen in Paris: strongly symbolic in subject matter.

Grayle found himself angrily envying the sureness of Cesari's workmanship: the drawing was exquisite, the brushwork superb, and the use of color bold; the handling of space masterly.

One painting caught his attention and he stopped before it. The tall, lithe figure of a woman in a Byzantine robe, her stance regal, her expression imperious, pointing a commanding finger at a man groveling before her, his face raised in adoration, fear and awe.

He knew immediately who the woman was; a face recognized from Irene's family album.

Had she really been that arrogant? Or was it only what Claude Cesari had wished her to be?

Grayle turned his head slightly at the sound of Cesari coming into the studio, his tread slow and heavy. The old man halted just inside the doorway, looking at Grayle and the picture he stood before. After a moment he asked: "What is your name?" His voice still trembled, but he knew what he was asking.

"Nicholas Grayle."

Cesari nodded, thinking about it. He looked at the picture, and then back to Grayle. "Are you Nina's boy?"

"Yes."

The old man nodded again, gazing at Grayle's face. After a time he said, "I was a very good painter . . ." He intended to say more, but Grayle watched the words get lost inside him. Finally, Cesari walked to the armchair and sat down, facing the canvas. He picked up a brush and held it, his attention focusing on the painting he had begun.

Grayle knew he had been utterly forgotten.

The shock he'd experienced on finding the man like this gave way to a helpless fury he had known, all too well, since childhood. He'd been prepared to confront him, at last; but it was too late. The man was safe in his own silences, his mind's retreat. Grayle could not identify what was left as the enemy he'd known so long.

His anger threatened to break through his habitual control. He was relieved when Cesari's wife motioned him to follow as she went out of the room. She didn't stop leading the way until they were outside on the terrace. Then she turned and faced him.

"You should not have lied to me about wanting to buy his pictures." There was no genuine anger; she might have been chiding a child who needed a lesson in basic manners.

"That was unkind. And unnecessary. I would have let you in if you had told me the truth."

"I told you I wanted to see his work. That was true."

"But you let me *think* you were a collector coming to buy. That was false. The same as a lie, you understand?" She sighed, studying his face. "You look very much like her. It brings everything back . . ." Her sudden smile was rueful. "But, my God, that was long ago . . ."

"I'll go now," Grayle said tightly.

"Yes." She opened the red door for him. "You could come back, you know. Later, sometime. I would be interested to talk with you, if you wish. But right now I am still too annoyed. I am sorry . . ."

Outside the walls, Grayle took a deep breath to steady himself, and headed for the village. There was a bus to catch, if he was to reach the train back this evening. The trip from Paris had cost him time he should have been working, and money he needed for his rent and paints. Both had to be made up for.

He was quite sure he would never return to Claude Cesari's house. Not to look at him again, nor to listen to what his wife had to say. He'd thought to lay a ghost; he'd been defeated by one. His pace quickened as he walked away.

Nora, returning from the beach, saw him striding from the house and frowned, wondering. When she reached the red door she paused with her hand on it and looked after him again, just before he vanished in the direction of the village.

It was to be almost three months before she saw him again. And by then, Victor Royan had met him.

2

It was, like Nora Cesari's, a chance meeting. Victor Royan's came while he was prowling the dark belly of Paris in search of trouble, three hours after midnight, in one of the ancient, crooked streets crowded between the massive iron hulks of the covered food-markets in Les Halles.

The central markets were boiling with noisy activity at that hour. Trucks and horse-drawn wagons were jammed to a standstill in every access route, horses drooping wearily in their traces. Under the strings of electric lamps inside the markets, throngs were milling between pavilions bulging with all that was needed to feed a daily hunger of monstrous proportions: endless rows of slaughtered animals hanging from hooks, mountains of wine barrels, crated oysters and sacks of mussels, prairies of vegetables and fruit, acres of butter, eggs and cheeses, tubs of blood, hills of fish, plucked chickens and dead rabbits.

A carnival of gluttony which in turn fed Victor Royan's savage misanthropy. As did what he found outside, between the markets: the beggars, vagrants and other rock-bottom poor scrounging for scraps of food; the prostitutes servicing Les Halles doing their peak business; the thieves and hoodlums eyeing slumming tourists from dim doorways.

The arcade of the Street of Innocents was the logical center of this night carnival. It had been the charnel house of the ancient cemetery upon which the markets had been erected, after the remains of over one million corpses had been removed. Passing a small group of men in the deep shadows of the arcade, Victor was conscious of their heads turning, watching him, assessing his clothing and manner.

He smiled, and swung his silver-handled ebony cane with a tightening grip. Ready to be attacked; perhaps desiring it.

He strolled, lazily alert, into Rue de la Ferronerie. It was lined with pushcarts whose vendors were inside the halls buying the wares they would hawk through their neighborhoods at daylight. There was a workers' bistro across the narrow street. On impulse, Victor threaded between the pushcarts and entered it.

The place was full: butchers, teamsters, clerks and saleswomen from the markets; farmers, hucksters, pimps, porters. Victor elbowed a spot for himself at the bar and ordered a brandy. Downing it with a single swallow, he ordered a repeat. This one he drank slowly.

Grayle, seated on a stool in a corner, at one end of a long common table, studied the way Victor stood there: a tall, gaunt man of about forty, wearing an elegant cape with a velvet collar, his stance arrogant, his cane held like a swagger stick. A lean, aristocratic face ravaged by dissipation; the eyes bitter and the mouth a twist of despair.

Victor Royan paid for his two drinks from a thick wad of bills. As he stuffed the wad back in his pocket a bulky-shouldered man in a flashy suit moved in on him with a knowing smile: "This is no place for a man with money, my friend. If you're looking for something special, I could show you where."

Victor grinned at him, his spirits lifting. "Could you really?"

The man moved closer, his voice lowering: "Girls—real beauties, thirteen-fourteen years old. Or if you like little boys . . ."

"I wouldn't go to Paradise with you," Victor cut in. "You're too ugly, too stupid, and your breath stinks. Also your body. Don't you ever wash?"

The man stared at him, taking seconds to absorb it. His face darkened, and his left hand closed into a fist. The right hand reached into his back pocket.

Victor continued to smile at him, waiting. Something in the smile bothered the man. After a long hesitation, his right hand came away from the pocket, empty. He turned with a soft curse and shoved through the crowd, out of the bistro. Victor put his back to the bar and leaned against it, losing his smile, staring at nothing.

Grayle pushed aside his empty wine glass, turned to a fresh page in his small sketchbook and began to draw. His large hand moved swiftly, with delicate sureness, no motion wasted; each line final, each shading precise. When he had the full figure completed he began a separate impression of the face, beside it. Victor remained where he was, not moving, seeming lost in a private world. But when Grayle finished and turned the page, he left the bar and came over.

"May I see it?"

Grayle rested his shoulders against the wall behind him and briefly searched Victor Royan's expression. Then he turned back to the page he'd just used, and reversed the book on the scarred table. Victor pulled over an empty stool and sat down, studying the face and figure Grayle had drawn.

"Not very flattering . . ." After some seconds he added quietly: "It's excellent work." He looked at Grayle, faintly puzzled, taking in the faded blue porter's cap and overalls, stained with blood and wine no washing could remove entirely. "You're a Strong One?"

Les Forts—the Strong Ones—was a nickname the porters of Les Halles were proud of, for they earned it. Before being accepted into the tight guild, each passed a test that included carrying 450 pounds of pig iron in a basket for 250 meters. They were the ones who could handle casks of wine and whole sides of beef single-handedly.

Grayle shook his head. "The Corporation won't take foreigners. I'm just a *coup de main*. An extra the *Forts* can hire from their own wages, when they need helpers on a job."

"Ah—you're American." Victor looked down at Grayle's impression of him. "And viciously observant. A Goya grotesque. I'll buy it. How much?"

"It's not for sale."

"Why not?"

"I need it."

"For what?"

"I don't know yet."

Victor looked at him again, thoughtful. Then he gestured at the empty wine glass. "Another?"

"If you're buying. Red."

Victor called to the barman for a glass of red wine and another brandy. "And a dozen raw oysters," he added. To Grayle: "We can share, half and half. If you're hungry."

"I'm hungry," Grayle said flatly.

Victor touched the sketchbook. "May I look at the rest?"

"Yes."

Victor began to leaf back through the pages, pausing to study each sketch—an old woman's face, a broken chair, a shuttered window, a Percheron pulling a milk cart. The drinks came, and the plate of opened oysters. Grayle took an oyster and gulped it, picked up another.

Victor remained absorbed in the sketches, turning the pages, taking his time with each. "You have a magic hand."

Grayle shrugged. "That's the tool."

"Of course. Everything depends on what you do with it." Victor reached the last sketch: a vagrant slumped in a doorway, his face raised in drunken anger. "Do you know what *any* of these studies are for?"

"Not yet." Grayle finished the last of his six oysters. He washed it down with a swallow of wine.

"I know a book publisher I can introduce you to. He pays not too badly for illustrations, I believe."

"It's not for me," Grayle told him. "I use my body to earn money. The rest of me is for my own purpose and pleasure."

"Like a whore." Victor Royan's smile was sardonic. "The cunt for sale but not the kisses."

Grayle said judiciously: "That's not a bad comparison."

The bistro owner, a scrawny man wearing a black derby and leather apron, came from around the bar to them. "Yank, I'm running out of the white. Bring me up a barrel, will you."

Grayle took his sketchbook as he stood up. He wrapped it in a cloth that had been waterproofed with paraffin, and stuck it deep in a pocket of his overalls as he headed into a back room. Beside the toilet was a closed door marked Private. He opened it and descended a steep flight of newly constructed wooden steps, bending his head under a crumbly stone arch.

The cellar below had been a burial vault, seven centuries ago. Four men sat in it around a table, playing cards by the light of a kerosene lamp. Each was an organizer of one small aspect of the quarter's underworld enterprises. Grayle opened a trapdoor in the floor behind the player who got a percentage on every lemon that moved through the markets. The steps into the wine cellar were stone, deeply worn. There were further subcellars below this; every time the owner of the bistro needed more space he dug and found them. It was said that if you dug deep enough in these places, you'd find passages connecting most of the cellars in Paris.

Crouching, bowing his head, Grayle got a secure grip on a barrel of white wine, and dragged it off the stack onto his shoulders. Straightening a bit, he turned with the weight balanced carefully and went up the stone stairs one slow step at a time. When he was up with the card players he said through clenched teeth: "Shut the trapdoor." The lemon prince reached out and closed it behind him as Grayle trudged up the wooden steps.

Grayle set the barrel in place on the skids behind the bar and straightened himself all the way, flexing his shoulders. He wiped his palms dry on his overalls, as the patron thanked him and asked what he'd like to eat. Grayle looked toward the end of the long table. Victor Royan was gone. His glass was empty but his half-dozen oysters remained, untouched.

"I've got my meal for tonight," Grayle said.

"Then I owe you. Tomorrow night."

"Or the next." Grayle took a chunk of bread from the counter behind the bar and went back to his stool with it.

He had finished the other six oysters and was eating the last of the bread when one of the porters from Les Halles came in. A short man with an enormous width of body and small hands and feet. He was called the Ox. Tipping his blood-spattered cloth cap to the patron's pretty wife behind her cash drawer, he scanned the men in the room and settled on Grayle: "A couple hours' honest labor, *américain*?"

Grayle finished off his wine and got up. Another man who'd been waiting to earn a little money helping the *Fort*s grumbled loudly, "Why pick a foreigner?" Grayle stopped and looked at him, his face becoming expressionless.

In the sudden quiet of the bar the Ox told the man, "You can fight him for the job, if you wish. Personally, I would not advise it."

In the first weeks that Grayle had come to Les Halles for work he'd had several fights for offered jobs. The way he'd fought had been recounted to others by witnesses. "Not a man to tamper with," they said. "A crazy."

The grumbler stayed where he was, his attention on his drink as Grayle followed the Ox out of the bar.

It was after six in the morning when Grayle finished the last job. His muscles and bones ached. Two hours hauling the skinned bodies of sheep and pigs; one hour of unloading oyster crates. His overalls and gum boots were soaked with the drippings. Pocketing his wages, he headed out of Les Halles toward the Seine.

Housewives and owners of small cafes were already coming on foot in the opposite direction with their big baskets, to buy cheaply from what was left over when the wholesale marketing ended. A small jazz band was still playing for diehard tourists inside the Au Père Tranquille. At a sidewalk table out front two men in tuxedos and two women in dark furs were sleepily drinking and smoking as the streetcleaners moved past along Rue Pierre-Lescot, getting started with their job of hosing and sweeping away the night's market gore and garbage.

Grayle carried his reek of blood and seaweed through the sweet, tangy odor of Rue des Prêcheurs, where colorful displays of cut flowers flowed between grimy banks of seventeenth-century buildings. He reached Boulevard de Sébastopol and trudged between the loaded pushcarts and horse-drawn huckster wagons carrying their day's wares from the central markets.

Victor Royan was slumped drunkenly at a sidewalk table

of a corner cafe, paying a waiter for a second bottle of champagne. The recipients of his largesse were an elderly pimp known as the President, and three of his young whores, slender leggy flappers wearing the latest permanent waves and short skirts. He didn't appear to notice Grayle walking past into Rue des Lombards.

Less than fifty feet in, Grayle came across Daniel Verdier, sprawled unconscious on the cobbles against the bulging base of an ancient house at the corner of narrow Rue Quincampoix.

He lay on his side, one outflung hand touching the wall, legs awkwardly angled. Grayle squatted down and rolled him over on his back. The lean body was utterly limp. The young, gently handsome face had an ugly pallor. Grayle placed a hand flat on his narrow chest.

A girl of about eleven was scrubbing the stone steps of a house just inside Rue Quincampoix. "He's not dead," she said. "I asked the men who left him there. Just drunk, they said."

Grayle felt the heartbeat slowly under his palm. "What men?"

The girl raised and lowered fragile shoulders. "Hard numbers. Didn't care who saw them. One gave me five sous, just like that. For nothing. Then they went away. Very cool."

She stopped scrubbing, and watched with deep interest as Grayle went through Daniel's pockets. No money. He leaned close and smelled Daniel's breath. Knockout drops. Grayle nodded toward a house that catered to all-night gamblers. "Did they bring him from there?"

The little girl became wary. "I'm not sure."

Grayle was. Daniel lived in the same courtyard as Grayle, and worked as a cook in a restaurant in Les Halles. And had a sporadic, usually disastrous addiction for gambling. His wife, a beautiful acrobat several years his senior, was away with a traveling circus. Daniel had obviously collected his week's pay that night and decided to invest it in a card game. Either he'd gotten too lucky at the wrong person's expense, or had begun to suspect he was being cheated. Whatever the reason for their slipping the drug into his drink, there was nothing to do about it. Except get Daniel home.

Standing up, Grayle walked back to the boulevard. He stationed himself at the curb near the table where Victor Royan was listening vaguely to a story the old pimp was telling him. Scanning the wagons diverging toward various sections of the city, Grayle searched for one of the hucksters from his own neighborhood.

He had been waiting for a short time, without spotting one he knew, when Victor Royan spoke up sharply in excellent English: "Are you having some trouble?" He had risen to his feet, leaning on the fancy cane, his face ashen.

Grayle read the man's expression with a short, penetrating stare. "You're not as drunk as you look."

Victor's smile was mocking. "No, just weary. And bored. It's not easy for me to get drunk when I have these white nights. What were you looking for?"

Briefly, Grayle explained the situation.

Victor considered, and shrugged. "Nothing else of even minor interest has happened so far. Drag out your friend, and I'll find us a cab. Least I can do for a budding Daumier."

Grayle nodded, and went back for Daniel.

3

The taxi Victor had hired came to a stop on Rue Mouffe-tard in front of a bistro named Le Soldat Perdu. The lost soldier referred to was one of the exhausted thousands who had failed to survive Bonaparte's cold and hungry retreat from Moscow; his fallen figure had frozen into the Russian snow.

This was an old neighborhood, and an even older street, having been laid down by the conquering Romans back when Paris was a primitive village named Lutece. The thick wall built to protect Paris in the twelfth century ran through this neighborhood, though little of it remained visible; many buildings were constructed of the stones removed when cross streets were cut through it, and others clung to its disjointed remnants, mounting over and burrowing into them. The quarter now housed the lowest working classes, but Rodin had been born at one end of this street where Grayle lived, and Verlaine had died at the other end. At that time of the morning it was lined with pushcarts and vending stands, and crowded with people buying their day's food.

Madame Bobichon was having her first beer and fifth cigarette of the morning, at a table in front of Le Soldat Perdu, when Grayle and the cab driver climbed out and reached for the limp figure of Daniel in the back seat. Still plumply pretty in her fifties, Madame Bobichon had bought the bistro for her husband and herself with her savings as a young prostitute in Marseilles.

"What happened to the boy?" she asked as Daniel was dragged from the taxi. Grayle told her. She nodded sagely.

"I have something that will help him." She flicked her cigarette into the gutter and went inside as Grayle and the driver carried Daniel through a door in a wide wooden gate next to the bistro.

Victor Royan climbed out wearily, entered the bistro and ordered a strong coffee, laced with brandy.

Through the open rear door he watched Madame Bobichon cross the uneven cobbles of a courtyard, and enter a seedy little hotel. The other side of the courtyard seemed to be the back of some kind of warehouse. At the rear of the courtyard was a bakery, and next to it a two-floor house with a tiny, beautifully tended garden.

Grayle and the cab driver came out of the hotel as Victor finished his coffee. He paid for it and went through the rear door to meet them.

"He'll be all right," Grayle told him. "Madame Bobichon is bringing him around. Thanks for your help."

Victor paid off the driver, adding a liberal tip. "You can pay your thanks," he told Grayle as the driver left, "by letting me have a look at your work. As I said, it was a dull night."

Grayle gave him another of those short, calculating stares. Then he said, "I have to clean up first. The hotel has a bathroom they let me use." He gave Victor a key and gestured at a back door of the warehouse. "You go in and up the stairs to the top." From a jacket pocket he drew a thick chunk of sausage he'd lifted in Les Halles, giving that to him, too. "I'll get bread from the bakery and we can have something to eat before I get down to work."

Victor took out a coin and offered it.

Grayle's eyes went to the coin, then back to Victor's face. "You paid for the cab. I can afford bread." There was no special emphasis in the way he said it, but Victor experienced a rare moment of embarrassment. He put the coin away and turned toward the rear of the warehouse.

As he did, his left leg gave way. He stumbled, and just managed to catch his balance with the aid of the cane.

Grayle eyed him. "It's four flights up. Can you manage that?"

Victor smiled sourly. "The legs aren't that bad. They just refuse to cooperate sometimes, when I get tired." He straightened himself all the way. "A German machine gunner in the Marne tried to shoot them off, and almost succeeded. But not quite. Were you in the war?"

"No, I was exempt. Because I was in the merchant marine. Mostly sugar runs as it turned out, between Baltimore and Matanzas, Cuba."

"You missed something."

"I don't think so."

"Yes, of course, someone like you wouldn't need it. But for someone who has never *had* to do anything, it was an extremely exciting experience."

"Painful way to get your excitement."

"Oh, most of the time it's not that painful. When it is, I just begin wandering all night. Drinking as I go." Victor's slight grimace was self-deprecating. "I become irritable and quarrelsome when the nerves shriek too much, you see. I prefer taking it out on strangers rather than on people I care for."

Grayle read the erosion of self-esteem in the eyes, the set of the mouth. "You could get yourself killed that way," he told Victor soberly.

"Yes?" Victor Royan laughed softly. "Well, that would be another interesting experience, wouldn't it." He walked away to the back entrance of the warehouse, not using the cane again as long as he was in Grayle's sight.

There was only one door at the top of the four flights of narrow, time-worn stairs, and the key Grayle had given him opened it. But Victor still thought that he had entered the wrong room. It was a storage loft. Most of the floor space was covered by piles of Persian and North African carpets. Tapestries and rugs of better quality hung in layers from three walls. Huge mirrors with ornate gilded frames leaned against them.

Victor walked through an aisle between piles of carpets and parted the hanging tapestries that formed a fourth wall. He had come to the right place. Grayle's part of the loft formed a large, high-ceilinged room, lit by a wide win-

dow tilted to the sky between exposed rafters in the slant-
ing roof.

What struck Victor immediately was how unusually neat
and clean it was. No paint drippings on the plank flooring,
no dust in corners, everything just so.

The flea-market furnishings used little of the space. There
was a wide mattress on the rough wooden floor, with a
cushion at one end and a blanket neatly folded at the other.
A long linoleum-top table and a cane chair. A standing
closet with two drawers in its base. The few kitchen utensils were in a battered brass tray at one end of the table,
next to a big enamel basin and a tall pitcher of dented tin.
At the other end was a brass oil lamp.

One of the two straight walls was almost covered by
black-and-white sketches of various sizes, drawings similar
to those in Grayle's sketchbook, pastels, watercolors and
studies in oils on squares of cardboard.

Near the opposite wall was a handmade easel. The
stretched canvas waiting on it was empty, and, Victor
noted, of expensive quality. Beside it, on a massive wine
barrel were a square of window glass used as a palette, two
jars filled with top-grade brushes, a bottle of solvent and
assorted tubes of oil paint of the best brand available. It
was obvious where most of the money earned in Les Halles
went.

Victor walked to the long table and put down the sausage Grayle had handed him. Then he turned to look fully
at the large, unframed paintings against the wall.

There were eight on the floor leaning against the wall,
and above these three more hung side by side. And in each
of them he saw concentrated power. Each had the quality
of an arrested moment in time, drawing him in.

It was some moments before Victor Royan's critical faculty reasserted itself. Deliberately, he began to isolate the
techniques involved: the interaction of volumes and linear
forces. The dynamic strength of composition. The controlled energy of the firm, disciplined brushwork. The bold
richness of color—and the tension between the rigor of the
draftsmanship and the impact.

Victor moved closer, for a critical examination of the three pictures Grayle had chosen to hang on the wall.

The one that drew him first was the painting later acquired by the Museum of Modern Art in Paris. Grayle's name for it was *The Sorceress*: a middle-aged woman with a turn-of-the-century dress and hairstyle, seated at a table, staring straight out of the painting with an expression that was fixed, almost frozen. She sat there, stiffly erect, shoulders pressed against the chair-back. Her hands lay palms up on the table before her. Between them ten tarot cards were spread in the pattern of a cabalistic tree of life. The beaded table lamp in the foreground was on, but its glow was barely discernible in the harsh sunlight pouring through a partially curtained window behind the woman. Victor's immediate impression was that she was dead. Then he decided she was in a trance.

He had difficulty tearing his eyes from hers, to move on to the next picture.

The scene was an open cafe terrace, the square behind it instantly recognizable as the Piazza della Signoria in Florence. A beggar, a waiter and a woman seated at a table between them, with the fountain in the background dominated by the statue of Neptune. The strong sunlight was of a kind Victor had seen nowhere in Italy or France, though he had experienced something akin to it in Greece. The shadows cast by it had an unnatural solidity, like a dream-world intrusion.

The beggar was an old gypsy woman in a shapeless tattered dress, a red shawl wrapped around her head, one hand planting a cane firmly on the paving stones, the other hand held out palm up, waiting. An age-scarred brown face, immobile in its arrogant patience. The waiter stood in his soiled white jacket trying to argue the beggar into going away; annoyed and worried, unsure. Between them, seen from the back, the young well-dressed woman sat concentrating on stirring her coffee. Behind this stabilized trinity stood the tall white figure of the god Neptune, bearded face slightly averted, two pigeons perching on his head. All four figures—god, waiter, beggar and seated woman—seemed united forever inside an arrested ritual.

Victor moved to the next painting. The more he looked at it, the more disturbing it was. *The Night Walker*, a painting which was later to cause some to associate Grayle with surrealism.

The foreground: a lamp-lit city street at night, at the entrance to a Parisian *passage*, one of the block-long shopping arcades roofed with glass. The subtle, motionless illumination within the *passage* seemed to be moonlight seen through shallow water. A man was walking away through the interior. At the other end of the *passage*, harsh sunlight burned through fog on a rocky sea-coast lashed by a stormy surf.

Victor spent less time before this painting than the other two. He did not like the memories it evoked in him. He turned from it to examine what was on the opposite wall.

The smallish oil paintings on cardboard were carefully executed copies of old masters. A group of watercolors studied sea and sky; others were of circus performers. Among the black-and-white drawings were sketches of street scenes; some in Paris, others from London, Florence, Sienna and Arezzo. Of special interest for Victor was a group of pastels: attempts to capture the colors of twelfth- to fourteenth-century stained glass, the chalks applied with a vigor verging on violence. Three were from the cathedral windows of Bourges, two from Chartres, another three from Canterbury.

He was standing before these when Grayle came in through the hanging tapestries. He had changed to shoes, slacks and shirt, and was carrying a loaf of crusty bread. From his other hand dangled his boots and overalls, washed and drying.

"You found an odd place to live," Victor said.

"Cheapest I could get with enough space to work." Grayle put the bread on the table and went to hang the wet clothing on a wire strung from the beams under the skylight.

Victor gestured at the street sketches. "I see you spent some time in London and Tuscany."

"Six months."

"What did you live on there?"

"Savings. I made some money with several trips on a rum-runner, before I came to Europe."

Victor smiled. "So that insane Prohibition law in America does serve some purpose. I understand people are making fortunes from bootlegging."

"I didn't make a fortune—but enough to take care of the time in London and Florence, and my first two months here in Paris." Grayle took two glasses from the table and filled them from a wooden plug-spigot in the wine barrel which served as a support for his painting materials. He put the glasses of wine on the table and rested a hip on its edge. "Have a seat. You look ready to fall down." He opened a knife with a wooden handle and cut the bread in half.

Victor walked over and lowered himself into the only chair as Grayle cut one of the bread halves down the middle and picked up the chunk of sausage. "Only the wine for me." Victor's voice had a dragging rasp. "I can't eat that this early."

Grayle cut thick slices of sausage into the opened half of the loaf. "I need it. I have to begin work soon."

"Aren't you tired?"

"Yes—but sometimes that helps." Grayle took a bite of the sandwich.

Victor tasted the wine, tentatively. It wasn't what he was used to, but it wasn't bad. He looked at the three paintings on the wall behind the empty canvas. "They surprised me," he said slowly. "Even after what I'd seen in your sketchbook. You must have started very young, to be this far along, at your age."

Grayle nodded. "And I had a good teacher."

"You can *learn* a great deal, yes. But this, some of it you had to be born with."

Grayle thought of the senile old man in Brittany. "Probably. What is your background?"

"In art, you mean? My father and grandfather were collectors. In the same way they'd buy more land or machinery for our factories. Sound investments. But shrewd, at times. My father was on to some of the impressionists before their work cost real money."

"And you?"

"I'm not interested in collecting. I studied art history . . ." Victor shrugged. "One was expected to attend a university, you see. I had to pick some subject."

"But you like my work."

It was said flatly, but with a satisfied undertone that touched Victor. He leaned back in his chair and regarded Grayle. "I could introduce you to a dealer whose opinion would be of more use to you than mine. Pauline Renard. If you don't know her, you should."

Grayle took a drink of wine. He put the glass down and said, "No. Not yet."

"Why not?" Victor demanded irritably. "Your living standard could obviously do with some improvement."

Grayle moved a hand in a careless gesture. "I'm a simple person. With simple needs."

"And the world is not ready for your revelations, is that it?" The sarcasm was thick now.

Grayle laughed. "The world's ready. It always has been, always will be. So it'll wait until *I'm* ready. What you see here is all I've got. That I'm satisfied with. Not enough."

"At least Pauline can tell whether she is interested in seeing more."

"And if she is, I'd be tempted to push faster than my ability allows. To concentrate on finishing off a picture so I can get on with the next. Some painters work fast, I can't. I get too facile, and lose something."

"If Pauline Renard likes your style . . ."

"I might become afraid to change it," Grayle cut in, "when a change might be right for me." He shook his head, an emphasic negative. "I need to get a lot more done, first. So I'm so sure of where I'm going that nothing can knock me off the rails. My own rails."

Victor watched him bite off another chunk of sandwich. "I think you are ignoring the possibility that you can still learn something from others."

"I still learn," Grayle told him quietly. "From Dürer, Van Gogh, Rouault . . . I steal anything I can use. Anything that feels right for me."

"That still leaves room for direct advice and discussion with an expert."

Grayle washed down the last of his sandwich with wine. "Words are one kind of language. Art is another. They don't translate well, in either direction." He glanced at the big window in the slanted roof. "I have to start soon. There's a phone in the bar downstairs. Or you can send a kid to find a taxi."

"I'll phone home for my car." Victor put a hand on the table and shoved to his feet. His legs were quivering. "Come down and I'll treat both of us to coffee. It will help to keep you awake."

He was surprised when Grayle accepted.

They were at a table outside the bistro, Victor's coffee again laced with brandy, Grayle's just a very strong double.

"It won't take long for my car to get here," Victor said. "But you don't have to wait till then. I'll be all right."

Grayle stirred two lumps of sugar into his double espresso. "It's been a long time since I had anyone to talk to about art—or anything else."

"I thought art and words don't mix."

"I said they're not the same language. They don't substitute for each other." The humor in Grayle's sudden grin surprised Victor. "Anyway, you can't believe everything I say. Some of it's just trying ideas on for size."

"Don't you know other artists?"

"One. But usually I don't like talking with anyone in the field, in any capacity. You wind up talking technique, and what sells, and it gets too inbred. With someone like you it's simpler—someone who knows about art but isn't *in* it."

Victor shook his head. "You won't get anything from me but discouraging thoughts in the end. I think you are exceptionally talented. But in an area that no longer has any meaning. Art is an empty profession, unless you have gods to fill it."

Grayle's smile was smaller now, reflective. "I think I've found some."

"I know you do. But you are very young. It is an illusion. The gods are all quite dead." He drained his cup and slumped a bit in his chair. "I decided, sometime during the war, as I watched men being ground to raw meat by machines we created: humanity is nothing but a virulent disease infecting the skin of the earth. Which makes your profession rather pointless."

Grayle took a sip of coffee and said mildly, "You like to try ideas on for size, too."

"Where do you think God is?" Victor demanded angrily. "Now that we know he's not out there in the stars? Inside ourselves? Freud has had a long look in there, and all he found was mud, filth and garbage."

Grayle stretched his arms and looked with pleasure at what was around them: at the delicious colors of the fruits and vegetables on the sidewalk stands, at the throngs of people filling the narrow street between the stands. A scene he could usually count on to bring himself back to the joy of life when other things, inside him, grew too dark. "I think Freud found what he was looking for," he said. "Others found other things."

Victor waved a hand at the crowded street, his expression puzzled. "I don't know what you see here. What I see is that life is ugly."

"Ugly or beautiful, it's what we've got. And so far nobody has come up with anything half as interesting."

Victor gave him a twisted smile and shook his head wonderingly. "You remind me of the peasants in Normandy, around my family estate where I spent my childhood. My wife lives there much of the time now—but I seldom go back. The poverty of the area is too depressing. And yet those peasants still find excuses for enjoying something in their lives—I've never understood how or why."

Grayle looked up the street. "Is that your car?"

Victor turned his head. A long, shiny-blue Packard Phaeton was pushing very slowly through the crowds, people barely shifting out of its way as it touched them. Victor nodded, remaining seated, watching the automobile inch nearer.

The woman driving it was young, perhaps twenty. She had a pretty, freckled, snub-nosed face. Pale golden hair, cut short, formed straight bangs across her forehead, and the bottom ends curved in slightly against her cheeks. When she finally managed to get the Packard to the curb in front of them, she climbed out looking angry. She was a small, slender woman, wearing a severely tailored black velvet jacket and trousers, with a ruffled white shirt fastened at the collar by a red bowtie.

She stood with fists on hips, studying Victor critically. "Well, I've seen you in worse shape after one of these nights." She said it in English, with a Cockney flavor. "At least you're not bleeding all over your clothes." She shot a cold glance at Grayle. "Does he have any money left?"

"Don't be vulgar, Jill," Victor admonished mockingly. "My new friend here is an artist, not a crook."

"One doesn't necessarily cancel the other," she pointed out tartly.

Grayle smiled. "No, it doesn't."

"This one," Victor told her, "is almost as much of a mother as you. He was trying to warn me I could get killed if I keep on like this. Familiar?"

"Who cares?" she snapped. "You'd do it to yourself, if you weren't such a driveling Catholic."

"Lapsed," he reminded her. "And unrepentant."

"Those are the worst." She turned on her heel, getting back into the car, behind the wheel. Glaring straight ahead through the windshield, waiting.

But Victor seemed in no hurry. He glanced obliquely at Grayle. "What do you think of my chauffeur?"

"Pretty."

"Come, now, she is much more than that. The way she draws the boys—and other exquisite girls, which is even better." The lechery in his smile was weak. The exhausted, dissipated face was haunted. "She is also very intelligent— and right about lapsed Catholics. The superstitions cling. Nobody breaks easily with Rome."

Grayle said offhandedly: "Not with anything that goes in deep, early enough."

Victor studied him for a moment. Then he used the cane to help himself to his feet. "We're off to London tomorrow. Until autumn. Will you still be here?"

"Probably."

"I may drop in to see you again when I return. Unless that would annoy you."

"It won't, if I'm not working. If I'm working, I'll say so."

Victor nodded and got into the Packard beside Jill. Grayle watched her drive him away, then finished his coffee and went into the courtyard and up the stairs to work.

4

He didn't hear from Victor Royan again until the second Friday in September, the day Nora Cesari entered his life.

Through much of the night before and until early that morning he had worked in Les Halles. Seven full hours of heavy labor that had left his body drained and cleared his brain. It had also earned him enough money for his back rent, and to pay what he owed Madame Gaussin for the dinners he ate at her house but no immediate debts. He bought bread, and carried it and a whole salami and a ball of cheese he'd taken from the central markets up to his room in the warehouse. Like a man laying in a food supply to resist a siege. Actually, it was a continuing siege, which had already gone on for a very long time.

After hanging the cheese and salami from a ceiling beam, Grayle turned first to the wall with the canvases he considered finished works. There were now twelve of them. The eight that Victor Royan had seen resting against the base of the wall were still there. But a new painting had been added to the three hung on the wall above. Grayle called it *The Three Fates*.

It was a triptych, within a single horizontal canvas. In the left portion a peasant woman in her forties stood in an open doorway, drying her hands on her apron, watching a boy of about nine playing with a dog in a village street. In the middle portion a voluptuous nude stood against the opened skylight of his room, her shoulders at the height of its lower sill, arms spread, resting lazily on the sill, head tilted back and slightly turned to look at the noontime sky. The foreground was taken by the shadowed head and shoulders of a man looking at the woman's offered body.

In the third part of the painting, a lovely girl of about fifteen was rowing an old man across a stream toward a dense, dark forest.

The lines of one portion of the canvas flowed into the next, integrating them. There was a flow also of the quality of light: the strong, pale shine of early morning; the molten glow of noon; the murky light of evening.

Grayle knew it was effective. But it had been over a month since he'd finished it. More than four weeks that an empty canvas had been waiting on his easel.

He turned and crossed the room to look at the sketches, studies and watercolors on the opposite wall, his eyes slitted as he searched for what he knew must be there, willing it to reveal itself to him. For almost an hour he stayed there, his hard-boned face taut, alert, scanning the studies covering his wall. But the frustration that had gone on for far too many days and nights continued. None of the sketches would combine for him, and he couldn't force them to. There was nothing to end the emptiness of the canvas waiting on the easel behind him.

He turned, at last, toward the easel. And stood there studying the empty canvas; slowly scanning its surface, his mind feeling over its pattern. His hand reached out, and took hold of the chair by the table, swung it around before him, its back to the easel. Straddling it, he lowered himself onto its caned seat, his forearms crossing on top of the chair's back, his lhin resting on them. Watching the empty canvas with the stoic calm of a fisherman, curbing the impatience and anxiety.

It *would* come. That he knew.

But waiting was hard; too damned hard . . .

He turned his head slightly, looking past the empty canvas at the painting he called *The Sorceress*. The corners of his mouth tightened slowly. She was exactly as he remembered: sitting there rigid, hands inert on the table, with the familiar cards, spread between them, eyes staring at him.

Check resting on his crossed forearms, he stared back at the woman who had raised him.

* * *

The hill against the back of the clapboard house seemed to push it forward. The roof tilted, the porch supports were at an angle. When the sharp winds came through the shallow valley along the creek out front, the place shuddered. The attic flooring groaned under Nick's mattress at night. Between winds and hill, the whole thing was bound to come crashing down sooner or later. But the house had held its own for seventy years before he came to live in it when he was three, and it was still there when he went away.

Irene called it "the shack." It was in an overgrown wooded stretch along Old Man's Creek, in the New Jersey farmlands some forty miles from Camden and Philadelphia. The house had no gas, electricity or running water. There was a pump out front, kerosene lamps and candles for light at night, a wood-burning stove, a single fireplace for heat in winter and an outhouse in the dense bushes to one side of the house: a cold dash in the winter, and a wet one during the frequent rains.

The woods hid the place from the nearest neighbors, up by the road out back. In front of the porch there was a small yard with an old split-rail fence. Beyond it the ground sloped down to the creek, where Irene kept her rowboat tied to a makeshift dock. Mostly the creek yielded catfish; edible when nothing else took the bait.

But the creek held something else. Exploring along its east bank he discovered an overgrown Indian burial ground, where a little digging turned up shards of patterned orange pottery, bits of human bones and flint arrowheads. Eventually he had a whole cigar-box full of them. They had started Irene telling him the legends and rituals of various Indian tribes, one of the odd things she knew a lot about. Her stories fascinated him, and there was a period of his childhood when he religiously copied the ritual prayers certain tribes used to help the sun to rise, and the moon to renew its cycle.

The elementary school, when Nick became old enough to go, was on the edge of the nearest town, a two-mile hike from the shack. Nobody from town ever dropped in to see them. In the years Nick lived there they had only one regular visitor, who came all the way from Philadelphia.

People in town considered his aunt a crackpot. Irene Grayle was a lean, overintense woman with strong features, strong opinions and a sharp understanding of human nature. Jack, the man she was supposed to marry, had died at the age of twenty-nine, the year Nick was born. The idea that she could find another man went against her nature. She was passionately in love with Jack, and the fact that he was dead didn't alter that. Which probably accounted for her loyal sympathy for Nick's mother. Both sisters had lost their men in the same year.

Irene explained who his father was when Nick was seven.

"He came over from France for an exhibition of his paintings. He was very popular, then. Sold a lot in New York and Chicago, before coming to Philadelphia to show what he had left. We went to see it, with Jack. He was so handsome, and a charmer. Like you'd expect, with a Frenchman. And with Corsican blood. Your mother was crazy about him from the first look. She went after him, no holds barred. Well—she got him."

"I don't care about any of this," Nick told Irene flatly.

"You have to *know,* sooner or later. He liked her, too. No question about that. Stayed a whole month after his exhibition was finished, just to be with her. When he left, he promised he'd come back for her."

She'd discovered she was pregnant after he was gone, and had written to France to tell him. He'd written back that he'd come as soon as he could. But he never did, even when she wrote him about Nick's birth, and eventually he stopped answering her letters. She had brooded about it for almost two years before she decided to leave Nick with her sister and go over to get him, borrowing every cent she could to pay her passage.

"She found out he was married," Irene explained. "It broke her heart."

"I don't care," Nick told his aunt.

"Don't be so hard on your mother, Nick. She was so unhappy. Some day you'll understand."

Later, Nick was to understand that his mother had stayed on in France for months as his father's mistress, before he'd dropped her for another. And that *that* was when she'd drowned herself.

At one point Irene told him about the night his mother had appeared in the kitchen of the shack, when Nick was asleep in the attic. Her ghost just standing there, checking on whether Irene was doing a proper job of raising him.

"If she cared so much," Nick said angrily, "she should have hung around and watched me grow up. She didn't, so why should *I* care?"

Irene rented the place from a farmer who didn't want the trouble of clearing the land around it. The rent wasn't much, but neither was what she earned doing an astrology column for five newspapers in New Jersey and Pennsylvania. To supplement that, Irene charged for answering letters from readers who wanted their individual horoscope charted.

Nick was never sure that she entirely believed in astrology.

"It's not a mechanical fortune-telling system," she told him once. "It's more like what Freud is studying, only from a different angle. Like tarot and the cabbala. These methods go way back in history; and they're all just ways of trying to analyze the influence of certain universals: the different situations mankind comes up against, the forces of nature on us."

Nick was eight when a boy in the schoolyard taunted him about Irene during recess, explaining with malicious pleasure what kind of crackpot she was. Nick kicked him in the stomach. The boy folded like a broken stick, throwing up as he landed on his knees, clutching at his agonized middle. Two other boys, friends of the one he'd kicked, tried to jump Nick. He spun away from them, sprinting out of the schoolyard. They went after him eagerly, a pair of dogs running down a cat.

Nick saw what he needed and stooped to grab it. The two boys were almost on him when he twisted around swinging the stick in a vicious arc. It caught one boy across the side of the head, and he fell against the other. The boy

he'd struck slumped to the ground with blood streaming
from his head. The other backed off hastily, and Nick did
not go after him. He just stayed there watching, twitching
the stick.

It took the doctor summoned by the school principal
twelve stitches to close the wound in the boy's head. By
then Nick had reached home. Several hours later a policeman showed up. The parents of the boy with the stitched
scalp were saying that Nick was either dangerously unbalanced or just naturally vicious, that he should be put either
in a loony bin or a reform school.

"That's ridiculous," Irene told him firmly. "They attacked him, he only fought back."

"With a stick. That's not fighting fair."

It was Nick who pointed out, matter-of-factly: "There
were two of them, against one of me."

"But," the cop reminded him, "after you knocked the
first one down it was one to one. Other kids say you were
still ready to use the stick."

It wasn't the first time that Irene had been worried
about the way the boy could erupt in reacting to a situation; she knew she had to find a safe channel for that
streak of violence. But right now, she had to protect him.
"Officer," she said, "you have intelligent eyes. When were
you born?"

Startled, he told her the date of his birth.

"What time of day?"

The cop told her that, too, after some thinking. When he
left half an hour later he knew some interesting things
about himself.

Nick wasn't sent to an asylum or reformatory; he returned to the school, and no one provoked him again with
cracks about Irene. The kids with bullying tendencies used
them elsewhere, others treated him with new respect. The
teachers found him unchanged: a poor student, his
thoughts generally elsewhere in class, and he got low
marks. His real education continued to come from Irene.

He knew her extensive repertoire of folk tales by heart
before he learned to read. For basic information she started
him early on the first volume of an old Encyclopaedia Bri-

tannica, and over the years he worked his way through the others in alphabetical order. For the rest, Irene had her own prejudices about what a well-informed person should know, and she was a natural one-to-one tutor.

By the time he was twelve they had worked together through Shakespeare, Dante, Euripides, Plutarch and the Old Testament. For lighter reading he had her volumes of poetry, mysticism, Kipling, Conrad, Mark Twain, George Bernard Shaw, Dickens and Dumas. In addition: her own observations on the ways of mankind, animals and plants; the forces of nature, God and the universe.

The lessons in art, he got from Rita, the visitor from Philadelphia.

Rita Moser would come out to spend a weekend in the country with them every few weeks, sometimes more often, depending on whether her husband, an officer on a merchant ship, was away on a trip or not. And, as Nick eventually learned, on whether she had any particular friend she was interested in during his absences.

It turned out that she, too, had been enamored of his father; but briefly. She'd first met Irene while hanging around his exhibition in Philadelphia day after day.

"He was something, that Frenchman. I fell for him like a ton of bricks. But your mother—there was the most determined girl I ever met. I didn't have a chance against her."

In Nick's private opinion that proved there was also something wrong with his hated father's taste in women. He had seen his mother's photos in Irene's family album, and she wasn't bad; but Rita was all warm softness and easygoing humor. She was small, curvy and dark, with luxuriant raven-black hair. Her rich brown eyes fascinated him, and he loved the smell of her perfume. The atmosphere around the shack was considerably lighter when she was there.

She was a free-lance illustrator of children's books. During one period she came out to the shack almost every weekend because Irene wanted to work on an illustrated book on the philosophical and psychological aspects of astrology. But in those days the market for anything having to do with the occult was very small; they never managed to find a publisher.

Nick was nine years old when they were working on the astrology book. One Saturday afternoon while Irene and Rita were out on the porch firing the single-shot .22 rifle at sticks floating past on the creek, Nick began using Rita's pencils and pad to copy one of her illustrations. He worked with absorbed concentration, and he was almost finished when the women came back inside. Rita examined what he'd done, and gave him a few technical pointers. But only a few. The next weekend she brought him a sketchpad and pencils of his own, together with a small book of Dürer drawings.

During the next two weeks he spent most of his time copying the Dürer illustrations. Rita studied what he had done, keeping her comments to a few essentials. On his tenth birthday her presents were a box of watercolors and another of oils, with brushes for each, and basic instructions on how to use them.

It had always been her habit on her weekends at the shack to wander along the creek looking for subjects to draw and paint: trees, leaves, wildflowers, tricks of light on the surface of the water. Now Nick always accompanied her. For a long time he worked on whatever subject Rita chose for herself, learning by comparing results. She kept her advice and criticisms minimal, allowing his skills to develop in their own way and time. She gave him sticks of pastel and charcoal, and began assigning him subjects for when she was away: a stone, a cup, his own hand.

The year he was eleven he spent most of the summer at Rita's house in Philadelphia, close to the Delaware River docks. Most days she took him to the Fine Arts Museum to copy the paintings of the masters, and draw the sculptures there.

Toward the end of that summer Rita began sending Nick to the museum without art materials. He would choose whatever sculpture or painting excited him, spend an hour studying it, then go home and attempt to reproduce it.

In 1913 the Armory Show was held in New York, and Rita took Nick to see the new directions European artists had been exploring—from Impressionism through Blau Reiter to Cubism and Dada. Nick's head swarmed with Gauguin, Rouault, Matisse, Picasso, Duchamp, Redon, Monet, Van Gogh, Munch, Rousseau, Delaunay, Kandinsky. With the aid of the catalogue bought by Rita, he immediately began work on paintings inspired by them. Rita looked at the results with both pride and a tinge of envy.

"Don't ever go to an art school," she told him. "They'll cripple what you've got, trying to squeeze it to fit their mold. Maybe it'll take you longer this way, but you'll come out of it your own man."

Nick's aunt also watched his progress, with little comment but obvious approval. There'd been no violent outbursts since he'd become so absorbed in his art work.

Two months after the Armory Show Nick woke up late one morning, wondering why Irene hadn't called him for breakfast and school. When he got downstairs he found her just as he'd left her the night before: at the table with the cards, the lamp still burning weakly. She looked frozen in place, her eyes staring straight ahead. She didn't react even when he began shouting, and at first he thought she was dead. But then he discovered she was breathing, slowly but steadily.

He picked up her hand; it felt unnaturally heavy, and when he let go it dropped like an inanimate weight. He ran the two miles to town for the doctor.

Irene was taken to a hospital in Camden, where Nick was asked a lot of questions, including whether he had any other family. He gave them the name of Rita Moser—and the phone number of the drugstore on the corner at the end of her block. She got there in an hour.

Irene showed no sign of getting better in the hospital. The doctors couldn't figure out exactly what was wrong with her. They guessed that it might have been brought on by her thinking too much about the supernatural, which could have aggravated some kind of brain trouble that had lain dormant for a long time; probably hereditary.

She was moved to the state asylum, where she was to spend the rest of her life. Rita helped Nick pack his few belongings, and took him back with her to live in the house in Philadelphia.

The canvas on Grayle's easel was still empty when he finished a lunch of cheese, salami and bread. He left his room. His brain had become too restless, infecting the rest of him with a need for physical movement.

He went swiftly down the back stairs of the warehouse and into the courtyard, heading toward the Seine. He reached the Quai Voltaire and crossed the Pont du Carrousel, entering the Louvre. He stopped before Caron's *Massacre of the Triumvirs*. Its skillfully orchestrated violence fitted his mood, and he fed on it. The next picture he chose was Cimabue's *Virgin with Angels*. But the calm authority of its architectural massing of faces and halos upset him, and he left the building without seeing anything else.

It was five o'clock in the afternoon when he returned to Rue Mouffetard. Madame Bobichon spotted him crossing the courtyard, and came out the rear door of the bistro with a note for him. It was from Victor Royan, an invitation to the opening of a one-man show at the Renard Gallery. "The works of the artist in the gallery may not be of interest to you," Victor Royan had written, "but Pauline's private collection in her apartment upstairs will be. Paintings you won't have seen anywhere else. She is having a cocktail party there for a small number of friends. Use my name and come up. In addition to the pictures you'll want to look at, there will be abundant food and liquor. From eight o'clock on."

Grayle thrust the note in his pocket and trudged up the stairs to his room. The invitation was tempting, but his body was heavy with fatigue and his head swirling; bed was more tempting. He sprawled across the mattress and let his eyes close, passing out almost immediately.

Four hours later he was wide awake, still tired but his brain too active to let him slip back into sleep. Grayle went down to the courtyard and across to the hotel, where he paid for the use of its bathtub. There was still a clinging weariness in a brain that refused to relax as he toweled himself dry. Getting dressed, he went into the bistro and had a coffee at the bar.

The empty canvas waiting in his room was very clear in his mind. He knew every faint ridge and indentation in its surface; he was not ready to face it again, not yet. He needed something to eat. And then he wanted to get drunk, a luxury he could not usually afford. Digging Victor's note from his pocket, he checked the address.

It was almost ten when he got there. The gallery was still filled with well-dressed people, most of them holding cocktails and paying little attention to the paintings on exhibit. These were severely geometrical compositions using strong primary colors. A slow scan of the walls told Grayle there was nothing new here that he wanted. He moved to the rear of the gallery. An elderly woman in a lavender gown sat beside a miniature palm tree in a square ebony pot, winding up a phonograph. She was watching the crowd in the gallery with sleepy disdain. Grayle used Victor Royan's name and she pointed to a doorway behind her.

It opened into a small foyer where a curving stairway led to the floor above. A young woman in a light green dress and dark green hat was coming down the steps. She had a snakeskin purse in one hand, and an almost-full bottle of whiskey in the other. Her supple figure moved with a dancer's blend of controlled strength and careless ease.

She stopped when she reached him, barring his way. Her preoccupied frown changed to recognition. Grayle took a moment longer; he'd had only the one glimpse of her on the beach, some distance away.

She had an odd, intriguing face, framed by unruly black curls. Hard Nordic features, contradicted by lips that made him think of an equatorial plant. Her long, very steady eyes regarded him, deep gray and difficult to read. They hid too much.

"The beach out near Cape Chèvre," she reminded him. Her voice had a dark texture that belonged more to the passionate mouth than the careful eyes.

"I remember you."

She smiled, but was aware of the way he was observing her. She found herself wondering what he saw. "Are you a new addition to the group?" She indicated the apartment above, and was unable to keep the faint disdain from her voice. "One of the art lovers?"

Silently she cursed herself. That had sounded so brittle, so glib. He would think she was stupid and superficial. Why did she always become so awkward whenever she met anyone who really impressed her?

But he was smiling. "Not the way you mean. I'm a painter."

"What's your name?"

"Nicholas Grayle." He was sharply aware of her closeness, the timbre of her voice.

"I'm sorry, I don't know your work."

"Few people do."

Nora Cesari cursed herself again. If she didn't talk at all, she wouldn't keep saying the wrong things. "My mother thought at first that you were an American art collector."

He didn't understand what she was saying. "Your mother?"

"The house in Brittany near the beach," she explained. "I saw you leaving it. I'm Claude Cesari's daughter."

Something cold formed in Grayle's throat. He looked down, so she couldn't see the change in him.

Nora thought he was looking at the bottle in her hand. She had taken it from Pauline Renard because she was out of whiskey at home, and she had felt a sudden need to get drunk, all by herself. She had decided there was nothing for her upstairs but more meaningless entanglements and she already had enough of those. A marriage that was finished but wouldn't end, lovers who came too easily and palled too soon, ambitions that lost their direction. She had come down the stairs with a savage longing for solitude, to try somehow to reduce her life to something it could grow from again.

But she kept looking at Grayle, puzzled by his silence. "It was nice of you to go all the way out to Brittany, just to pay your respects to my father and see his work. I remember when he was famous, and people came all the time.

But that was when I was a child. My mother was pleased with your visit, even though it turned out you hadn't come to buy any of his paintings, just to look."

So her mother hadn't told her the truth. Grayle looked at her eyes again. "What's your name?" He spoke carefully, controlling the dizzying surge of pressure within him.

"Nora." She hesitated. The mood in which she'd left Pauline's gathering was dissolving before this man. She reminded herself angrily that this kind of thing had happened to her before. And she knew this one wouldn't solve anything, either.

Yet she didn't bid him good-bye and leave. Instead she found herself saying, "I'd like to see your work. Unless it's important for you to attend Pauline's party. I'm afraid I'm just not up to any more of that."

"No, it's not important to me." The desire she'd stirred in him had turned bitter.

That senile ghost of a man was still there, still enmeshing his life with hidden snares. The old thwarted fury seized him again. And out of it grew an uncontrollable need to strike back—through this girl.

The intensity of it surprised him. But it was there. He savored it. His smile hid it from her.

"Let's go," he said.

She didn't catch the quiet undertone.

5

He stood beside the bed as the dawn seeped through the skylight of his studio.

The night had been warm, and the blanket was bunched on the floor at the foot of the bed. Nora lay half-curled on her side, her supple figure turned toward him, arms and legs sprawled limply. Her face was relaxed now, the dark hair disheveled luxuriously around it, the soft curls flowing across the arch of her throat. The mouth was childish in sleep, her full lips parted.

He looked toward their clothes thrown across the chair, the whiskey bottle on the table. They'd finished it without noticing, absorbed in talk. Nora had been enthralled by his paintings, studying them with awe. They'd discussed other artists they both admired. He'd told her about the rum-running days that had earned him the money to come to Europe, and about Les Halles. She'd told her a bit about the mood that had driven her from Pauline Renard's party.

When the bottle was empty, they'd gone to bed. She'd no longer needed to be alone. And he'd no longer remembered his anger.

Grayle looked again at her asleep on his bed. The daylight strengthened by degrees, touching parts of her, deepening the shadowing of other parts. Graceful, long-muscled thighs . . . small, oddly shaped ears . . . ripe, resilient breasts, the nipples delicate . . .

The image of the old man who'd been father to both of them intruded. Anger shook Grayle again. But none of it was directed at Nora. The tenderness he experienced, looking at her now, shocked him more than had the savage desire to do harm which had originally caused him to bring her here.

He wondered if she would ever come to him again, when she found out the truth. And if he would ever feel as alive as he did right now.

He went to the skylight and picked up a large sketch pad leaning against the base of the wall under it. He put it on the table and opened it to a fresh page. Taking a stick of charcoal, he began his first drawing of Nora Cesari.

When the drawing was finished, Grayle detached it from the pad and laid it on the table, beside the bottle. Nora rolled over in her sleep, her face turning away from the early sunshine entering the skylight. He began to draw again: the long, slender curve of her back, the flare of the raised hip and the plump, firm buttocks. The way one foot was tucked behind the knee of the other leg.

He placed it beside the other drawing and began to dress. Boby's bar downstairs would be opening about now, and Nora had said she had to rise early for a morning appointment. Grayle took the tin pitcher from the end of his table, and went down to the courtyard.

He filled the pitcher from the pump, got croissants from the courtyard bakery and went into the bar. Nora's car was parked out in front of it, half up on the sidewalk: a Sainte Clair V-8 coupé with a rumble seat. She obviously had money, or a friend who liked giving expensive presents.

Madame Bobichon's husband, whom the neighborhood called Boby, was behind the bar this morning. Grayle asked him to fill one of the thermos bottles he kept under the counter with café au lait.

After washing herself awake with the water he'd poured in the bowl, Nora sat at the table, wrapped in his old raincoat, eating the breakfast he'd brought for them. She was still sleepy with contentment, and she didn't feel any urge to talk about what had happened.

She looked at his works on the walls of the room, and then at him. He stood leaning against the skylight, the sunshine behind his head and shoulders. She said, finally: "I don't know if I really managed to make you understand what your paintings make me feel."

Grayle smiled at her. "Yes, you did."

Nora felt herself blush, and it had been a long time since that had happened to her. She lowered her eyes from his to the two charcoal nudes he'd done of her asleep. "And these—are they your way of saying how much you liked what *I* do?" Immediately self-anger welled up in her, and she growled, "I'm sorry, that was such a stupid thing to say. I didn't mean it to be, but . . ."

She looked again at the paintings on his walls, seeking desperately to change the subject and make him forget what she'd said. "I'll boast someday, about being one of the first to see these. They make me think of dreams I've had, and could never remember."

His smile was something that flickered and was gone.

She was resting her chin on one hand, gazing deeply at the pictures behind the blank canvas on his easel. "It's the *people* in them," she said finally, groping for what it was she felt. "They are very real, but at the same time they evoke something separated from reality, hidden from the eye. That's what your work is really about, isn't it."

"It's whatever you see in it. The only thing that matters is if they make you see *something*."

Nora's attention shifted from one picture to the next. She pointed with her coffee cup at one of the eight paintings lined up on the floor against the wall. "Who is the girl in that portrait?"

It *was* a portrait, but an odd one: the head and shoulders of a young woman, held fast in a moment of passing an antiqued mirror. Her pretty profile, the features small and sharp, held a startling depth of repressed sadness, and a wariness of age far beyond her years. That was the profile turned to the viewer. The profile reflected in the mirror held a bloom: the healthy optimism of arrogant youth. An art critic would later dub this picture *Remembrance of Times Past*.

"She's someone I use as a model, occasionally," Grayle said. He gestured at his *Three Fates*, on the wall above it.

"She also posed for the nude in the middle panel of that one."

Nora looked at the voluptuous figure, with the head tilted back to regard the sky, the face almost hidden. She asked, with a forced casualness, "A friend? Or just a paid model?"

"A girl who lives on this courtyard. I pay her, when I can. She works in a brothel over near the Panthéon."

"Oh." Nora looked again at the two drawings of her on the table. "These make me look beautiful, too. May I have one of them?"

"No, not yet."

She stopped herself from asking why. Picking up her wristwatch from the table, she strapped it on. "I have to go now; and after that I have a very full day and evening. Then I promised my mother to spend a few days with them out in Brittany." She glanced at Grayle, the question in her eyes. "I'll be back in four days, at the most."

He stiffened, then forced himself to relax. If she told her mother about meeting him, she would come back knowing the truth. But there was nothing he could do about that, until it happened. "I'll be here," he told her. He found himself looking forward to her return, no matter what feelings she brought with her.

"I hope so," she said softly. She stood up and took off his raincoat, acutely aware of his watching as she put on her own clothing. "Have you a comb?"

He gave her the one from his back pocket, and she picked up her hat and car keys, going through the hanging tapestries into the rug-storage room. She was standing before one of the mirrors, using his comb to bring some order to her dark curls, when he came through. Grayle turned his head slowly, observing the way she was reflected from different angles in a half-dozen of the big, gilt-framed mirrors against the walls.

She gave him back his comb and said, "I'm glad we've met." She took his face between her hands and kissed him. "I'll be back. Only three days." Her hands left his face and she went out quickly.

* * *

Grayle went into his room and used the water in the bowl to wash his own face, drying himself with the towel still damp from Nora. He kept his mind away from what he would have to deal with when she returned. Picking up the nudes he'd done of her, he tacked them to the wall with the other studies, between the Rodin sketches and the group of pastels.

Then he lay down on the bed, shutting his eyes and letting himself drift. Looking at the darkness inside his lids and waiting for the emergence of what he felt coming. Searching for it, but not too hard; mostly letting it come in its own way. One part of him secretly observing its development, out of the corner of his eye, while the other part of him remained aware of the scent of Nora in the fabric of the mattress under his cheek.

He lay that way for almost an hour. When it came it had nothing to do with the drawings he'd done of Nora. But it didn't take him entirely by surprise. Some part of him had known for a long time what his next picture would be.

It was to take him fourteen days to finish the painting. He was to call it *The Drowner*.

Five men crowded precariously into a rowboat in danger of capsizing amid the surging waves of a turbulent ocean. The light obscure; the sky hidden in churning masses of storm cloud, the colors brutally somber.

The composition was boldly basic: the boat with its crowded figures dominating the undulating horizontals of sky and water—with a broken diagonal begun by a slash of light through the clouds in the upper left, and continuing through the figure of a man struggling in the sea in the lower right, trying to reach the boat.

The features of the swimmer were Grayle's. Under him, just below the surface of the water, was a woman's hand, reaching out of the depths, grasping at his ankle.

Sometimes, while he was at work on the picture, he found himself remembering where it came from.

6

The house in the Bridesburg section of Philadelphia was part of a block of identical attached two-floor red brick homes, with shallow porches and tiny yards in back. The neighborhood was flanked by a Kopper's Coke plant and a chemical factory, and there were days, even in the worst heat of summer, when they had to keep their windows closed against the soft coal dust and sulphur fumes.

The neighborhood was predominantly Polish and German, most of the men skilled or semiskilled factory workers. Harry Moser, Rita's husband, was the only one who didn't come home every night after work. He had risen to the position of chief mate on a cargo ship by the time that Nick Grayle came to live with them. A short, stocky man with the arms of a gorilla and a cheerful, blunt-featured face, the skin sun-bronzed and leathery from too much salty wind.

Rita and Harry Moser had no children and were unlikely to have any, because Rita apparently had a condition that prevented her from becoming pregnant. The problem had to be Rita's, Harry pointed out, since he had a number of illegitimate kids in various port cities around the world. But he said this with gentle humor, not really minding. And he didn't mind when Rita brought Nick into their home. It gave Harry a kid to teach carpentry to, between voyages, in the shop he'd fixed up in a shed behind the house.

Nick developed in return an attachment for Harry almost as strong as his feeling for Rita. But other than that he grew up the loner he had been as a child. Sometimes Rita worried about the way he didn't make friends nor seem to want any. As though he found it hard to trust anyone else.

Harry shrugged it off: he knew men like that aboard ships, and they did all right for themselves, having found a way of life that fitted what they were. The boy obviously had a driving need to belong to someone and something; but it was intensity he required, not variety. Nick had Rita and Harry, and his painting.

His grades in school continued to be poor, while he concentrated on his real studies: refining his drawing skill, developing his technique with oils, enlarging his grasp of color, expanding what he could do with it. On Sundays when the weather was good, Nick and Rita would have picnics in Fairmount Park, spending most of the day painting landscapes and sketching people having picnics and ball games. When Harry was between voyages he went with them, playing catch with Nick while Rita prepared their meal in the open, joining pick-up baseball games while they were painting.

For his study of the human figure, Nick continued to use the sculpture in the museum, and Rita's book of anatomy. But when he turned sixteen, he began slipping a neighborhood girl into the house on afternoons when Rita was away seeing publishers. The first time, the girl was surprised to find the reason he'd given her was the real one: that all he wanted of her unclothed body was to capture it with pencil and paintbrush. By the third time her surprise turned to anger, and she demanded payment. Nick paid her from then on, with nickels he earned hauling and unloading at a local junkyard over weekends.

Rita caught on to what he was up to, studied his first attempts with a live human nude approvingly, and was as surprised as the girl to learn that Nick used her as a model and nothing else. She began looking at him thoughtfully.

It was some weeks later when Harry was away on a trip to South America that Rita came home one morning after spending the night with a friend Nick knew to be male. He glowered at her through the rest of the day, until she told him to stop it, he was making her nervous. Then Nick just stood there, his fists clenched at his sides, staring at her, refusing to put in words the jealousy and passion over-whelming him.

Rita met his stare, took his hand and led him firmly up the stairs to the bed in his room. It was the most beautiful, tender and revealing experience of his life. And it continued so.

But before long, guilt about Harry began nagging at Nick. Rita explained why there was no reason to feel guilty. "What do you think Harry's doing in all those ports he hits? I don't want him to tell me, and he doesn't want to know about what I'm doing. As long as neither of us feels a need to boast about it, it's okay. Harry and I can go on loving each other, our own way, when we're together. Hell, Nick—life is there to be tasted. Otherwise it's all such a waste. It's a new century and a new world. People are supposed to be free, as long as they don't hurt each other. And Harry and I don't."

It was always in Nick's room that he spent his nights with Rita; never in the bed belonging to her and Harry. She had her own personal code of right and wrong. So it was in Nick's bed that she whispered one night, with her face buried against his throat, about something she'd once read in a French novel: "Only the last love of a woman can satisfy the first love of a man. And vice versa, Nick. You're my last lover."

Harry was already talking about giving up the sea, which aggravated his increasing trouble with arthritis, to move to the milder climate of California and start a carpentry and home-decoration business together with Rita. If he sensed what was going on between Nick and his wife, he never showed it.

And when Harry was home, it became Nick's time to fight the demon jealousy, alone in his bed, eventually taming it to a stoic acceptance of what must be. The situation changed when Nick graduated from high school at seventeen and signed on permanently as a deckhand aboard Harry's ship, to pay for his own clothes and art materials, and his share of the rent and food. From then on, he and Harry were always back in Philadelphia at the same time. Rita's feeling for him became confined to warm glances, and an occasional tender hug. For Nick, their relationship became a delicious, gentled memory, the torment gone.

World War I interrupted Rita and Harry's preparations for the move west. The American merchant marine discovered a shortage of licensed, experienced officers, and Harry felt a duty to continue as long as the conflict lasted. Nick continued to sail with him, rising from ordinary seaman to able seaman, most of their trips between Cuba and Baltimore, carrying cargoes of sugar.

The month the war ended, Rita and Harry made the move to California. Nick stayed on in the merchant marine, using a cheap boardinghouse in Baltimore between trips, trying to save money—toward a purpose that had grown in him for a long time. Ever since the Armory Show in New York, back in 1913, Grayle had known he would have to go to Europe, and immerse himself in the art there, before he could consider his apprenticeship over and try his strength as a full-time painter.

But merchant marine pay was low, even when he rose to bos'n's mate, and his savings account grew with excruciating slowness. Prohibition had been in effect for some years when he ran into a former shipmate who had gotten a job on a rum-running vessel, carrying liquor from the Bahamas through the Coast Guard blockade off the shores of New England and New York. The man told Grayle of an opening on his vessel for an experienced sailor, and Grayle left the merchant marine and joined the rum-runners.

The *Sarah II* slid through thick night fog with Grayle at the wheel and Petersen, the skipper, beside him giving terse instructions in a quiet voice.

Petersen was a fat old-timer with a pockmarked face and a keen feel for foul-weather direction and distances. According to his calculations they had just crossed the line into the territorial waters of the United States. Which was bad, if the Coast Guard spotted them. Petersen was taking the chance, searching for better visibility closer to the coast. Inside this low-clinging fog, there was no hope of making contact with the speedboats the bootlegger was scheduled to send out to off-load the *Sarah II*'s cargo.

Sarah was the name of Petersen's wife. *Sarah I* had been the sleek, two-masted fishing schooner in which Grayle had made his first three rum-running trips from the Bahamas.

The first two had considerably fattened his bank account. The third had ended in disaster when they were intercepted by two fast powerboats manned by armed hijackers, each boat mounting a heavy Lewis machine gun. Outnumbered and outgunned, lacking the speed to get away, the *Sarah I* had fought its losing battle and wound up wrecked on the Block Island coast, one crewman killed and others wounded, cargo a dead loss.

Petersen had taken Grayle and the other survivors to Brooklyn to strike a bargain with his biggest customer. The bootlegger agreed to finance a new vessel, better suited to the increasing dangers of the trade, in exchange for a new payment deal. Petersen already knew the vessel he wanted. He bought it with the bootlegger's advance, and named it the *Sarah II*: a sixty-five-foot cruiser with triple screws, three 450-horsepower Liberty motors capable of hitting over thirty knots when driven all-out. Two Lewis guns were mounted fore and aft; there were four sub-machine guns and two marksman rifles, and a supply of hand grenades. They now had a vessel that could outrun anything the Coast Guard had, and deal with all but the strongest concentration of hijackers.

But they didn't head south to the Bahamas this time; the *Sarah II* had a new destination. Just before the Prohibition law had gone into effect, a number of Kentucky distilleries had been dismantled and transported to Montreal. The first stocks of liquor distilled in the new location had now had four years to mature, and the Canadian operators were moving it in bulk to their dockside warehouses in St. Pierre harbor. That was where the *Sarah II* went for its cargo.

Its first trip was completed with no real trouble. They left a Coast Guard patrolboat behind without half trying, and when a speedy hijacker hove into view it looked them over and swung away to find easier game. The *Sarah II* delivered the liquor on schedule, and the profit resulted in a healthy increase in Grayle's savings.

This was the second trip.

The heavy fog swirled away from the *Sarah II*'s bow, and closed in again solidly behind the stern. Petersen kept the engines at slow as the boat angled closer to the unseen tip of Long Island, easing through the soup in search of visibility. When it came it was sudden: the boat sliding out of the fog into a relatively clear patch of night, like going through a moist wall.

There were thick banks of fog on either side, but toward the coast only separated clouds of mist. Petersen rang down for full-astern, and then had the engines idle while he peered through binoculars toward the shore. The boat rolled heavily in the choppy swells. Grayle couldn't make out any shoreline; but when a pair of red and green lights blinked in the prearranged code, he could see it without binoculars. Petersen had his signalman blink back the answer. The blinker was just starting when a man on lookout yelled a warning.

They all heard it at the same time: the throbbing of giant engines, the direction difficult to place because of the diffusing effect of the fog. Petersen let the binoculars fall to his chest and rang the engine-room for full speed ahead. A U.S. destroyer, a long World War I four-stacker, materialized out of the fog some distance to starboard.

Petersen growled an order, and Grayle spun the wheel. The boat leapt into motion with a sharp swing to port. It was going at top speed when it dove into the protection of the fog, and the destroyer was lost to sight. They were racing away through the heart of the fog when the four-stacker's cannons thundered.

It was blind shooting. But one of the cannons got lucky. The *Sarah II* jumped and slewed around as a shell smashed away part of its stern at the waterline. Then it was wallowing sickeningly, with only one screw still turning, the ocean pouring into the hold.

Grimly, Petersen snapped an order for Grayle to steer toward land. The boat responded sluggishly, its bow lifting out of the water as the stern settled.

Neither the shore nor the destroyer was visible when the last engine quit. The boat lost any semblance of forward motion, and the sea increased its grip. Petersen shouted the order to abandon.

The *Sarah II* foundered with startling abruptness as Grayle left the wheel to help with the lowering of the lifeboat. A heavy wave slammed into him and hurled him into the ocean.

He came up spitting water, his eyes burning from the salt. The *Sarah II* was gone, and he couldn't see the lifeboat, or anyone else in the sea near him. Taking a deep breath, Grayle doubled himself below the surfaec and dragged off his shoes, letting them sink away from him. Then he straightened, treading water, turning slowly, squinting into the fog. When he did spot the lifeboat, it was far off to his right, being rowed away from him.

Grayle tried to shout after it. Each time, waves slapped water into his opened mouth. When he finally managed a yell, his voice had become a rasping croak that did not carry. The boat kept on, leaving him behind. But its progress was slow, the rowing hampered by the running swells, the choppy surface. Grayle swam after it, putting all his strength into trying to catch up, desperation injecting jolts of heightened energy into his arms and legs.

For a time he seemed to be closing the distance. Then he collided with something large and yielding. The body of a man, floating head-down, face completely submerged. Pulling the corpse out of his way, he went on after the crowded boat. But he was no longer closing the distance. The driving panic of his first effort had taken its inevitable toll: his arms and legs were losing their initial power.

Grayle was not trying to catch up any longer, only to follow the boat. They'd have a hand compass; they'd know the direction to the mist-hidden coast. He continued to swim strongly, but without urgency now, to husband his reserves, pacing himself to last the distance.

The lifeboat kept getting farther away, and finally vanished. Grayle swam toward the point where he'd last seen it, praying that he would not lose his sense of direction. His head began a dull pounding that drove tiny needles of pain into his eardrums and the back of his eyes.

His arms and legs were becoming heavy, their muscles limp. Each stroke required a separate effort; it took concentration to keep his face above the surface. The swells began rolling him. His throat ached from the sea water that got in through his nostrils and clenched teeth; his eyes were almost blinded with salt. There was a roaring now in his ears, and flashes of bright color inside his skull. His legs were sinking . . .

He found himself remembering about his mother, her body never found, drifting forever below the surace of this same ocean. In his childhood she had often come in dreams to crouch on his lower legs, her face horrible; that was when he would wake shrieking, and why he could never tolerate the weight of a folded blanket across his feet when he went to sleep. Now she came from the sea beneath him, to grab at his sinking legs, trying to drag him down to her.

The shock of terror drove him to the final convulsive effort, making his legs kick wildly, his arms flail. His sinking hands touched something solid below him. Crazed hope burst out of exhaustion to pull him forward a few more yards, until his knees, too, were moving over hard-packed bottom. Grayle crawled a bit farther, into shallower water.

He stayed there a long time, on hands and knees, the surf lapping around his arms and thighs, gulping air into his tortured lungs, his head hanging. Then he crawled the rest of the way out of the water, up onto the dry sand of a dune, and passed out.

When he came to, he was sprawled out on his back, looking up at the night sky. Through the clouds he could see the position of the moon. He hadn't been unconscious long. Sitting up, he dragged off his socks and shook the caked sand from them. Getting his bare feet under him, he stood up. His legs were still heavy, little tremors running along the muscles and twitching the nerve ends. He stuck the socks in a back pocket and slapped drying sand from his shirt and trousers.

Neither the boat nor its crew was in sight, in either direction. Wherever they had beached it couldn't be far from here, but Grayle didn't want to hunt for them. The destroyer had certainly radioed ashore. There'd be police soon along this stretch of Montauk beach. Grayle headed inland, away from the sea.

When he was far enough from the beach, he began following a dirt road. It led to a small village. He bypassed it and kept walking in the direction of New York, letting the warm night air finish drying him. By dawn Montauk Point was far behind him. Two hours later he reached a town with a general store, filling station and bus stop. The bills in his pocket wallet were still damp and stiff with ocean salt, but there was enough for his immediate needs. He bought a pair of sneakers, had a big breakfast in the diner next to the filling station and took the noon bus the rest of the way to Manhattan. On the way, he made his decision.

He was finished with rum-running. The increasing vigilance of the government and violence of the hijackers had raised the risk above a level he wanted to deal with. The threat from both would continue to grow: the Coast Guard would acquire faster vessels and the hijackers heavier weapons. Grayle had other things to do with his life than to spend it in prison, and he had no intention of dying in a gunfight.

He figured that he had enough in his savings account now to last him a year in Europe if he was frugal. That would have to do.

Grayle managed to sign on a tramp freighter bound for Great Britain. When the freighter reached Cardiff he jumped ship and took the train to London. He spent three months there, and then three in Florence, before he settled in Paris.

It was 1924 when Grayle left America. He was twenty-six years old. It was two years later that he met Nora, and began *The Drowner*—the last of the thirteen works which were to be the only paintings of his that the world would know about for the next two decades.

7

The cold blue of an autumn sky was framed in the tilted skylight window, with clouds like flecks of bleeding wool. Grayle laced his fingers under his head and continued to lie there on his mattress, coming awake as he gazed at that framed sky. Trying to resolve that special light into combinations of oil paints. And failing. And remembering Van Gogh's exasperated cry before a country sunset: "How does God *do* it?"

Grayle turned his head to look at what he'd accomplished so far, with his first two days and nights of work on *The Drowner*. A disquiet stirred in him, brief but sharp. He switched the feeling off and got up from his bed to wash his hands and face with cold water from the bowl on the table. To mix the critical faculty with the creative before a painting was finished was folly. The first invariably intruded on the second, weakening it. He had learned long ago that the only way was just to keep working to the end, almost mindlessly. There were paintings he'd despaired of, which had seemed sickeningly inert, but had sprung to life with the final touches.

He dressed and folded the blanket neatly at the foot of the mattress. It was the first night he'd really needed the blanket. He thought of the winter coming. Remembering the previous one, when he'd had to lay a carpet over the blanket to fight the cold at night, and had painted wearing woolen gloves. But that was still a couple months ahead, with luck. Grayle poured the water from the bowl into a tin bucket and carried it down to the courtyard.

He left the bucket upended beside the well and got two breakfast rolls from the baker. He ate them with a large coffee in the bar. Both the rolls and the coffee were on credit in this period during which he did not go to Les Halles in search of work. So were the dinners he ate each evening at Madame Gaussin's little house inside the court-yard, and the apple he got from a pushcart vender on Rue Mouffetard, as he set out for a short, brisk walk.

He wasn't the only one in the neighborhood getting by on credit. The number of workmen unemployed was on the increase. Shopkeepers who didn't give credit didn't do much business.

He climbed the cobbled street to Place Contrescarpe. In front of the bistros, university students were doing their homework in clusters around tables to which they'd pur-chased tenancy with a single coffee. Under the plane trees groups of idle men in shabby clothes argued world econom-ics and growled vague threats concerning inept politicians. Grayle circled down the slope via twisted passages between jumbles of grim, ancient houses, where the air carried whiffs of the slaughterhouses some blocks away.

Reaching Saint Médard, he turned back toward Rue Mouffetard across a square that had been the church's graveyard. The government of Paris had destroyed it two centuries before, frightened by the swift-growing sect of hysterics who gathered there to go into convulsions around the grave of their saint.

Governments had to be fatally shortsighted, Grayle thought, to crush sects like the Convulsionists. Everybody in this world required some means of escape out of the crushing pressures of their lives: some hiding place where for short periods Hell could not find them.

Grayle returned to his courtyard behind Le Soldat Perdu, filled the tin bucket with water and lugged it up the flights of narrow steps to his place. Then he advanced on the easel and got back to work.

Always, during those first days of work on *The Drowner*, there lurked in the back of his mind the inevita-ble confrontation with Nora. But he had other visitors, be-fore he saw Nora again.

* * *

The first was Tonton. But Grayle could never regard Tonton in the same category as any other visitor. Because he always came when Grayle was working on a painting. And when he came, he always did the same thing.

Tonton had the small bakery in the courtyard. Grayle didn't know any other name for him, and doubted that anyone along Mouffetard did. He was just Tonton—Uncle. A quiet, solitary man, with a dreamy sadness in the thin face whose swarthy complexion was accentuated by silver-gray hair. Living to himself, speaking little, baking his cakes and bread and remembering past horrors.

He was a Greek, from the Turkish port of Smyrna. When the Turks began, in 1918, their systematic slaughter of all the Greeks and Armenians in their country, he had squeezed his wife and daughter and himself aboard one of the vessels carrying refugees across to the nearby Greek island of Chios. The blood-inflamed Turks had followed, and the people in the port of Chios had jammed themselves into the church for God's protection. God did not hear their cries.

Tonton had told Grayle in that gentle voice of his that the walls of that church were now lined with the skulls of the slaughtered, so no Greek would ever forget. Tonton had survived because he was one of the first to fall, with a head wound; he'd been buried out of sight under the piles of corpses that fell in the hour that followed. When he'd been extricated the next day, he'd learned his wife and daughter had been hacked to death after being repeatedly raped. He murdered two Turkish troopers before slipping away from Chios; but that had not relieved his hate, nor his shame.

He had left Greece, seeking some place where what had happened was not known and he wouldn't have to talk about it. And he'd found the French Foreign Legion. They'd shipped him to Algeria to fight the rebels, granted him French citizenship near the end of his five-year enlistment and given him a medal for ferocity in battle. He'd come out with most of the money he'd earned over those five years, and invested it in the bakery behind Rue Mouffetard.

Tonton came, this time, late in the afternoon. Like everyone around the courtyard, Tonton knew when Grayle was painting a new picture. It was obvious in his altered daily routine: the fact that he did not go to Les Halles for nights on end, even in the way he walked and spoke, with a preoccupied quality.

As usual, Tonton brought with him a fresh-baked loaf of bread and an apple tart. These he placed on Grayle's table. They would not be added to Grayle's bill. It was a ritualistic offering for what followed. He would sit and watch Grayle work. He never made any comment on Grayle's paintings, neither while he worked nor at any other time. Whatever he got out of watching Grayle at work was his own private affair. Usually he would remain for about an hour and then get up, still without speaking, and leave.

Grayle had been concentrating for a couple hours on strengthening the tonal values of the sea and foundering boat, when Tonton arrived this day. For perhaps half an hour he continued at it, barely aware of the baker's observing presence, until his eyes felt burned from dealing with the colors so long, and he could no longer properly judge the results. Automatically cleaning the brush he'd just been using, Grayle put it down and walked to the open skylight window.

Its lower sill came just below his shoulders. Grayle rested his arms on it and looked down at the crazy-quilt of crowded roofs and chimneys. Close by, the upper foliage of a chestnut tree burst out of the masses of stone, tin and brick. Near it, three cats were sunning themselves atop the blackened wall of a fire-gutted tenement.

Tonton stood up and said, "Let's go down. I'll buy you a coffee."

Grayle turned to look at him. The baker's sure instinct for his moods no longer surprised him. Picking up the tart Tonton had brought, Grayle ate it as he led the way out.

They sat down at one of the sidewalk tables. Madame Bobichon, the inevitable cigarette trapped in a corner of her lips, brought out their order. A double café for Grayle, hot chocolate for Tonton. Grayle stirred two lumps of sugar in his cup and relaxed, observing the street and letting his mind clear. Tonton talked quietly about his years as a Legionnaire, not expecting response from Grayle. He loved the Legion, in spite of its harsh discipline, its grinding desert marches, its use as a suicide force easily replenished from the world's bountiful supply of exiles, unemployables and hunted criminals. It was the Legion that had used up all of his hate and shame, returning him to the world as one of the most gentle people Grayle had ever met.

The Legion had even taught him his baker's trade—while he was recuperating from bullet and saber wounds sustained in an ill-conceived night attack on a rebel stronghold in the Harrar. And it was the Legion, too, which had removed the burden of Tonton's past. No Legion recruit had a history, unless he chose to discuss it. Recruits were even assigned false names to protect those who'd assumed them out of necessity.

Tonton told Grayle about the *cafard*, that strange craziness into which Legionnaires could sink from too much desert and heat, mixed with too many secret memories. He recounted the story famous among them of a trooper who had fired his rifle at the back of his colonel's head, missing by a centimeter. The colonel had turned, looked calmly at the man who had just tried to murder him and seen the *cafard* in his eyes. He sentenced the man to six days' solitary confinement on bread and water as punishment for having missed his shot at such short range.

Tonton laughed softly, shaking his head, and finished his chocolate. He stood up, and looked at Grayle's eyes. "Always beware the *cafard*, Monsieur Grayle. It is important to distract oneself, from time to time. I seldom see you laugh."

Grayle smiled at him. "That has always been a problem, Tonton. Even when I was a kid, I took myself too seriously." He gave it some thought. "I never had any talent for telling jokes, for instance. And I could never remember any that I heard. Usually, I fail to understand the point."

"I was not speaking of jokes," Tonton said. "For grown men there are other amusements." He placed a hand on Grayle's shoulder, and then went away through the courtyard, to his bed in the hotel. For a baker, workdays began at three in the morning.

Grayle sipped the dregs of his coffee and continued to sit there, not allowing the waiting canvas to enter his consciousness. A taxicab pulled to the corner at the foot of the street. Victor Royan climbed out, followed by a slim woman in a gray suit and hat of understated elegance. They came up the street, Victor swinging his cane, the woman a black-beaded handbag. When Victor saw Grayle, he slowed his step for a moment, taking the woman's arm and whispering to her.

She was in her fifties, wire-thin and darkly beautiful. Huge sleepy eyes, the careful mouth of a professional gambler, slim hands charged with nervous energy. Black hair extremely short, shaved at the back of the neck: a style begun recently by the lesbian crowd around Montparnasse and adopted by the chic avant-garde. When they reached the table she took the chair vacated by Tonton, crossing her legs and looking up at Victor, waiting mockingly. Her eyebrows were plucked to long arches.

Victor introduced her uneasily: "This is Pauline Renard. I do remember what you told me, but I still think you should know each other. And since you didn't meet at the gallery the other evening"—an angry smile twisted his mouth—"damn it, I want Pauline to have a look at your work. She has *promised* me not to say a single word."

Pauline Renard turned her head and met Grayle's look with banked humor in the huge eyes. A woman who liked a good fight, he decided.

She said, "I had to swear an oath, by all I hold holy. Which means my bank account, I suppose." Her voice had a raspy toughness. "I think you are both ridiculous. And *your* attitude, of course, is insufferable. Conceited and naive. I wouldn't have been dragged here except for my curiosity. Not about your paintings. About you. It is the first time I've known Victor to care this much about anybody of the male gender. Is he becoming human—or senile?"

Grayle said, "I don't think you'd find my kind of work of interest."

"You don't know me," she pointed out crisply, "so you can't possibly know that."

"I know what your gallery is showing."

"You mean right now? I happen to think Gerard Rosnay is a very talented young artist."

Victor said sardonically, "I'm sure he has talent, in bed."

Pauline Renard gave him a poisonous smile, "More than you had, when you still had some." And to Grayle: "Why don't you like Gerard?"

Grayle made a small gesture with one hand, as expressive as a shrug. "I have nothing against him, or for him. Constructivism isn't a type of art I have feelings about."

"And you think it's all I care for? Do I look such a fool? My personal taste in current artists has *some* range. Say, from Bonnard to Kandinsky to Christian Schad . . . Is that enough for you?"

"You've left out Darius," Victor reminded her.

"I never leave him out of anything. But a dealer isn't supposed to keep talking about her husband."

Grayle sat up straighter.

Pauline Renard observed his changed expression with a cynical smile. "Ah, suddenly impressed. Don't be—it has no bearing. And Darius is not really my husband. Only as near to one as I'll ever have. Well?" she went on acidly. "It is your move, and the meter is still running in our taxi-cab."

Grayle took out his key and gave it to Victor. "You don't need me there for this."

Pauline Renard stood and took the key from Victor's hand. "I don't need either of you. I'd prefer to have a look without having to listen to another publicity onslaught. Just tell me where it is."

As she disappeared into the courtyard, Victor sat down and laid his cane across the center of the table. "I hope you don't mind too much, my bringing her here?"

"It's done, so don't worry about it. I understand that you're trying to help me."

"Well, thank God for that." Victor called into the bar for a calvados. "It could have been accomplished so much more easily if you had met Pauline the other evening as I'd planned. Instead of allowing Nora to kidnap you."

Grayle looked at him. "Word travels fast, in your circle."

"Gian-Carlo and Nora Pattara are old friends of mine." Grayle frowned. "Pattara?"

Victor considered his expression. "Did Nora use her maiden name? She's been doing that quite a bit lately. A wish for independence." He hesitated. "She didn't mention having a husband?"

"It didn't come up."

"Ah. Well, don't let it trouble you. Gian-Carlo—such things amuse him. Quite sensible, considering the amount of time she spends alone while he is off to other countries dealing with his family's publishing empire." Victor hesitated again. "Your modern permissive husband. The only thing he is never going to give her is a divorce. That is the Good Italian Family side of him. In those families divorce doesn't exist. They find—an arrangement."

Grayle took a moment. "How long have they been married?"

"About six years, I believe." Victor studied him. "Nora is a lovely girl," he said carefully, "but with too much undirected energy, and too many changing whims. Take her latest, for example: to become a professional photographer. She's quite good at it, actually. But the only pictures she's managed to sell so far have been to Gian-Carlo. For a guide to Paris his firm published. Which doesn't do much to establish her as independent of him."

Grayle sat in silence.

Madame Bobichon brought Victor's drink out. Victor paid her and downed half of it before resuming: "The real trouble between Nora and Gian-Carlo, I'm afraid, is that the poor girl still believes in love. She can't accept the substitution of quiet friendship." He sipped at his drink. "I have perhaps known Nora better than most. So I would certainly understand if you find her interesting. But I would advise you to be careful there. As I mentioned, her whims are changeable. Extremely. People have been rather badly hurt in the process."

Grayle wanted no more of this. He forced lightness into his tone: "Some time ago you accused me of trying to mother you. Now it's you wanting to play mother."

Victor's smile was a trifle embarrassed. "Well, I suppose that is what friends tend to do with each other, isn't it?"

"I suppose." Grayle's thoughts went to the woman studying his work upstairs—and from her to Darius Kreschevsky, an artist he admired. He liked the powerful social realism of his early paintings, woodcuts and lithographs, the joyous colors of the abstractions to which he had turned in his old age. "What *is* the connection between Darius and Pauline Renard?" he asked Victor.

"Now? I'm not really sure what to call it. She was his mistress, long ago. For quite some time. Darius was the one who taught her about art, and introduced her to everybody of any importance. Then he launched her career by making her his agent. Of course, she couldn't have had a better foundation to build her business on. As it turned out, *he* couldn't have found a better agent. Their personal relationship?" Victor thought about it. "Now they live separately, most of the time, but consider themselves an inseparable unit." He thought about it some more, and shook his head. "When two people remain strongly attached to each other over a long period, in spite of everything . . . does anybody else ever really understand what is going on between the two of them? Except perhaps themselves? Perhaps."

Grayle cut in sardonically: "You do take a lot of words to say two people get along with each other."

Victor laughed. "Yes, I have a tendency to split each hair in four parts, as they say. I am an incurable thinker; not a man of action, like yourself."

"I don't spend much time thinking about what's going on inside me, if that's what you mean."

"Perhaps it is safer not to?"

Grayle considered that. "Maybe."

Pauline Renard returned and gave Grayle a short, hard look. Keeping to her promise, she said nothing. But before starting off down Mouffetard to the waiting cab, she placed her business card on the table before him.

Victor glanced from it to Grayle as he rose to his feet. Taking his cane, he raised it in a kind of salute before striding away after her.

8

Nora Cesari arrived the following day.

Grayle saw her when he returned from his morning walk. She was maneuvering her car around the trees in the center of Place Contrescarpe, angling to enter Rue Mouffe- tard. When she spotted him crossing the square to her, Nora swung two wheels up onto the sidewalk and shut off the motor.

He stopped beside the car, looking in the open window. "Come on up."

Her hands gripped the steering wheel. She looked at him with a bewildered expression. "No," she answered quietly. "Please get in. I want to talk to you."

Grayle walked around the car and got in the front seat beside her, shutting the door and turning to look at her. What he saw was her profile. Her hands had fallen from the steering wheel to her lap, and she was gazing ahead through the windshield.

He waited, and at last she spoke. Her tone was tightly controlled: "That was very unfair of you, not telling me the truth about us the other night. What was it—a way of inflicting a bit of vicious revenge, through me?"

"What did your mother tell you?" Grayle asked her steadily.

"What she should have told me the first time: the truth. I told her about meeting you. That I liked you—very much. I could see it frightened her. She said I shouldn't like you *too* much. And she explained why." Nora forced herself to look at him. "It seems we're related."

"Not really." He wanted desperately not to deal with

this. But there was no way to avoid it without losing her completely. "We've never met before. Neither of us even knew the other existed. That's hardly what you can call a relationship. We're strangers to each other. Or, we were."

"You knew," she insisted harshly. "When you took me to bed. You knew I was your sister."

"Only half," he said heavily.

Her control broke: "Good Christ! *Why* didn't you tell me?" Her voice faltered. "I want to know—was it what I said? Your chance for vengeance—a desire to hurt?"

"Not to hurt you." He spoke softly, seeking the right words. "Just to hurt *him*. The way he hurt me—from a distance. And even that was gone, when we . . ."

She looked away from him, through the windshield, her slender hands taking hold of the steering wheel again. "I've done things people call immoral; and some more than that. But I can't deal with this. I can't handle incest." Nora shook her head. "It won't happen again," she said firmly.

Grayle's hand reached out and took hold of her chin, turned it until she was looking at him once more. "I don't want to lose you."

She didn't pull away. But there was no give in her expression. "It won't happen again," she repeated. She heard her voice become uncertain: "But if you want to be my friend, my brother . . ."

Grayle let go of her chin. "I want to keep seeing you. I want to draw you again."

Nora drew a harsh breath. "I've spent hours thinking about this. The only excuse I can find for not hating you is that you *are* my brother. But . . . I know so little about you." She hesitated, and her voice became gentle: "What was your mother like? My mother told me a bit, but her viewpoint has a certain prejudice, naturally."

"All I know about my mother is that she was a selfish bitch. With an overinflated idea of how much guilt her suicide would cause your father."

Nora stared at him. "Are you always so hard on people? I hope not. And by the way, my father is your father, too."

Grayle shook his head. "I don't feel it."

"Nevertheless, he *is*. At least biologically. And that does make me your sister." She forced a small smile. "At least, half."

His smile was genuinely amused. "Biologically."

Nora leaned toward him, and the sincerity in her voice surprised him: "Please be my brother—really. I've been thinking about that, since my mother told me. I'd like someone I can confide in, be honest with. A big brother."

"That's not what I feel."

"You will if I work at it," Nora insisted. "I have inherited at least a little of my mother, after all. She hasn't wanted many things in her life, but what she wanted she got, and kept. Icelandic women have a reputation for strong character. You knew she was from Iceland?"

"No, I didn't." But it added to the contradictions Grayle kept seeing in her: this mixture of Arctic and Mediterranean seas in her blood.

"That was where Papa met her," Nora told him, seizing gratefully on this new topic. "He'd gone to Iceland because he'd heard about the fantastic scenery, and she posed for one of his paintings. She was so much younger than him, but she decided very quickly that she was going to become his wife. And with all the other women who'd made that same decision, she was the one who got him."

She regarded him with taunting humor, suddenly; her smile deliberately wolfish. "And don't forget, I'm half Icelandic. So when I decide I want you for my brother, it is really useless for you to resist me."

"It won't work out that way, though. Not in the end."

Anger flared in her. "You're so sure of that. You're always so sure of everything, aren't you?" But the anger died in her, as swiftly as it had come. "I envy you that. It's so obvious, in your face, your manner, your work: that absolute sureness of direction."

"Sometimes," he put in mildly, "the direction is not so sure."

"But it is. Even when you think it's not. You are such a healthy man. Strength of motivation. Single-minded, undeviating drive. The sense of purpose I lack."

Grayle said: "You have your photography."

Nora fell silent, lowering her hands to her lap. "I suppose it was Victor who told you about that."

"Yes."

"And about my husband, too, I imagine."

"What he told me is that you're quite a good photographer. I'd like to see your work."

Nora looked down at her hands. "I'm not really sure if it is my *work*. Or if it will turn out to be just another thing I'm playing at. I start things with such enthusiasm. And then . . ." An angry grimace. "They just—wither. No, that's not right. It is my interest in them that withers. Lovers, professions—even angers. I can't sustain. *Mea culpa.*"

Grayle watched her raise her head, glaring through the windshield as she thought about what she was saying. "First, I wanted to be a dancer. Passionately—until my marriage. And when that went wrong, I entered medical school. Gian-Carlo approved, encouraged . . . and two years later I ran out of interest and quit."

Nora drew a ragged breath. "Now it's photography. And I don't want it if I'm not going to have enough motivation to become a professional. I already have too many things I'm an amateur at. Including love." Abruptly, she looked at her watch. "I'd better go."

As Grayle opened the door her hand stopped him. "You do understand that I meant what I said before? We . . . it can't happen again."

Grayle climbed out of her car. Before he shut the door he told her, "Bring me some of your pictures to look at, the next time you come."

She came again two mornings later, carrying a thick cardboard portfolio tied with thick ribbon. She was breathless from running up the steps.

"I can't stay . . ." She stopped as soon as she'd stepped inside the storage area of his loft. "I have to catch the next train to Berlin. Me and my camera! I have a commission, to shoot a series of pictures for a private collector."

Nora broke her excitement with a wry grimace. "A ghastly job, actually—but for a lot of money. *And* a chance to see Berlin. I'll tell you about it when I get back. Maybe it won't be so ghastly, after all."

She handed Grayle the portfolio. "Some of my pictures to look at, while I'm gone. You asked to see them."

He took the portfolio and held it in the crook of his left arm, looking at her. "When will you be back?"

"Ten days to two weeks. It's exciting, I've never been to Berlin. They say it's the most interesting city in the world." Quickly, she kissed him lightly on both cheeks. "I have to run now."

"Enjoy it."

Nora gave the portfolio he was holding an anxious glance. "Some of the pictures might shock you—but I hope not. I almost didn't include them."

Grayle smiled, and caught her chin in his free hand, kissing her lips, briefly. "Third one, for luck."

She turned swiftly, and ran down the stairs.

That night, when he had finished the day's work on his painting, Grayle took Nora's photographs out of the cardboard portfolio. He spread them across his table, under the light of the lamp.

They were superb, technically and in emotional content. He spent a long time studying them—learning from them. Especially a group of photographs of alcoholic vagrants. The one that hit him hardest was of two old men in torn remnants of clothing, huddled together at the corner of a wall in a rubbish-littered lot, passing a bottle between them. Their grimy faces were as empty of hope, or fear, or desire, as the wall against which they leaned.

He pinned this one to his wall, and took down a watercolor he had done in London. One of his favorites: a family of street entertainers, dancing in homemade spangled costumes. It was more than a fair exchange: Nora could make another print, from her negative; he could not.

Grayle slipped his watercolor into her portfolio, with all of the photos except two. These he looked at again for some time. One was a sensuous study of a nude girl, seated on a satiny cushion, absorbed in watching the painting of her toenails by a woman's slim hand entering the picture from its left border. The nude girl was Victor Royan's chauffeur, Jill.

The second picture was an extreme close-up of two women's profiles. One of them was Jill, again. And the same satin pillow. The other woman's head rested on it, and Jill's face bent over her, kissing her on the lips. Just the two profiles, and the light kiss—but disturbingly erotic.

Grayle put the two pictures back in the folder with the others. But he continued to think about them.

Grayle finished painting *The Drowner* late one night, and sprawled across his bed and slept for the next eleven hours. It was late afternoon when he woke, with a ravenous hunger. Breakfast used up most of what was left of the salami and cheese he had laid in before starting the picture. That night, he changed to his gum boots and overalls, and went back to Les Halles.

Over the following days he settled into a regular routine. His nights were spent at Les Halles, the days were given to sleeping and taking long hikes through different quarters of Paris. He always had his sketchbook and pencils with him. When something intrigued his eye or mind, he stopped to draw it. Usually it was something he saw. But more exciting for him were subjects observed in the past, filtered through memory so only certain elements remained. Two of the drawings he did in this period were memory portraits of Nora Cesari.

For more than a week Grayle did not allow himself to begin thinking about what his next painting would be. And during that time he did not take a long look at the picture still drying on his easel.

Gradually he paid off his debts: to Tonton and Boby's bar, to Madame Gaussin and the fruit vendor. His rent was due soon, and that was going to be harder. Flamel, the owner of the carpet warehouse, had originally rented the space to Grayle for a comfortably low rate, with the idea that Grayle could compensate by serving as night watchman. But Flamel had discovered that Grayle was usually away all night. He announced that in all fairness he must insist on a raise in the rent, almost doubling it. Finding an equal amount of space with good natural light would be difficult. Grayle decided he would have to pay the increase.

So he continued to go to Les Halles, night after night. But the job situation there was becoming tighter. The growing number of unemployed workmen in Paris increased the competition for jobs as part-time helpers. Porters who continued to use him pointed to the competition and lowered the wages they paid accordingly.

Grayle had slept off a long but not-too-lucrative night at Les Halles, and then taken a hike out to Buttes-Chaumont. Stopping to make sketches when something caught his interest. But mostly just walking. Letting intimations of a new painting find their own way, not forcing or dwelling on any of them. Not yet; it wasn't time for that yet.

"Don't try to understand too much," Irene had told him, so long ago that he couldn't remember the occasion. "Most things that matter can't be understood. We just don't have the equipment. Our ability to reason beyond simple mechanics is highly overrated. What we do have is an extraordinary gift to feel things. But most people let it atrophy, and have to depend on their rudimentary reasoning faculty."

It was interesting, how much of Irene remained, after so many years and so many other people.

He returned to Mouffetard at seven in the evening and there was a note from Nora, slipped under his door: offering to treat him to dinner at the Rotonde, at eight-thirty. Grayle put on his only suit, brought from America, and walked over to Boulevard Montparnasse to meet her. He took her photo portfolio along.

The Rotonde was on the same block as the Cupole, Dome and Select: four expensive cages in the Montparnasse zoo of international cafe society. With journalists and tourists scurrying between them in search of the successful artists, writers and theater personalities who were the star attractions.

It was not a neighborhood Grayle cared for. It offended

a puritan instinct in him that had nothing to do with any morality that normal people would have recognized as such.

He knew there were some exceptional talents in this zoo. But they seemed to share with the rest an irritating fragility of self-assurance that required constant buttressing in the form of being gaped at and gossiped about. Hence the extreme eccentricities of dress and flamboyance of manner—aped by their lovers, hangers-on and patrons. The other publicity-seekers and dispensers didn't offend Grayle. They didn't matter, one way or another. But the talented ones did. They gave too much of themselves here that should have been given to their talent.

It was a cloudless evening, but the breeze stirring up dust along the boulevard had too sharp a cold edge for dining outside on the terrace. Nora was waiting for him at a table near the interior staircase. They could hear a jazz group playing from the grill room upstairs. She was charged with excitement about her stay in Berlin, and began with her first impressions of the city—the feverish blooming of all the arts, the decadence of high society's antics, the underlying menace in the political atmosphere.

By the time their meal arrived she had launched into her professional triumphs, telling Grayle about them with a self-mocking restraint.

Der Arbeiter-Fotograf, a new Berlin magazine of photography, had bought three pictures from the portfolio she'd taken with her: light-and-shadow studies of Parisian courtyards. A German anarchist journal had taken six of her photographs of French vagrants, beggars and unemployed workers. Though the journal couldn't afford to pay for them, her name would be prominently displayed with the accompanying article.

She had also met a German representative for Michelin. He had been impressed with her pictures, and had given her an introduction to the firm's director of advertising in Paris. "That's where the real money is in photography now," Nora told Grayle as they ate. "In advertising. I have an appointment for tomorrow. If I can begin getting that kind of work . . ." She rapped her knuckles on the wooden arm of her chair, for luck.

Nora shot Grayle an apprehensive glance, and made a self-deprecating grimace. "I know—I sound like money is the most important thing in the world for me. But please understand, it hasn't felt very nice, being totally dependent on a man who . . ."

She didn't finish it. Grayle watched the pain at work in her. "If it hurts so much, don't talk about it."

She was silent for a moment, looking at her plate, her fork toying with the food. "I've always suffered from three excesses which do not mix very well: romantic novels, convent training and worldly ambition."

"Convent?"

"That was when Papa's work was being exhibited all over Europe, and he had to travel a lot. Maman began worrying about the seriousness of his love affairs. So she began tagging along with him on the trips. Leaving me in a convent, for longer and longer stretches. Between the time I was nine and fifteen."

Her soft laugh contained nothing pleasant in it. "The girls had to wear *two* sets of underwear all the time. And we had to change clothes and take baths in the dark, so we wouldn't see our own bodies. The nuns used to make surprise tours of our rooms at night, to make sure we were each in our own bed, alone. Arms spread apart, hands not touching the body—that was especially important."

Nora paused, searching Grayle's face. "The horror of anything sexual was dinned into us repeatedly—if a bit vaguely. And it worked. God, how it worked. For years afterward, I had this thing inside me—like a hidden chain that allowed me to go only so far, and then pulled me up short. What they used to refer to as natural feminine modesty—and now label frigidity." She paused again, and then added quietly: "Gian-Carlo got me over that. He was very good for me—until I became pregnant."

Grayle sensed how deeply it still troubled her, how badly she needed to tell someone about it. "What happened?"

"I had a miscarriage." Nora's tone had become flat,

robbed of emotion. "Gian-Carlo has hardly touched me since then."

"Was it a dangerous miscarriage?"

"Bad enough." She made a face. "It frightened him . . . or disgusted him. The doctor doesn't know if I can ever get pregnant again." She looked at Grayle, and saw only concern in his eyes. Frowning at her clenched hands on the table, she made her fingers open. "Perhaps it would have come to this anyway." Her voice was very low. "Perhaps he was already becoming bored with that aspect of me, only I didn't realize it. He says he still loves me and I'm sure he thinks he does. But sexually—he's had a number of mistresses for that."

Her shrug was careless, but her expression was not. Grayle couldn't stop himself from probing: "Then why stay with him? If it's just because he supports you . . ."

"It's not that easy. You don't understand, this is some kind of sickness with him. He cares for me deeply, in his way. I think it would destroy him, and I can't do that to him."

Grayle felt the jealousy in him, biting. "Because *you* still care for him."

She nodded slowly. "God, I was in love with him. The first time I saw him . . . He'd come out to the house to ask my father for rights to publish some of his old drawings. I was eighteen, and I thought he was the most beautiful thing I'd ever seen." Nora stopped herself, glanced up at Grayle. "You don't want to hear any more of this."

"No," he admitted.

"I don't blame you." She drew a breath, finished the wine in her glass and suddenly smiled. "Enough."

"Good." He returned her smile, and refilled her glass. "You haven't mentioned the commission that took you to Berlin."

"Oh, the commission went well enough." She made a small gesture of boredom. "Tiresome, but well-paid." She watched Grayle as she continued: "A wealthy German lesbian wanted a very private album of photographs, of her favorites." She was still watching his expression. "At least you're not shocked. I'm grateful."

Grayle shrugged. "Everybody is entitled to his own brand of strangeness, as long as he allows me mine."

"It was Jill Ferguson who introduced me to this German woman. I think you know Victor's mistress . . ."

"I've met her." Grayle indicated the portfolio he'd brought along, resting on a chair beside their table. "And I saw your photographs of her."

Nora's eyes slid away from his. "Jill *is* fond of Victor, in some odd way. But her lesbian side is very strong. She . . . has a sort of revolving harem." She hesitated again. "I was never part of it—but I was on the edges of it, for a while."

Grayle took a sip of wine. Nora asked him, suddenly, "What is your relationship with Victor?"

Grayle thought about it. "He's a friend, of sorts . . . and he understands art."

"As long as it's nothing else. I don't much like Victor anymore. He's a twisted man."

Grayle was amused. Now she was warning him to be careful of Victor Royan, as Victor had warned him about her.

When he didn't say anything, Nora told him, "Jill used to be the mistress of Victor's wife. Perhaps you knew?"

"I don't know anything about his personal life."

"The problem was, Jill likes to be in control, and so does Victor's wife. So Jill switched to Victor. Who is perverted enough to enjoy her bossiness. And to enjoy her harem." Scathingly, she added: "It gives him so many pretty young things around the house all the time, to play with. That is your friend Victor."

"I have the feeling," Grayle said drily, "that my friend Victor doesn't have many pleasures in life. By the way, I stole one of your photographs." He told her which of them was now pinned to his wall.

Nora's pleasure in his appreciation of her work was immediate. She quickly opened her portfolio to look at the watercolor he was giving her in exchange. She gazed at it for some time, before looking at him again. "I'll take it to be framed in the morning," she told him softly. "Thank you."

Over their dessert, Nora told him more about what she'd found in Berlin. The disturbing things: the poverty, panic and savage battles between the extreme left and right.

She had taken some pictures that caught this violence. But not many. "My Graflex is too confining and too conspicuous." She told Grayle about a miniaturized camera she'd come across in Berlin, called a Leica. "That's what I need. I want to be able to document what's going on in the world."

"You mean the world of politics." Grayle shook his head. "Stick to your posed pictures—they're beautiful, and meaningful. Politics—what seems important today will be forgotten tomorrow."

"People's lives hang on what is happening today. It's impossible not to care. One must take some kind of stand."

"What stand would you take on the political struggles of the fifteenth century? Do you even know what they were about? But we do know the art of that century. Because that lasted. It's the only thing that did."

Nora knew he was wrong, but there was nothing to be achieved from arguing the matter. It was simply that their motivations were quite different. Grayle was searching for his own private vision of the world. While she wanted to be an interpreter of what she saw changing that world.

As she paid the bill, Nora glanced up and caught the way he was looking at her. "I wish," she said with a faint sigh, "that I didn't keep having this feeling you're humoring me through all this talk about so many things that don't actually matter to you. This feeling that what you're really doing is just waiting patiently for me to forget what we are and fall into bed with you again."

He smiled a little, looked down at his hand on the white tablecloth, turned it over and looked up into her eyes. "Maybe I am," he told her.

Outside, he watched her taxi carry her away. Then he walked back to Rue Mouffetard, changed to sweater, overalls and gum boots, put on his work cap, and headed toward Les Halles in search of another night's employment.

* * *

He did not go looking for her during that autumn in Paris. Always, she came to him. Grayle let her have her try at creating the relationship she'd wanted between them, but he had little faith in its enduring that way. She was not entirely wrong, he thought: something of the unusually strong sense of belonging he felt for her had to do with the blood tie between them. But he couldn't forget the way her body had felt that night.

She came, one afternoon, to tell him she would be away from Paris again for more than a week. "We finally sold the house in Brittany," she explained as he let her in and shut the door behind her. "I have to help my mother with the moving."

The house they were moving to was the one in which Claude Cesari had been born. A small place that had belonged to his family for several generations; part of a village in the south. It was a cheaper place to live, and with the sale of the Brittany home there'd be enough money to get by on. Nora's mother had wanted to make the move since Cesari's pictures had stopped selling and they'd had to live on dwindling savings. But Cesari had never liked the village he'd come from, and refused to accept the permanence of his altered fate.

"But now, of course, he doesn't quite understand what's happening. So . . ." Nora let what she'd intended to say end there. She was looking at the new painting on Grayle's easel.

For some time she said nothing, turning her head once to glance at Grayle, and then back to the face of the struggling swimmer in the painting. Finally she asked: "The woman's hand there, trying to pull you under . . . your mother?"

The sharpness of her intuition startled him. After a moment, he said, "I thought so, at the time."

Nora's eyes looked into his, briefly. She walked over to the two portraits he'd drawn of her from memory, studying them. "When did you do these?"

"While you were in Berlin."

"Do you remember everyone this vividly?" She didn't wait for an answer. "The mouth is so ugly." She turned her face to him. "Is it really that ugly?"

He reached out a finger to trace the outline of her lips. Her eyes narrowed, but she didn't move. The touch of his fingertip was light, memorizing. "I got it wrong. Wait . . ."

Getting a sketchpad and soft pencil, he gestured Nora to the chair. Resting a hip against the table, he began to draw her mouth. Only her mouth.

It was quite easy. He had never seen a mouth with such a separate identity, so strongly defined.

When he was finished he turned the drawing for Nora to look at. "That is your mouth."

"Is it? Good God, if I were a man I would jump on me and rape me—just for that."

"Hasn't anyone?"

She laughed. "It never occurred to me that it was my mouth that was to blame." Her eyes came up from the drawing to Grayle's face. "I really came here to ask if you'll go out to Brittany with me, to help with the moving. There's so much to be packed. And Papa, he may be a problem, when it comes to leaving."

Grayle stiffened, but kept his tone normal: "Sorry, I can't."

"My mother has been waiting to talk to you again. She feels guilty about being rude to you that first time."

"I deserved it. No reason for her to be guilty about it."

"Father isn't going to live much longer, you know. If you are ever going to make your peace with him . . ."

"I have no more argument with him, so there's nothing to make peace about."

"Won't you *please* come—as a favor to me?"

He didn't answer. She saw the stubbornness of his refusal in his eyes, and felt sharp annoyance rise in her. It took an effort to stop herself from putting it into words.

Always, she kissed him when they parted. But this time she didn't.

* * *

Grayle went back to what he'd been doing before she came: staring at his painting of *The Drowner*. It was dry enough, now. He put his hands on it, testing. Then he got a pair of pliers and began removing the tacks fastening it to the stretcher. When the canvas came free he spread it on the floor and rolled it up tightly, and tied a knotted string around it.

He tucked the rolled canvas under his arm, left the building and went to see Maurice Fourrest.

9

Above the Gare de l'Est the strings of heavy barges fed through three cargo canals into the Bassin de la Villette. Grayle came up out of the métro near this juncture of canals, and turned to walk along the edge of a wide man-made canyon floored with railroad sidings.

On the top of one embankment squatted the municipal building where paupers who died in Paris were prepared for burial. Directly across the railroad trench from it rose a six-floor apartment house stained dark gray by the coal smoke. Maurice Fourrest lived on the fourth floor. He took time responding to Grayle's knock.

"I was sleeping," he mumbled, the green eyes watery. Trembly fingers adjusted the loose knot of a flowered silk neckerchief, its ragged ends dangling over a brown shirt with missing buttons. The sculptor's walk was slow and unsteady. Maurice was two years older than Grayle and looked two decades older. Drugs and alcoholism had finished the wasting of a face deeply pockmarked in childhood.

As always, Grayle felt awkwardly huge beside Maurice's slight, still-graceful figure.

They had met in the Rodin Museum, where during one period Grayle had gone every day in an effort to discover the secret of Rodin's transformation of stone, clay and metal into living flesh. Several times he noticed Maurice wandering about, studying the sculptures like old acquaintances. He came over at one point to stand behind Grayle, watching him sketch.

The first words he said were: "Real, genuine, living cunts. Not just the standard mount of Venus. Cunts with juicy, open lips—nobody but Rodin had the nerve to do that."

And, with no comment on Grayle's drawings, he had suggested they adjourn for a drink. Later, when Grayle had looked at Maurice's work, he'd acquired a respect for him that he felt for few artists he met. They'd become friends, and Maurice was the only one in Paris that Grayle turned to for criticism.

Grayle scanned the sculptures that took up much of the large main room overlooking the railroad canyon.

"Don't bother looking," Maurice rasped. "I haven't done anything new. Marble costs too much, and casting has become impossibly expensive."

"There's still clay."

"A waste of good money that could contribute to getting drunk."

Grayle gestured with his rolled canvas at a small poodle seated on a cushion in one corner of the room. "That's new."

"He belongs to Ghislaine. She moved in here. I can't pay the rent anymore, and she decided there was no point trying to keep two apartments going." Maurice dropped exhausted into a chair, and glared at the poodle. "It's practical for her. Sometimes clients want to take her out to the country for a weekend. This way she's sure there's somebody home to take care of the dog."

Ghislaine was a prostitute who worked several middle-priced hotels. A strapping, good-natured farm girl whom Maurice had used as a model for many of his nudes. In those days he had still been making money, doing commissioned portrait busts. But drink and drugs had begun to sap his ability to flatter his subjects. It was some time since he'd had a commission.

"That dog hates me," Maurice said heavily, still staring at it.

"It's just a dog."

"He hates me," Maurice repeated. "And I hate him. We just sit here, looking at each other, waiting for Ghislaine to come home and feed us." He watched Grayle lean the rolled canvas against the wall. "A new painting?"

"Yes." Grayle went to Maurice's work-closet and got a box of tacks.

"Have you changed your style?"

"No."

"Then I don't want to look at it. I'm depressed enough with my own disaster. We're too late. Both of us. The times have passed us by, before we've even begun. Which leaves a simple choice: change and conform to current trends, or accept being left behind in yesterday's garbage. I'm in the garbage. If you don't have the sense to get out of it, I don't want to look at your work."

Grayle snapped the string from the roll of canvas and held out the box of tacks. With a disgusted sigh, Maurice dragged himself out of the chair and took it. Grayle unrolled the canvas against the wall, holding it up as high as his arms could reach. Maurice climbed on a stool and thumbed tacks through the top of the canvas, into the wall. Then he got down and crouched, pushing tacks into the lower corners.

As Grayle stood aside, Maurice walked to the windows and turned to contemplate *The Drowner*. Grayle watched him.

"I don't like it," Maurice said, finally.

"Why not?" The question was probing; Grayle was after information, not admiration.

"I told you, your work is out of step with current history."

"I'm not interested in why other people won't like it. Why don't *you?*"

Maurice went slowly back to his chair and regarded the painting again. "It is damn good work, Nick. But too explicit. You are still storytelling. You have to become more simple. Pick a simple subject. Anything. A table—or a woman's rear end. If you feel something about it, you'll make it felt by others."

"I haven't found a table I feel that much about." Grayle walked to one of the windows and stood gazing through it, fists thrust in his pockets.

Across the canyon of railroad tracks, big-bellied clouds

were slowly moving into the clear evening sky, massed one against the other. The strong sunset hidden behind them transformed the clouds into a rare exhibition of all the shades of cold gray, ranging from charcoal black to pure white.

Had anything he had ever painted contained that much simple power? Grayle doubted it.

Beside him, Maurice said softly, "Do not mistake me. You should have no difficulty at all in being accepted by an established, accepted movement."

Grayle's smile was acid. "The surrealists, you mean."

"They have the press, the galleries, public attention. And with your obvious talent, sensibly directed, they would be delighted to have you."

Grayle walked back to the canvas and began removing the tacks. "I'm not a joiner, Maurice. Not a sociable type. I like being left alone."

"And lonely. So, if you don't want my sage advice, don't come here asking for it." Maurice looked at his trembling hands and asked, with no change of tone, "Do you have any money, Nick? I know a man I can get absinthe from."

Grayle shook his head. Since France had declared absinthe illegal, the price had shot higher than cocaine. "Not that kind of money. Enough for a bottle of wine. Cheap bottle."

Maurice grimaced. "Perhaps it will help." He grasped the arms of the chairs and heaved to his feet. Grayle retied the rolled canvas, and followed Maurice out with it. The poodle stayed on its cushion, watching them leave.

In the narrow street behind Maurice's tenement a bistro called Les Petits Amis was huddled between a pipe foundry and a lumberyard. The patron took Grayle's money and filled a bottle with house wine from a barrel behind the bar. They sat at a table with a sheet of tin nailed across its top. Grayle poured himself half a glass and left the rest to Maurice.

The bottle was more than half empty when Maurice spoke again, hunched forward with his elbows on the table, his head down: "Perhaps you are right. About the surrealists. They'll soon be passé. Join the future. This will be the year of Constructivism. It's growing, fast."

"You think my work lends itself to that direction?" Grayle asked him impatiently.

"You can *change*," Maurice said harshly. "Start painting with a ruler, a scissors, T square and a drafting compass. Or buy some architectural blueprints and just add colors to the various squares, oblongs and circles. No, better not have circles. Too personal."

He took hold of the bottle and refilled his glass. Some wine slopped over. With exaggerated attention, Maurice wiped the puddle with his hand and licked the wine from his palm. "Too personal . . ." he repeated, and raised his glass with both hands, drinking it down.

"Constructivism is akin to sculpture," Grayle pointed out. "Why don't *you* join up?"

Maurice put his glass down carefully. "Too late. It is too late for me." He took his hands from the glass. The fingers were jerking, out of control. "Too late for wine, also. It does nothing." He looked at his quivering hands and silently began to cry.

Grayle leaned his elbows on the table and took Maurice's hands in his own, holding them tightly. After several moments Grayle said quietly, "I know a place where we can probably get you some absinthe without having to pay for it. Or something else just as effective."

Maurice's head came up and the brimming eyes fastened on Grayle. A pilgrim might have looked that way at a remnant of the True Cross. His whisper was barely audible. "I would be very grateful, Nick."

Victor Royan's Paris home was one of five around a private courtyard behind Saint-Germain-des-Prés. Elegant eighteenth-century brick houses, each raised on a base of heavy stone from the sixteenth century. Grayle stood at an open third-floor window, framed by heavy curtains, looking down into the courtyard. Yellow light from an old-fashioned gas lamp gleamed on wet cobbles. It was raining now: a thin, steady drizzle. The wind coming in through the window, clearing the room of the opium smell, was turning cold. Grayle looked up at the clouded night sky, thinking of the hours ahead of him at Les Halles.

He closed the window and turned back to the room. It was a small library-study, furnished in the heavy, luxurious style of the 1890s. In spite of all the bookcases, it made Grayle remember pictures of plush Third Empire brothels.

Maurice was asleep on the large sofa, curled like an unborn baby. Grayle had loosened his neckerchief and removed his shoes, leaving them on the thick carpet. The pipe Maurice had been smoking rested in an ornate ivory ashtray, beside the bottle of absinthe, still almost two-thirds full. It hadn't required much to do the job.

Grayle looked at a porcelain-faced clock on a brocade-covered section of wall between two bookcases. He'd have to leave in about an hour, and he doubted that Maurice would come around by then. But he'd be in good keeping, here. He hadn't found Victor at home. But Jill was there, entertaining a friend. Her response to Maurice's suffering had been immediate, sympathetic and exceedingly efficient.

Making himself comfortable in a dark leather wing chair, Grayle picked up the cup of tea Jill had made for him before disappearing. It was cool now. He sipped it, eyes half closed. There was nothing to be heard of the night city outside the thick walls of the house. Only the ticking of the clock, Maurice's breathing and the faint sound of a Victrola playing in one of the bedrooms on the floor below.

Jill came in, and regarded Maurice critically. "Well, it seems he's doing just fine, now." She kept her voice low. "You can call me Doctor Ferguson."

She was wearing a black velvet evening gown with slim shoulder straps, open down to the base of her spine. A very long rope of matched pearls was looped around her throat and flung with studied carelessness over her left shoulder. Her pale golden hair was a bit disordered now.

"You can speak normally," Grayle told her. "It won't wake him."

Jill moved closer to the sofa, and nodded. "Probably won't wake up for hours."

Grayle finished the cool tea and returned the cup to its saucer on the Louis XV desk. "I'll have to leave before that."

"Don't worry, he'll be all right here. I'll look in on him from time to time. And see he gets home safely, when he does come around." Jill turned to look at Grayle, her expression calculating. "You're more tender than I thought. A good friend. That's a relief to know."

Without anything at all to prepare him for it, she sat down in his lap, and wound her slender arms loosely around his neck. Deliberately, her eyes wide open, she kissed his mouth.

His hands went automatically to her back, and found a surprise: under the smooth skin there was solid muscle, brick-hard. It gave a perversity to the softness of her pointy breasts against his chest.

He raised his hands to the sides of her small head and carefully drew her face from his. "You did say Victor will probably be home soon?"

"Yes, I did." She was smiling at him, quite calm about it. "Are you worried? Don't be. Victor would be pleased."

"You're quite sure of that."

"Quite sure. It would be the closest he could get to you without actually turning queer. And he couldn't let himself go that far. Both of you making love to me is the nearest we can manage, as things are."

Grayle laughed softly. "And you'll do anything to make him happy."

"Yes." She said it simply. Resting an elbow on his shoulder, Jill leaned her cheek against her fist and watched his eyes. "He likes you enormously, you know. Says you're a man who's fashioned a world entirely your own." Her tone was slightly mocking: "I can even quote him exactly: You're a man following your own way with an obstinacy solid as oak. How do you like that?"

A dark-haired woman appeared in the doorway. The clinging white satin of her dressing gown flaunted the lovely figure. Her aristocratic features were pinched with annoyance. "I thought you came to play nurse—to the other one."

Without looking at her, Jill said, "I told you to stay in bed and wait." Her tone was flat, without emotion.

"What I just may do is go home."

Jill smiled at Grayle and said uncaringly: "Go home."

The woman turned away, furious. When she was gone, Jill impishly rubbed the tip of her nose across Grayle's and whispered: "She won't leave. Wanna bet?"

Grayle stood up, lifting her with him. He kissed her lightly and set her on her feet. "It's all right. You've been worrying I might use Victor, hurt him somehow. I won't. You don't need insurance."

"So you say."

"So I say."

She nodded, finally. "Right. Well, then, back to the stables."

"Stables?"

Jill gave him a bland look. "She likes to be exercised under control. A bit like Victor, really."

Grayle watched her saunter out, her hard, saucy buttocks moving in a deliberate burlesque of provocation.

The teapot on the desk was still half full. Grayle refilled his cup and drank. It was quite cold now. He put the cup down and wandered over to the bookshelves, examining the titles, not eager to leave. There was a bit of time left before he'd have to, and it might stop raining.

On one shelf there was a small stereopticon, and a single box of glass slides for it. Curious, Grayle took them over to the desk and sat in the swivel chair behind it. Slipping the first slide into the viewer, he held it up to the light of the desk lamp and looked into it.

A scene from the war leaped into view: two German soldiers carrying a wounded man on a stretcher, between buildings that had been almost totally demolished by cannon shells. The stretcher bearers were hunched over as though expecting another shell to come their way at any moment. The wounded soldier had one arm dangling from the stretcher, hand trailing along the ground.

The feeling of being *inside* that scene, caused by the three-dimensional quality of the image, struck Grayle with unexpected force. He studied the slide for some time. Then he drew it out, and slipped the next one into the viewer.

This one was of a French soldier hanging in a tangle of barbed wire at the top of a muddy trench. One of his arms had been torn away and lay in the mud below the dangling boots, the hand resting against the barbed wire. Most of the face had been shot away. Again, the feeling of being *there* was shocking.

There was nobody, living or dead, in the third slide. It showed part of what had once been a dense forest. What was left of it: splintered tree stumps, a welter of shredded chunks of wood, severed strands of barbed wire, churned earth. No single battle could have done that. This piece of land had been fought over, back and forth, time after time. The devastation was absolute.

Grayle found himself thinking of the sketches he'd done of Victor Royan, the first time he'd seen him. He knew, quite suddenly, what his next painting would be.

When he lowered the viewer he saw that Victor had come into the room, and was standing by the desk watching him.

"Are they all of the war?" Grayle asked, gesturing at the box of slides.

"Yes, I collect them. Disgusting hobby, I know . . ." Victor looked at Maurice curled up asleep on the sofa. "Jill just told me about your friend."

"I hope you don't mind my bringing him here. He was in pretty bad shape."

Victor walked to the sofa and gazed down at Maurice. "He has a certain resemblance to me, don't you think?"

"No. The poor never resemble the rich."

"You think not?" Victor strolled back to the desk, lowered himself to a half-sitting position on it and looked at the slides. "You find them interesting?"

"Very."

"They serve to remind me of things no photographer could possibly have recorded. Like the time my legs were shot out from under me. I lay there in a shell hole for two days and nights, unable to move, with the decaying corpse of another man sprawled on top of me."

"Not pleasant."

"No, but not as bad a memory as some others. For some reason, the worst is a young lieutenant who was telling me about the girl he was in love with when he was quite suddenly killed."

Victor paused, not looking at Grayle, gazing vaguely in the direction of the window behind him. "He was smiling a bit shyly while he talked about it, as I recall. During a lull in the fighting, which had gone on for almost thirty hours, relaxing all of us to the point of euphoria. And then, that single shot. I never understood where it came from. The bullet caught the boy in the back of the head and went through and cracked his forehead but didn't come out."

Remembering, Victor's voice acquired a kind of awe: "The look on his face, as he fell toward me, very slowly—I don't want to die like that. With that look on my face. So—surprised. The thought terrifies me, sometimes. I want to know it is coming."

"Even to go looking for it?"

"Sometimes. Why not? I want to be *prepared*. When I remember the expression of surprise on that boy's face—sometimes it's so vivid I can't sleep, or make love. Or . . ." He didn't finish it.

Grayle was studying his face. He said, carefully: "But you like remembering. Don't you?"

"Yes, I do, God help me." Victor lowered his eyes to Grayle's. "You see, in the war I was motivated; I had a way to use my drives. Oh, I understand how ridiculous it sounds. But I've got as much bottled up inside me as you do. Maybe everybody does. Only you have a means of getting it out, of expressing yourself. I don't, except through action."

"In war."

Victor's smile was self-deprecating. "What else is there? I can't be an artist. No talent. I'd like to be an anarchist or communist, but I don't really have that kind of faith; it would be faking. Sports? Too silly. Work? I'd be faking again, because I don't need to work, I'm too rich. I can't become a criminal; same reason."

"Give away all your money, Victor. There is salvation for you in poverty. It supplies a number of motivations. Urgent ones."

This time Victor's smile was genuine. "One of your more endearing traits: a complete lack of sympathy."

"Victor, do you still have your uniform, from the war?" The question startled Victor. "Yes . . . why?"

"I'd like to see what you look like, wearing it. I have an idea for a painting."

"You want to do a portrait of me in uniform."

"I don't know if it would turn out to be a portrait. I do want to use you as a model."

"And make me immortal?" Victor laughed quietly. "I wouldn't mind that. Not at all."

"Immortality, I can't guarantee. But I do want to try doing the picture."

"The uniform is in the south. A place I have, in Menton. But as a matter of fact, this is opportune. I'd intended to tell you: Jill and I are going there in a couple weeks. My legs don't like the Paris winters. I was going to ask you to come down with us. It would be a new world for you to paint. Green the year round; flowers, lemon trees, the sea and mountains. And the light and purity of color—well, you've seen what some of the impressionists got from the region."

"I can't live in somebody else's household, Victor. You could bring the uniform when you come back."

"We won't be returning to Paris until late spring. You could live entirely to yourself there. I have a gardener's house that isn't being used, some distance from the main house. Too small for my present gardener, who is also my caretaker and has a wife and children. I had to make a separate apartment for them, in the main house."

Grayle leaned back in the chair, brooding on it.

"There is more maintenance work around the estate than my caretaker can handle," Victor told him. "I'd intended to hire help for him. That could be you. I'd pay you what I'd have to pay anyone else. Not much, but enough to buy your food, a few extras."

"That still leaves the money I'd need for paints, canvas, new brushes . . . and they all come high." Grayle got out of the chair. "I have to go look for work now. Let me think it over. This may not be the right time."

"On the other hand, it may be. Exactly the right time."

10

A dismal October wind howled through dark, narrow streets and lashed him with black rain. Water streamed in sheets down old stone walls and the corrugated iron shutters of closed shop-fronts. It overflowed through the gutters and bubbled like lava over engulfed sewer inlets. Somewhere behind him in that savage dark a church bell tolled. Much nearer, off to his right, the tower of Saint Étienne-du-Mont took up the tolling: four in the morning.

It was the third night in a row he'd worked Les Halles in a downpour, and walked home through it. But it was the first time he'd quit work before dawn. He was shaking with fever, his face burning and his hands and feet numb. Holding his balance by hunching forward with the cold rain pelting into his back, Grayle went down the slanted, slippery street, heavily but steadily.

What he needed, he knew, as he turned into the total darkness of his courtyard, was a very hot bath. But it would be hours before one could be had in the hotel, so that was out. He trudged up the back steps of the warehouse, and began stripping the drenched clothing off as soon as he entered his room. The water had run down inside his boots and even his stockings were soaked.

Shivering in the cold damp of the room, he walked naked to the table, got a match, and lit the lamp. He grabbed a towel and began rubbing his clammy flesh vigorously with it, all over. When he was dry he continued shivering. He filled a glass with wine and drank some of it. Then, out of ingrained habit, he went back and picked up the clothes he'd dropped on the floor. They left a wide puddle, and immediately began creating another under the line below the skylight where he neatly hung them to dry.

From the other room, he dragged a rug and spread it on his bed over the blanket. Then he blew out the lamp and dug himself in under both blanket and rug, and let himself pass out.

It was still dark when he came awake, with a violent need to urinate. His laugh was hysterical. He hauled himself off the bed, wrapping the rug around him as a toga, stumbled through the other room and fumbled his way down the steps to the toilet. When he'd relieved himself he turned to go, then abruptly turned back, dropped to his knees and vomited. It cleared some of the fever from his blood, but his weakened legs had difficulty getting him back up the stairs.

When he woke again it was day. Some part of the afternoon, he estimated. The light was dim, rain still slashing at his skylight window. It came to him that he'd been wakened by knocking on the door in the other room.

"It's not locked," he called. He had to try again before it carried. His skin felt cold and unnaturally dry, and his head was throbbing.

Nora came into the room and stopped, staring down at him. "What is the matter with you?"

Grayle sat up, pulling the rug tight around his shoulders, shivering inside it. "I caught a cold. Maybe the flu. Will you get me hot tea from the bar downstairs? Laced with honey and rum. They'll know where to get the honey. And a lot of aspirin—there's a pharmacy to the left on Mouffetard."

Nora touched a hand to his forehead. "You need more than aspirin."

"Whatever you can get . . ." Grayle rolled down on his side and plunged back into sleep.

It was Daniel who woke him, sitting down on the edge of his mattress, carrying a tin cup and brass teapot. Grayle forced himself up on one elbow and took the cup when it was filled. His hand didn't tremble, but his head was stuffed with lard. The honey and rum in the hot tea improved that, almost immediately. But he was still shivering.

"Your friend went for medicine," Daniel told him, waiting with the pot ready. "Interesting girl."

Nora returned while Grayle was drinking a second cup. "Wait a second, don't drink all of it." She took a paper packet from a small prescription box, unfolded the paper and emptied powder from it into his tea. "Now drink. All of it."

Daniel put the teapot on the floor and stood up. "Tonton will bring up some soup from Madame Gaussin, later. I have an early shift at the restaurant. Don't lock the door, I'll check on you when I come home."

"I'll be here." The words came out tight, because Grayle's jaws were clenched to keep his teeth from chattering.

Daniel gave Nora a seductive smile as he left. Grayle drank the rest of the tea down in two gulps. In spite of the honey, it had become bitter.

It was night when he woke again. He couldn't remember if Tonton had come with the soup, but there was no hunger in him. Nor any strength in him, either, though his temperature had gone down a bit, and his brain was somewhat clearer.

Rain no longer beat at his skylight window. The moonlit outlines of passing clouds moved slowly across the walls, the floor, his face. And over Nora, asleep on the bed beside him.

Nora carried her Graflex camera, tripod and film case through the cool sunshine of Grayle's courtyard, and lugged them up the stairs toward his studio. They were heavy and bulky, but she was strong enough to carry them easily. Strong, and a fighter, she sometimes imagined; and these were her weapons. Like a Viking's battle-ax and knife, Arthur's Excalibur and shield. Weapons to be wielded with ferocity and cunning against the enemy in glorious battle.

Childish, but she knew that the desire behind it was not. She had always wished she were a man. A darkly dangerous, untamable breed of male. Whose need for violent action was fulfilled, instead of trapped inside a steaming kettle without a spout. They never quite left one, those childhood daydreams: to whet one's strength against barbarian hordes, hurricanes, dragons, jungles, mountains. To be a man. Curiously, it was that which had made her lesbian experiments unsatisfying. She needed to be with men, one of them in the camaraderie of mutual endeavor; accepted by them, admired by them.

Who would dream of being Guinevere, when one could dream of being Arthur? A man could be a porter in Les Halles, or sail the world in the crew of a tramp freighter, prowl exotic cities seeking adventure, cut through to the heart of the Amazon. How often she'd put herself to sleep imagining herself Admiral Nelson; and how well she'd understood Lady Hamilton, absorbing him like a boa constrictor. It was the nearest poor Emma could get to *being* Nelson.

The scope of success didn't matter. It was the unlimited possibilities she'd always longed for, restrained only by the range of one's vision, and determination. Being a woman was just so damned restricting. The scope of activity so narrowed.

She wished she were—Nicholas Grayle. Not for his art; she had her own. For his ability to do anything at all he wanted with his life. And then to utterly change it, if he wanted to, or opportunity tempted, or fate demanded. She wanted to become him: absorb him into herself.

Now *there* was a wicked notion, she told herself mockingly as she reached his door. Positively and undeniably incestuous. She opened the door and walked in. With her weapons.

A sharp clicking noise woke Grayle. He opened his eyes and stared at the sunlight against the ceiling. His temperature felt normal, or close to it. And so did the rest of him. It had been three days and nights. And she'd been there, tending to him, more of that time than she'd been away. He turned his head to look for her—and saw her behind the camera.

It was tilted on its tripod, bellows open, the Tessar lens

angled down at him. Sitting up, he ran a hand through his hair.

"Stop that," Nora ordered. "I want the real you."

"The real me doesn't usually lie around sick for three days."

"It is one facet of you. Leave your hair alone."

Grayle dropped his hand and smiled into the lens, letting her take another picture. Then he glanced toward the table. "Anything to eat? I'm famished."

"That is good news." She came over and briefly felt his forehead, picked up his wrist and expertly took his pulse. "Well enough for a real meal, I think. Stay there and be patient. It may take me a little time."

As soon as she'd left, Grayle swung off the bed and stood up. He felt weak, but staying in bed any longer wouldn't help that to pass. There was water in the basin. He used it to wash his hands, face and neck. Drying himself, he got into slacks, shirt and an old sweater. He sat in the chair and got his feet into wool stockings. He was putting on his shoes when someone knocked at the door.

Grayle called out to come in, and heard the door open and close. He stood up and went through the hanging tapestries to see who it was. A tall, beautifully dressed man was standing among the piled carpets, looking puzzled. Pitch-black hair and slanty green eyes. Handsome, thoughtful face.

"Are you Nicholas Grayle? I'm Gian-Carlo Pattara. I hear you've been quite ill. You seem to have recovered."

"Pretty much," Grayle said stiffly. Resentment rose in him; the man had no business intruding here, uninvited. He had to force the politeness: "Come in. Nora has gone to get me something to eat. She'll be back soon."

Pattara followed him, his glance around the studio perfunctory. "Well, you certainly couldn't have had a more devoted nurse than Nora's been, could you?" His glance, when it returned to Grayle, was guarded. But the question lurking behind the mannerly facade was obvious. "But then, I understand you're her newfound brother."

"Half-brother," Grayle said sharply. It was becoming

difficult to keep the antagonism down. The man hadn't believed Nora's story, had come here worried that she'd found a lover she was becoming *too* involved with.

"Yes. So Nora tells me. Funny story."

This time Grayle's anger showed: "Not to me."

Pattara's eyes stayed on Grayle's face, and then something inside him relaxed. He took off his hat and said quietly, "I apologize, bad choice of words. I meant *strange*, brother and sister, just discovering each other's existence."

"That it is." Grayle put a clamp on his anger. He had no quarrel with this man. More reason to be sorry for him. He was worried and had reason to be. He'd be losing Nora soon enough, one way or another.

"I understand of course that there could be nothing amusing about . . . the tragedy of your mother." With his guard down, there was something shy in the handsome face.

"It was long ago," Grayle said, dismissing the subject. He was under control now. He sat on the edge of the table and gestured at the chair. "Have a seat. I have some wine, if you don't mind the ordinary bar stuff. About two months old."

Pattara laughed. "No, thank you. My taste buds are too spoiled, I'm afraid." He looked at the paintings. "May I?"

"Of course."

Pattara strolled over for a closer inspection. When he turned from them his nod was approving. "Excellent craftsmanship. Really fine. I envy you. Has Nora told you? I frequently employ artists to illustrate our books. Some very good artists."

"So I've heard."

"I just brought out a lovely edition of Daudet's *Sappho*, illustrated by Pierre Rousseau. Perhaps you have seen it."

"No, but I know his work. He's good."

"If you would ever care to do some illustrations for us, please come to see me. I'd be most interested."

Grayle quelled another brief surge of antagonism. "I'll remember the offer. Thanks."

Pattara strolled across the room to look at the sketches, pastels and watercolors. He took time with a number of them. "I inherited my profession," he said quietly, standing before the drawings of his wife. "I sometimes wonder what I would be doing, if I hadn't. If I would have anything of my own to offer. Something *you* don't have to wonder about."

"No. I didn't inherit anything."

Pattara turned his head slightly, observing Grayle with a slight frown. "Didn't you? I think you did."

Grayle didn't like the implication; but he found that he couldn't be angry at Nora's husband for saying it. Whatever was wrong with the man, he didn't have any squeamishness about speaking directly.

Nora came in carrying a filled paper bag and a hot stew in a tin pail. She stopped, surprised, when she saw Pattara there.

He smiled at her fondly. "I thought I'd drop by and pick you up on the way home. Since we're having guests, and there are preparations."

Nora set the food down on the table, frowning a bit. "I was going to come a bit later, Gian-Carlo."

He nodded, accepting it without irritation. "That's all right. Actually I can take care of the preparations myself." He swung the hat in his hand, toward Grayle. "To be honest I really came by because I was curious about Monsieur Grayle. You were right, his work *is* exceptional."

Nora relaxed fully for the first time, returning her husband's smile. "Oh, I suppose I might as well go with you, since you're here. And the light is getting bad." She looked to Grayle. "Can I leave the camera? I want to take a few more pictures, next time. But don't touch anything."

Pattara told Grayle: "You are very welcome to join us at home this evening, if you care to. Some old friends, quite nice. If you feel well enough now."

"Not that well," Grayle said politely. "But thanks for the invitation."

"And the offer I made earlier. Don't forget that."

Grayle thought about Gian-Carlo and Nora Cesari while he ate, and then took a short walk around the quarter.

When he returned he was more tired than he'd expected, and went back to bed. There was a book on Celtic folklore, in English, which he'd bought at a secondhand stall along the Seine. But he couldn't maintain his attention. He took a sketchpad and tried to do a drawing of Nora's husband. But it didn't work out and he put the pad aside, lying back with his hands under his head and his eyes open.

He was tired, but not sleepy. And he missed the presence of Nora.

She came the next day. And the next. They began taking walks together; strolls which lengthened as his strength returned.

She asked him, once, what he'd thought of her husband.

"I liked him."

"Yes," she said, "everyone does."

They let it go at that. Nora told Grayle about her parents' move, and about the mountain village they were settled into now. Claude Cesari had been confused about what was happening, but he created no problems during the change of domicile.

"I don't think he recognizes where he is now," she told Grayle. "Anyway, he doesn't go out at all. His legs have become too uncertain to take walks. Most of the time he sits and looks at his paintings. I'm not sure he often realizes they are his own."

"Does he work at all?"

"No. Not anymore." Nora bit her lower lip. "It's hard, seeing him like that. Harder on my mother, naturally, since she has to be with him all the time. But I think it is more of a shock for me, only seeing him occasionally. He was always such a dominating man, so sure of everything . . ."

Grayle didn't say anything to prolong that conversation, and Nora didn't push it. He told her about Victor's offer of a place in the south. But he still hadn't made the decision whether to go when Victor and Jill headed for the Riviera. The invitation remained open; and Victor left his viewer and slides of World War I with Grayle, who began using them to make preliminary sketches for the painting he had in mind.

On clear days Grayle and Nora took to going on joint explorations, hunting subjects they could photograph and sketch together. Their favorite places for this became the Luxembourg Gardens and the Bois de Boulogne.

When it was rainy they went to museums. There were long stretches when they hardly spoke; and these were their closest periods, when words weren't needed, each sensing the other's thoughts and feelings, in the deeper sharing of silences. Increasingly, they found they enjoyed being together. They were good for each other, each supplying what the other needed. She had a high-strung, restless temperament. His solidity drew in her scattered drives, centering her. Just as he could feel her power of drawing him out of his self-absorption, relaxing the rigidity of his fixed singleness of purpose.

He was alone in his place one cold morning in late October, working on a sketch from one of Victor's slides, when Maurice Fourrest showed up. There was a look of bemused shock in his ravaged face, and his manner held an uncertainty unusual for him.

"I've done a terrible thing. I don't understand why."

"What is it?"

Maurice slumped in the chair, hands falling limply to his thighs. "That horrible little dog. Ghislaine's dog?"

Grayle nodded. "I remember."

"Last night I couldn't stand it anymore. The two of us sitting there, waiting for Ghislaine. That dog constantly watching me. Hating me. Me hating him back, the hate screwing down tighter and tighter . . ." The tired voice had a curious lack of expression. "About five o'clock this morning I filled the sink with water. I picked him up by the neck and stuck his head in and held it down until he drowned."

Maurice raised both hands, letting his sleeves fall back, looking at the deep scratches in his forearms.

Grayle was careful to keep emotional reaction from his voice. "Did you put some alcohol on that?"

"Don't worry, Ghislaine kept that dog cleaner than I am." A croaking laugh, cut off sharply. "I left him there in the sink. And then I just sat and waited for Ghislaine to come home." He let his arms sink. "I don't understand why. I need her, and I knew how she'd react."

"A lot of screaming, I expect."

"Mostly that I must be insane. Nick, she's thrown me out. For good."

"It's your apartment, Maurice."

"She pays the rent. I can't. And if I don't move out, right away, she says she'll get somebody to cut my throat. She has friends who would probably do it."

"Perhaps she'll get over it."

"No. She won't. And Nick—she says if I don't get my sculpture out of there, she'll let me know what she felt, coming home and finding her dog like that. She's going to start smashing my sculptures, one by one."

"Where would you move them?"

"First of all, I can't pay anybody to haul them away."

"Where would you move them?" Grayle repeated.

"My parents live just east of Paris. A small farm, did I tell you?"

"No."

"They won't be overjoyed to have me back in my present circumstances. But they won't be able to refuse me." Maurice sat with downcast eyes. "I could put everything in the barn. Temporarily."

Grayle went out and put through a phone call to Nora, and explained briefly why he needed a short-term loan. He made a fair estimate of the amount, and gave her Maurice's address. Then he walked up to Place Contrescarpe to see what he could find. There was a ponderous old Percheron waiting in front of a bar, attached to a big wagon used to haul vegetables from Les Halles to this quarter. Its owner was like the horse: old, heavy and strong. He was known as Grand-père; and having sold all his produce he was in the bar having a drink before going home to sleep.

Grayle told him the situation, and the cause of it; in detail, making it interesting enough to override Grand-père's desire to stick to his regular routine. They argued price, and settled for a bit less than Grayle's estimate.

* * *

Nora was waiting with her car outside Maurice's tenement, when Grayle, Maurice and Grand-père arrived with the horse and wagon. She followed Grayle and Grand-père up the stairs to help carry down the sculptures. Maurice waited by the wagon, afraid to face Ghislaine.

Nobody answered Grayle's knock, but the door was not locked. He went in first, and found Ghislaine in bed, lying on her side, face to the wall, but not asleep. Hunching down beside the bed, Grayle spoke quietly to her for a time. She didn't turn to look at him, and didn't answer. He gave it up, and started with one of the bigger sculptures, carrying it out with Grand-père's help. Nora followed them with a smaller piece. When they went up for more, Maurice went with them.

The wagon, when full, didn't have room for two of the pieces. They were wedged into Nora's rumble seat, and Maurice drove out with her, to prepare his parents. Grayle followed with Grand-père, much more slowly.

The farm was small, intensely worked, drab. The house was old and solid. The barn was newer, and wouldn't last as long. Maurice was waiting in front of it, with Nora. His parents stayed by the house, watching with resentful resignation as their son's works were carried into the barn, their eyes like stones that had been buried in the earth for thousands of years.

Nora paid Grand-père the agreed amount, and drove Grayle back with her into the city. He looked back as she pulled out, at Maurice standing there, staring after them.

"Perhaps," Nora speculated, "he'll be better off out here. It just might be good for him, staying away from the city for a while."

"No, it won't," Grayle said flatly. "I have the feeling he's never going to do any more work." He faced forward, gazing through the windshield at the road ahead.

"I feel so much pity for him," Nora said. "At the same time I hate him for what he did. I know the two feelings shouldn't exist together, but . . ."

"Opposites don't cancel each other. They feed each other. Love and power, imagination and calculation, male and female—one can't exist without the other."

She gave him a slow sidelong look. "I'd say male and female can exist quite well without each other, more often than not."

"Not for very long, or nothing living would be left. We're constructed so the two form a single unit. Either is incomplete without the other."

"There are times when I'd prefer to be incomplete, and tranquil."

Grayle shrugged. "Opposites clash, as well as interact. That doesn't alter the fact both are needed. Take photography. You need both light and shadow. If you only have one, you don't get a picture on your film."

"You're a male without a female. Are you incomplete?"

"I'm an aberration. Maybe painting is a substitute."

"Or, it may be that not everything has to have its opposite."

"But it does. Anything unopposed too long corrupts itself. Sentiment becomes masochism, initiative becomes sadism. Logic becomes insensitivity, desire becomes gluttony."

And because some of this went far back into his childhood, Grayle began to talk to Nora about his memories of Irene.

It took him three nights at Les Halles to pay back the money he'd borrowed from Nora. She used the money to take them both to an excellent dinner at a small restaurant on Montmartre, tucked in a small passageway behind Sacré-Coeur.

She was in a mood to celebrate. A meeting with the director of advertising for Michelin had gone well.

Another cold rain was sweeping the city, but a crackling fire in the restaurant's fireplace gave the place a cozy warmth. The smell of woodsmoke and the candles glowing on their table gave their meal a special intimacy. Grayle told Nora about glancing through his book on Celtic folklore earlier that day, and coming across some lines he remembered with surprising clarity from his childhood.

"It seemed odd," Grayle said, "telling you about Irene just the other day, and then finding that riddle she'd taught me, so many years ago." And he recited it.

Heaven's Above, Heaven's Below;
Stars Above, Stars Below;
All that is Over, Under Shall Show;
Happy are thou, whom the Answer Know.

Nora was staring at Grayle. She said, bemused: "I'll tell you something even odder. When I was helping mother pack for the move, I found a diary I kept when I was fourteen, and began to read it. On one page there is a quotation I'd copied—I have no memory at all of where I got it from. And I've been wondering why it impressed me enough to fill a page with it."

"The same lines?"

"Exactly the same."

Nora recited them back to him, but in French, word for word.

Grayle said, after a moment, "We meet in strange ways, you and I."

"Yes, don't we."

And then, quite abruptly, it was finished.

She came to his place early in the morning, shortly after he'd returned from Les Halles. There'd been a phone call from her mother. Claude Cesari was dead.

Her voice was strained, her face drawn; but she hadn't been crying. She watched Grayle as she told him. She didn't expect a conventional "I'm sorry" from him, and didn't get it. He said, "You knew it was coming."

"Yes. I imagine that is why I'm not taking it as hard as I should. I'll probably pay for that, when it really hits me, later."

Nora walked to the chair and sat down, experiencing an exhaustion that had something anticipatory in it. "The funeral will be the day after tomorrow. Gian-Carlo is driving down there with me. His car—there's more than enough room for you."

"No."

"I'm not *asking* you to," Nora said harshly. "You *have* to come, this time. He was your father, too."

Grayle said, very gently: "No, he wasn't."

She looked up at him, regarding him with a depth of cold hatred that startled her. "If you don't—we're never going to see each other again. Never."

He looked at her with a disquieting kind of mindless absorption. "I'll be sorry about that."

And he was. But that didn't alter his decision.

That night he didn't go to Les Halles. Instead, early in the evening, he went to see Pauline Renard, at her gallery on Rue d'Astorg.

"I can't sell your work," she told him. "Not for enough to make it worthwhile, for either of us."

Pauline Renard looked across the desk at him, interested in what he'd say to that. Grayle looked back at her shrewdly, and said nothing, waiting. The office behind her gallery was small and functional. There were only two pictures on the walls. A Bonnard nude, the colors luscious enough to taste. And a solarized photograph of a maple leaf by Man Ray, cool and elegant.

"What do you need the money for?" she demanded. "I thought you were doing well enough. Working at Les Halles, leaving yourself free to develop your painting as you see fit."

Grayle told her about Victor Royan's offer.

"Not a bad idea for you," Pauline Renard said. "You'll discover color and light down there you'll find hard to believe."

"Victor said that. If I'm to go, I need a certain amount of money."

Pauline Renard leaned back in her chair, tapping the desk top with a gold pencil. "You don't fit into any of the recognizable schools of art currently selling well. You're not a cubist, not a surrealist, not a constructivist . . ."

"And not a purist or futurist. I'm not inclined to have labels stuck on my work."

"If at least your work had some social significance for our time. But it doesn't."

Grayle gave her a steady look. "Neither does music. Some artists look for their inspiration in the newspapers. I'm not a journalist."

"You are a vain man." There was a testing edge to the art dealer's tone. "Vain of your profession. All around us people struggle, starve—while you glorify your individuality."

"That is true."

"And it satisfies you?"

"It has to. It's what I am. A painter." Grayle paused, and then added in another tone of voice. "You looked at my work, and left me your card."

"Because . . ." The gold pencil stopped its tapping. She studied him. "Vlaminck told me a story a couple weeks ago, apropos of artists who work most of their lives to regain something they lost in learning the techniques. He knew a woman who'd had so many lovers she couldn't remember half of them. She was complaining that now that she'd finally learned how to enjoy herself in bed with men, she wished she could be a virgin again. Somehow, you've managed to remain a virgin. And," she added, "you just *may* turn out to be one of the best painters I've met in my lifetime."

"But?"

"But you don't have enough work ready. If I could sell the paintings you've done, they wouldn't bring enough at this point to make up for your losing them. For the time you invested in them. Not after my percentage, which would be twenty-five percent. If I'm being generous. To earn enough to make selling them worthwhile, you have to have more. So I can stage a full-scale publicity campaign, and a serious show; to force the prices up."

"I work slowly," Grayle said.

"That is obvious, and not necessarily a liability, in the long run. If you are willing to wait, and work, and wait some more. Until you have a real body of paintings to show. Another year, say."

His gaze was penetrating. "Are *you* prepared to wait that long?"

Pauline Renard's laugh was surprisingly musical. "Yes, as a matter of fact. But I don't have your financial pressures."

"And what's to be done about that?" Grayle asked her coolly.

"You'd have to sign a contract making me your sole representative. And allow me to have all the paintings you've done so far. Not to sell. Only to use, carefully, to gradually stimulate interest in you."

Grayle nodded, waiting for the rest of it.

"The amount I would be able to advance would, I'm afraid, be quite small. But enough, if you continue to live as frugally as you do now, to carry you for perhaps five or six months. At which point I would want to see what you have done in that time. Allowing me to reconsider our relationship, and your prospects, if need be."

"That's generous enough."

"No, I'm not a generous person, Monsieur Grayle. I am a businesswoman. And I believe I might, just might, make a great deal of money out of you in years to come. You do understand, what money I give you until then is an advance, against earnings. That means I expect you to pay it back, out of your earnings from sales. With six percent interest."

"I hope you'll be as sharp when it comes to selling my work."

"That depends entirely on how many people want it. We'll see. When do you need the money?"

"Now."

The following day Grayle delivered thirteen rolled-up canvases to Pauline Renard, along with a number of his sketches, drawings, watercolors and pastels.

There was a cold, dark fog crawling through Paris when his train pulled out of the Gare de Lyon at nine that night.

11

The January breeze was a sun-warmed breath on her face and arms as she skirted the sculpted hedge-maze behind the sprawling orange-red villa. She pulled off the straw cloche hat with its flared brim and shook loose her dark curls. Trellised vines overhead cast changing laceworks of shadow against her sleeveless white-cotton tennis dress as she mounted graveled steps between rising terraces of lily ponds.

She came to a path that switchbacked its way up the hillslope through narrow rock gardens of cactus, agave and Barbary figs, flanked by cypresses and umbrella pines. High above, the limestone cliffs of the Italian frontier were backed by the Provençal Alps. Behind her, below Victor Royan's estate, red tile roofs of several other large villas lay partially submerged in shrubbery, trees and flower banks descending to a stony beach and tranquil sea.

Along the upper limits of the estate ran a wide terrace of orange and lemon trees, with a rusted wrought-iron arbor leading to the gardener's house: a narrow two-room dwelling against a steep part of the hillslope, one room on top of the other. The lower part had a heavy wooden beam over the door; a squared tree trunk sunk deep in the stones and mortar of a wall that had been restored in various places over various centuries, giving it a patchy appearance. Lizards darted across a side wall that got most of the sun, between small cactus plants growing wild out of chinks in the stones.

Steps led up to the room above, which projected beyond the top of the lower room, one corner supported by a whitewashed pillar, the other sunk in the hillside. In the shade of this overhang Grayle was seated on a three-legged stool before his easel, face and arms sun-bronzed, at work on a new canvas.

Nora stopped under the end of the arbor to one side of Grayle, just behind his range of vision. He was adding faint touches of Veronese green and burnt umber to his painting of a slim woman leaning against the white pillar that held up one corner of the room above. The nude figure was barely sketched in as yet, the face merely outlined; only the pillar was finished, with a lizard clinging to it, jewel-like in a spattering of sunlight.

A faint metallic clicking noise reached Grayle. He turned on the stool and saw Nora, and the instant pleasure that came into his expression injected adrenaline into her. He got to his feet, smiling at her. The way she stood there, in a pool of lavender shade enclosed by molten sunshine, reminded him of a half-wild colt poised to break into a run.

"How long were you watching me?"

"Long enough to take a shot of your work in progress."

He looked for the camera, and Nora grinned and turned the hat in her left hand, showing him the small camera it had concealed. "I went and got it. The Leica. Cost me everything I've earned the last month. Which was considerable. I finally got the commission. Four advertising pages for Michelin, with the good old Graflex."

"Congratulations. It looks like a toy."

"But it is not. Shutter speeds to three-hundredths of a second. Thirty-six negatives in a single loading of inexpensive motion picture film."

"You'd make a good salesman."

Nora laughed. "I do love it. I can make ten shots with this *toy*, in the time it would take to get two with the Graflex."

"I'd like to see what my work looks like in your photograph, when it's developed. Are you a guest in the villa?"

She shook her head. "Friends of mine have a converted fishing barge in Menton harbor. They're in Paris at the moment, so I can use it while I'm here."

Grayle began cleaning his paintbrush, first with a turpentine-soaked rag, then soap and water and another rag. He did it deftly, his attention staying on Nora. "How long will you stay?"

"A day or so. I'm on my way to join Gian-Carlo in Milan. Family gathering, a latish celebration of the New Year." She finished awkwardly: "I decided to stop by here on the way. I wanted to see you."

They both knew by then that neither was going to bring up the subject of their father's funeral, two months past. Not now, and perhaps never.

"I'm glad." Grayle licked the brush to a sharp point, squeezed it dry between thumb and finger and put it aside. "Let's go for a walk, up in the hills."

She nodded, and he picked the canvas off the easel, with both hands at the edges, carring it with automatic caution into the downstairs room. Nora stepped into the doorway. He was using the room entirely as work space, and the room above for his living quarters. There was no connecting interior stairway. Grayle leaned the canvas against an unused wall, and went out for his brushes, paints and palette.

Nora looked around the room. In one wall was a deep window with a view on the sea and sky. A longer wall was taken up by two large finished paintings. One radiated with the colors of flowers that seemed to quiver in the predominant greens, grays and blues of a hillside against the sea.

The second finished canvas froze her nerves. A portrait of Victor Royan in an army officer's jacket and cap, looking straight out of the canvas at her, with a faintly surprised smile. The smile was somehow more unnerving than the war-devastated landscape of splintered trees and smashed houses around him; where two small figures in the background carried another on a stretcher, past a corpse caught in a tangle of barbed wire. Above this: a spring sky of incredible beauty.

Nora sensed that the painting represented a step forward in Grayle's work; but it horrified her. The way certain crucifixion pictures of the Middle Ages had, when she was a child.

* * *

They hiked together up to the small stone village of Gorbio, perched under the ruin of its old castle on the peak of a foothill a few miles above Menton. From the shops on the little square, Grayle bought a picnic lunch: bread, goat cheese and black olives, with a bottle of local wine. Following a sheep-trail that wound between forested hills toward the higher slopes of the mountains, they found a spot for their picnic: a tree-shaded level of wild grass, beside a small stream, where low ferns grew along both banks.

Carpenter bees hummed around them as they sat in the grass, and Nora opened the oil-papers holding the olives and cheese. Grayle got a wood-handled claspknife from his pocket and sliced the crusty bread for them. The goat cheese coated their mouths with saltiness, and they passed the wine bottle back and forth until it was empty. They listened to the silence as they ate, absorbing the feel of sheltered isolation.

Below them, unseen from here, were the winter centers for wealthy sun-seekers, strung along the coast: Monte Carlo for those who enjoyed gambling and ladylike whores; Nice and Cannes for the party-hounds and marriage seekers; Beaulieu for yachtsmen; Cap d'Antibes for beach lovers with small children; Menton for the reclusive. Above the foothills, the Maritime Alps rose into the true Alps, increasingly crowded by those who wanted as much company as possible with their snow and four-star chalets.

Grayle and Nora were in a forgotten region between: sloping forests and pastures and farmed terraces, rocky cliffs and gorges and lonely streams. Where civilization was represented by isolated peasant villages perched on steep hills, stone houses and gray-slate roofs, densely grouped for defense against the Moors and Saracens and Turks, marauding inland from their beached war-galleys centuries ago, in search of loot, food and slaves.

They didn't speak much. It didn't seem necessary. After their meal Nora sat resting against the trunk of a pine tree, drowsy with the wine, eyes almost closing. Grayle stretched out on his back in the grass beside her, languid in the gentle sun-warmth piercing through the foliage overhead. Her head was bent, the full lips parted, the long eyes gazing down at his face.

They refreshed themselves by washing their hands and faces in the stream before moving on. The water was icy cold, coming down from a spring somewhere in the higher mountains, bringing the flavor of snow with it. Nora began wandering in a slow circle, stopping occasionally to pick flowers. Grayle sat on a low rock and watched her. She moved, as always, with a controlled grace.

Her circling stroll brought her back beside him. She stooped to pluck one more wildflower, adding it to the tiny bouquet she'd gathered: vivid little ancestors of domesticated roses and orchids. She straightened with a slow, heavy, graceful turn, holding the miniature bouquet out to him, a breeze stirring her dark curls, the sunlight caught by her eyes. Raising her white cotton skirt to kneel in the grass, she watched him carefully insert it in a buttonhole of his opened shirt.

An hour later they came upon a shepherd bringing a flock of sheep down a heavily wooded slope. A young man, with stocky legs and a long, thick torso; his skin like the material of a brown shirt that had been hung out to dry in the sun too often. About thirty sheep were already down past him, following the path toward Grayle and Nora, led by a black donkey and a goat with a clanking tin bell around its neck. The shepherd was scanning the dense trees and underbrush above, looking for more.

There were two mongrel dogs with him. He growled at one of them, an odd noise that had no relationship to human speech, and he gave the other a trilling whistle. The first dog dashed up the slope to the left, the second to the right. Minutes later one of the mongrels appeared, driving four sheep ahead of it down the slope. Then, higher up, a larger group of sheep appeared among the trees, with the other dog barking at their heels.

They came halfway down, and then began to detour along the slope in a wrong direction. The shepherd called out. The one lower down spun around, racing up to help the other turn the straying sheep back in the correct direction.

The shepherd turned to stroll after his flock, wishing Grayle and Nora a good evening in passing.

The setting sun was a horizontal slice of fire through a chink in a streak of black cloud, low on the horizon, when they came back down to the edge of the sea. The coolness of evening was already sliding down the mountains to the water. They stopped off at Grayle's place, to pick up a jacket for him and a sweater for Nora, just in case.

They had dinner in a seafood restaurant at the foot of the old town, behind the market, facing the little fishing harbor of Menton. An excellent bouillabaisse, with Provençal wine. Their table was at one of the windows, with a view on the small square at the land end of the seawall, where elderly fishermen and farmers were playing boules under a string of lanterns.

Over the harbor a seagull hung suspended on an invisible current of updraft, slowly rose higher without a quiver of its outstretched wings. The smaller fishing boats rested on the cobbles on the inclined quay a hundred yards from the restaurant, painted bright red and blue, green and yellow. The colors were gradually lost in the murk of thickening night. Against the darkening sky the mountains turned inky purple, and then black, but their peaks remained clearly defined. When Nora and Grayle left the restaurant, the sky was a living darkness sparkling with stars, the Milky Way a misty curtain carelessly flung among them.

The fishing barge was tied up near one end of the dock. It was one of the largest vessels in the little harbor, with two stubby masts and a long, low upper cabin and wheelhouse. The interior had been converted into an Aladdin's cave of Oriental voluptuousness, its flooring covered with Persian carpets and a multitude of Turkish pillows and cushions.

Nora lit a Moorish lamp of pierced bronze and bits of colored glass. She sat down cross-legged on one of the embroidered pillows, and looked up at Grayle, her face almost devoid of expression. Then she lowered her head and struck a match, touching the flame to a stick of incense on a low tray of ornately patterned brass. He settled beside her, half-reclining in the cushions, watching the play of multicolored lamplight on her bare arms, round and firm. His fingertips and tongue felt swollen.

She leaned across him to reach a cognac flask from a shadowed alcove. Filling two small liqueur glasses, she drank hers quickly. Grayle sipped slowly, his eyes on her moistened lips. Nora wasn't looking at him; there was a queer, concentrated expression in her eyes, and the corners of her mouth had deepened. Reaching into the alcove again, she drew out a curved pipe. There was a small ivory box on the brass tray. When Nora opened it the odor of hashish cut through the smoking incense. With practiced neatness she packed the pipe full, her nail polish gleaming darkly in the lamplight.

Lighting the pipe, she sucked at it deeply, holding in the smoke, and offered the pipe to Grayle.

He shook his head.

Nora gave him a look of discontented amusement. "Haven't you ever?"

"I don't need it."

She took another drag, and then extended the pipe again. "Please," she insisted softly, "I feel strange doing this alone." The pinched concentration was leaving her face.

Grayle took a puff, liking the smell but not the taste. Nora watched, smiling lazily, as he took another puff. He handed the pipe back. "It's wasted on me," he told her.

When the pipe was finished, Nora continued to hold it for a time, sitting hunched forward, staring at the wisp of smoke drifting from the incense. Then she straightened out her long legs and turned her torso slowly, leaning across him to put the pipe away in the alcove. She stayed that way, hand extended into the alcove, her body resting against him, her head lowering to his shoulder. Her breathing became slow, harsh. Grayle took the softness of her breast in his hand and felt the beating of her heart.

She made a quiet sound, deep in her throat. Her hands gripped at his upper arms, feeling the tensed hardness there, her fingers tightening with nervous strength. Her cheek turned against his shoulder and her teeth bit delicately into the flesh of his neck.

He turned against her, forcing her down, his mouth greedy and his hands exploring, commanding. Nora dragged her face from his, her hands going flat against his chest, with a testing pressure. She saw his eyes, darkly alert, searching hers. He held her, easily, not allowing her to twist away; and she felt the strength in him, controlled and directed, reach into her blood and marrow, taking possession of her.

Her laughter was soft, exultant. Her swollen, parting lips caressed his mouth, tongue darting and tasting. Her body submissive and demanding in turn, responding to his.

The violence of it left them limply entwined, indolent with pleasure. Neither wanting to move. Grayle lying with his arms around her naked waist and hips, his hands holding her buttocks and his face heavy between her thighs. Nora sprawled among the cushions, smiling at the vessel's curved beams above her, one leg curled around his back.

She was shocked by what she had done; but exalted, delicious with sin. Over and over she had told herself that this would never happen again. But there was no need to wonder why it had: for so long she'd suspected that only a sense of sin could infuse sex with some ultimate feeling for her. The deep, dark sin she had longed to taste—and now she had.

She had caused it this time—she couldn't blame it on him. Yet this time, also, there was no confusion about whether he'd wanted vengeance or wanted *her*. It was the most wanted she had ever felt. Excitement continued to swell in her. She had dared, and taken the forbidden flower, thorns and all. And there was no poison in the thorns; only an exhilarating narcotic.

But it frightened her, too, and she raised herself on her elbows, staring down at Grayle's head. "I'll never stay with you, you know."

"Won't you?" His voice was quiet, relaxed, as if his words had nothing specific to do with hers. It was sound he was making, answering her sound, like one bell in a tower answering another.

"No," she whispered shakily, "no chance at all of that; not at all. You do understand that, don't you?"

"Do I?" He turned himself sleepily, like a great cat, raising on one hip, looking at her breasts, taking them tenderly in his hands and holding them.

"I'm not to be depended on," she warned him. But she knew it was herself she was trying to protect. "Not for long. You know what I'm like."

"Yes." He bent his head and rubbed his cheek along her inner thigh; then looked at the smooth flesh there, studying it.

Nora rested a hand on his head, fingers in his hair. He took it and turned it over, the back of her hand in his palm. The fingers of his other hand traced her palm and his eyes followed the lines, as though reading her there.

"It would be impossible." Her voice broke. "You know that."

"Yes." He took her in his arms and drew her to him, kissing her throat, a hand going to the small of her back, the other taking hold of her belly. Her arms wound around him, clinging, her mouth and legs seizing on him.

There was nothing hurried or brutal this time. They had worshiped at this shrine before, and knew the sweetness of it beforehand: his strength mastering her, and her hunger overpowering him. And lying afterward together, laden with satiety, her breath cool against his neck, and his hands memorizing her flesh.

12

From three in the afternoon Grayle worked on his new painting, strengthening the nude figure leaning against the pillar. He forced himself to concentrate on what he was doing.

After Nora had left, he'd spent until two o'clock with Jacques Lorenzi, Victor's caretaker, sawing and chopping firewood in a strip of forest up along the base of the cliffs, and dragging it down to the estate with the help of Lorenzi's donkey. But he'd finished still preoccupied with the previous night.

The more he thought of the feelings it left in him, the more he sensed that the blood relationship only strengthened his need for her. The rules were not for them; of that he was certain. He had been born outside them; could not exist within them.

And now, at last, she must feel that way too. She'd known the barrier, and deliberately broken it. But—she had left.

She'd come back, he told himself fiercely. Only a last, faltering vestige of self-protection had made her deny they could ever stay together. That would pass. She'd come back. He had to be patient, wait her out.

Grayle settled down to the painting outside his lower room, but he was dissatisfied with it. He looked at the three nude studies of Jill beside the canvas. Something inherent in Jill's figure which had made him decide to use her, was missing in his painting. Grayle put down his brush, and was scowling at what he'd done so far when he heard Jill coming.

She was riding a tall black horse with a silvery mane and tail. Grayle stood up and called to her. She dismounted below the other side of the little house, and tethered the horse to the pump.

Climbing to Grayle's patio she asked, "Where's Nora?"

"Probably in Milan by now. She took the morning train."

"So soon? She just got here yesterday."

"Will you take off your clothes? I want another look at you. Same pose."

Jill eyed him questioningly as she stripped, with as little inhibition as an eel. "You don't look moody—so I assume she'll be back."

"One of these days."

Jill couldn't read any answers in his tone. She gave him an exasperated look before going over to stand against the white-washed pillar. Her recollection of the pose was exact, perhaps because it was her own: one foot planted flat, the other crooked, giving her pelvis a jaunty tilt. The golden hair of her sex was dense and silky, ends stirred minutely by a warm breeze.

Grayle sat hunched on the stool by his easel, examining her deceptively soft, satiny flesh. He knew the brick-hard muscle structure concealed inside it; and that was what he wasn't getting on canvas, what had to be hinted at, somehow, without resorting to exaggeration.

From her position at the pillar, Jill looked at his canvas. "When do you get to my face? I do hope you're not going to make me look silly."

Grayle continued to look at her, not taking up a brush, not turning to his canvas on the easel. What she'd just said, he decided, might be the key. The hardness hidden inside that sheath of smooth flesh would have to be suggested in her expression, more than with her body. He looked at what he'd done with her face in his three studies of her. Then at her again. "Turn your head a bit, to the left."

"Profile?"

"No, not quite. That's it."

She held still, and Grayle studied her. Finally he told

her to get dressed. As she put on her underthings, she asked him: "Wouldn't it be simpler if you painted me directly, while I'm here? So you could get me just right?"

"An exact copy is not what I want."

Jill got into her riding clothes. "Why not? I'm not exactly a flop, especially my figure. It has been known to meet with approval."

He grinned at her. "That's you. A painting is supposed to have something of the artist in it, too. For that, I have to allow time; time for you to pass through me, would be one way to put it."

"Sounds indecent."

"I guess it is, in a way."

Jill's humor gave way to anxiety as she pulled on her boots. "I'm going to look for Victor. He's been out riding somewhere in the hills since breakfast. With that goddamned stallion he dotes on. I hate that horse. Unpredictable."

Grayle understood her worry. Jill had been riding since she was a child. Victor had only taken it up the previous year, and hadn't found it too interesting. Until this year, when he'd discovered the stallion, a new acquisition in the stables on the next estate. It was a strapping buckskin-colored horse, high-strung, with an obstinate temper. Since then, riding had become a daily passion for Victor: a battle of wills between him and the horse. It was, Grayle suspected, akin to Victor's prowling of Paris at night, looking for trouble. But with the buckskin the challenge was more direct and dependable. With the odds slightly favoring the horse, since Victor was still learning.

"I wouldn't mind," Jill growled, "if he took a spill. Teach him what he's playing with. Do him good. But a *bad* fall wouldn't."

She sauntered off, down to her black horse.

Grayle went inside his workroom to get a sketchpad and pencils. The sketch he'd done in Paris of Nora's mouth was in an open box on his table. Grayle looked at it for some time, before going out again.

* * *

Nora came again five days later. This time she bypassed the villa late in the evening on her way up to Grayle, not letting Jill and Victor know of her presence. Her friends were back on their converted fishing barge in the harbor, preparing to move it to Spain. Nora spent the night with Grayle in the upper room of the gardener's house—almost defiantly this time, as if to exorcise any remaining feelings about their relationship. But still ready to flee.

And she was gone again the next morning, on her way to Paris.

Grayle still held to his certainty that she would be back. Meanwhile, he worked; painting more steadily than ever in his life, forcing it now. Perhaps because Pauline Renard had the first thirteen paintings, and he needed to have his own work around him. He finished the canvas of Jill, and began another. Painting every day, whenever he was not needed to help Lorenzi with maintenance jobs around the estate.

He had never worked so uninterruptedly. And he had never slept so little. The hours were charged with purpose. In two months he finished four more pictures.

In those two months Nora came twice: on her way to Rome, with an assignment to take photographs that were to be part of a book on the Fascist government. And on her way back to Paris with the pictures she'd taken; which got her barred from returning to Italy, along with the book's author.

Grayle never asked her to stay longer; not in words. But before she took the train back to Paris, Nora asked if he ever expected to live there again.

Grayle gave it thought before answering her. "Not for another year, at any rate. Victor has said I can stay on here, even when they're gone. I'm working well here. I don't want to break it."

"I see."

"And I understand," he added slowly, "that for *your* work, you need Paris still."

She nodded and said: "That's true."

But she thought about it, during her journey to Paris. And it was still on her mind when she arrived there.

* * *

On rare occasions, Victor Royan climbed from his villa to see how Grayle was coming along with his work. And to look silently at the portrait Grayle had made of him. He never made a comment about what he saw, content merely to know he contributed some part in what Grayle was doing.

Twice in February Victor and Jill went away: short trips to Madrid and Capri. When they were at the villa, Victor continued to ride the buckskin stallion almost every day. But he complained that it was getting less exciting; the horse no longer fought him. Several times they had parties at the villa, to which large numbers of people came from all along the Riviera, some from as far as Paris and Vienna, staying as guests at the villa for some days. Grayle was always invited, and never went, and Victor didn't push him.

Victor had promised Grayle solitude in which to work, and he gave what he'd promised. His feeling for Grayle had never been based on a need for his company or conversation, but on a feeling for his work, and a desire to feel a participation in it. Here he felt a real one, for Grayle was working more steadily than he had in Paris, getting more exciting with each picture. And this satisfied Victor.

Grayle noted that Victor's relationship with Jill seemed to have grown closer. There was no evidence, here, of the "harem" he'd been told about. From Jill's manner when talking about Victor, Grayle got the impression that her lesbian affairs were gradually losing their emotional validity for her.

In Grayle's life, during those first two months of 1927, there was a new relationship. Victor's caretaker, Jacques Lorenzi, began inviting Grayle to have dinner in the side-apartment of the villa he shared with his wife and children. These invitations Grayle accepted, and a relaxed, mutually respectful friendship had grown between the two men, starting with their learning that each had been a merchant seaman. Lorenzi had wound up as captain of a small freighter with a regular run from Marseilles to Casablanca.

On his final trip he'd been carrying field cannons and shells for the French army in Morocco. There'd been a fire aboard, and an explosion, and six of his crew had died when the ship sank. The accident was attributed to lack of proper safety measures by the captain. Lorenzi had lost his license, putting an end to his twenty-six-year career at sea.

He had become a taciturn man. But his wife made up for that. She loved to talk and had considerable skill as a storyteller, though her command of French was still patchy. Lorenzi had met her in Casablanca, and married her on one of his last trips there. She was a Berber, from the Atlas Mountains in the heart of Morocco. Plump and very pretty, in spite of the tribal tattoos on her cheek bones and forehead.

The tales she told over dinner in the little apartment were mostly of her native village, mixed with bits of Berber history and folklore. It was at these dinners that Grayle acquired his first smattering of Arabic and Berber phrases.

Pauline Renard came to look at his work the second week in March. It was almost five months since he'd left Paris, and the money she had advanced Grayle was nearly used up.

She studied each picture with a cool, judicial eye. Taking her time. Frowning a great deal, the high-curved forehead wrinkling with concentration.

In the end she said: "We need more. At least twice this much, just for me to begin with."

"We said a year," Grayle reminded her.

"Yes, we did. All right. But in the meantime I want to take some of these back with me, to show around."

"No," Grayle told her flatly. "That wasn't part of our agreement. I still need these around me. All of them."

Pauline Renard didn't like it. But she looked at his face, and accepted his decision. When she left, he had a check from her that would keep him going for another three months. At which point she intended to have another look at what he'd accomplished; and he'd promised to have chosen certain of the pictures he could temporarily part with.

By the end of March he'd finished two more, to add to what he'd done since he'd arrived at the little gardener's house above the Mediterranean. That made nine.

Nora didn't come back again until the first week in April. But this time she came to stay.

13

Six days before Nora arrived, Victor Royan was thrown by the buckskin horse he thought he had conquered. Thrown badly, as Jill had feared.

The hospital of Menton was off to one side of the Old Town, stretched out on a high terrace with the densely wooded foothills of the Maritime Alps building up behind it. Grayle and Jill, waiting in wicker chairs on the second-floor arcade, looked anxiously to the nun who finally opened the front door of Victor's room.

She shook her head as she came out to them. "He is out of surgery but I'm afraid it is still much too soon to predict anything. I'm sorry, I know it is hard, but you will just have to be patient."

The buckskin had chosen a wicked place to throw Victor: a narrow cliff-trail he'd been negotiating with Jill riding behind, and an almost-sheer fall of some fifty feet below them. Victor's skull had been fractured against a boulder. The first question they were waiting to have answered now was whether he was going to live or die. If he lived, there would be the question of how much brain damage he had sustained.

The nun looked at the crushed cigarette butts on the red-tiled flooring around Jill. Mouth thinned to stop herself from chiding, she strode along the arcade and came back with a terra-cotta dish, into which she dropped the butts as she picked them up. She gave Jill a sharp frown, and left the dish beside her.

Jill continued to chain-smoke when the nun was gone,

eyes fixed on the patterns of the wrought-iron railing directly in front of them. She hadn't cried; her expression was more puzzled than anything else. She didn't look at Grayle when she reached out to take his hand. He twined his fingers around hers and gazed at the sea below. There was a low, stiff wind. The surface was like churned milk.

"I was really in love with him." Her voice was strained, and lost. "I don't know why. He was ridiculous; nothing was normal with him. Everything about him was wrong, crazy. But I was in love with him."

"He's not dead yet."

"But he will be."

"You don't know that," Grayle told her.

Victor wasn't dead when one of the doctors came out to send them away from the hospital that night. But he acknowledged that they were still unable to predict whether Victor would ever come out of coma.

"Come back in the morning," the doctor told them. "Not before nine. By then we should know more." And: "I've spoken to his wife by phone. Madame Royan expects to arrive by noon. She's arranging to fly down with a brain specialist from Paris. I know his reputation; a very good man."

Grayle and Jill left the hospital and walked down through the cramped covered passages of the Old Town, following the twists of Rue Longue and descending the wide staircase below the church of Saint Michel. There was a cafe still open on the Quai Bonaparte, and they ordered the only meal being served: a plain beef stew, with bread and wine. Jill hadn't eaten since breakfast, and both felt hungry when they sat down to the dinner. But neither was able to finish half of it. Even the wine didn't sit right, and they left most of the bottle untouched.

They followed the curving promenade along the Bay of Garavan, and turned up just before the frontier, climbing the Chemin Vallaya. There was nothing they could find to say to each other when they reached the villa. Grayle left her there and continued the climb to the gardener's house.

138   MARVIN H. ALBERT

The wind had turned, becoming a mistral blowing down out of the mountains, sweeping any trace of mist from the night air and causing the stars to blaze with unnatural brilliance.

Grayle lit a small fire in the corner fireplace of his upstairs room; just enough to draw the chill from the thick walls. The fire was down to smoking embers when he finally stretched out on the bed.

He did not sleep. When footsteps sounded on the exterior stairway, climbing from his little patio below, he knew who it would be. He'd been expecting it.

Jill stopped just inside the door, waiting while her eyes adjusted to the darkness. "I can't be alone now. Please, may I stay with you?"

"You can stay," he told her. "But I won't be of any use to you. Not tonight."

"That's up to me," she told him fiercely, and tore off her clothes as she came through the darkness to his bed.

There was no passion in the efficient sexuality with which she aroused him. There was only her need for release, and his giving of it. Direct, impersonal and abrupt. And yet, with an odd kind of tenderness there, as well. It was done with quickly. And then they lay together staring at the dark, Grayle's arm sheltering her while they waited exhausted for the dawn.

Jill was asleep when it came. Grayle was careful not to wake her as he got out of the bed and dressed. He went outside and watched the red ball of the sun lift above a turbulent sea into a bleached sky.

His sense of loss, though so different from Jill's, was almost as total.

Victor's wife arrived at the hospital with her Paris specialist in the early afternoon. Victor remained sunk in his coma, neither dead nor alive. Grayle left the hospital and walked back to Victor's estate.

He was filling a basket with oranges and lemons that had ripened on the trees flanking the arbor when Victor's wife appeared shortly before sunset, climbing up from the villa. She was a tall woman in her thirties, with a lean elegance and beautiful reddish hair. She had Jill with her. Grayle put down the basket and waited as they reached him.

"He's going to live," Victor's wife told him. "But he hasn't regained consciousness. It is a coma that *could* continue for weeks, even months. No one is willing to hazard a guess, at this point, as to whether his mind will be normal when he does come out of it."

It was a matter-of-fact appraisal of the situation, by someone who was used to controlling her feelings.

Jill stood there beside her and said nothing; very small in comparison, almost childish. Her expression was defenseless, her spirit gone.

"I'm having him moved to a hospital in Paris tomorrow," Victor's wife went on. "I've arranged to hire a special airplane fitted with a hospital bed. We'll accompany him, along with Doctor Masson and a nurse. Victor will have a better chance there."

Grayle nodded, saying nothing; having nothing to say.

Unexpectedly, she asked if she might have a look at some of his paintings. When Grayle showed her into his workroom, Jill remained outside, her head bowed, staring at the ground.

After some minutes of inspecting his work, Victor's wife said in a tone of polite apology: "Not my sort of thing, I'm afraid. But that doesn't matter. Jill has told me how much it meant to Victor, helping you. I'm sure he would want to know he has continued to, if . . ." She stopped herself, and calmly changed the word: "*When* he recovers. I'd like you to stay on here, if you would care to."

"I don't know."

"You should stay. Jill says Victor was enormously pleased at how well you worked here. You can continue to help Lorenzi with his maintenance jobs, if that makes you feel better about it. Or not, suit yourself. It costs us nothing for you to stay; the place is here, and if you go it will only be unused." She gave him a smile that had assured strength behind it. "Do stay. For Victor's sake. When Victor recovers, your being here can be my present to him."

"I have to think about it.".

"Of course. Do." She walked outside and took Jill's hand. Jill allowed it to be taken, not looking at Grayle. Victor's wife told him, "You don't have to make your decision before we leave. Just stay, as long as you wish."

She smiled again, and turned and led Jill away by the hand. Grayle remembered what Nora had once told him about them. Now there was no question about which one was in control.

Five nights later Grayle sat outside the lower room of the gardener's house, listening to the ten o'clock Rome-Paris express train come out of Italy and race past below.

He'd left a lamp on in his workroom, and its light through the open door outlined his figure as he sat there on the stool, leaning forward with his elbows on his spread knees, watching the night. There was a canvas he'd begun work on before Victor's accident, waiting in there to be finished. He had spent some time looking at it, without being able to resurrect the feelings that had started him working on it. Nor could he find any impetus inside him, to begin again with a different canvas.

He had just about decided that the time had come for him to move someplace else. Anyplace else. The dead feeling here had invaded him too solidly; and there was no sign that it would lift.

The villa below was invisible in the darkness: not a single window light, anywhere. Full of unused rooms now, except for the small side-apartment; and the Lorenzis always went to sleep early. The hoot of an owl sounded, somewhere quite close, above the gardener's house. The hooting was repeated several times: mournful and insistent. Then it stopped, leaving the night to the chorus of crickets and frogs, and a couple of nightingales singing to each other.

An automobile pulled in to the front of the villa. It stopped, and the noise of its idling motor came up faintly to Grayle. Then motor and lights were switched off. Grayle rose to his feet. He walked through the arbor and started down toward the villa.

They met as she came up the graveled steps between the terraced lily ponds. For several seconds they only stood there looking at each other in the scattered moonlight.

"You know about Victor?" Grayle asked her.

Nora nodded. "I saw him, at the hospital in Paris. I'm sorry, Nick."

"Yes, well . . ." He let it go; the words had no meaning in them, and he found ones that did: "I am, too. But it happened, and there's nothing can change that now. He hasn't come out of the coma?"

"No change at all."

Grayle made an angry sound. "Stupid bastard. He didn't have much. Now it's nothing."

"He may recover. It may just be a matter of time."

Grayle heard, this time, the tired weakness of her voice. "You drove your car all the way down from Paris?"

"All the way. I'm exhausted." And then, quietly: "*Are you going to stay on here?*"

"I was thinking about leaving."

"I hope not," Nora told him. "I have two suitcases waiting in the car. Plus a case of film. And my cameras. Both of them."

His eyes narrowed on her, but he couldn't quite make out her expression. The shadows, tangy with the scent of breathing vegetation, patterned her face with a delicate mask.

"I had an idea for a book of photographs," Nora explained, "about all the forgotten villages in the mountains just behind the Riviera, where everything still goes on pretty much as it has for centuries. I even thought up a good title: *Another Way of Life.* I tried a number of publishers—not Gian-Carlo, though. One of them finally gave me a contract; and a very small advance."

"Does Gian-Carlo know?"

Nora hesitated. "He knows about the book, and that I'll have to be down here for some time to do it. But I'm certain he understands that it is more than the book involved." Another hesitation. "I'll have to go back to Paris in three or four weeks, anyway. To develop the film I've taken in that time and see how much of it is what I want. When I do, I'll make it clear to him. I may even have my darkroom equipment shipped down, at that point. *If* we're staying."

Grayle put his arm around her, and turned her with him, starting down the steps. "Let's bring up your things."

14

In the first three weeks Nora was with him Grayle finished two paintings, and began worrying that he might be forcing his work too fast. Over the same period Nora photographed the villages of Castellar, Saint-Agnés, Gorbio and Roquebrune. She used her old Graflex to photograph the ancient stone formations of the villages and to do posed portraits of certain villagers. The Leica was used to catch the way of life in the villages; their citizens moving through their normal daily routines. Nora took her time; in no hurry to be finished, though her desire to take news photos of current events remained. That, she had decided, would wait until such time as Grayle returned to Paris.

The first time Grayle accompanied her was on the Sunday she drove up to begin recording the life in Eze, perched spectacularly on a spire of rock fifteen hundred feet above the Mediterranean. He was between paintings, and Jacques Lorenzi did not believe in working on Sundays. While Nora moved through the climbing passageways of the village, setting up her shots, Grayle did sketches of her at work. He had five of them done by the time the weather suddenly changed.

Until three in the afternoon the only clouds were far out to sea, and the old stone walls of the village were drenched in sunshine. Then, while Nora was snapping pictures of an old woman leading a donkey loaded with cement sacks, Grayle noticed the black clouds rising between the peaks of the inland mountains. Soon there were flashes of lightning inside the clouds. The resonance of the thunder's vibrations radiated down the valley around the spire holding the village aloft.

By three-thirty the mountains were in fog, barely visible, as though carved out of immobile smoke. The wind rose sharply from the mountains to the sea. Grayle and Nora climbed down to her car as the mist rolled into Eze, people moving through it like shadows. The storm moved in as Nora drove down the hills to Monaco. When she turned onto the coast road the horizon was a swirling cloudy green between black sea and dark gray sky. They entered Menton in a downpour.

Nora parked alongside the covered market, and they dashed inside to buy food for that night and the next morning. Carrying their purchases, they ran out across the cobbled street, sloshing through puddles before they reached shelter under the wide tin awning in front of the Cafe du Commerce. They took the only dry table still unoccupied, ordered two small glasses of calvados, and sat there watching the rain and listening to it ring on the metal sheeting above them; savoring the heat of the calvados inside them, turning their heads to smile at each other. Sharing the exhilaration. And rising without a word between them, to make the dash back to the car, and the drive along the promenade and up to the estate.

Their clothes were soaked through by the time they climbed to the gardener's house. Grayle lit a small fire in the lower room, just enough to keep the damp from his paintings, while Nora ran up the outside steps to start a bigger fire in the upper room. She had her clothes off and was drying herself before its blaze when Grayle came in and began stripping.

Nora used the big towel to help him rub himself dry. By then the dry warmth of the room was enveloping them, and Grayle reached for her. Nora backed away, teasing, holding the towel up between them. There wasn't much room to move around in. Grayle, lunging for her, struck his hip against a corner of the table and cursed. Nora laughed and let the towel go, grabbing him and falling across the bed with him.

They made love with a sweet ease that had grown from

continuity—and with no questions left about what their love-making meant. It was there, and had to be recognized.

Nora was no longer surprised when he got up, shortly after, and began efficiently preparing their meal on the little kerosene stove in front of the fireplace. Nor at her own lack of sleepiness when she got up to help him with it. At the beginning of their three weeks together she had been somewhat disturbed by the way Grayle would sometimes, after they had made love in the daytime, soon leave her and go down to paint or draw. And that at those times she herself often felt stimulated to work. In Nora's previous experience, when lovers really satisfied each other, they fell asleep.

"Love is positive energy," Grayle had told her. "Giving and getting new energy from each other."

"*Are* we in love?" And then, when he only threw her a look: "Sex without love can be quite exciting, too."

"But it leaves you drained and tired. I don't know if people fall in love because of the energy they get from each other, or get the energy because of the love. But it's there, and it works in both directions, like everything in this world. And probably the next."

"You do have some bizarre ideas. Where do you pick them up, sir?"

"The Tree of Life," his tone mock-serious, "teaches all things, about the ways of man and nature." And he'd explained about the cabalistic Tree of Life, with its ten centers and twenty-two paths that would explain everything, if only they could be totally understood. But which even in its simplest meanings explained much: the roots drawing nourishment out of the earth and sending it up to the branches, the branches drawing nourishment from the sun and sending it down to the roots. "It works both ways, or not at all. Everything does."

They had learned so many things from each other in those three weeks together; they knew each other so well.

Grayle knew about her following funerals as a child; and haunting graveyards. And that her only female idol had been the "sacred monster," Sarah Bernhardt. He knew that

Nora could cure herself of illness with her mind, from the time she'd gotten a sharp pain in her abdomen a week after her arrival, and gone to sleep feverish. He'd wanted to take her to a doctor, but she'd insisted on trying sleep first. He'd wakened her in the middle of the night because she'd been moaning, and she mumbled without opening her eyes, "Let me sleep, I've just found out where the trouble is, now I can work on it." She'd slept, and been entirely better in the morning.

And Grayle had known, then, that he'd found a new sorceress.

There were also things about her that he learned anew each time, as he did again late in that stormy Sunday night: the slant of her long gray eyes when they mocked him, and the power of her mouth and loins, while the hot embers of the fire crackled and the rain still drummed on the shutters and tiled roof.

But just before he fell asleep, he found himself thinking of the one thing they never talked about, anymore: Gian-Carlo—and Grayle's feeling that Nora's still being attached to her husband was the real sin.

When he woke, just before dawn, the rain had stopped. It was the recurring anxiety that wakened him: that he had pushed his work too hard, too fast. That there might be nothing in any of it. He left the bed and dressed without waking Nora, stepped outside and closed the door quietly behind him.

Dawn light filtered weakly through dense mist that hid sea, sky and all but the nearest hill. The air was chilly and soggy, drops detaching from the mist and dripping. Grayle went down the steps and entered his workroom. Striking a match, he lit an oil lamp and turned up the wick. He carried the lamp in one hand as he went to inspect the paintings he'd done since coming to the south. One by one he examined them, critically. Was it only his awareness of how hard he had been forcing that had made him anxious, or was it something in the pictures themselves? Or simply that no matter what he achieved he was always reaching for more; that the result could never quite match his goal?

Grayle was still not certain of the answers when he finished, and saw the chinks of daylight in the shutters had become stronger. He extinguished the lamp and put it down, threw open the shutters. The mist was lifting heavily, revealing the surface of the sea out to a wall of low, solid fog. Only wisps of the mist still clung to the nearer hills. Dollops of water trickled from trees emerging in sharp outline.

Grayle watched the cliffs to the left become visible, halfway up. Out at sea the roof of mist raised above the top of the distant roll of fog, revealing a long, uneven strip of sky: brilliant gold and blue.

Turning quickly from the window, Grayle snatched up his box of watercolor paints and brushes, a small jar of water and a sketchpad. He carried them outside and swiftly set to work to catch those extraordinary layers: that dazzling strip of sky caught between the roof of mist and the dense roll of sea-fog.

It was not a precise rendering; the scene was changing while he painted, and he had to work too fast. What he did was more in the nature of hasty notes, to catch the contrasting colors and shapes. It was all gone before he finished. But what he'd gotten was enough, together with his visual memory of it.

He rinsed out his brushes as the sun rose above the distant wall of sea-fog, fat and red, radiating fire. The trees around him were still dripping, but the air had become noticeably warmer. A smell of coffee came from the room above. Grayle stood up and placed the watercolor face-up on the stool, and went back up the steps.

The bread they'd bought in the market was already on the table, sliced and thickly buttered, along with an opened jar of grape jam. Nora saw his preoccupied face, and silently poured the coffee in two cups, placing one in front of him as he sat down. He watched her as he ate, absorbing what he saw into something else that was inside his head and very remote from her. And she still didn't speak when he finished the breakfast and went out again.

When Nora descended the steps half an hour later,

Grayle was seated outside his workroom, studying a newly stretched canvas on the easel before him. The canvas was blank, but she knew he saw something there. Propped against stones on the patio close around him were the drawings he'd done of her the previous day in Eze, and the watercolor study he'd just finished.

Nora rested a hand on his shoulder and bent and kissed him. They still hadn't spoken when she went down to the car, to drive back up to Eze with her cameras. Grayle began to paint an hour after she'd left: a portrait of Nora, fused from the drawings and memory, against that strange sunrise.

It was eighteen concentrated days before he began to get what he wanted with it.

Nora waited six weeks for the visit to Paris that she had originally intended to make after three or four weeks.

She had received three letters from Gian-Carlo in that time. All in the same tone: caring but unworried; looking forward to her return but patient; certain she *would* be back together with him, when her work in the south was completed. He meant, Nora knew, that she'd come back to him, as always, when she became bored with the lover he realized she must be with on the Riviera. Gian-Carlo was aware that Grayle was there, and that she was seeing him; but Nora doubted that it occurred to her husband that Grayle might be that lover.

Nora left her car, and took the train to Paris. She stayed four days, and then returned to Grayle, bringing her developed film with her. But she hadn't done any of the enlargements in Paris. That she intended to do in Menton, when the equipment she'd arranged to have shipped down arrived. Grayle had found a room for rent in the Old Town, that could be converted into her darkroom.

During her time in Paris, Nora went to the hospital to check on Victor Royan's condition. As she approached his room she met his wife, coming out of it, and it was from her that she learned about Victor. He was still in a coma, but he'd had another operation, and since then he'd begun to have periods approaching consciousness. The doctor was now hopeful that he would respond to further treatment.

Nora had only met Madame Royan twice before, and had found her intelligent but too cool to like. She hesitated before asking, "Have you seen Jill, recently?"

Madame Royan nodded. "She is staying with me, now." She left it at that.

Nora didn't see Gian-Carlo while she was in Paris, because he had gone to New York on business. She was relieved, though she berated herself for her continuing cowardice. She had told Grayle that this time she was going to make the final break from her husband, and everything inside her had been knotted in anticipation of Gian-Carlo's response.

But he wasn't there, and instead she left a note for him to find on his return from New York. A short note, lacking in details, but honest enough as far as it went: she was leaving him, and was with Grayle. Fervently, Nora hoped it would be enough—that the ugly scene she had feared was not merely being delayed.

The night after she came back to Menton, Nora and Grayle were invited to the Lorenzi apartment for dinner. For Grayle, it turned out to be a lucky dinner. The next morning police arrived to question him. During the previous evening a considerable amount of jewelry had been stolen from a nearby villa, while the Swedish couple who owned it were off partying in Monte Carlo. Though there was nothing to indicate that Grayle was involved in the robbery, he was a foreigner, a stranger to the area and without a steady job. So the police were naturally curious about his movements at the time of the robbery.

Nora and the Lorenzi family were able to provide his alibi. Still, the police spent five hours searching the estate before apologizing for the inconvenience and leaving. The stolen jewelry was never recovered.

Gian-Carlo arrived six days later.

* * *

Grayle was in his workroom late that afternoon, stretching a new canvas, when Gian-Carlo stepped inside the open door. Grayle put down the hammer and nails he'd been using, and rose slowly to his feet.

Gian-Carlo looked at the paintings that hung and leaned against the wall. He continued to give them more than casual attention as he spoke, avoiding Grayle's eyes: "You have done a considerable amount of new work since coming down here." There was nothing in his voice but polite interest. But the pain was writ plain, in the tension around his mouth and eyes.

Grayle nodded, watching him warily.

"I think they are even better than the ones I saw in Paris," Gian-Carlo said. "Really very exciting."

Grayle was conscious of a faint sound of movement from the room above. Nora had spent the day installing her newly arrived equipment in what was to be her darkroom, and she had returned tired.

"Madame Royan asked me," Gian-Carlo said, "to tell you how pleased she is that you've stayed on here."

"Any further improvement in Victor?"

"He's responding very well. He has periods of consciousness, and begins to recognize people. There's real hope for a full recovery of his faculties. But it will take a great deal of time."

Gian-Carlo glanced, finally, at Grayle's face; but almost instantly he looked away, to the open window. "I'd like to see Nora," he said quietly. "Do you know where she is?"

Grayle told him, "The room above." And when Gian-Carlo looked around for a stairway: "The steps are outside, to the left." His voice was devoid of expression.

Gian-Carlo's eyes turned to him again, briefly. The mixture of pain and embarrassment in them was terrible. Turning away, he went out and climbed the steps.

Grayle walked outside and sat down on the three-legged stool, hunching forward and staring down at the sea. His face was wooden, and his eyes were almost closed.

Nora was stretched out on the bed, wearing only her

slip, half-asleep when Gian-Carlo stepped inside the upper room. She sat up quickly, wide awake.

"Hello, Nora." Even as he said it, he was conscious of how ridiculous the conventional greeting sounded, and he smiled awkwardly. Pulling out a chair, he sat down heavily and placed his hands neatly on the table, looking at them.

Nora swung her bare feet to the floor, sitting on the edge of the bed with her hands gripping the mattress on either side of her. "Why are you here, Gian-Carlo?"

"I want you back," he said simply.

"What for?" Nora demanded raggedly. "You don't need me, don't use me, don't love me . . ."

"I do love you, Nora. You know that."

"Not in any way that is of any use to me, Gian-Carlo."

"I can change that. Nora, I want you back. I still love you. And you love me; I know you do."

"Not that way—not anymore."

"But you did."

Nora whispered viciously: "I was crazy for you."

"Until he took you from me."

"No one took me from you, Gian-Carlo. What is wrong between us happened long ago."

His hands clenched into fists on the table, and he raised his head with a flash of anger. "I've always allowed you all your little affairs . . ."

"So you'd be free for yours."

"None of that matters, Nora. The only important thing is that, finally, we belong to each other."

"But we don't."

"If that were true," he told her slowly, "I wouldn't want to live."

Nora's mouth became ugly with scorn. "The ultimate blackmail? Don't threaten to kill yourself, Gian-Carlo, because I'll hate you for it. Let me be your friend. Don't destroy that, too."

He leaned back in the chair and, looking at her, he began to cry.

* * *

It was getting dark when Nora came down the steps. Grayle stood up and looked at her, expressionless. "How is he?"

"Very bad. He keeps crying. Nick, he has a suite in a hotel in Menton. I'm going to drive him there, try to calm him down. I don't want to leave him alone until I'm sure he will be all right."

"Be careful. If he begins to sound violent . . ."

"He won't hurt me, don't worry about that. He only needs time, to get used to it, accept that it can't be changed."

Nora flung her arms around him suddenly, burying her face against his throat. Grayle's hands went to the back of her head, and her waist, holding her against him. She drew a deep breath, and kissed him, and pulled away. "I'll be back, but it may take all night. Please say you understand."

Grayle looked at her. "It'll be all right," he said, trying to convince himself as he watched her go back up the steps.

She came down with Gian-Carlo. His face was tight. He didn't look at Grayle as they went past him, down to Nora's car.

Nora kept talking gently to Gian-Carlo as she drove to his hotel, but he didn't respond. There was a bottle of whiskey in the living room of his suite, and he began drinking as soon as they entered. It was after he'd finished a quarter of the bottle that he began to talk again: pacing the room, alternately pleading and weeping and reasoning, while Nora sat on the sofa and tried to talk him back to normal.

By midnight he'd fallen silent, slumped in a chair and continuing to drink, staring at Nora piteously. She leaned back, emotionally exhausted, resting her head on the back of the sofa and covering her burning eyes with her hands.

Gian-Carlo waited for a considerable time, watching her, until he saw that she was deeply asleep. He stood up and left quietly, went down to the lobby and summoned a taxi.

* * *

The smell of smoke wrenched Grayle out of sleep. He was on his feet beside the bed before he was fully awake, swaying and confused. Trying to grasp what dream it was that made his heart thud so violently. But the smoke was no dream.

By the time he reached the bottom of the outside steps the entire workroom blazed with firelight. Gian-Carlo had just thrown the last contents of the can of kerosené across a painting when Grayle flung himself into the room. It was the last one, the portrait of Nora against the sunrise. All the others were already being consumed by flames. And in a corner, all of Grayle's drawings and watercolors, thrown in a haphazard pile, were curling into ashes, the fire running up the painted walls to lick at the ceiling beams.

Grayle threw himself at Gian-Carlo with an animal scream. The cigarette lighter in Gian-Carlo's hand was snapped to flame as Grayle's weight slammed against him, driving him staggering away from the last canvas.

But it was too late. The kerosene drenching the painting exploded into flames with a soft, fat noise, all of it at once. Gian-Carlo twisted with shocking strength in the grasp of Grayle's hands, and crashed the emptied kerosene can across the upper part of his face and forehead. Grayle fell back against his work-table, and partway across it, his vision blurring and blood running from his fractured nose.

"Now you'll know," Gian-Carlo told him, "how it feels to have the only thing that matters to you destroyed by another man."

The odd thing was, his voice was not much different than it had ever been with Grayle: quiet, controlled, thoughtful.

Grayle's clearing vision filled with the spectacle of the multiple fires around him, consuming the work he'd accomplished; all of it, disappearing in flame and smoke. His right hand closed around something hard.

Afterward, Grayle said that he wasn't aware the hammer was in his hand, until he saw it strike the side of Gian-Carlo's head.

He stood over the body for some time, dazed, until the

flames began to burn at his skin. Then he walked outside, leaving the dead man behind.

Much of the body was consumed in the spreading fire that gutted the lower room, and part of the one above. The charge that it was a deliberate attempt to destroy evidence of the murder weighed heavily against him at the trial.

15

Grayle had been in his cell in the House of Detention in Nice for a week when Inspector Rives, assigned to conduct the preliminary investigation of the homicide, came in carrying a bottle of cheap champagne and two glasses.

It was Inspector Rives who had arrived at the police station in Menton, with two uniformed cops, to remove Grayle to Nice, where the Préfecture in charge of the Maritime Alps area was located. He was a solid, capable-looking man with weary eyes that regarded Grayle with neither animosity nor pity. Grayle had become accustomed to his unfailing courtesy. But the bottle of champagne was a surprise.

"Today all of France is celebrating a renewed love affair with America," Rives explained as he sat down on the edge of Grayle's bunk beside him. He put the glasses on the floor and began working at the cork. "Charles Lindbergh has just landed his monoplane at Le Bourget Airport."

Grayle's frown of incomprehension surprised Inspector Rives: "You do not know of him? A fellow American, and a great pilot. And today the greatest hero in France. He has become the first pilot to fly across the Atlantic, all alone; America to French soil. So now we have two Charlies we love; Lindbergh joins Chaplin in our affections. And today no American in France can pay for a drink, anywhere."

Rives popped the cork and poured the foaming champagne into their glasses. "So—I toast you, American." They clinked glasses and drank.

"No interrogation today?" Grayle asked him.

The inspector shook his head. "It would not fit the mood

of this day." He added, as he refilled their glasses: "Besides, there is not much more to be done, here. Tomorrow I will go to Paris for some days of background investigation. But from what has already been determined . . ." Rives took a sip from his glass, not finishing what he'd begun to say.

Grayle finished for him: "You don't think much of my chances."

"That is not for me to say. The Public Prosecutor has the dossier I have assembled. All the information in it has been passed on to the Judge of Instruction assigned to this case, and has also been made available to your attorney. What they make of it all is between them and you."

Rives hesitated, and then said in the same careful tone: "This is a day to be kind to Americans. So I will offer some advice that I am not empowered to give. If you were to reveal that I had done so, I would deny it, and make matters even more difficult for you in retaliation."

Grayle watched him without comment.

Rives studied his face a moment, and then resumed: "I have as much respect for artists as any Frenchman. But to give the burning of some paintings and drawings as a reason for killing a man . . . No, Monsieur Grayle, it is not acceptable. The destruction of a small amount of property and the destruction of a human being do not equate. This is not a moral judgment I am giving you, please understand. I merely give you some practical advice."

"Which is?"

"A crime of passion—*that* a French court can understand. I have known people to admit to a crime of passion, and walk out of court exonerated. In any case, sentences tend to be quite lenient, with crimes of passion. A few years . . ."

Inspector Rives lowered his voice, even more: "Gian-Carlo Pattara had a beautiful wife. You fell in love with her, and she with you. Passionately. Then the husband came, and threatened to take her away from you. Perhaps even threatened you personally. Perhaps he threatened her. And perhaps she was frightened by these threats into agreeing to leave you and return to him. The possibility of losing her drove all reason from your mind. And in that moment of jealous insanity, you killed him. Without thinking. To keep the woman you love. That, Monsieur Grayle, is your only possible effective defense."

Grayle did not explain to him that the woman he would have to claim was responsible for his crime of passion was his half-sister.

But Inspector Rives found out by the time he returned from Paris. The information was passed on to the Public Prosecutor; and to the Judge of Instruction, who was responsible, under French law, for a detailed examination of the case for and against the accused. It was also made available, on the same day, to the attorney Nora had hired to defend Grayle.

The attorney's name was Girard Rossi. It was a name that commanded respect among the lawyers and news reporters of that time. He was a tough, canny old courtfighter. And he did not like what he had just learned; as he made plain to Grayle in their next meeting.

They met in an interview room at the House of Detention. It was a small room. The only window was in the closed door, so the guard who was required to remain outside during the interview could watch them without hearing what they said. There was a long table, covered with green baize; a low divider along its top and a larger one below, to make passing anything across the table difficult.

Grayle sat in the single wooden chair on one side of the table. There were two armchairs available on the other side, and attorney Rossi had chosen the more comfortable. But he didn't sound comfortable with the information that had been supplied to him.

"Incest—that will not sit well on the stomach of the court." Rossi quickly raised a hand to forestall Grayle's objection. "I know—I spoke to Madame Pattara this morning. She is only your half-sister; until quite recently you were complete strangers; neither of you ever seriously considered yourselves related."

A stab of a forefinger in Grayle's direction. "Nevertheless, the blood relationship does exist. And incest remains an extremely disturbing word, for many. Your three judges will not like it. Your jury will despise you for it. And your attorney cannot use a crime of passion as your defense because I do not want to dwell on it in your trial."

"I never claimed that I hit him because of Nora," Grayle pointed out. "He destroyed my work. Everything I've done . . ."

"Property," Rossi interrupted, unknowingly echoing Inspector Rives, "does not equate with human life."

"I'm not talking about property. I'm talking about my work, my life."

"Two years ago," Rossi told him softly, "a man in Paris went into the Louvre and deliberately slashed a painting by Rembrandt. He was given a harsh sentence: three months in prison. As I've said, destruction of property—even if that property is a work of art acknowledged by the entire world to be a masterpiece—cannot be regarded under the law to have a significance remotely comparable to the destruction of a human life."

"I didn't intend to kill him."

"Of course not," Rossi agreed firmly. "That is the nub. It was an act of sudden insane fury. Which you were incapable of controlling." Rossi leaned back in the armchair and contemplated the dingy brown ceiling. "The incest aspect of the case may even be of help. A man who would sleep with his own sister must be mad, to begin with."

"I won't let you use that."

"You'll have to. If I don't bring it up, the prosecution will. At least if I'm the one, I can use it to support my statement that what you did was the act of a man gone mad."

"I may have been, when I hit him. *Will* that help, even if it's true?"

"If the court believes it. With your background, they may: mother a suicide by drowning; your aunt in an insane asylum."

Grayle's fingers dug into the green baize of the table. He felt himself sinking deeper and deeper into filth—and a premonition of doom.

Nora's visits were painful for him. She could not hide her terror at the possibility of his permanent removal from her life, and he could not persuade her that she was not to blame. He was grateful for the chance to end her visits when, on the fourth one, she shook his stoicism with something she had just learned. Discussing it, they agreed that if it was discovered by others it would make their relationship look even worse. It was decided, finally, that it could only be kept secret by her leaving the country.

She went to stay with friends she could trust in Scotland, and did not return until a week before his trial, by which time her secret was safe.

While she was gone the strength of the case against Grayle became increasingly apparent.

His interrogation by the government's Judge of Instruction went on day after day, consuming months. Each morning he was taken from the House of Detention, in a police van, to the Palace of Justice, an imposing three-centuries-old structure built by the Duke of Savoy. In the office of the Judge of Instruction Grayle was seated in a leather-padded armchair before the wide desk, and his left wrist was manacled to the radiator beside it. Grayle's right hand was left free so he could sign transcripts of his statements, and thumb through pages from the growing dossier which the Judge of Instruction occasionally passed across the desk for his inspection. The interrogation always went on until noon, recessed for lunch, and resumed until evening.

For Grayle, these sessions were a quagmire that spread without end.

But it did end, finally, in the last month of 1927. The Judge of Instruction presented his completed dossier to the Chambre d'Accusation, along with his own recommendation.

Grayle's trial for murder began on the twenty-second day of January, in 1928. Unlike the preparatory interrogations, it did not take long.

There were no unexpected moments of drama. The questions put to Grayle by both the Public Prosecutor and the President of the Assize Court were little more than rephrasings from the Judge of Instruction's detailed interrogation:

"How many of your paintings were lost in the fire, Monsieur Grayle?"

"Twelve. Plus quite a number of drawings, watercolors, sketches . . ."

"Do you remember the paintings you did?"

"Of course."

"Each one?"

"Yes."

"Then you could paint them again, couldn't you?"

No answer.

"And much more easily and quickly than the first time, since you already know the subjects and would only have to repeat, to copy from memory?"

"No."

"Why not?"

"I could never do them again."

"That is difficult to understand. However . . . will you please tell us how many paintings you have sold, so far in your career as an artist?"

"None."

"How much have you earned, in your lifetime, from your paintings?"

"Nothing, so far. I never tried to sell them."

"You never tried? Perhaps because you were afraid, with some reason, that no one would buy them?"

"That was not the reason."

"Let me understand: You have sold nothing and earned nothing from your paintings? Yet you consider a dozen of them more valuable than a man's life?"

"I didn't mean to kill him. I told you, I didn't realize I had that hammer in my hand until after he was lying there on the floor."

"You say you didn't intend to kill him—but you didn't pull him out of that fire with you, did you? You left him there to burn?"

"There was no point in trying to pull him out. He was dead."

"How can you be sure of that?"

"It was obvious."

"Are you saying you didn't leave him there in the fire to make certain that he died?"

"He was already dead."

"Are you aware that men have been known to survive, in the war, even after being struck in the head by several bullets? So you can't be certain he was dead, and neither can this court."

"He was dead."

"You didn't leave him in the fire to make sure of that?"

"No."

"Or perhaps you hoped that the evidence that you had killed him would be burned with his body?"

"No."

There was a second prong to the prosecution's attack, and it was honed to a sharp point with skill: "According to information received, Madame Pattara, the widow of the man you killed, is your sister? Is this true?"

"*Half*-sister."

"But by blood? Not merely through legal connection? That is, you and Madame Pattara had the same father?"

"Yes."

"When Madame Pattara, your sister, left her husband, she moved in to live with you, her brother—is that correct?"

"She stayed for a time in the house I was using."

"This house has how many rooms?"

"Two rooms."

"One of these rooms was entirely a workroom, is that correct?"

"Yes."

"Was there a bed in it?"

"No."

"So, in this house which you both shared, there was in fact only a single room in which to live, to sleep?"

"Yes."

"And Madame Pattara, your sister, and wife of the man you killed, lived with you in this one room? Which contained only a single bed?"

"There was no place else."

"And would it be fair to assume that you lived together in this one room, with only one bed, in an intimate relationship?"

No answer.

President of the Court: "You are required to answer the question put to you, Monsieur Grayle."

Question rephrased by the prosecution: "You slept with Madame Pattara in the same bed—as brother and sister, or as lovers?"

"We didn't know each other until quite recently. We'd never even met until little more than a year ago. We came to care for each other."

"Care for each other? You mean you became lovers?"

"You use the *words* brother and sister, but that's all they are in this case: just *words*. They didn't really apply."

"The laws of nature do not apply to you? Nor the law of man? Of every civilized country in the world?"

"I don't understand the question."

"*Do* you understand the meaning of the word—incest?"

"Yes."

"Would you agree that incest is a disgusting affair? Repugnant to every decent normal human being? And even among most wild animals, by whom it is shunned by instinct alone, forgetting for the moment God's seal against it?"

"There was nothing like that."

"Let me phrase this as simply as possible, Monsieur Grayle: You were in love with your sister, enough to have intimate sexual relations with her and consider that the laws of God, nature and civilized government against incest did not apply to you? And you knew your sister loved you, enough to leave her husband to live with you as lovers? And that she would continue to care for you after her husband was killed?"

"I don't know the answer to that."

"Don't you? Well, did you know that Madame Pattara's husband was quite well off, financially?"

"I knew he had a good business; that his family had money."

"A great deal of money. And you realized that in the event of the death of Madame Pattara's husband, she would be certain to inherit a certain portion of that money? Certainly enough to continue to live comfortably?"

"That is an arrangement I know nothing about, if it exists."

"You do know, however, that since Madame Pattara cares for you, to put it mildly, you could expect her to continue to do so after you killed her husband? And that if you were to need financial assistance in the future, Madame Pattara would give you that assistance, having become capable of doing so because of the death of her husband?"

"I don't know any of that. I've never considered any of it."

"But you do know that *she* is the one who is paying for the services of Monsieur Rossi, the extremely talented and also extremely expensive attorney whom she has hired to defend you?"

"I couldn't afford to hire a good attorney myself."

"Precisely."

And with that the prosecution was content to rest for a time; patiently waiting until the time for his summation, to link together the two prongs of his attack.

As part of the testimony for the defense Attorney Rossi called Pauline Renard, to counter the prosecution's claim that, since Grayle had never sold anything, the paintings destroyed in the fire had been worthless.

She testified that she had considered Grayle's work so valuable that she had become his agent and dealer, and had even advanced him money so that he could continue to work—because she had been certain, as a businesswoman, that she would reap great profits from future sales of his work. And she quoted large sums which had been offered to her, recently, for each of the paintings by Grayle which were in her possession.

The prosecution countered by asking how many of Grayle's paintings Pauline Renard had managed to sell *before* Grayle killed Gian-Carlo Pattara. The answer: none.

But Pauline Renard explained that this was solely because she had not attempted to sell them before; waiting until Grayle would have completed a larger body of work before she intended to launch him on the art market.

Whereupon the prosecutor summoned two rebuttal witnesses: a Parisian art critic and an art dealer with a greater record of success than Pauline Renard. Both stated flatly that the sole reason for the sudden upsurge of interest in buying paintings by Grayle was the notoriety surrounding the murder and trial. People wanted to buy his works because they had become objects of morbid curiosity. The value of Grayle's work, as art, remained unproved.

The defense summoned only one other witness on Grayle's behalf: Nora. Under Rossi's questioning, she testified that on the day and night before the burning of Grayle's work and the death of Pattara, her husband's state of mind had been savage, verging on insanity. That she had stayed with him in an attempt to calm his violence. That he had deliberately waited until she'd fallen into an exhausted sleep before sneaking away from the hotel and into Grayle's workroom, clearly with the intention of revenging himself on Grayle.

The prosecutor's cross-examination destroyed her testimony through insinuation: Clearly, a woman whose own state of mind was so unbalanced and unnatural as to allow her to indulge in an incestuous affair was not capable of giving a true account of another person's state of mind. Not capable even if a woman of such proven perverted morality could be trusted to tell the truth.

There was further ammunition to be used against her: "I understand that you betrayed your husband with a great many other love affairs in the past? Is that true?"

"There *were* others."

"Many?"

"A number. They didn't mean anything. Just . . . affairs."

"I see. And did your late husband know of these other lovers?"

"Sometimes he did."

"And did he react to them with insane rage? Did he

attempt to physically attack these other lovers of yours? Or try to destroy their property in revenge?"

"No, because he knew they were just passing affairs; that I would always come back to him."

"So, in fact, your husband was actually quite indulgent about your love affairs, all your infidelities? According to your own testimony, it would be quite out of character for him to become, as you claim, violently jealous of this latest affair?"

"With the others, he knew they would pass, that they didn't really mean anything permanent."

"The others were merely little sexual infidelities, while this one was a deep sexual love, with so solid a basis that your late husband could be quite sure it would never end?"

"Yes."

"This affair—with your brother."

No answer.

"Putting aside the reasons for the difference for the moment, would it be true to say that at no time in the past did your husband ever act in the way you claim he did in this case?"

"Yes . . . because he knew this time I would never return to him."

It was in the final summation that the prosecution joined the two sharpened prongs of its attack: "We have no proof at all that the fire which destroyed twelve of Monsieur Grayle's paintings was, in fact, started by the murdered man, Gian-Carlo Pattara. We have only the statement of his killer, Monsieur Grayle, that this was the case. Against which we have testimony, by Madame Pattara herself, that her husband had never—*never*—reacted in a violent manner to any of her love affairs.

"So, we must consider another possibility, as to what actually occurred on that fateful night: the possibility that Monsieur Pattara went to see Monsieur Grayle, in an entirely reasonable state of mind, to see if he could dissuade Monsieur Grayle from continuing this repugnant, incestuous affair with Madame Pattara. And that at this point it occurred to Monsieur Grayle that he could make his own future secure, if he were to kill Monsieur Pattara. And

166   MARVIN H. ALBERT

that, in fact, he did kill him, as he has himself admitted under oath. But—*before* the fire.

"What I am suggesting, and what you must consider, is the possibility that Monsieur Grayle killed Monsieur Pattara, and then *himself* set the fire, to serve as his excuse. We know now, for a fact, that Monsieur Grayle was a would-be artist who had never managed to earn a single centime for any of his paintings. Under this circumstance, what was the cost to him, of burning a dozen of these financially worthless paintings—if this could assure his future?

"Madame Pattara herself has testified to her certainty that this love she felt for her brother was an abiding one, which would continue. Monsieur Grayle knew that. He also knew that she was certain to inherit at least a comfortable income after the death of her husband. And the realization that Madame Pattara, once she became a widow, would then be in a position to support him, extremely well, could not have failed to occur to him.

"That, I am suggesting, is what we are dealing with here: not an uncontrollable act of fury, in a moment of madness caused by seeing Monsieur Pattara burning some of his work—but a calculated act of murder, the reasons for which he then attempted to contort and confuse by himself setting fire to the paintings."

Against this, Attorney Rossi's summation for the defense, though starting from a strategically inferior position, established certain strong points of its own: all the evidence and testimony given in this court proved that Monsieur Grayle had been a man single-mindedly devoted to his work as an artist. Even utterly obsessed by it: his work was his life, and even more important than his life. A man so devoted to his work, so obsessed with it, could not possibly have himself destroyed a major portion of it, for any practical reason. Such a man could, however, be driven temporarily mad at the sight of his work, work which to him was holy, being destroyed by another man.

Absolutely no evidence had been presented in this court that disproved Monsieur Grayle's version of exactly what had happened on that fateful night. He had been awakened by smoke, and had discovered the enraged husband setting fire to all the work he had accomplished with such painful devotion and time-consuming dedication. He had tried to stop Pattara from burning the last painting left, but Pattara had used a weapon to knock him away—and even that last work had been set on fire. And Grayle, maddened by the raging flames consuming everything he lived for, had struck without consciously intending to, unbalanced by his terrible loss.

Finally, and most important: There was no proof—none at all—that what Monsieur Grayle had done had been a premeditated act.

It was these facts—and not the prosecution's clever hints and flights of fictional invention—on which the court must now base its deliberations.

16

The three judges of the Assize Court retired with the nine jury members to deliberate and reach their decision. Their combined number was both traditional and sacred, reaching back thousands of years into prehistory: to primitive, frightened minds searching for some form of order in the chaos around them. The twelve signs of the zodiac, the ritual number for the year, for the chosen tribes, for the hours of the day and the hours of night. And for determining the fate of an accused man. After four hours the twelve emerged to pronounce their verdict on Nicholas Grayle: Guilty.

But the degree of his guilt, announced by the President of the Court, did not require the death penalty. One thing had saved Grayle from the guillotine. The twelve agreed with his defense attorney on the most vital point: there was no proof that the murder had been premeditated.

Grayle was sentenced to twenty-five years of penal servitude in a hard-labor penitentiary in central France.

There was an eager squad of news photographers waiting outside the Palace of Justice to shoot pictures of Grayle as he came out, handcuffed to one of the officers conducting him to the police van. The pictures they took of him appeared next day in papers all over France; and then in other countries, including the United States.

Only one of the photographers in front of the Palace of Justice managed to catch a shot of a different subject, trying to fight her way through the crowds and police cordon to Grayle: Nora Cesari, at that point the most notorious woman in France.

* * *

Two days before Grayle was to be transported to the old prison of Rennes, to begin his sentence, he sent a message to Inspector Rives. They met in the same interview room where Grayle had spent so many sessions with his defense attorney.

Grayle was seated on one side of the long table. Inspector Rives took a chair on the other side, got out a small, flat tin, and opened it. He balanced the tin on the partition running along the top of the table, to serve as an ashtray, and took a pack of cigarettes from a jacket pocket.

"What can I do for you?"

"There was a jewel robbery outside Menton last year. From a villa belonging to some rich Swedes. Remember?"

Inspector Rives had to think. "Vaguely. It wasn't my onions, so . . ." He finished with a shrug.

"It happened shortly before I was arrested. Some police came and questioned me about it. And they did a search of the estate where I lived. But they didn't find any of the missing jewelry, and they couldn't turn up any evidence that I'd ever been near the Swedes' villa. So they finally gave up on me." Grayle leaned back in his chair. "They still haven't found any of that jewelry."

Rives let smoke drift from a corner of his mouth, squinting at it and waiting.

"I did it," Grayle told him. "I broke into the house just after dark, when I knew the Swedes were off to some party. The jewelry—I took all I could find. Hid it in three different holes, up in the hills just under the Italian border. And hurried back down for dinner with the caretaker on the Royan estate, to set up my alibi."

Rives looked at him through the smoke, expressionless. "That's it? All of it?"

Grayle nodded.

"It's still not my onions," Rives told him. "I can pass what you've said on to whoever was handling that case. I would have to ask around to find out who. Is that what you want me to do?"

"Yes." Grayle was poker-faced. "I'm going to spend all of my life that matters in prison anyway. I might as well clear this up while I'm at it."

The inspector's laugh was cynical but uncaring. "Shit! All you're trying to do is delay being stuck in Rennes. I don't blame you. It's a hell hole. Had its last modernization about a century ago." Rives took a deep drag at his cigarette. "You know, if you really did it, it'll add more years to your sentence."

"I'm thirty years old," Grayle said. "If I manage to survive twenty-five years in Rennes I'll be fifty-five when I come out. And I'll look and feel seventy-five. With nothing behind me anymore and nothing ahead of me. So what's the difference."

"You have a point." Inspector Rives looked at his cigarette, decided it was getting too short, and crushed it out in the tin. "You wouldn't be the first to confess to other crimes after conviction, for the same reason. If you really stole that jewelry, the investigation, interrogations and trial could use up another year before you'd have to go into a hard-labor prison. But if you're bluffing, you won't be able to keep it up more than a week."

"I stole those jewels," Grayle said.

"You'd have to be able to prove that to keep it in motion any time at all."

"If I'm the only one who knows where the jewelry is, I guess that's proof."

"True." Rives stood up, closed the tin and slipped it back in his pocket. "All right, I'll pass it on to whoever was stuck with the case."

"Thanks."

Rives went to the door and opened it. He paused and looked back at Grayle before going out. "Good luck."

•

It was late afternoon before the arrival of the detective who'd been in charge of investigating the Swedes' missing jewelry. His name was Lorron, a tall, skinny man with a harried face and stringy yellow hair. He had a detailed map with him of the area between Menton and the Italian border, and he spread it out before Grayle in the interview room.

"Show me where you say you hid the jewelry."

Grayle studied the map for a considerable time, scowling over it. "I don't understand much about reading maps . . ."

"You don't have to know much," Lorron told him snappishly. He pointed a finger. "This is Menton. And over here, this is the Italian frontier. It runs along this line. These are the cliffs, there. And down here, that's the sea. You only need two details to help you. Right *here* is the Swedes' villa. You left there with the jewels. And you say you hid them close to the frontier—that's this line up here. And then you came back down to the Royan ville, *here*. Now all you have to do is show me the route you followed from this spot to this, with your finger."

Grayle tried. Finally he drew a smallish circle with his finger, close to the line marking the frontier. "Someplace in there. I'm pretty sure that's it."

Lorron made a weary noise. "You know how much territory that little circle covers? We could spend a month trying to dig that area up."

"I just can't make the relationship, between what I remember and all these marks on this map. I could show you the three hiding places, easily enough, if I was there. But on this map . . ." Grayle shook his head, angrily. "It's not the same. It doesn't *look* the same."

"You must have marked the spots you used to hide the stuff," Lorron said heavily. "So you'd be able to recognize them quickly, later. You aren't dumb enough to just dig holes in places that you couldn't be sure of spotting when you went back."

Grayle gave him the answer to that in detail. One hiding place was under a large flat stone between two tall fir trees. Another was inside the roots of a dead scrub-oak, at the base of the cliffs. The third was a hole he had dug under some creeping juniper bushes, at the edge of a wild grove of pines.

Accurate descriptions, each of which might fit a dozen different locations. Lorron gave him a sour look as he folded his map. "I'm not going to spend all tomorrow climbing around up in that. You'll have to come along and show us where you hid the stuff."

"I won't have any trouble, once I'm there. A few minutes, that's all it will take."

"That had better be true," Lorron warned him. "If we go up there, and it turns out you *can't* spot the right places . . . I'm going to get the notion you've just been playing games with us. And you won't be feeling good by the time I bring you back here. Not good at all."

Grayle remained seated in his chair, after Lorron had left, staring fixedly at the opposite wall of the interview room. When the guard came in and tapped his shoulder, it took a moment for Grayle to rouse himself, and stand up to follow the guard back to his cell.

Grayle watched the sea as the black Renault carried him from Nice to Menton along the coast road. There was a strong wind from the mountains, chopping the surface with whitecaps.

Lorron, sitting in front beside the uniformed police driver, had come to get him shortly after nine in the morning. Grayle was in the back seat between two other uniformed cops. His wrists were tightly linked together by handcuffs, which were attached by a short length of chain to the cop on his right. It was ten o'clock when they entered Menton.

The police station was on the narrow Rue Saint Charles, attached to one side of the city hall: an imposing two-floor brown and red building that had once been a gambling casino. Grayle was locked in a small cell while Lorron consulted with the Commissaire of the Menton police.

As usual, these matters took time. There were transfer authorizations to be filled out, signed and properly stamped. There were questions of jurisdiction to be settled, officially. There were two local cops to be chosen, who knew the wild area along the border where Grayle claimed to have hidden the stolen jewelry. By the time all this red tape was taken care of, it was almost eleven-thirty.

Grayle was taken outside and put in the back seat of the car, between the same two cops who'd accompanied him from Nice. Lorron spread his map across the top of the car and showed the local cops the area Grayle had indicated as the place where the jewelry was hidden.

"We won't be able to get anywhere near that with the car," one of the local cops told Lorron. "We can drive up a path to about *here*. After that, it'll be a climb on foot. Rough climbing. Could take an hour and a half, two hours."

The other local cop agreed. "I don't much like the thought of doing that on an empty stomach." He looked at the clock on the city hall. "Almost time for lunch, anyway."

Lorron agreed they'd best get the meal inside themselves before starting up.

The city hall faced on Place Ardoino. On the other side of the square was the Cafe Lugano, a favorite place for municipal functionaries to take lunch. Lorron chose a large table in the shade of the pillared arcade outside the cafe. Grayle was seated beside the cop to whom he was chained, on one side of the table. The chain was lengthened a bit so both could eat without awkwardness; but Grayle's wrists stayed manacled together before him. Lorron sat at the side of the table to Grayle's left, and the police driver took the right side. The other two cops sat across the table from Grayle.

A man condemned to spend most of the rest of his life entombed inside a place as grim as Rennes Prison was traditionally allowed a certain amount of indulgence beforehand. Grayle ordered steak, salad and red wine. When his steak arrived it was one of the cops across the table from him who used the sharp knife to cut it up into little pieces. The cop kept the knife when he was finished, passing the plate across. The only utensil allowed Grayle was a fork, which he used to eat each piece of meat in turn, chewing thoroughly, taking an occasional sip of wine, his manner apathetic.

The others were used to prisoners in this state, and did not let Grayle's mood disturb their own. They ate heartily, exchanging stories of past cases and exploits. When his glass was empty, Grayle casually leaned forward and reached for the wine bottle. His manacled hands shot past the bottle and snatched up the steak knife from the other side of the table. He jerked himself backward in the instant before the police could adjust to his abrupt action, and slashed the knife at his throat.

He had spent a long time calculating exactly how it had to be done, to cause enough damage for his purpose and yet not prove swiftly fatal. The blade missed the vital point of his throat, seemingly because of the haste of his attempt: its sharp point dug into the side of his neck and ripped down, digging just deeply enough. The blood that spurted from the wound stunned the others around the table.

He jerked the knife up and made another feint at his throat; but by then the cops were reacting: hands caught at his arms, twisted. Grayle slumped in his chair and let the knife fall, his blood spilling out and his eyes dulling as the police surged to their feet, cursing viciously and dragging him from the chair. Grayle gave them no resistance, but his legs went limp under him and they had to carry him to the car. One of the cops tried to stem the flow by keeping a napkin pressed to his slashed neck during the wild ride up to the hospital. But it did little good; the napkin in the cop's hand were soon soaked with blood, which dripped steadily on the back seat of the car.

Grayle was semiconscious when they reached the hospi- up to the hospital. But it did little good; the napkin and the emergency ward decided, and gave Grayle a transfusion while medicines were applied to disinfect the gaping wound and slow the bleeding. Grayle's heartbeat and blood pressure were almost back to normal by the time they put him under anesthetic. The wound was stitched shut and heavy bandages taped across it. He was still unconscious when they gave him a second blood transfusion to replace what he had lost.

It was night when Grayle came to. Within seconds of his eyes snapping open, there was no trace of vagueness or confusion in them. By the moonlight filtering into the room he could see that it was similar to the one that had been used for Victor Royan; but with certain differences.

There was no door leading to the outside arcade-corridor. Instead, a small window, with iron bars across it. This room the hospital had obviously set aside for patients considered potentially dangerous, insane, or perhaps just too difficult to be trusted.

Grayle's narrow bed was quite comfortable, except that his left wrist was handcuffed above his shoulder to the iron bedstead. There were three other beds crowding the room, two of them occupied. The man in one of them had a wrist manacled to his bedstead, like Grayle. He lay flat on his back with his eyes wide open, mumbling incoherently to himself. The third man in the room was not manacled to his bed. He sat upright against two pillows, playing a game of solitaire on the sheet by the light of a small lamp beside his bed. The glow of his lamp revealed the sunken face of great age, skull-like.

Grayle turned his head to look at the clock on the wall above the closed door to the inner corridor. The movement caused a burning stab of pain across the side of his neck. The black hands of the clock pointed to five minutes past ten.

The very old man who was playing solitaire suddenly pushed the cards off the sheet with a snort of impatience. His movements were shaky as he slid out of his bed. He almost fell in the process of getting hold of the crutches leaning against his nightstand, and anchoring them firmly into his armpits. He used the crutches to help him walk, one uncertain step at a time, to Grayle's bed.

"Hey! You decided to live?" The old man's voice was weak and cracked. "You'll like it here. Better than going to a theater. Everybody's crazy." He chortled at his own wit.

"Are you?" Grayle asked him, his voice weak.

"Sometimes. I act like a baby, sometimes. Sometimes it's funny." His grin was upsetting. But there was no mirth in his blurred eyes. "If you have to piss, there's a chamber pot under your bed. Want it?"

"No." Grayle indicated the other handcuffed man, with his free hand.

"A dangerous type," the old man said. "A shepherd, crazy like all of them are. But he suddenly got worse.

Tried to strangle his wife. Shepherds shouldn't have wives.
What do they need women for? Sheep are better for that,
and they don't argue." The old man gave a crackling laugh.

The crazed shepherd appeared not to have heard. He
went on staring at the dim ceiling, mumbling to himself.

"A dangerous man," the old man continued. "Like you.
They say you murdered somebody. Did you?"

Grayle gave a small nod.

"And you tried to kill yourself to keep from going to
prison. Don't blame you. It's a lousy life, anyway."

"You don't look dangerous," Grayle said. His wound
hurt savagely, but the rest of him felt sound enough. The
sense of weakness was ebbing. "Why are you here?"

"I get bored in one room all the time," the old man
whined. "I like to get out, wander around. They don't like
that."

Grayle glanced toward the closed door.

"Locked. They keep it locked, the sons of swine. The
sisters, too. Bitches, all of them."

"Police?"

The old man grinned at him knowingly. "I know what
you're thinking. But you're out of luck. There's a cop in a
chair outside the door. All for you."

"Just one?"

"They take turns on guard out there. Why would they
need more than one?" The old man nodded to the handcuffs securing Grayle's wrist to the iron of the bedstead.

There was a noise outside, a key being turned in the
door lock. The old man quickly turned to hobble away toward his own bed. But the door opened before he reached
it.

A young doctor entered, followed by a nun and the cop
who had cut Grayle's steak for him outside the cafe that
noon.

The nun admonished the old man: "You should be
asleep by now, you know that."

The old man crawled obediently into his bed and drew
the sheet all the way up, covering his face. The nun
snapped out his lamp, and came over to help the doctor
examine Grayle. His pulse was taken, his arm strapped to

record his blood pressure, one of his eyelids raised for an examination of his eyeball, a stethoscope used to listen to his heart.

"Coming along fine," the doctor finally announced. "Strong constitution. Tomorrow," he told the cop, "you can take him away."

"You pig," the cop told Grayle quietly, "you made a lot of trouble for us with that trick." But he didn't sound vindictive about it. "I suppose you had to try. But you didn't cut deep enough to succeed. So it was all for nothing."

"I'm very thirsty," Grayle rasped.

The nun crossed to the other end of the room, filled a glass with water from a carafe, and brought it back to Grayle. She helped him raise himself enough to drink. He finished half the glass. "Can you leave the rest, please?"

It was the cop who answered: "No. No glass anywhere near you. No more chances to try bleeding yourself to death."

The nun replaced the glass near the carafe on the stand across the room, and followed the doctor out. The cop went out last. After the door was shut, Grayle listened to the key being turned in the lock.

There was another sound, outside the hospital: a freight train on its way into Italy. Grayle didn't have to look at the clock to know it was now half-past ten. He had spent a lot of time listening to the trains passing through this area, from the gardener's house up in the Royan estate. He knew their schedules by heart.

The next train through would be coming in the opposite direction. a very long freight train, coming out of Italy, bound for Toulon and Marseilles. At five minutes past eleven. It always slowed considerably before entering the tunnel a short distance from the hospital.

Grayle sat up on the bed, fighting the weakness. "Old man," he called softly.

The old man pulled his sheet down away from his face, and propped up on one elbow, squinting at Grayle through the moonlight.

"Where did they put my clothes?" Grayle asked him.

The old man gestured at the closet in the corner. He giggled. "Are you really going to try it? Really?"

"Listen to me," Grayle said quietly. "Please listen."

The old man listened. From time to time he chuckled, delighted.

Ten minutes later he was at the inside of the locked door, banging against it with one of his crutches and screaming: "Help! He's killing himself! Help!"

A chair clattered in the corridor outside. The key snapped in the lock. The door was flung open, the cop stepping inside cautiously, a hand ready on his holstered pistol, peering through the gloom toward Grayle's bed.

Grayle dangled over the side of the bed, hips and legs and free hand sprawled on the floor, the rest of him hanging from the wrist manacled to the iron bedstead. His head sagged.

"He pulled off the bandage!" the old man was babbling. "Ripped his wound wide open again! With his fingers!"

The cop charged across the room with a snarl that was half fury, half panic. He dropped to his knees on the floor beside the bed, reaching with both hands to lift the limply dangling body.

Grayle's free hand came out from under the bed, swinging the chamber pot in a vicious, twisting arc. It thudded against the cop's head, hammering him face-down to the floor.

The cop's hands groped under him, trying to force himself up from the floor. Grayle struck again, with all his strength. The cop's head hit the floor, rolling. But his hand was still moving, automatically groping for the holstered gun. Once more Grayle drew back his right arm and swung the pot, slamming it across the back of the bent head. The hand stopped groping for the gun, went limp on the floor.

Panting, the side of his neck throbbing, Grayle dug into the unconscious man's pockets with his right hand. He found the key to the handcuffs and pulled it out, got his bare feet under him and stood up. An instant later, his left wrist was free. He ran stumbling to the closet, began yanking his clothes from it.

His shoes were the last things he dragged on. Leaning against the wall, his head swirling and his fingers fumbling, he got the laces knotted. Then he stepped through the doorway. The corridor outside was empty and almost dark, a single lamp showing at the far end. Grayle turned back to look at the crazy old man.

"Thanks . . ." His whisper was hoarse. He sprinted through the inner corridor, away from the lighted lamp, and hurried down a flight of dim stairs. He bumped into a nun about to mount the stairs from the landing below, staggered past her and down another flight of back steps. Under his bandage, the wound had begun to bleed again. He kept going.

Behind him, the nun he'd run into started to shout. The first person to reach the room Grayle had escaped was the nurse in charge of that corridor. The cop was still unconscious on the floor beside Grayle's empty bed. The shepherd still lay as before, staring at the ceiling and mumbling to himself. The old man was back in his own bed, the sheet drawn up to cover his face.

Grayle went out a back window on the ground floor, and dropped into the garden behind the hospital. He crossed it, climbed a low fence, and vanished through the darkness into the dense wooded slope above.

During Grayle's trial at the Palace of Justice, Nora Cesari had taken a room at the Negresco Hotel in Nice. She remained there, even after the trial had ended in his conviction and sentence to Rennes Prison.

She was waiting for something, the police decided after Grayle's escape from the hospital in Menton. Detectives were stationed at the Negresco's telephone switchboard, to monitor every call to or from her room.

The search for Grayle, concentrated at first on the area immediately around Menton, was soon spread farther afield as it failed to turn up any sign of him. Someone remembered that a freight train out of Italy had come through Menton shortly after Grayle vanished; and that the train always slowed before entering the tunnel near the hospital. By the time the train was stopped and searched, it had reached Toulon. And Grayle was not on it. If he had been, he could have dropped off anywhere along the line.

One line of police thinking was that the Menton area was the one Grayle knew best, and that he could still be holed up there, somewhere. Local patrols continued to comb this area. But at the same time, photographs of Grayle were circulated throughout France, and to each adjacent country; especially Italy, with its frontier so close to the point of Grayle's escape.

The difficulty was that a man could so easily change his appearance: grow a beard, put on glasses or a false mustache, wear a hat with a low peak. As for the bandaged wound across his neck, it could be concealed under a common scarf or neckerchief. But no matter how he disguised himself, nor how far he managed to run, eventually he would run into a situation where someone would demand to see his identification papers. And it was doubtful that Grayle had the kind of contacts needed to obtain false papers.

There was, however, one way he could get out of the country without having any identity papers demanded of him. A ranking officer of the French police automatically checked on this possibility; a purely routine formality, from which he expected nothing but a purely formal denial. And that was what he got.

A colonel of the Foreign Legion, at the reception center of Fort Saint Nicholas in Marseilles, blandly gave the Legion's standard response to all inquiries about recent recruits: nobody named Nicholas Grayle, or answering his description, had been processed through Fort Saint Nicholas during the past week. Since the last batch of recruits had been shipped to Oran, it was unfortunately impossible to have a look at them. By now they were on their way through Legion headquarters, at Sidi-bel-Abbès, to remote outposts throughout Algeria and Morocco.

That still left the possibility that Grayle might arrive as a recruit at some later time, both agreed. The police official presented a picture of him, just in case. The colonel thanked him, shook his hand and dumped the picture in a wastebasket upon the policeman's departure.

The day after this pointless exchange of official courtesies, Nora received a phone call from Grayle in her room at the Negresco. It was a short call, with no time to trace where it came from.

Grayle said: "Nora, I need your help now."

"Yes. Are you all right?"

"I'm fine. Do you still have your car with you?"

"Yes."

"I want you to drive it up to Bourges. Be there in two days, is that possible?"

"I can do it."

"Good. The day after tomorrow, after sunset, be at the place in front of the cathedral. Stay there, I may be quite late."

"I'll wait there."

"It may be a long wait, you understand?"

"Yes, I understand."

"Good-bye, Nora."

"Good-bye. Take care of yourself."

That was all, and a detective at the Negresco's switchboard got every word of it. By the time Nora checked out of the hotel, the police in Bourges had been notified. By the time she drove north out of Nice they had begun spreading their net through Bourges, searching to find if Grayle were already in the city; posting lookouts at all approaches in case he was still on his way. Making certain that, in either event, once inside the city he would never get out again.

And while this was going on, two unmarked police cars tailed Nora all the way from Nice to Bourges. She did not appear to be aware of them.

When Nora, on the appointed evening, went to the square in front of the Bourges Cathedral, it wwas already surrounded by a ring of hidden police, in readiness to close the trap as soon as Grayle appeared. Nora wandered about the square, aimlessly, for about an hour. Then she went inside the cathedral.

Several plainclothes detectives were already inside, before her. Others took positions covering every exit. When it grew dark, Nora walked outside and sat down on the steps of the cathedral. She continued to sit there, for three hours; not moving, not appearing to become impatient.

Finally, she stood up and crossed the square to check into a small hotel. She had dinner there, eating little, and then went to her room. In the morning she checked out, got into her car and continued north to Paris.

It was quite obvious that Grayle's call had been a gambit, to concentrate the hunt for him in the north, while he went in a different direction. But there was no way the police could prove that Nora had been aware the call sending her north had been a trick. She answered their questions with triumphant silence, and no action could be taken against her.

She continued to be shadowed, spasmodically, over the following year, in the faint hope that she might yet lead the police to Grayle. But that never happened. The Ministry of Justice, when pestered by newsmen, continued to declare that sooner or later Grayle was bound to be caught. But that never happened, either.

Nicholas Grayle was never seen again.

All that was left behind, to show that he had ever lived, were the works he had left with Pauline Renard. And a daughter named Pascale, born to Nora during the month before Grayle went on trial.

Part 2: ISHMAEL

"*Man is a creature that can get accustomed to anything, and I think that is the best definition of him.*"
—Dostoyevsky

"*Life being what it is, one dreams of revenge.*"
—Gauguin

17

Captain Edouard Verdier filled a short, curved pipe from his half-empty pouch. If the supply convoy didn't reach his post in the next few days he would be out of tobacco. He had never smoked much; but with duty so deep inside what the French army officially designated as "The Zone of Insecurity," in the heart of emptiness, small vices grew into essential diversions.

Dismissing that particular worry for the moment, Verdier stood outside his quarters and watched the sun set. The Legion bugler had sounded retreat and the first night guards had taken their positions. The searchlights had been switched on in readiness for the coming darkness, and the hum of the post generator was the only sound in the pervading silence. Verdier used the moment for a break in the unpleasant report he'd been filling out for the past three hours. Watching the sunsets was something the captain did almost every evening. He found it necessary, for mind and soul.

Verdier was equipped by breeding and training to endure with few nervous twinges a life of professional monotony. But the visual monotony of the desolate, stony flatness surrounding his post was another matter. It could, if not relieved occasionally, crush a man.

The long barrier of the Atlas range, far away, formed a northern limit to this vast plateau. To the south the plateau dropped into a depression filled with the slowly shifting dunes of the Sahara. *Bahr-belà-mà* the Arabs called it: the waterless ocean. Between this sea of sand and that chain of mountains, spreading in every direction from the point where Captain Verdier stood, there was nothing but the immense flat emptiness, alien to life: the high desert of the Guir Hammada. An unrelieved table of stones, cinders, clay and dust.

The Moroccan outpost which Captain Verdier commanded was on a slight rise. Its cannons looked down on the oasis and its Berber village, where a shallow afterthought of the River Ziz surfaced briefly on its journey south to a final death in the sands. Thin though the river was here, it had cut deep. And it had cut wide, during the rains that fell every four or six years. High, crumbling red banks rose on either side of the wide riverbed, which was almost entirely dry now. Down between these banks, running the length of the trickles of water, was the miracle: the luxuriant palms, argan trees and tiny farm plots.

The village and its own defense towers, built from the same ochre-red earth as the high banks on either side, spread through the oasis. Intact buildings mingled with the melting ruins of older ones. The very oldest had long ago melted down into mounds indistinguishable from natural hillocks.

Captain Verdier watched the rays of the setting sun transform all of it to a pure, pale gold: the village walls, the stone barricades and barbed wire around his post, the dust swirling above the vast plateau. Darkness would come within minutes, quite abruptly. Then he would have to go back inside and finish his paperwork, by lamplight. The long, detailed report made necessary by the return of Lieutenant Jaloux from a trek north to the foothills of the Atlas.

The orders had been for Jaloux to examine approaches to the point where a new road was to be thrust up from the south into the mountains. The planned road was intended to enable armored vehicles and heavy guns to reach into difficult areas protecting Berber tribes who still refused to surrender to the Sultan and his French "protectors."

Lieutenant Jaloux had taken with him eighteen of Verdier's Legionnaires and two Zouave guides. He had returned with sixteen Legionnaires and one Zouave.

Everything lost had to be accounted for by Captain Verdier in his written report to his superiors in Marrakesh: one missing Lebel rifle, canteen, bayonet, sixty rounds of 8-mm. ammunition, etc. And—three men dead.

Officially, only two of them could be definitely reported as dead at this point. The Zouave scout and one Legionnaire had been killed outright by Berber snipers hidden in the cliffs above one stretch of Lieutenant Jaloux's line of march.

The other Legionnaire, posted as a sentry outside Jaloux's last night-camp, had simply not been there at dawn. Captain Verdier had listed the man as missing, with the strong presumption that he had been taken captive by rebel infiltrators. Verdier could only hope that this missing Legionnaire was also, by now, mercifully dead.

Berber rebels who managed to capture a Legionnaire alive usually gave such a job to their midwives, who were experts at prolonging it. Their ministrations were concentrated on surface areas for as long as possible. They worked deeper inside the body only after all the outer nerves had broken down completely and no longer communicated the agony. At some point during their work the genitals would be severed and stuffed in the mouth. After they were finished, a matter of several days and nights, the head would be chopped off and placed neatly between the thighs.

The enlistment papers of the Legionnaire Jaloux had last stated that he was a Canadian, named Ishmael Moser. Neither the nationality nor the name listed meant anything, of course. Except, perhaps, as an indication that the man might have had some education and an odd sense of humor. Verdier had read Melville in translation. He could imagine the impulse that could cause a recruit to choose that particular first name.

There was little else that Captain Verdier could guess about this "Ishmael Moser"; and even less that he knew. Except that he'd been filled with the kind of anger that most recruits came to the Legion with—but he had never lost any of it, the way so many others did. He'd given a fair amount of trouble, never learned to settle for the discipline as easily as others. Willing to work hard but balky at taking orders he didn't agree with. He'd gotten more than his share of Legion punishments, start to finish.

But other than that—he had been a good soldier, even by Legion standards: quick to learn what was required, equipped with an enormous amount of physical and mental endurance, neither shirking nor foolishly brave in battle, but steady and dependable. And he had managed to pick up an unusual grasp of the Arabic and Berber languages during his four years and seven months of service, which had made him quite useful as an interpreter with the natives.

About the man's past, before the Legion, Captain Verdier knew nothing. Nor did anyone else in this post, he was sure. That was unusual. Most of Verdier's Legionnaires, in a post as depressingly isolated as this, sooner or later dropped in one night for a visit to his quarters. To be offered a glass of cognac and an understanding, noncommital listener. And to offer in return their various guilts, memories and dreams. As though their captain was the nearest substitute they could find for a priest. But this Canadian, Ishmael Moser, whatever his real name and nationality had been before the Legion, had never come to him for this kind of sharing and unburdening. Which made him either a very special kind of madman—or a more accomplished stoic than Verdier considered himself. Or perhaps both.

Again, as the night came and Captain Verdier went inside to finish his report, he hoped fervently that the man was at least finally finished with his dying.

Somewhere, a stone fell. The sound as it struck the rocks in the dust-dry streambed echoed sharply through the deep, narrow gorge.

Grayle became as motionless as the boulder against which he sat, concealed in its shadow. His hands came to rest, lightly, on the rifle across his thighs, and after that no part of him moved again. Except his eyes, studying the gorge below.

Some hundred yards east of his position the gorge made a tight bend. The sound, he thought, had come from just beyond that point. But nothing came around that bend.

And no wisps of dust rose behind it to indicate the movement of man or animal. The sound was not repeated. The silence stretched, broken after some minutes by the cry of a small hawk.

He continued to wait, the boulder against his back, his senses alerted, his finger touching the trigger of his rifle. Something had made that stone fall. And he was entirely alone here, in confusing terrain which his quarry knew intimately, and he did not.

He could not see or hear them. But he knew they were there, somewhere around him. The vital question was: did they know *he* was there? If they did, what he was trying to do would be finished before he could begin it.

His sole chance lay in seeing them before they knew where he was. He had to initiate the meeting, to exercise some control over how it happened. Otherwise there was no possibility of surviving it.

Grayle waited, watching and listening. He looked more than a decade older than his years. Burning suns and the abrasion of wind-blown sand, long periods of dehydration and thirty-five-mile marches with an eighty-pound pack and rifle, had aged and hardened him. His face had become gaunt, the eyes permanently inflamed and habitual wariness in the set of the mouth. Lines were gouged deep into the dark, weathered skin. Any trace of spare flesh had been eaten from his figure; what was left was there because it was functional, required for endurance and survival.

He could smell the breath of the Sahara, far behind him to the south. It was carried on a wind sweeping over the flatness of the Guir Hammada to spend its force against the mountain barrier. Nomad herdsmen below the Atlas called it "the wind that burns the trees." Grayle smelled it, but could not feel it. His hiding place among the high rocks was too deep within the labyrinth chain of the mountains. The wind from the Sahara was hurled back on itself by the southern flanks of this barrier.

Where Grayle waited, cool air from the depths of the gorge under him made the heavy Legionnaire's coat he wore just right. But he did not remove the kepi protecting his head and eyes from the intensity of the noon sun. Four years of marching, working and fighting under that sun had taught him what it could do to a man who left his head uncovered too long, even where its strength seemed diminished.

Grayle was afraid as he waited, alone in these mountains. But that was something else the Legion had taught him: controlling fear was a skill that could be learned until it became almost automatic, like any skill; and he'd had a great deal of practice.

Controlling the rage triggered in him by the Legion—that had been another matter. His anger had acquired a life of its own, over the years. It couldn't be killed except by tearing out its roots; and he couldn't do that because they'd become part of his life-support system.

Both the rage and the fear could be *used*, for the cruel pleasure of striking back with gun and bayonet. That was the final lesson the Legion had given him, now that all else had died with Gian-Carlo, and he'd lost both art and Nora. But he needed to be more than what the Legion had tried to make of him: an anonymous fighting machine with no separate identity or purpose of his own; a life without meaning or future.

Nor was there any hope of using the new identity given him by the Legion to achieve a different kind of future. Others had tried that and failed. Grayle knew all the stories about former Legionnaires who'd left North Africa with their new names and impossible dreams only to be recognized as wanted men, after some weeks or years. And to find their new future shrunk to the size of a prison cell. A different identity was not enough. A considerable fortune was required for a man to have even a remote chance of pulling it off.

Grayle had chosen his present goal with much thought and preparation; his job now was to reach it alive.

A pair of large ravens drifted past him, quite close. They swooped down inside the gorge, to the spring that trickled from the base of the cliff opposite, almost directly under his position. He watched them drink from the small, shallow pool around the spring.

Grayle's increasing thirst asserted itself, but he ignored the impulse to take a sip from his canteen. He had drunk deeply from it earlier; and he would do so again in the midafternoon, though that would use up what remained in the canteen. Experience had taught him that sips of water left a man still thirsty, and increasingly unable to concentrate on anything else. Better to slake the thirst completely, and for a period leave the brain free to deal with what was necessary for other survival problems. If the gorge was still empty when night came he would descend to the spring, drink and refill the canteen. As he had the previous night. And then climb back to this spot of high cover, to wait through another day.

The spring was the reason he had chosen this position for his waiting. In this land of thirst it was a treasure that would draw anyone whose route came within a half day's march of it. Sooner or later, the ones he wanted would come here.

Long before Lieutenant Jaloux had posted him on sentry duty two nights before, Grayle had made his decision. Only the need for the right opportunity had kept him waiting. It had come when the Berber snipers began harrying the Legion column as it snaked through the foothills.

The controlling power inside this part of the Atlas chain was a cagey, stubborn old chief named Brahim ben Hamid, known as Abd-el-Rahman—"Slave of the Merciful," one of the ninety-nine names of Allah. His was a loose confederation of tribes who continued, with startling success, to resist the inroads of the French pacification policy.

Another chief, of a similar confederation farther north, had recently been pacified. The French had captured him and turned him over to the Sultan. He had been mutilated and then stuffed into a cramped cage on wheels so the Sultan could have him dragged along wherever he went, and miss no stage of his slow, agonizing dying. Survivors from his broken confederation slipped south to join Abd-el-Rahman, whose continued success proved that he still possessed *baraka*—the divine luck which the Berbers believed more important than anything else. And the increase in his forces proved it still further.

The Berber snipers had killed a Legionnaire marching directly in front of Grayle, late in the afternoon. The Zouave guide had been hit late the following morning. Grayle had added it up: the snipers were using the night-time, while Lieutenant Jaloux was camped, to hurry ahead and take positions commanding the line they thought Jaloux would follow the next day. The snipers had no way of knowing that Jaloux intended to turn away, due south across the desert flat, the following morning.

Grayle had slipped away from his sentry post and moved through the night toward the area where he estimated the snipers would be—had chosen a position high above slopes strewn with boulders, and settled down in deep cover.

Shortly after dawn the Legion patrol came into his line of sight, heading away from the mountains, south over the Guir Hammada in the direction of the post commanded by Captain Verdier. Grayle fixed his attention on the area closer below him, scanning the slopes. The patrol led by Jaloux was getting smaller in the distance when the snipers began to emerge from cover behind the boulders.

There were five of them. They gathered together and watched the patrol increase the distance, until they were certain it would not turn back. Then the five snipers headed the opposite way, through a break into the interior of the mountains. Grayle followed them.

He stayed a good distance behind, trailing them by the footprints they left and the dust they raised. Careful in his own movements to raise as little dust as possible. Four hours inside the mountains he came to a place where the signs were easy to read: the snipers were now mounted on donkeys and horses they had left tethered here.

After that they began increasing the distance on Grayle. He moved as swiftly as he could on foot, but fell steadily farther behind. In places there were fresh tracks to keep him on their trail. But across stony stretches he rediscovered their direction only when he came upon the droppings of their animals.

These led him into the gorge. At the spring he found unmistakable signs of their stopping to refill their water-bags and let the animals drink. Grayle had filled his can-

teen from the spring that fed the still-clouded pool, and
shoved on. An hour later he reached a place where the
gorge opened out in a number of different directions the
riders could have taken. He'd circled around for some time
before giving up. He had lost them. Returning to the spring
and its little pool of water, he had climbed to cover against
the base of the boulder above the gorge.

That had been yesterday. He was still waiting.

The two ravens suddenly veered away from the pool below. They flew swiftly, up out of the gorge, and vanished.

A scruffy-looking donkey came around the bend in the
gorge, head down, picking its way delicately among the
sharp stones. It carried filled sacks in a double basket hung
over its back and down its sides. And a rider.

The rider sat with one leg crossed, his foot resting on one
filled sack, on the same side as the other leg which dangled
and kicked at the donkey to keep it in movement. The
most comfortable position for a long trek on a donkey, easier on legs and rump than riding astride it. The man wore
a grimy old djellaba, which covered him loosely from head
to shins, leaving only hands, sandaled feet and weathered
face exposed.

It was a Berber face. No one knew the origin of the
Berber race: some said Europe, others Persia. All Grayle
had been able to learn was that they had been here since
before recorded history; tending their sheep and goats, and
forcing caravans using these mountain passes to pay tolls;
mixing their blood with every other race that came
through: the Roman Legions, Arabs, the black slaves
bought or looted from the Sudan and Senegal. The result-
ing mixture was a short, sturdy, handsome people; men and
women with brown skin, neatly chiseled features and beautiful eyes.

The man on the donkey might have been a herdsman,
returning to his flocks from a village market. Except that
he was carrying a Lebel rifle. He even had "Rosalie," the
regulation-issue épée bayonet, in fixed position, ready to be
put to work. The lean, sharply-pointed blade flashed in the
sunlight as it bobbed with the plodding movements of the
donkey.

Grayle knew there were only two ways a Berber who was not attached to the French army could get his hands on a Lebel: steal it or kill for it. The penalties imposed by the French on anyone who lost one were so severe that no trooper was likely to report back without his, unless he was in no condition to report back at all.

Grayle stayed very still, watching. The donkey reached the pool at the spring and stopped to drink. Its rider looked up, in Grayle's direction.

Grayle's nerve ends jumped. It seemed that the Berber was looking directly at him. But Grayle was hidden by the deep shade under the boulder. The man on the donkey was looking a bit higher.

Grayle's fingers tightened on the rifle across his thighs, but did not raise it. He couldn't risk the faint sound that might make. There had to be someone up there, behind his position.

Whoever was there apparently gave an all-clear signal. The rider below slid off his donkey and turned to call out: a short, hard sound. It might have been a word, but Grayle couldn't make it out.

One by one, sensibly spaced, eighteen Berber warriors rode into sight around the bend of the gorge. Five on donkeys, the others on barbs—strong, fast mountain ponies. The hooves made a monotonous crunching noise as they advanced steadily over loose gravel and stones; and then became silent as they crossed a stretch of soft, clayish dirt.

Grayle forced his shoulders back against the sharp ridges lacing the boulder's surface. His breathing became shallow, teeth forced together to keep it slow and quiet.

Grayle studied each rider just before he passed directly beneath him. Some carried Lebels and others had Mausers or Winchesters. Not a single traditional Berber musket. Each wore a sword and long dagger. The last rider led a saddled, unmounted barb.

The man riding point carried himself like a man accustomed to leading. He remained alert as he reined to a halt at the spring, scanning the length of gorge ahead, and the sloping walls on either side. He was the last to dismount.

Standing erect, letting his mount drink from the pool while
his followers filled their waterbags, he raised his head and
looked at a position somewhere above Grayle's.

It was Grayle's first clear look at the face of Kaddour
ben Salah, one of the most experienced fighting chieftains
in Abd-el-Rahman's confederation. Grayle had heard that
face described, and it was unmistakable. It had been rendered hideous by a livid, diagonal scar from a saber that
had destroyed the left eye, torn the bridge of the nose and
distorted the right side of the mouth.

Grayle put a clamp on the tension trying to rise inside
him. He kept still, part of the boulder and its shadow. Kaddour ben Salah's remaining eye continued to squint in his
direction. Grayle heard something: a very faint scraping
somewhere behind his boulder. Then a few pebbles rolled
past, down to his right, stirring up some dark-red dust.
Grayle drew a breath and held it.

The lookout came down the steep incline carefully, legs
and arms spread for balance, a Lebel in his left fist. The
face was young and lean; intent now on rejoining the band
beneath, no longer alert to anything but the difficulty of
the descent. His route took him around Grayle's side of the
boulder. Grayle rose to his feet and put the muzzle of his
rifle into the small of the young man's back.

"Don't move and don't drop your rifle." Grayle said it in
the Shelha dialect used by the Berbers of the southern Atlas and the desert below.

The young lookout's back muscles jerked, causing the
barrel of Grayle's rifle to move slightly. Then he froze in
position.

Kaddour ben Salah must have spotted the freeze and
snapped an order, though too softly for it to reach up to
Grayle. Suddenly the men below were in motion, taking
cover behind their mounts, rifle barrels angling upward
across the saddles.

But none of them fired. Grayle was behind the frozen
lookout and still deep inside the boulder's shade. He had
begun to sweat profusely. Every move he made now had to
be exactly right.

Holding his rifle in place with his right hand, he took off his kepi with the other and sent it spinning, high above the gorge. He watched it fall, the white neck protector flapping like a flag of surrender. Hoping Salah would accept that he intended it as that.

The men below remained behind their mounts, rifles pointing. The lookout started to turn his head.

"Don't," Grayle warned, and the head stopped turning. He reached out with his left hand and took hold of the young Berber's rifle. "Let it go."

Slowly, reluctantly, the Berber's fingers forced themselves open. Grayle drew the rifle from them. Now he had two.

His shout carried sharply, reverberating within the confines of the gorge: "I have come to join you!" He had practiced these phrases often, and he pronounced each word distinctly. "No one is with me! I come alone! I bring secret information for Abd-el-Rahman! Vital for his cause!"

There was no reaction from the bottom of the gorge. None. Grayle allowed a few seconds for what he'd shouted to sink in. Then he pressed the muzzle of his rifle into the back of the young lookout, propelling him forward. "Go down and join them. Do it now."

The young Berber took a step away; then another. Shoulders hunched high, expectant of a bullet striking between them. Grayle shifted both rifles, grasping them by the muzzle-ends of their barrels. He spread his arms wide to either side, each Lebel dangling from a fist, stock hanging toward the ground. Making it impossible to get either weapon into position to fire quickly enough to matter. He stepped out from the boulder's shade, letting them see him that way. Then he started down after the lookout, arms still spread wide apart, the rifles hanging, every part of him exposed, an unprotected target.

18

Kaddour ben Salah may have issued another order. Grayle didn't hear it. But the rifles below remained silent. Their barrels, resting across the saddles, moved with Grayle's slow, steady descent, keeping him in their sights. When he reached the floor of the gorge he stopped and waited, maintaining his exposed, spread-armed stance.

Salah stepped from behind the protection of his pony and advanced toward him, his rifle balanced in the crook of his left arm. Grayle held his position, waiting. Salah stopped, the single eye in the hideous face studying him. The young lookout stood beside his chief, head down.

Ignoring him, Salah snapped an order. Two of his men emerged from cover and circled to either side of Grayle. He opened his hands as they snatched at the rifles, and then let his arms fall. At Salah's next order, Grayle unbuckled his shoulder straps and the belt holding his bayonet, canteen and leather ammunition-pouches. He gave this to one of the men. The other searched him, quickly and efficiently, and then nodded to Salah. The others were coming from behind their mounts now. Salah sent two of them to search the clifftops overlooking the gorge, one to either side.

The young lookout growled, "There are no others up there, I swear it."

Salah told him carelessly, "Hassan, go tend to the animals. Keep them together."

Hassan threw Grayle a look of hatred and hurt pride, before turning away to obey.

"He's right," Grayle told Salah. "I came alone, as I told you. Since I found you, I could have led others to you—*if I* intended you harm. If I had done that, you would all be dead or prisoners by now. But I came to join you. To offer Abd-el-Rahman my allegiance and my rifle. And the information I spoke of. Information it is important for him to know, or his enemies will overwhelm him."

Salah regarded Grayle thoughtfully, without surprise or scorn at his stated desire to change sides. Treason was a concept that had little meaning for a Berber. Lust for independence was too ingrained in them for that. And independence, for a Berber, meant more than a refusal to submit to the control of whoever claimed to rule all of Morocco.

It meant that each tribe was independent of the others. If they joined together, it was for reasons of temporary self-interest. Or because they were enthralled by some leader's powerful personality and *baraka*. Berber independence even applied within the tribe: each family considered itself a separate unit, cooperating with the rest only as long as it suited them. And even within the family, independence meant each member acting as he saw fit. One could change allegiance if one wished—and was able to. He might be killed in the attempt, but no one would consider his attempt as treason.

A year earlier, the sons of a powerful old chieftain in the Middle Atlas told their father they intended to quit him and join the French. "I will be defeated by the French in the end," he had agreed with his sons. "But I am too old in my ways to change now. I will fight until I am killed. You wish to survive, and for my line to survive. That is sensible. You have my blessing."

His sons had become part of the French force that had finally destroyed the old chieftain. After the battle they found their father's body, mourned over it and buried it with honors. But their sorrow over his death contained no guilt. And no one considered what they had done as betrayal.

So Salah considered Grayle's offer, as he watched the cliffs flanking the gorge. When the scouts appeared, to signal the all-clear, he gave his considered answer.

"We have enough men," he told Grayle. "One more or

less makes no difference to our chances. As for your rifle, I already have it. As to your information, tell me and I will decide if it is worth conveying to Abd-el-Rahman. Also, whether it contains any reason to preserve your life for a time."

"The information is secret. It is for Abd-el-Rahman to hear first. It is for *him* to decide what to do with it—and who else should know of it."

Salah gestured at the ground before him. "Sit down."

Grayle lowered himself to the ground as ordered.

"Take off your boots. They will fit one of my men."

Grayle pulled his boots off and put them aside, not taking his attention from Salah's face.

"Now everything else," Salah commanded. "Good cloth should not be wasted."

Grayle hesitated, and then began to strip. When he was naked, Salah regarded the knife-slash across his chest, the spear wound in his shoulder, the scar cut by a bullet down his left thigh. Salah was an expert at reading the history of such scars. But all he said, as Grayle sat naked before him, was: "You know, at least, how to obey."

Grayle's voice remained quiet and steady as he quoted an Islamic proverb: "One must kiss the hand one cannot cut off."

Smiling, Salah's face was more horrible than when it was stern. "So it is written." It did not take long for his men to spread-eagle Grayle on his back, bind his wrists and ankles to stakes driven into the ground. Salah drew his dagger and squatted down beside Grayle's face. "Since you will not tell *me* the secret information, perhaps I must take you to deliver it to Abd-el-Rahman. But in that case I must first make certain that you will not be a danger to him."

"Abd-el-Rahman has defeated entire armies." Grayle kept his voice controlled with a harsh effort of will. "Why would he need to fear facing a single man?"

"A thousand enemies outside the house are safer than one within it," Salah quoted. And then, with no change of tone: "I am going to blind you. The loss of one eye is nothing, as I can attest. But to lose both of your eyes, that, I think, would be very bad."

"It is also written," Grayle said through clenched teeth, "that to defeat the helpless is more shameful than being defeated yourself."

Salah nodded mockingly. "But also that to show kindness at the wrong time leads to injustice. And that if you do no good, you will meet with no disaster. You see? So much is written that in the end one must choose, oneself, what is correct for any situation."

He made a gesture with his free hand. Two men crouched to seize Grayle's ears and hair, holding his face tilted upward. The point of Salah's dagger lowered to Grayle's right eye. It was not a bluff.

Grayle unclenched his teeth and got the words out: "I will tell it to you."

"Good." Salah waited. His dagger did not move.

Grayle told him about the road the army planned to build from the south into these mountains. And the route it would take. Through places that were now negotiable only by a man on foot, or with a donkey or mountain-bred pony. And the purpose of the road: to carry armored cars and trucks and heavy guns into the heart of Abd-el-Rahman's hitherto inaccessible stronghold.

"When will they begin this road?" Salah asked. "And when do they believe it will be completed?"

Grayle told him that, too.

Salah was silent for a time. "Is there anything more?"

"No. That is everything I know about."

Salah drew the dagger away from Grayle's face. "Very well, then. I will convey what you have said to Abd-el-Rahman." He studied Grayle for a moment, and then said quietly, "And now, if you have nothing further to tell, I think the time has come to kill you."

There was no change in Grayle's expression as he regarded Salah's disfigured face, framed by the cliffs above, one sunlit and the other dark. "Abd-el-Rahman will not be pleased to hear of my death. The information I brought does not end my usefulness to him. And I advise you not to parcel out my uniform, either. He'll have a use for that, too. With me wearing it."

Salah considered the possibility. Finally he said, "Perhaps—*if* you could be trusted. But I think the danger is too great. You may, after all, be only a very clever spy. Or one cleverly instructed."

"That is for Abd-el-Rahman to decide. Or are you wise enough to make his decisions for him?"

Grayle had kept his voice steady as he spoke, but one of the men crowded around them pointed between his thighs and said, "Look, that is the one place it is impossible to hide fear. See how his manhood shrinks."

Another man laughed. "It tries to hide itself inside him."

Salah looked up at them. "Never mock the fallen. They may rise again."

The man who had laughed was still grinning. "I will stake my life on it, *that* will never rise again, if you let me cut it off."

Even Salah joined in the laughter the joke provoked.

Grayle spoke as though he'd heard none of it: "You know a Legionnaire can do things none of the rest of you could. Only consider the places I could go, where you could not."

The scarred face was still twisted by a smile when Salah looked down at Grayle, but there was no humor in his voice. "You are very persuasive," he said slowly. "You may wish that you were not. A knife across the throat is an easy way to die. That is my way. If Abd-el-Rahman decides against you, there are those around him who have ways to make your dying last for a long time. A year. Even longer."

"*Inch'Allah*," Grayle said.

As God wills.

A deep grave. Not yet closed forever. But the opening was small, and very far above him. Most of the time it was sealed.

Once a day—he *thought* that was the interval—the heavy rock that closed the opening was rolled back, letting in some air and dim torchlight from the underground dungeons above. A basket was lowered at the end of a long rope, down to where he waited for it, at the bottom of the pit. There was always water and a piece of tough bread in the basket. Sometimes there was also a bone, from a lamb or goat. With shreds of meat to gnaw from it, and marrow to be sucked out.

He would drink all the water first, and drop the bottle back inside the basket. Soon, the basket would be pulled up. Usually, when there was a bone, he had eaten the last shred of meat from it before the rock was pushed back in place. Then he would eat the bread slowly in the darkness, and crack the bone between his teeth to get at the last morsel of marrow. And then he would wait. Another day: if the intervals between feedings did indicate the span of a day.

There was room at the bottom of the pit for him to lie down, if he curled himself tightly. Room to sit, with his knees drawn up close to his chest. The rest of the time he stood. And waited.

He'd kept track of the feedings. When he calculated that he had been down there for twenty days, the terrifying suspicion began to gnaw at him: nobody had told Abd-el-Rahman about him—and no one ever would. Salah and his band had gone on another mission and been killed. Who Grayle was, and the reason he was here, was unknown to anybody else up there in the fortress he had never seen.

Salah had kept him blindfolded on the trek into this area; a precaution against his leading others here if he escaped. When the blindfold had been removed, Grayle was already underground, in the dungeons; and Salah was no longer with him. There were only the burly prison keepers, the low-burning torches which revealed some things, and the shadows that hid others: the cages of iron bars into which living men were crammed with decaying corpses, the chains from which others hung bleeding and burned, the unseen cells from which voices screamed and sobbed and whimpered. And the pit into which Grayle had been lowered, standing in the basket and holding onto the rope with both hands.

It was a grave, where he was buried inside the living rock of the mountains, with nothing but the dark, and the faint sounds of unending agony from above, and his own stench. Sometimes, Grayle shouted demands to see Abd-el-Rahman when the rock above was rolled open. No voice ever answered him. They were too used to the cries of prisoners, the demons of this subterranean region, and had long ago stopped listening to the words. The food basket would be lowered, pulled back up; the opening sealed again.

Grayle remembered, very dimly and very long ago, there had been a man named Victor Royan, who had claimed that Hell was actually the world. Or had the man been quoting someone else who'd said it? Now Grayle knew it was not true. The world was only a Purgatory. *This* was Hell; and he was condemned to the bottom of its deepest pit.

Not even condemned, like those suffering and dying in the dungeons that were the only world he could be certain existed above him. Merely dropped into a hole beneath the earth, beneath even that Hell of the damned up there, and forgotten.

But he would not allow his brain to accept that he might be forgotten forever. He forced himself to regard it as a period, of unknown length, that must be gotten through. And he concentrated on keeping his body from deteriorating.

There was only one form of exercise possible: climbing. Leaning with his hands against one side of the pit and his feet against the other, he would work his way upward. It was slow, heavy work: halfway up, and then back down. Every muscle in his body would be trembling by the time he reached the bottom. But when the muscle fatigue lifted he would do it again. As often as he could manage; knowing that if he let his strength drain away his mind would go, too. He had to hold on rigidly to a single article of faith: the waiting would end.

He considered trying to escape, and rejected it. It was just possible that he could work his way to the top of the pit and hang on there, until the rock was rolled away for his next feeding. But the guards up there knew their business. He had seen that when they'd lowered him in here.

There would always be one of them standing by with an iron club, while the basket was lowered. He might be able to grab the guard's ankle and dump him; avoid having his skull crushed as he scrambled out of the hole. And then? The only way out of the prison up there was locked, from the outside. He had seen that, too.

A suicide try: to be reserved until a time came when he could no longer hold on to the faith that this pit was not his final destiny. Grayle had not yet reached that point; not quite. He waited, he slept, he made the climbs at regular intervals; clinging to a certainty that he could no longer allow himself to examine with the powers of logic.

When the rock was rolled aside on what Grayle judged to be his twenty-first day in the pit, it was not food that was lowered in the basket, but another prisoner.

The basket was drawn up empty, and the opening closed. In the blackness, pressed together by the confines of the pit, Grayle tried to question the other man. Only meaningless sounds answered him. The other's hands probed him. His left hand was found, grasped, pulled up to the newcomer's open mouth. The man's tongue had been ripped out.

The next time water and food was sent down, it was exactly the same amount that had been Grayle's portion alone. The two men shared it.

The fourth time the basket was lowered to the two men cramped together in the pit, like twins in an unyielding womb, they fought each other for what it contained. Grayle was the stronger. Three feedings later the unseen sharer of Grayle's pit gave up the struggle. Three more, and he was dead.

Grayle screamed the news to those above. He was not answered. The basket was withdrawn, the opening sealed. Grayle crouched in the dark with the corpse under him and ate.

19

The Master of Dreams sat in the sunlight on the hard dirt outside the main gate of the fortress. At this altitude, so early in the morning, his old flesh and bones absorbed the warmth with pleasure. The Master of Dreams was not a native of these mountains. He came from far away to the southeast, near the Hoggar, in the very heart of the Sahara. A dream of his own had brought him here, to join himself to the destiny of Abd-el-Rahman. He did not know the ultimate purpose of this pilgrimage. Perhaps he would not even recognize when he fulfilled it. But he was here. Waiting, and earning his food by the practice of his profession.

Below him the flat roofs of the village, like red-brown cubes piled haphazardly atop one another, descended the steep slope to the stream that twisted its way through the high valley. In the distances all around the fortress that crowned the rugged hill, there ranged the jagged ridges and peaks of the higher mountains. On the highest, the morning sunlight gleamed off snow. The Master of Dreams saw none of this.

His skeletal fingers rested lightly on a page of the Koran opened on his crossed legs. His watery eyes peered through the new steel-rimmed glasses that partially dispelled his misted vision at the prettily tatooed face of the young Berber woman crouched before him, revealing the dream that had come to her in the night.

Even crouching, she held herself superbly; retaining much of the proud, figure-flaunting posture Berber girls learned by carrying burdens on their heads from the age of three. But the habitual pride was gone from her lovely young face, banished by the shame as she spoke softly of her dream.

"I was alone in my house. There was a knock at the door and I opened it. A man stood there. Tall, wearing a great robe of purest black. A terrible face, ugly and powerful, but his eyes were warm on me. I told him my husband was not home. He said he knew, and stepped inside, closing the door behind him. He opened his black robe and enclosed me within its folds, drawing me to him."

She shuddered, and after a moment went on haltingly: "I was crying, but I could not deny him. My blood boiled with the feel of him. I . . . gave myself to him, with passion, still crying. When he left me, he stopped in the door-way—and he laughed. I awoke drenched in sweat, and still crying."

Lowering her eyes, she murmured: "The laugh of that man in black burns in me still. It was the thing that shames me most."

The Master of Dreams considered what she had revealed, his fingertips wandering idly over the page of his Koran. "What is your name, child?"

"Ayesha."

The Master of Dreams interpreted in silence the secret numbers contained in the sounds of her name. Ayesha waited patiently, watching the old man calculate the meanings of those numbers.

If either of them noticed the emergence of Bou Idriss, Abd-el-Rahman's black vizier, from inside the fortress gate, they didn't show it. The attention of the young woman and the Dream Master remained fixed.

Bou Idriss withdrew to a point where he could not hear their low voices. Though he had come on a matter of importance, he waited there for them to finish, out of respect for the old man seated on the ground. Though he, himself, was even older—much older. Some believed he had lived a full century—that was not quite true—but he had to lean on the thick staff he carried, to support his years and obese weight. Sometimes when his black face twitched with anger, he would wield that staff as a club, with a skill and speed astonishing for a man of his great age and eunuch's fat.

"Do you know this man in the black robe?" the Master of Dreams asked the young woman crouched before him.

"No. Master . . . I have never seen such a man. If he was a man," she finished with a shudder of horror.

"Do you love your husband?"

"Oh, yes," Ayesha told him. "He is young and strong. A fierce warrior, but tender with me. And good-humored. His laugh when we make love is like a song."

"Like the laugh of the strange man in black?"

Ayesha, surprised, thought about it. "No, I don't think so. It was different. My husband's laugh never shames me. It delights."

"Do you ever lust after other men?"

She gave a small shrug, a faint smile. "Sometimes, when I see one who is young and pretty. There is no harm in that, if I never show it."

The Master of Dreams had completed his calculations. "Does your husband have a black robe?"

"No. He has a new one that is pure white, of beautiful material and workmanship. A reward from our lord Abd-el-Rahman."

The skeletal fingers traced a line in the opened page of the Koran. "A final question: When you woke from this dream, was it morning or almost dawn—or the middle of the night?"

"It was the darkest part of night. I couldn't sleep again, and it was hours before the sun came up."

"Ah . . ." It was a sigh of relief. "A good sign. The Prophet has said, 'The truest dream is one you have near daybreak.' Dreams that come late at night often foretell their opposite, since night is opposite from day. Your husband's robe is white, and that of the man in your dream was black. This stranger may in reality be your husband, returning unexpectedly from a battle in which he has distinguished himself. If so, this will be some years from now."

"But . . . this man in black, he looked nothing like my husband."

"Years and wars change a man. Your dream may mean that you will still long for him, no matter how his appearance changes with time. And his laugh: the proof that he will still delight in you."

Ayesha's smile was short-lived. "You are certain? The dream does not signify that one of The Others has seen and desires me?"

The Berbers had their own term for a demon, or evil spirit. It was *djinn*. But they seldom spoke it aloud, for fear that this would summon one of them. Instead they referred to them as The Others, or Those Who Hate Salt.

"I feared . . ." she hesitated. "I have heard that The Others do come, sometimes, to taste the flesh of mortal woman. Is that not true?"

"That is the other possible meaning of your dream," the Master of Dreams acknowledged. "For the Prophet has also said that a good dream is from God, and a false one from the Devil. To ward off this danger, there are three things you must do. First, when you leave me, you must spit three times over your left shoulder; and then tell no one else of this dream. No one."

She nodded, and he leaned forward to touch a copper amulet in the necklace of coins she wore. It was decorated with two triangles and five small eyes: a common protection against the Evil Eye. "For the next seven days and nights you must never take this off, even when you sleep. That is the second protection. The third is this: On the next night of the new moon, you must fill a bowl with water and carry it to a secluded place. Put it on the ground and tear fresh grass which you will throw to the new moon, an offering of fresh green life. Then strip yourself naked and call three times: 'O new moon, come look at me and find me pretty.' This will draw the rays of the new moon toward you, and they will fall also on the bowl of water, giving some of its power to it. Drink from this water, and pour the rest over your head, letting it run down your body. Then dress yourself, return to your home, and for the next seven nights do not go outside again between sunset and sunrise."

She was comforted by the precise instructions. "Thank

you, Master." She rose gracefully and turned away. Stopping, she spat three times over her left shoulder. Then she made her way down a sloping, shadowed passage, into the close-packed village, her carriage erect, radiating sensual awareness.

The Master of Dreams smiled after her, remembering ones like her from his youth. Then he turned his gaze on the black vizier, who had had any chance for such memories removed from him at the age of four. "Bou Idriss, you honor me with your presence. Have *you* had a dream, at last?"

"Abd-el-Rahman has had one. It disturbs him."

"Ah." The Master of Dreams made a small sack of the ragged square of cloth on which Ayesha had left her offering: a small quantity of raisins, figs and nuts. He used a forked stick to help himself to his feet. "Tell me truly, Bou Idriss—you never dream?"

"Only waking dreams," Bou Idriss said. "And those I can interpret for myself." He had great respect for this teacher's special talent; for his long experience, sharpened by natural insight. But Bou Idriss confided his personal secrets to no one. Some, he even hid from Brahim ben Hamid, the boy he had raised, loved and saved, and who had grown into the great Abd-el-Rahman, with his help.

"Perhaps you are right," the Master of Dreams said, studying the sagging fleshiness of the eunuch's blue-black face. Bou Idriss came from even farther away than he: the Sudan. Slightly mocking, he added: "After all, it is truly said that the guess of a wise man is more to be believed than the certainty of a fool."

"But you are not a fool." There was no answering smile. Bou Idriss was not a man who smiled.

"No, but I am so much younger than you, Bou Idriss. And a man older by a day is wiser by a year."

Bou Idriss cut the exchange by turning to lead the way into the fortress, leaning a bit on the staff, but his step oddly light under the burden of his squat weight. The scrawny Master of Dreams followed him, hobbling along with the aid of his forked stick.

* * *

Grayle rolled over on his back, stretching his arms and legs far apart across the tiled floor, luxuriating in the steaming heat sucking the poisons from the opened pores of his body. The Master of the Hamman stirred the coals of the brazier fire with a long poker, and Grayle watched the reflections of its leaping flames in the steam rising to a bright blue ceiling.

Stars glistened in the mosaic of the ceiling: the constellations of Orion and the Great Bear. Golden Venus and red Mars. The walls of Abd-el-Rahman's hamman were decorated with orange trees and palms. Under Grayle was the sea. His left hand rested on a fish and his right on a seahorse. There was a spray of seaweed under one foot and his other touched the tentacles of an octopus.

It was not orthodox. But a man of power could indulge certain whims. "Everything that gives pleasure," ran a bit of Arab cynicism, "is forbidden." And relics of Berber paganism persisted, drawn from a past much older than Islam.

The Master of the Hamman poured a bucket of water across Grayle's arms, head and torso. One of his apprentices, a slim, naked boy not more than nine, emptied another bucket over Grayle's legs and lower body. The water ran down his flesh, taking the sweat with it. It spread over the tiles around him, turning to steam. Grayle rolled up onto his knees. Water from two buckets sloshed across his back.

He became dizzy when he stood up. His heart thudded, and his pulse was not normal. Release and anxiety. He didn't care. He savored the moment. The other apprentice, a boy of about twelve, began patting him dry with a long, thick towel. Grayle took it from the boy and finished the drying himself. They gave him a freshly laundered djellaba to put on. Its light cotton fibers scratched his skin. The older apprentice knelt with a pair of slippers, old but still serviceable. Grayle slid his feet into them. Two of Abd-el-Rahman's personal bodyguards conducted him out through an underground passage. The hamman was underneath the fortress, like the prison. But in another area. Another world.

One of the bodyguards led Grayle through the passage. Thr other followed him. They were lean men with hawk-like faces. Each carried a drawn sword. Grayle had no illusion about how many seconds he would survive if he attempted a move that alarmed them. He had seen Berber partisans show off by dispatching a flying insect with a flick of a blade. When the passage widened they shifted to either side of him.

Steps led up to a covered arcade surrounding a small courtyard. Grayle had been too long underground to adjust quickly to the dazzle of sunshine. Needles of pain stabbed his eyes before he could narrow them almost shut. He stumbled as they moved along the arcade. The bodyguard on his right gripped his arm with his free hand, leading him.

They entered a foyer, went through a short enclosed corridor, stepped into another open courtyard. The sunshine blurred Grayle's vision, but he glimpsed the beauty of greenery and flowers, heard the music of water splashing in a fountain. Then they were inside another corridor. It led to a third court, larger than the others. Two fountains; flowering plants growing out of huge urns geometrically positioned. They crossed between the fountains, to an open arcade with slender white pillars. The entrance of Abd-el-Rahman's reception chamber was wide, with three arches. Grayle's eyes felt better as soon as he stepped inside the shade of the room.

The walls were covered with blue and yellow tiles to the height of his head. Above that, lovely white scrollwork, verses from the Koran, rose to an intricately carved and painted wooden ceiling. Green-tiled flooring and a Persian carpet. Darkly colorful Berber rugs covered a low divan that ran along three walls. A single window, with a painted wooden grill, framed distant sky and mountain peaks.

A man of about sixty, his white silk robes embroidered with gold and purple, sat under the window, preparing mint tea in a pot on the low table before him. He paused, looking up as Grayle entered.

Physically, he was of average height, with a thickset fig-

ure and wide, fleshy face. He reminded Grayle of a faintly
smiling Budda: the strong, well-padded bulk, the placid
appraisal, the thoughtful quietness. Even the large ears,
flat to the head, with heavy lobes.

Abd-el-Rahman pointed to a yellow pillow on the carpet
on the other side of the low table. "Please, seat yourself."
His French was a good deal more cultured than Grayle's.
That didn't surprise him. Everyone knew the Berber chief
had taken his university education in Paris.

Grayle kicked off his slippers before stepping onto the
carpet. He lowered himself to the pillow, crossing his legs.
His guards left their slippers on the green tiles at the entrance and took positions behind him, to either side. Abd-
el-Rahman returned his attention to the preparation of the
mint tea. He selected with care the herbs he put into the
pot, taking them from a bowl held by a black slave on one
knee beside him. He had unusually thick fingers, the
thumbs abnormally short. Hands that could crush bones.

Bou Idriss sat to Abd-el-Rahman's right, where the divan cornered, his old, squat figure resting against the other
wall. His eyes, studying Grayle, were almost hidden by the
swollen, glossy fat of his face. Grayle took him in, briefly.
He had seen only one other eunuch during his years in
Morocco. This one was black, too; blacker than the slave
with the bowl. Grayle's eyes swung back to Abd-el-
Rahman.

He had finished with the selection of herbs. Taking several big lumps of sugar from the bowl, he put them in the
teapot, pushing them down with the herbs. The slave rose
quickly and took the bowl away. Another came to clean
Abd-el-Rahman's fingers with a damp towel. The first returned with a large kettle of steaming water which he
poured into the open teapot slowly; and stopped the instant
the Berber chief raised a thick finger.

Abd-el-Rahman put the top on the teapot and settled
back to let it steep. He put his hands together and linked
the thick fingers, resting an elbow on a pile of small blue
cushions. There was absolute authority even in that pose as
he regarded Grayle. The look of someone who knew every-

thing that might happen; who had seen it all before and dealt with it before, well enough that he was still alive, and in command.

Grayle understood who he was without having to be told. That authority was unmistakable. What the Moroccans called *shih*—a gift from God of awe-inspiring inner certainty, strength and vitality. Grayle had seen that kind of impenetrable quietness before in certain officers. Men would follow such a man, even to their deaths.

For his part, Abd-el-Rahman noted Grayle's sunken eyes and the smears of darkness under them, the trembling of his hands. Quite natural, considering the condition and length of his confinement. What interested him more was that the Legionnaire's flesh had not wasted away to the extent to be expected.

"How are you called?" he asked Grayle.

"Ishmael."

Abd-el-Rahman's small smile was reassuring, warming. "Indeed? That is a name that augers well for you." His voice, like his manner, had a special quality to its quietness. "Ishmael was the son of Abraham by an Egyptian concubine, Hagar. He became an ancestor of the first Muslims. But his father, Abraham, had a wife who was jealous. For her, Abraham cast Ishmael and Hagar away, into the desert. They were almost dead of thirst when a miracle created a well before them."

"I know the story." There was a bitterness in Grayle's tone, and Abd-el-Rahman noted it. "It fits well enough."

"The story . . ." Abd-el-Rahman repeated the phrase thoughtfully. "You do not believe it is true?"

Grayle answered carefully: "I think it is true, for those who believe."

"Believe," Abd-el-Rahman told him. "It will help you. It is said, for example, that I am in direct line of descent from Mohammed. I believe it. Is it true?" A small shrug. "A man may come from far away, and say anything about his ancestry. Perhaps some will not believe him. But his sons grow up believing. And in time, so does everyone else. Ishmael—it is a good name."

He leaned forward and took up the teapot. There were three small glasses on the low table. He poured a bit of the tea into the nearest one, and took a sip from it. "Exactly right." He filled the other two glasses before his own.

Bou Idriss shoved himself along the divan, closer to the table, and picked up his glass. Grayle was aware of their eyes on the trembling of his hand as he reached for the glass nearest him. He closed his fingers around it and let the heat of the tea burn into his palm as he raised it. He took a sip, slowly put the glass down, and raised his hand from it, spreading his fingers. The tremor was gone.

"That was not a pleasant place, down there," he said softly.

"I am sorry you were kept there so long," Abd-el-Rahman said. "I have been away. It was only yesterday that I returned and learned of you from Salah."

Grayle took another sip of the hot tea and repeated it: "Not a pleasant place."

"It serves its purpose."

"If Hell serves a purpose."

Bou Idriss spoke for the first time: "Think of your words before you utter them. You are now on the Bridge of Alsirat, which leads from Hell to Paradise. You may go forward, or be sent back."

Grayle turned his head and stared at him. "I won't go back there," he said flatly. He looked at Abd-el-Rahman. "If you take me, good. If you don't, these men of yours will have to kill me. They won't get me back there any other way."

"Now he utters threats," Bou Idriss murmured.

Abd-el-Rahman said, "Salah did say he has courage."

"Courage is easy," Bou Idriss pointed out. "Most men have some. It is *intent* that is important here. I don't think he is to be trusted."

Grayle glanced at him again and decided he was being baited, to test his reaction. "Why not?"

"The French trusted you."

"They got their money's worth out of me for over four years and my enlistment is almost up. I don't owe any loyalty to their cause."

Abd-el-Rahman's eyes hadn't left his face. "Nor to mine."

"I am not interested in anyone's cause," Grayle told him. "I offer *you* my loyalty. You, personally."

"In exchange for what?"

Bou Idriss had put his glass down, hardly tasted. "What are you after that you could not get with the French? Wealth? Fame? Women? Revenge?"

Grayle sipped at his tea. "There is some of that in it, too, I suppose."

"And what else?" Abd-el-Rahman asked slowly. "*Why* do you wish to join me?"

"Why do you fight the Sultan and his French allies?"

"My reason is obvious, I think."

"No. There are easier ways for you to spend the rest of your life. Make your peace with the French general. Let him have what he wants, which is only the right of way through your territory. He'd give you his protection from the Sultan, along with a medal from France and his own personal gratitude. You could sit up here and have even more power; permanent and backed by a French treaty. Or take their payment and your own wealth, and enjoy yourself in Europe with it."

"Is that what you really came to tell me?" Abd-el-Rahman's tone had become kindly; deadly.

"I'm just stating your alternatives. Which makes the answer to my question not obvious at all. Why do you fight?"

Abd-el-Rahman finished the tea in his glass. He opened the teapot and signaled. More hot water was poured into it. He put the top back on the pot. "Let us say that a man has few possible outlets for what is inside him. I have been impotent for some years." There was a certain amount of mirth behind the answer; but not mockery, not even self-mockery.

Grayle drank the last of his tea. It had become luke-warm. "I have been impotent for almost five years."

"You do not speak of sexual impotence."

"Soon it would be time for me to reenlist. It would be the only way, other than with you, that I could stay in this country. Another five years of impotence. And beyond that the same again."

"Why can't you leave Morocco?"

"I killed a man," Grayle said evenly. He didn't add to it.

Abd-el-Rahman refilled Grayle's glass with hot tea, then his own. He glanced at the tea remaining in the glass of Bou Idriss, and put the pot down. "I see. And with me, what do you think to have?"

"A purpose, maybe." Grayle picked up his glass and took a sip. It was very hot, and still strong. "A life needs to contain certain unpredictable possibilities, or it is not a life. It is what a blade of grass has. A man needs more than that."

The dark bulk of Bou Idriss stirred impatiently. "Perhaps," he suggested, "it is simply that you hope a grateful Berber chief will reward you more richly than the French? Richly enough for you to leave Morocco and assume a new identity?"

"Perhaps." Grayle kept his eyes on Abd-el-Rahman. "If I serve him well enough to earn such a reward."

Abd-el-Rahman studied him with something more than curiosity. "Why did you kill this man you spoke of? Money or passion?"

"Not even those. A spasm of rage, dead before he was."

The eunuch regarded Grayle coldly: "That does not speak well of your character."

Abd-el-Rahman looked at Bou Idriss. "*You* have killed for such a brief spasm of anger."

"I have certain virtues, to set against that fault. Has he?"

Abd-el-Rahman sipped his tea. "I had a dream last night. It disturbed me. Perhaps it was only weariness after my journey. Or the news of the road which Salah gave me from you, though I know the means of dealing with that. I want to know if this dream has any special significance for you."

He leaned back on the divan, watching Grayle's face as he spoke: "In my dream, the light was strange. Such a light as I had never experienced before. I could not tell if it was day, though it was surely not night. When I stepped out into the open court outside my sleeping chamber, I saw what it was. Overhead, thousands of carrion birds wheeled low in the sky, blotting out the sunshine.

"There was no one in the court, neither guards nor servants. There was an utter silence about my fortress; and above it, no cries from the circling scavengers. I wandered through the fortress, searching, and found no one. I was alone in it, except for wild dogs racing through the courts and corridors. They rushed past me silently, intent on some search of their own, not seeing or smelling my presence.

"When I wandered into the lower level of the fortress, in the court of my reception chamber, I found something that had not been there before. A tree of unknown variety, full-grown, had burst upward through the paving tiles. It bore many kinds of fruit, but these were being eaten by flocks of ravens that attacked the tree as I approached it.

"Only one small fruit remained, on a slender branch. A black olive. A snake was twined around the branch, and struck at any bird that flew close, driving it away. But it did not strike at me, when I plucked the olive.

"I ate it, and was young again."

Grayle straightened his back, feeling the swordsmen behind him, their eyes staying on him. "Some of the symbols are obvious. Wild dogs, vultures, ravens—omens of evil. You could be more worried than you admit about the new road. Or, if you believe dreams tell the future, it is a warning of a bad time coming."

Abd-el-Rahman nodded approvingly. "Or, having already dreamed this bad time, I may have put it behind me. The dream ended with my youth restored." A wry smile. "That would be worth any amount of troubled times."

Grayle understood that his life somehow depended on the interpretation of this dream. But he could not guess at the answers expected of him. He had to stick with the truth, and hope it sufficed. He studied the Berber leader and found no sign of what the Moroccans called *ayyan*: trace of incipient weakness or fatigue. But the man was *not* young.

"That was only in your dream. No one can become young again."

Another encouraging nod. "True. A man's only youth is in his sons. And the snake on the branch—the serpent is the protector of rebirth, not renewed youth. But the single remaining piece of fruit? It was a black olive, remember."

"I remember. But it has no significance for me." Grayle probed the Berber's expression. "I think it has for you."

"And the tree—how do you interpret that?"

"A tree can mean many things. Life, destiny; the passage from desire to goal, the conductor between darkness and light, the relationship of the lower self and the spiritual, of the material world and God."

Bou Idriss growled, "He answers riddles with more riddles."

"My answers are riddles to *me*." Grayle's eyes did not leave the face of the Berber chief. "Because I have no knowledge of certain things which are known to you."

"A tree bears fruit only if it is nourished." Abd-el-Rahman pointed to the reception court behind Grayle. "There is little nourishment under those tiles, for the roots of so great a tree. A layer of barren clay."

Grayle seized on the drift of it: "And under that your dungeons, where I was kept. Such a tree needs deep roots."

"A dream tree," Bou Adriss said softly, "does not require roots."

"But I was down there," Grayle countered. "And I am not a dream."

"Nor were you in it." Abd-el-Rahman rose to his feet. "We shall see . . ."

A stairway led up between blind ochre walls. Grayle followed Abd-el-Rahman and Bou Idriss, with the two bodyguards mounting behind him, their swords held in readiness. A short corridor at the top, then a foyer and more steps to climb. These led past the lavish gilded grillwork of a window, from which could be heard the voices of unseen women and children.

At the top of the steps they emerged into a roof-garden, shaded by arbors of ivy and grapevines. It was surrounded by an arcade of arches and pillars incised with Koranic verses, leading to various rooms. A marble fountain in the shape of a sea serpent trickled water into a lily-pool. Twittering birds flitted from one piece of foliage to another. There was a view of distant mountain ridges, and of much closer formations looming above the fortress: convoluted spires and broken cliffs.

Abd-el-Rahman motioned for Grayle to sit with him on a shaded bench beside the pool. Bou Idriss remained standing, leaning with both hands on his staff that could be used as a cudgel. Abd-el-Rahman's secretary, a plump young man wearing Western clothes under his blue selham, came up onto the roof garden with a map of southern Morocco.

Salah had been vague about certain sections of the route the French intended to use in constructing the road.

Grayle was spreading the map across his thighs when a sentinel called down from the watchtower: "An airplane approaches!"

Abd-el-Rahman stood up, scanning the sky. The plane appeared, flying very high to avoid the peaks and clifftops around the fortress. Grayle identified it as a Spad-91 two-seater: one for the pilot and the other for the observer who would be leaning out, using binoculars.

"Only a reconnaissance plane," he told Abd-el-Rahman. "What you have to worry about are the Nieuport-Delage 29s the French have converted into single-seat bombers. I saw some at Ouarzazate. They've been fitted with Michelin racks that hold six of those little ten-kilo bombs."

Abd-el-Rahman shook his head. "They have already tried with those. Twice. The first time a pair of them. They learned the danger of coming in low between those formations with the valley downdraft. One nearly cracked a wing against that cliff, and was forced to pull away. The other managed to get quite near and my marksmen emptied their rifles into its motor. It crashed at the end of the valley, killing the pilot. The next time there were three and they dropped their bombs from a great height. None hit the fortress or village. A sheep was killed on the other side of the stream. They have not come back since."

Grayle watched the Spad making slow circles. "They can't see anything useful from that high, even with glasses."

"But they can spot me moving large numbers of men, if they happen to fly over at the right time. If my direction is anticipated they can block the route with their troops. Then the bombers can be used, to scatter us."

Grayle looked at the map he'd been given. "This isn't good enough. It covers too much territory. Not enough detail." He indicated the section, small on the map, between Abd-el-Rahman's domain and the desert. "If I can have paper, pen and ink, I'll do an enlargement of this area. And draw in the route."

Bou Idriss gave him his full attention. "You know how to make maps?"

"Yes."

Abd-el-Rahman looked at him, and put a hand on his shoulder. Grayle was disturbed by the pleasure the weight of it gave to him.

"That is a talent I can use. To instruct my men before battle, for example."

"If you trust me."

"That must be tested, of course." Abd-el-Rahman looked again at the circling plane. The time had not come yet to tell this man the meaning of the black olive. He was still not certain if Grayle was the one the dream had prophesied must be there to help when that future time of disaster came. Testing was required, to determine if the dream should be interpreted in that way.

"We will try you," he told Grayle. "One level of trust at a time."

20

A furtive war was being waged that night, south of the Atlas in the labyrinth kasbah of Ouarzazate, between the Foreign Legion and the Bat d'Af. It had begun in a bar, the night before.

The Bat d'Af—the *Battaillon d'Afrique*, made up of soldiers sentenced by the French army to serve in the Sahara as punishment for various crimes—considered itself the meanest body of fighting men in the world. The Legion had a similar opinion of itself. The previous night two Legionnaires had gotten into an argument with a dozen troopers from the Bat d'Af. The pair had been smashed apart with vicious efficiency, and would not be leaving the army hospital for some weeks.

This night, packs of Legionnaires and Bat d'Af troops were maneuvering between the close-packed buildings of the kasbah, seeking each other out. The war was being fought with mule-chains and lengths of steel pipe. So far three more Legionnaires had been hospitalized, and eleven members of the Bat d'Af.

Grayle kept to shadows, and melted into a dark doorway at the approach of a Bat d'Af hunting pack. He was looking for a sizeable force of Legionnaires. The hunters passed, disappearing in the maze of passageways. Grayle resumed his search.

The kasbah whorehouse, patronized almost exclusively by French troops, might at that hour be in the control of either side. A fifty-fifty chance. Grayle took it, and lost.

About ten members of the Bat d'Af were inside, searching the place for lone enemies. Grayle spun out of the doorway and ran. But they had already seen his uniform, and they came out after him.

He sprinted down one alleyway and into another. As his pursuers turned the corner after him, Salah and the men he had picked for this materialized out of the night shadows on either side. Their knives did their work on three of the Bat d'Af before the rest turned and fled.

Cursing softly, Grayle walked back to the three sprawled bodies. "They'll be back, with reinforcements."

The diagonal scar disfiguring Salah's face was twisted by his unpleasant smile. He liked this game. "Then this is the best place for you to wait." He sent several of his men up onto rooftops, to alert Grayle when the Bat d'Af returned in force. Others spread out to find the nearest body of Legionnaires, and report back.

The Legion had taken control of a bar on a small square several streets from the whorehouse. Most of them were inside getting liquored up. Two of them were taking their turn on watch outside when they heard it: a cry made famous long ago by an officer who'd led the way over a barricade and jumped into the middle of a nest of enemies:

"To me, the Legion!"

By the time the Legionnaire who'd shouted it raced into the square, with a Bat d'Af pack at his heels, some fifteen Legionnaires were pouring out of the bar. Grayle kept running full-tilt until he collided with the bodies of the Legionnaires, surging forward to meet the charge of the Bat d'Af fighters.

The square became a whirlpool of battling men, savaging enemies with a joyous ferocity punctuated by the clashing of chains and steel bars, the crunch of bones, cries of pain. It ended when the Bat d'Af retreated from the square, dragging its badly wounded along. The exultant Legion contingent began checking its own fallen.

Some had been only temporarily put out of action; these were dragged into the bar and given liquor to help their recovery. A smaller number were more seriously hurt, and these were carried out of the kasbah to be turned over to the army hospital. One of these was Grayle. Though blood was running down his face from a scalp wound, he was conscious. Two Legionnaires half-carried him north to the single dirt street lined by the jerry-built new town.

They were passed by a lieutenant leading an armed platoon of Algerian Spahis, heading on the double toward the kasbah. The colonel in charge at Ouarzazate had finally decided that too many troopers were being badly hurt for the matter to be considered a letting off of pent-up boredom.

The fort which the French had built a mile north of the kasbah held a vital strategic position between the Atlas Mountains and the Sahara, and between the Algerian border and the Atlantic coast. For this reason the garrison at the junction point of Ouarzazate was intended to be impregnable. Its walls were surrounded by linked tangles of barbed wire. At night the strong beams of tower searchlights swung over designated areas, covering all possible approaches.

But the sentries on duty at the main gate that night were expecting the wounded men being carried from the kasbah. And they knew the two men carrying Grayle. The cover story he'd prepared, about Captain Verdier sending him to Ouarzazate with a message for Colonel Boulat, proved unnecessary. The sentries allowed him to be dragged inside without even checking his military identification papers.

The hospital was a single-floor, four-room structure deep within the fort. Grayle and other incapacitated Legionnaires were lowered to the ground beside several unconscious troopers from the Bat d'Af. The Legionnaires who'd carried them hurried off, back to the kasbah war.

An army doctor and two orderlies opened the door and angrily took in the increased number of sprawled figures waiting in the dirt. They picked a man with a fractured skull, and carried him inside the hospital. It was five minutes before the doctor came out again with his orderlies to choose the next patient. Grayle was no longer there. His absence was not noticed, since they hadn't bothered to count the waiting bodies.

The shack containing the fort's generators was a hundred yards from the hospital. Grayle walked the distance steadily, not hurrying and not avoiding lights. There was nothing to alarm anyone about a man in uniform going about his assigned duties. As he neared the shack Grayle scanned methodically for anyone in a position to observe him. A sergeant was coming across the parade ground in his direction. Grayle passed the generator shack without changing his pace or manner. His face was wooden, his palms wet.

He stopped and went down on one knee to tighten the lace of his left boot, turning his body slightly as he did so. The sergeant was beyond the generator shack, striding away. Grayle walked back to the door of the shack. With his back concealing what he was doing, he drew a short crowbar from inside his coat. It was the work of a second to break the lock, step inside and shut the door behind him.

Minutes later the searchlights, and every other electric light in the fort, went out at the same time.

The response within the fort was automatic, but time-consuming. Flashlights were found, kerosene lamps lit, emergency lights hooked up to batteries turned on. They were far from adequate in an area that large: small patches dimly lit, surrounded by deep shadows and great areas of darkness. It was almost five minutes before the report reached Colonel Boulat, commandant of Ouarzazate: someone had deliberately damaged the generators; repair work had already begun but would take at least two hours.

The colonel's thought at the time was that one of his troops had gone berserk; something akin to the madness raging up there in the old kasbah. But he didn't take chances. The alarm was sounded, every able-bodied trooper turned out and put on the alert.

By then Grayle had broken into an explosives shed and pried open a case of dynamite. Salah and four picked men reached him, after dodging through areas of darkness between groups of assembling troops. They had cut through the outer barricade of barbed wire the instant the lights went out, used a ladder to climb the wall, and a knotted rope to scramble down inside. The ladder and rope had been left in place.

Swiftly, they dumped sticks of dynamite into canvas sacks they'd brought along. Grayle filled the one Salah gave him and headed for the rear of the fort. Salah and his four men followed, keeping a sensible distance behind.

The walls at the rear of the fort had been extended to provide a secure area during the night to keep the planes which operated from the field behind the fort. The rear gate had been made wide enough to wheel the planes in and out. Shut and barred, the gate was as solid as the walls.

There were four planes inside, bunched together: a Wibault-72 fighter, a Spad-91 used for reconnaissance, and two Nieuport-Delage bombers. They were parked next to a watchtower. There were two men posted on the platform atop it, with a Hotchkiss machine gun mounted on a heavy tripod. They also had a searchlight, which being battery-operated was still working.

The searchlight's swinging beam caught a Legionnaire running toward the tower, carrying something in a canvas sack hung over his shoulder. The beam steadied on him. He kept coming, making no effort to evade it.

One of the tower guards called down: "What's happened back there?"

"Trouble with the generators," Grayle panted. "Colonel Boulat said to get this up to you."

"What the hell is it?"

But Grayle was already climbing the ladder, with no breath left to answer. The question was repeated when he reached the platform and unslung the sack from his shoulder.

"Didn't tell me," he gasped, and put the sack down.

They knelt to open it. The crowbar came out of Grayle's coat and struck the nearest one across the back of the head, hammering him face-down beside the sack.

The other twisted around, snatching up a revolver. The crowbar slashed against his forehead. His revolver fell on the filled sack as he went over backward, off the platform. Grayle heard his body strike the ground.

His hands were busy at the searchlight wires, ripping them from the battery contacts. In the abrupt darkness, he groped for the revolver and stuck it in his belt. He heard Salah's team sprint past below, toward the planes. Grayle hung the sack over his shoulder again before starting down. Abd-el-Rahman was going to have a use for the dynamite.

At the foot of the tower he waited, drawing the revolver and holding it ready, listening for approaching troops. But Salah's team came racing back first.

There were ten-second fuses on the sticks of dynamite they'd planted. The explosions as the planes blew apart, one after the other, hit Grayle with hard blasts of hot wind. He ran from the tower after Salah's team, following the darkest shadows toward their exit point. Not the way they'd come in. By now the cut wire, ladder and descent rope should have been discovered. The troops would be concentrating there, waiting for their return.

They ran, instead, for a prearranged point along the rear wall. The men Salah had left outside had acted the instant the planes started exploding. A knotted rope hung down inside the wall; another down the outside.

Sentries in one of the corner towers spotted shadows moving over the top of the wall and began firing at them. Answering fire from six rifles in the darkness outside the rear wall blasted at the tower, diverting the sentries there just long enough. Grayle reached the ground outside close behind Salah, and followed him through a new break in the barbed wire.

They looked at each other as they reached the waiting ponies, and Grayle's laugh was as ugly as Salah's mutilated grin.

It was not until dawn that a tracking force could be sent out from the fort to try locating the escape route of the saboteurs. The tracks of the ponies were found. Followed, they led northeast, toward the Atlas. But the trail was lost before it reached the mountains, and could not be picked up again.

By then Colonel Boulat had been informed that a Legionnaire had taken part in the assault on the planes. Or at least a man who wore the uniform and seemed at home in it. A warning was spread, and for a time all units were on the alert for the renegade Legionnaire. But as the months of fighting Abd-el-Rahman's hit-and-run attacks passed, and the renegade did not reappear, belief in his existence dwindled.

By then Grayle had taken part in four more attacks, but dressed as a Berber. He never wore his Legion uniform again.

21

He drifted awake in the arms of his slave, her nakedness sprawled loosely against his under the warmth of the covers on his wide divan. No chink of daylight pierced the closed shutters. It was still night. The sleeping alcove of his chamber, which served as Grayle's all-purpose living quarters, was a cave of darkness. He could barely make out the girl's head, turned toward him on the silk pillows, her breath hot against his throat.

She was from the Harar, in Ethiopia, and had been named Toma by the master of the slave caravan who had sold her to the chieftain of one of Abd-el-Rahman's tribes. When her owner had been killed in battle, she had become available for resale.

Abd-el-Rahman had bought her as a present for Grayle six months ago, after a skirmish with an enemy tribe allied to the Pasha of Marrakesh. An enemy horseman had managed to swing in directly behind Abd-el-Rahman. The barrel of Grayle's rifle had deflected the slash of the warrior's sword from the back of Abd-el-Rahman's neck. The stock of the rifle had smashed the attacker's face, clubbing him from his saddle.

Nothing had been said by Abd-el-Rahman about Grayle's saving his life. Not even after the fight was finished. But several days later he had given Toma to him.

There were enough available Berber women in the village under the fortress. Young widows of slain warriors. Abd-el-Rahman had seen Grayle eye them in passing, and noted the way some of them giggled and boldly returned his appraisal. He had warned Grayle not to pursue the interest further, with any of them. His tone, as always, had been reasonable, but inflexible. For Grayle to ally himself with a Berber woman would mean creating a tie between himself and her family; and thus, automatically, with the tribe of that family.

"You must remain a foreigner among us," he explained to Grayle. "In that way your only loyalty is to me, because I remain your only protector."

But Toma also remained a foreigner, because she had given no children to her former owner, which would have attached her to his family. Being barren diminished her value enough to make her available for resale. But her value as a pleasure slave remained considerable.

Grayle understood the price paid for her, during the first night she presented herself to him in his chamber. He had grown accustomed to the tattooed faces of Berber women; the designs with which Toma's had been decorated by her first owner heightened the exotic splendor of her aquiline features. A small blue star high on each red-dyed cheek. Three black dots forming the points of a triangle on her forehead. A straight purple line from the middle of her lower lip down her chin.

Her dark eyes, heavily rimmed with kohl, had studied him uncertainly at first. Her smile had been tentative. But it became sure of itself, almost insolently so, as she watched his expression while she stripped herself before him.

The light of the candles made her black eyes sparkle, and gave a glossy quality to her smooth, dusky skin. Long legs and flaring buttocks, proud breasts that trembled with each breath, swayed with each move. The springy strength within that ripe flesh revealed itself in his first taking of her, responding with a savagery equaling his own.

Grayle stirred with pleasure under the covers against her sleeping figure. She moved, instinctively pressing closer against him, but did not wake. And he did not attempt to rouse and take her again. It was a satiated pleasure he felt now. She provided another outlet for his trapped rage; as violent as killing, as sly as treachery.

That was what Toma had become for him; but no more than that. He treated her always with a casual affection; as one might treat a favored cat, but never a horse one might have to depend on in an emergency.

She gave him back a cunning lust, and a playfulness that responded to a growing perversity in him—but never a returned affection. Never. His part in her life, as hers in his, remained strictly limited. But she was not dissatisfied to be his slave. Otherwise she would have demanded, as was her right by custom, to be resold to someone else.

Gently, so as not to disturb her sleep, Grayle withdrew himself from her arms. His nerves were too active for him to return to sleep, this close to dawn.

That morning he was to start out on a mysterious journey with Youssef, Abd-el-Rahman's oldest living son, and his second-in-command. Together with a small number of warriors specially chosen by Youssef. A very small number, to lessen the chances of their movements being discovered. Their route would be north, through territory controlled by the enemy tribes allied to the Pasha of Marrakesh. Their goal was even more dangerous: Marrakesh itself, where the Pasha had his city palace and the French command its headquarters.

Grayle had not been told the purpose of this trek. That had happened before, and each time it clawed at his nerves. It meant that after more than a year he was still being tested; that their trust in him remained limited and provisional. He didn't like the passive waiting, his position hanging in the balance of a fate he could not influence or anticipate.

Still, the periods of relative inactivity here were never long enough for brooding to get out of control. And they were spiced by the savage actions remembered, and expectation of the violence to come. His pleasure in that continued to grow—and it caused him to remember Victor Royan's horror-affection for his war. And made him rethink his own judgment of that sick attachment.

He thought about Victor quite often.

Never of Nora Cesari, though. There were some things he couldn't remember; because if he started he might never be able to stop.

Grayle's flesh pebbled in the cold night air as he slipped

out from under the covers. Quickly, he found his clothes
and put them on in the darkness of his room: the baggy
pantaloons, silk shirt and felt slippers, the brown wool djellaba with its heavy warmth, and over that the rich selham,
a black cloak of brocaded velvet. Pulling the cowl forward
over his head, he pushed aside the curtains at the entrance
of his chamber and stepped out onto the roof terrace.

Above the fortress the stars were growing dimmer, but the
light of the half moon was still strong. The pavilion in front
of Abd-el-Rahman's living quarters was on the other side
of the garden from Grayle's chamber. He could make out
the shadowy forms of the bodyguards on watch there, and
he knew they saw him emerge into the open. But they did
not stir at the sight of him; they knew who he was and
understood his position, however temporary it might prove
to be.

Only two other living chambers beside his shared this
roof terrace with Abd-el-Rahman's quarters: those of
Youssef and Bou Idriss.

Immediately to the right of Grayle's chamber was a
flowering hedge. And on the other side of it the interior
opening that dropped to the reception courtyard. He was
sharply aware, at this moment before dawn, of what lay
beneath that courtyard. He never forgot when he was inside the fortress—not when he was sharing food and coun-
cil with Abd-el-Rahman, not even when he was in the arms
of his slave Toma—the dungeon where there was no night
or day; where the damned lay rotting in their chains and
holes, and the sound of groaning never ceased. It was always there, just under him, waiting.

It was Bou Idriss who had explained who most of the
damned were, down there. And he knew, more than most.
Bou Idriss had been an emasculated child of ten when he
had been bought from Arabian slave-dealers by Abd-el-
Rahman's grandfather, and assigned to duties in the wom-
en's quarters. At the birth of the son who was to become
Abd-el-Rahman's father, he had been made the boy's
protector-companion. When the grandfather died, Bou Idriss had moved out of the women's quarters as adviser to
the eldest son, the boy he'd helped raise.

Together with a brother one year younger, Abd-el-Rahman's father had ruled this area and built one of the three most powerful tribal confederations in the High Atlas. Then the younger brother had turned on the elder one, striking without warning to usurp the supreme power. It was an old, recurring story in the blood-spattered history of Morocco. The elder had been murdered in the coup. So had his sons, to prevent them from growing into avenging rivals.

But one son escaped, spirited away by Bou Idriss, along with a treasure in gems and gold coins hidden for such an emergency. When the boy had grown into young manhood, the two had returned secretly from Europe. Slipping into the Atlas Mountains, they had begun the work which would turn the grown boy into Abd-el-Rahman.

By then his uncle had lost three disastrous battles with the forces of the Sultan. To the Berbers, this was a clear sign that he had also lost his divine luck. Abd-el-Rahman, advised by Bou Idriss, had begun his mission in a small way: leading the tribe of his mother against another tribe with which it had a territorial dispute. The other tribe had surrendered, and Abd-el-Rahman had shown mercy and wisdom: sparing all who surrendered, and absorbing them under his banner.

After he had won the next three small battles in a row, tribes began joining him without being summoned, and his power had risen swiftly.

The uncle had died in the final battle, along with most of the men who had supported his original coup. But some had been unwise enough to survive the battle. These, along with certain chieftains who'd refused to make their submission to Abd-el-Rahman after the battle, were the ones now inhabiting the prison under the fortress. A more sensible fate for them, Abd-el-Rahman and Bou Idriss had decided, than executing them immediately.

Bou Idriss used the term Grayle had once given those dungeons, in explaining this decision: "If there were no Hell, why would men act in such ways as to avoid going there?"

Grayle considered this history as he turned from the hedge and strolled through the roof garden. He knew Bou Idriss had told it to him for a reason, and that the reason was connected with the dream of Abd-el-Rahman. But he still did not understand exactly how he fitted into that dream, and what it was supposed to lead to in the end.

He remembered the time he had asked the Berber leader, "Do you really expect to win this war?"

"I expect," Abd-el-Rahman had answered simply, "to fight."

"And in the end?"

"What does that term signify? Was it the end when Caesar conquered Pompey? Or when he conquered Gaul? Or England? When he was killed? Or when Shakespeare wrote of his death? At the death of the last Roman to be called Caesar? Or the last Russian called Czar? The end—is not my concern. Nor any man's."

Grayle stopped by a low wall, gazing at the moonlit valley cupped within the mountains. Undulating brown slopes, black cliffs, white clouds. Absolute silence; except for the flat, hollow sound of water turning stones in the stream below the village. A chill, desolate beauty, akin to death.

He watched the first streaks of dawn color touch the night sky. There had been a time when he might have wanted to paint such a landscape. He remembered. But he could no longer feel the emotions that had driven him to it. And didn't want to. Now he was run by other impulses that cut him off from that past.

When he returned to his chamber, Toma was gone. She had wakened and returned to the women's quarters to begin her day. In a Berber community women had their own world, separate from the men. In this one it was not the inactive, confined world of the harem. That still existed, in both Arab and Berber Morocco, but it was a dying custom. Here, it had been discarded. Women were lovers as men were lovers: it was not a profession. They had their work to do: cooking and cleaning, farming the banks of the stream, tending the olive groves.

Toma would return to his chamber only when he sent for her to come. Not this night. Nor for many to come.

How many, he did not know, since he did not know the purpose of the journey on which he was about to depart.

Grayle threw open the shutters of his chamber. In the dawn light the colors of the land seemed lifeless to him. Mineral greens, dulled reds, threatening yellows. Even the vegetation along the stream, covered with dust, looked lifeless, though it wasn't. Only the stream itself was alive; not in its color, but in what it was—water, the life-bringer.

One had to look inside the fortress, in the courts and roof garden, to find colors that lifted the spirit: the bright colors of foliage, fruit and flowers, of tiles and painted wood. Miniature, artifical Edens, in memory of the one man had lost.

From the minaret of the village mosque, the cry of the muezzin began to summon the faithful to morning prayer. Grayle went to join the others in prostrating himself to the east, chanting that there was no God but God, and Mohammed was His Prophet.

He had accepted Mohammed without a qualm. God meant nothing to him, whether He was called that or Allah. And whether Mohammed was the Prophet meant less to him than what was in the mind of the Buddha-like Abd-el-Rahman.

The conversion had been accomplished without formality. It had merely been necessary to state his acceptance. Like most Berbers, Abd-el-Rahman was not overly strict in his observance of the Faith. He had demanded the statement of conversion only to avoid any trouble that might grow among his tribes from having a known infidel so close to their leader. When Grayle was with others he prayed and fasted when they did. Nothing more was expected of him.

When the prayers were done, Grayle joined Abd-el-Rahman, his son Youssef and Bou Idriss for the morning meal: hot broth and eggs, with flat corn bread and mint tea. It was Youssef that Grayle would be following on the mysterious trek to Marrakesh. He was, at thirty, a younger replica of his father: the thickset body and short, strong legs; the Buddha face; the straight, hard-edged way of thinking; the quiet way of expressing his thoughts; the understated certainty of being obeyed. He was the eldest of the three surviving sons from Abd-el-Rahman's wife.

He had had only one wife, though Muslim law allowed him more. As he'd once explained, with a dry mixture of good humor and good sense, "It is far easier to manage a thousand angry men than three affectionate women."

Concubines were another matter. They could not make the same demands on a man as his recognized wife. Abd-el-Rahman had had a number of them. The children they'd borne him were given the same status as those of his wife. The daughters, from wife and concubines, had all been given as wives to the leaders of other tribes, or their sons, to strengthen their ties to Abd-el-Rahman. The sons he had scattered to be educated in safe countries; a precaution hard-learned from his own youth. One was in England, two in Germany, two in Italy, one in America.

Only his eldest and youngest remained with him. The eldest, because he had to be trained to take his father's place one day. The youngest, because as the final fruit of his loins, he was especially dear to his father. His name was Ahmed, and his mother had been a slave. A young virgin of unusual beauty and tenderness, as black as Bou Idriss, who had discovered and purchased her from her mother. A present for his master, to stimulate his diminishing potency.

For a short time, it had worked: long enough for Ahmed to be conceived. His mother had died in giving him birth; thus guaranteeing her entrance into Paradise. The boy was now nine, and Abd-el-Rahman could not bear to part with him yet. But he was not present at this last meal before the journey. It was too solemn an occasion to be lightened by a father's indulgence of a high-spirited child.

Little was said during the meal. Only at the end did Abd-el-Rahman look at Youssef and say, "Come back to me, my son. You are dear to me, and I need your young strength." He shot Grayle a piercing glance. "I make you responsible for his safe return."

Youssef didn't like it. "My life does not depend on this man. I am in the hands of God."

"*Mektoub*," Bo Idriss murmured: one's fate has already been written.

"It has also been written," Abd-el-Rahman said flatly, "that this world is the booty of the cunning." He took Youssef's wide cheeks, so like his own, between his palms. "Be very cunning, my son."

Servants entered with kettles and towels to wash and dry their hands after eating. Youssef rose to his feet, and there was still some anger in the manner of his gesture to Grayle. "It is time. Come."

They rode from the fortress with Youssef in the lead, followed by Grayle and three Berber warriors. All five wore black camel's hair cloaks, old and ragged, over patched, dirt-stained djellabas, and much-worn sandals of plaited grass. Their mounts were seedy-looking donkeys, carrying double-baskets loaded with ripe olives. Their weapons were carried under the cloaks, where they were not conspicuous but close to hand.

On the other side of the valley was a vast slide of gray-and-white rocks. Skirting this, they rode up a mountain slope into a V-shaped cleft. Once inside its notch, they paused for a last look back at the stronghold of Abd-el-Rahman. Then they pushed on through the cleft, climbing by way of circuitous goat trails. By the end of that day they were inside the territory of their enemies.

Grayle woke that night with a knife at his throat.

22

Grayle felt the point of the knife first; and then the heavy hand placed over his mouth. He opened his eyes without moving any other part of him. In the dim moonlight filtering into the small cave he saw it was Youssef crouched over him.

Youssef saw the gleam of Grayle's opened eyes and withdrew the knife and hand. He touched a finger to his lips and rose slightly from his crouch. Not much, because the cave was too low for standing erect. Gesturing for Grayle to follow, he left the cave. Grayle gathered up his rifle and the cloak in which he'd slept, and crawled out after him.

The cave was one of a number of erosion pockets eaten into the clay slopes of a narrow ravine. Following Youssef past the tethered donkeys, and the holes in which the other three Berbers slept, Grayle checked the position of the stars. It was not time for his turn at night watch. Youssef still had more than an hour of his turn left.

The ravine made several twists. Youssef stopped in one of them and turned to face Grayle. He had sheathed the knife; but his rifle, picked up as he left Grayle's shelter, was held in both hands. He tilted his head at a flat-topped rock beside them.

Squinting, Grayle made out a small filled sack. "What is it?"

"Food for four days, and a can of water. Also, a pouch of gold coins and precious gems. The coins will buy you false papers, and passage to any part of the world you choose. A man like you can find ways to invest the gems and live out your years in comfort. Take it and go."

"On foot?"

"You found your way into these mountains to us on foot. You are clever enough to get out the same way."

"Why do you want me to go?"

"This is not the kind of life I want," Youssef said slowly. "Fighting like an animal. Probably dying like one. I cannot turn against my father, but I want him to make his peace with the French. For some reason I do not understand, your presence among us encourages him to continue fighting. I don't know why. But I do know that with you gone it will become easier to persuade him."

"And what will you tell him, if I go."

"The obvious. That you slipped away, during your turn at night watch."

"Why would I do that?"

"Who knows why a man like you does anything? Your reason for coming to us has never been clear. Your leaving would cause little surprise. I think you came in search of wealth." Youssef nodded again at the filled sack. "There it is. Take it and go."

"The bribe," Grayle told him evenly, "isn't big enough."

"You haven't looked."

"No. But I know it is not enough."

Youssef scrutinized his face in the moonlight. "Or, perhaps, it is that you don't believe my offer is genuine."

"Perhaps. In which case you could have a man posted to kill me, as I left."

"There is no one. I give my word."

Grayle's smile was thin. "The water in the can could be poisoned."

"I swear it is not."

Grayle let the harshness come into his voice: "This is a child's game. I am not a child. Nor are you."

"I see—you think the offer is only a tempting."

"I'm waiting to find out."

Youssef's smile held no more humor than Grayle's had. "You mean, if I kill you or not."

"If you *try* or not."

Youssef glanced down at the rifle in Grayle's hand, noting the way it was held balanced. Unperturbed, he raised his eyes to Grayle's face again. Finally, he sighed and lowered his own rifle in one hand.

"You are right—a child's game." He shook his head angrily. "I do not think that this test has proved anything, except that you are not stupid. Go back to sleep. You have another hour."

Youssef turned from Grayle and started up the slope of the ravine to resume his watch. Grayle moved to the rock and opened the sack. It contained stones.

Marrakesh sprawled on a vast, drab plain forty miles north of the High Atlas range, topped by the great Koutoubia minaret and surrounded by acres of irrigated palm groves. The three warriors Youssef had brought along as extra protection for their stealthy voyage did not enter it. They were left waiting some miles south, hidden with four of the donkeys, and all the rifles and swords.

Youssef had only his dagger as he approached Marrakesh on foot, leading the donkey on which Grayle's sagging figure was tied.

This city at the heart of Morocco, conquered and reconquered by the warriors of the Sultans, the Atlas and the Sahara, had for a thousand years been known as Marrakesh the Red. The reason the eight miles of fortified walls enclosing the old city were redder than most was never forgotten: their bricks had been made with a mixture of human blood. More than a hundred thousand captured enemies of the first Sultans had died supplying that blood. And the massive defense towers had been rendered invincible by the hundreds of heads embedded within them.

On the night of the full moon, anyone foolish enough to stand against one of these towers could hear the faint voices of those heads, begging for release. For unless a man's entire body were given a proper burial, he could never hope to enter Paradise.

It was late afternoon when Youssef reached the Bab Aguenaou, leading the donkey. But even if it had been late night of a full moon, Grayle was in no condition to hear voices so dim from the towers flanking the wide gateway. The gateway guards, advancing to ask their usual questions, were checked as Youssef cried out to them, pleading to be directed to a doctor inside. Grayle managed to raise his head a bit. What the guards saw made them back off hurriedly.

His face had a ghastly grayish hue, splotched with angry patches. Sweat poured down it, and his eyes were murky from the raging fever induced by the potion Youssef had given him to drink.

None of the guards was about to venture close to a disease that did that to a man. They wouldn't even risk looking at him directly again, after that first glance. With eyes averted from the donkey and its burden, they shouted and pointed instructions that would take Youssef to the nearest doctor: near the ruins of the ancient Bedi Palace.

Youssef passed between the towers into the city, and followed their directions until the gateway and its guards were out of sight behind him. Then he diverged, tugging the donkey after him into a shadowy side-alley. It turned into the oldest part of the densely built kasbah of Marrakesh, changing direction irregularly. At intervals there were narrow openings into dimmer passageways. Youssef turned into one of these, turned again and entered another.

Blank walls pressed in close on either side, broken only rarely by a locked door or shuttered window. The life behind these walls could be heard and smelled, but not seen. Deep within this maze, Youssef led the donkey on which Grayle hung into an even tighter passage. Here the walls seemed to lean overhead, allowing little daylight to enter.

It was a short passage, reaching a dead end at a heavy wooden door studded with large black nailheads and reinforced by thick bands of iron. Youssef pulled at a bent wire sticking out of a hole in this door. A brass bell sounded faintly inside. After some moments a peephole in the door was opened. There was more light inside than out, and a pair of eyes could be seen, peering through the opening.

"Tell Hassan," Youssef said, "that the son of the tree has come."

The peephole was shut. Youssef turned to the donkey and cupped a hand under Grayle's chin, lifting it to see his face. "Patience. You will have the antidote soon."

Grayle kept his teeth clenched and forced the words through them: "It better work fast."

Youssef's smile was benign. "Do not be anxious. The poison is not fatal in so short a time."

Grayle tried to curse him, but his throat had dried up.

When the heavy door was swung open the afternoon light came through it into the passage. Youssef pulled the donkey through, into a stable courtyard, and untied the rope from Grayle's waist. He called to the servant who was relocking the door to come help him. But when the man saw Grayle's face he stopped dead. Youssef snarled at him, but the servant stayed where he was, terrified.

Youssef locked his arms around Grayle and dragged him from the donkey. With a grunt of effort, Youssef lowered his sagging weight to the ground, as gently as he could. He snarled again at the servant, who edged over close enough to seize the donkey's lead-rope and take it quickly into a stable.

Getting out a small bottle, Youssef opened it and pressed the mouth between Grayle's parched lips. "Drink."

Grayle got his teeth around the mouth of the bottle and shut his eyes as the liquid burned his throat.

Resting on a rubber mat with his back supported against the wall of Hassan's hamman, Grayle took a deep breath of the hot steam as the last of the poison sweated out of him. Youssef brought a bucketful of water up out of the well and poured it over him, to wash away the last of the grime ingrained by the eleven-day trek to Marrakesh. Hassan, sprawled on one of the rubber mats, poured more tea into their glasses.

There was nobody else: only the three naked figures, perspiring in the lamplit steam. Hassan had joined them here because his hamman was the most private place in his house to get their business discussion over with.

Hassan was about forty, Grayle judged. A lean, balding Arab with a narrow face and hard, watchful eyes. His skin was pale and had acquired a softness from the easy years his wealth had bought him. But there was still a wiry strength in the way he held himself; and memories of harder years in those eyes.

In his youth, he had explained to Grayle, his knowledge of his descent from the Moors had inflamed his imagination and led him to seek out adventure.

"And profit," Youssef had added, softly.

"And profit," Hassan had agreed blandly. "Adventurers always seek something: money, women or glory. One of the three. I was not ambitious for fame, and only normally lustful. But I was, in my youth, very greedy. The poor are always greedy, and if cunning, they do what is necessary to satisfy that hunger."

He had won his wealth during the previous decade, as an agent smuggling supplies to the great uprisings of the tribes in the Riff Mountains, to the north along the Mediterranean coast. "Those were the exciting years." Hassan's eyes shone with the remembered glory. "It seemed then that nothing could stop us. When we swept all the way to Fez . . ." He finished with a sigh.

Grayle leaned forward to raise his glass from the brass tray. He drank the tea slowly. The ravages of the poison were gone from his system, but the taste lingered.

Youssef was regarding Hassan sardonically. "We? You are not a Riffian."

"True. But I was with them. And in the ecstasy of their victorious advance I did come to believe, at times, that I was one of them." Hassan took a sip of tea as the heady memories faded. "And then—we failed, of course. The Spanish had been easy. The Riffians almost drove them into the sea, as you know. But when they also turned south, against the French, the combination of enemies became too great for them. Their victories had made them drunk with power. All human ambitions should be carefully limited. Their final surrender was their awakening to this truth."

"And with that surrender," Youssef reminded him, "you stopped considering yourself one of them."

Hassan nodded, unoffended. "I remembered, in time, that I was an Arab businessman. Battles, victories, defeats—these are for warriors." He turned on Grayle a sad smile. "I, too, surrendered, when in 1927 I gave up all illusions of having a part in such things. I retired, from the fight, from politics. I bought this house. At times I buy a lovely young girl or boy, to renew briefly my own illusion of youth. I have enough wealth to last out my years. What more does a civilized man need?"

Youssef put down the water bucket and sprawled on one of the mats. "You need something more, it seems. Else, why have you at times sent word to my father, of the plans of his enemies against him?"

Hassan gave a rueful shrug. "At times a romantic nostalgia for the past overcomes my judgment. At such times it occurs to me that my comfortable life does not include something even a civilized man requires for his soul: a purpose for my remaining years. Then I find myself longing for the lost rebellion. Any rebellion. Such moods are ridiculous, of course. And soon over with. But, they induce the old excitement, when I hear the exploits of your great father."

"I have heard," Youssef said, "that when the Riffians surrendered, not all of the enormous quantities of arms they had captured were surrendered with them. Mountain artillery, mortars and machine guns, thousands of rifles and grenades, great stores of ammunition—all vanished. It is said they were taken secretly into the desert between Morocco and Algeria. And that they are still hidden there, awaiting another use, in another time."

Hassan took a slow sip of tea. "I, too, have heard of such a possibility."

"My father believes you may know where they are hidden."

"Your father is one of the few great men left in our world. Great audacity, luck and courage. And great wisdom. But in this matter he is mistaken. I do not know the hiding place."

"My father considered the possibility that he was in error about this," Youssef conceded carefully. "But he feels certain that if you do not know where these arms are, you have the cunning to find others who do know—and persuade them to sell their secret to you."

Hassan placed his glass neatly back on the tray, and appeared to consider. "If I am able to do this, it will involve great expense."

"This is understood. I have brought with me a small offering, to defray your first expenses. As to the final price, on delivery, you know that Abd-el-Rahman can meet it."

"Abd-el-Rahman is the favored of Allah. Words are bitter without money, and money a bauble without power. Your father is doubly blessed. But you understand that my search will take time. And it could be several months, between finding the arms and delivery."

"The need is not immediate. The arms are for the future, at the end of the coming winter."

Hassan inclined his head. "Then it is possible. How will we maintain contact?"

"When you locate the arms, send us word by the man you have used before. One of us will come, to work out the details of delivery. If it is not I who comes to you, it will be this man, Ishmael. Marrakesh is dangerous for the son of Abd-el-Rahman to visit too frequently."

"Truly." Hassan studied Grayle anew. "You are indeed a strange one for the great Abd-el-Rahman to choose to give such trust."

"Not yet, he doesn't." Grayle kept his face expressionless as he drank the last of his tea. But unease stirred in him. He was being allowed to overhear too much.

"If Ishmael is the one who comes to you," Youssef told Hassan, "he will bring back the ring you once gave my father, as proof that he has reached the stage of complete trust."

It was another test, Grayle decided. If he slipped away to pass on what he had learned here, only Hassan would be lost to Abd-el-Rahman. And the Berber leader had other agents, Grayle was certain, who were being assigned to the same search.

What *was* it that Abd-el-Rahman was waiting for to prove the validity of his dream?

Hassan rose to his feet and led them into an anteroom, where servants waited to towel them dry and help them dress. Youssef and Grayle were given silk robes and satin cloaks, slippers of embroidered felt. Hassan dressed much the same, except for the green fez, emblem of his title El Hadj, acquired by his pilgrimage to Mecca.

The three dined together in an upper room, reached via one of the balconies encircling the luxurious garden around which Hassan's house was built. After their meal, and the evening prayers, Hassan had servants conduct Youssef and Grayle to separate guest rooms. What Grayle found waiting for him was not entirely unexpected. Hassan had asked him, as they'd left the steamroom, if he had a preference between boys and girls.

The girl, resting among the cushions of the divan taking up half the small room, was perhaps fourteen years old. Her figure was concealed by the loose folds of a purple satin robe, fastened at throat and waist by silver buckles. She smiled as he entered and let the curtains fall together behind him. Rising gracefully from the divan, she stood beside a copper bowl filled with perfumed oils, warming on a small charcoal burner.

Her face had the darkness of a desert tribe; and a small, blood-red jewel adorned the ring that pierced her left nostril. But she was not tattooed. Her makeup was European: lipstick, rouge, mascara. And she spoke an unflawed French: "My master suggests a bit of diversion, to rest you from an arduous journey." Her soft voice, like her smile, was a practiced caress.

"Your master is a wise man."

Her smile deepened, creating tiny dimples at the corners of her small, delicate mouth. As she moved to him there was a tinkling sound, and he saw the tiny bells attached to the slim silver chains around her wrists. They continued to tinkle as she divested him of his clothing. He let her take his wrists and lead him to the divan. But when he tried to draw her down with him she stepped quickly back, roguishly shaking a finger at him.

"You must wait," she whispered.

Her slender hands went to the silver buckles at her waist and throat. A shrug of her shoulders, and the robe slid away from her, settling in folds on the Persian carpet around her bare feet.

There were slim chains around her ankles, too; and more tiny silver bells suspended from them. The adolescent slenderness of her budding figure was belied by a depth of experience in her calculating gaze.

She dipped both hands into the copper bowl. Judiciously, she observed his response as he watched her smear the warmed, perfumed oils into her firm, resilient skin. She did it slowly, until her supple body had acquired a silky, slippery glow. Then she dipped her hands into the bowl again.

Droplets of oil dripped from her fingertips and pointy nipples as she crawled onto the divan, pressing him back among the cushions and kneeling astride his hips. The jingling of the tiny silver bells took on a steady rhythm as her small, oiled hands massaged him.

When she left, two hours later, Grayle sprawled among the cushions staring sleepily through the small window beside his divan. A lamp burned in each minaret, guarding the Faith through the dark night. Every fiber of his being was relaxed and content; limp from the skills of her fingers, mouth and loins. Sophisticated skills, where Toma's were more primitive. Both gave joy; and the difference increased it.

The pleasures of the flesh: they drained the deeper poisons out of a man and left him whole again. He was ready for sleep, ready for the return trek to the mountains; eager for the fighting that was waiting there.

The Legion had given him the fighting, too, but without that special excitement. There, he had merely been one of a pack of wolves that had been trained to be a herd of sheep with a common purpose. And, with the years, he'd found himself functioning mechanically.

With Abd-el-Rahman the fact that he was different from the others—watched and judged separately, needing to use care with every word, every move—gave each thing he did a significance.

That this intensity of feeling was heightened when he staked his life against those of others, hacking at human flesh, did not trouble him. The pleasures of the flesh, he had learned, included destruction. It had a unique taste to it, that gave flavor to the other pleasures. So did construction; but that had been taken away from him.

Grayle reached out a hand and closed the shutters. He pushed the damp cushions away from him and slept deeply.

When they left Hassan's house the next morning, leading the donkey, they were once more dressed in their ragged djellabas and mountaineer cloaks. They did not head for the gateway by which they'd entered the city, but toward another where the guards would not remember them: the Bab Doukkala. Hassan had supplied them with a set of false papers to ease their passage out. And another set, for whichever of them returned when he sent word that the hidden store of arms had been found.

Their route took them to the edge of the great market square of Marrakesh: Djemma El Fna. The Meeting Place of the Dead—a name recalling a custom of the city's rulers, suspended only recently: the impaling of the severed heads of their enemies on stakes all around the square, where they could observe the carnival of the living that jammed this greatest caravan junction in Africa. Buyers and sellers from east and west, north and south; beggars, food vendors, child acrobats, holy men, musicians, public letter writers, storytellers, dentists, snake charmers.

Youssef and Grayle skirted the square, their hoods pulled forward over their heads to keep their faces shadowed. They stopped at the cubbyhole shop of a tobacco seller, for Youssef had a small vice to indulge. Going inside to buy a few packs of French cigarettes, he left Grayle waiting with the donkey. There was a stand outside, where Arabic newspapers were displayed. Grayle looked at them idly, not understanding printed Arabic.

A photograph on the front page of one paper held his attention: a young woman, squatting before a burning grass hut, holding a dead baby dangling in her hands. Her features reminded Grayle of Toma. But not the expression. The young mother was staring into the camera with an emptiness of emotion which verged into insanity.

When Youssef came out, Grayle asked him about the picture. Youssef scanned the headline above it and the print under it. It seemed, he explained, that Italy had launched a war to conquer Ethiopia. The picture had been taken in an Ethiopian village that had just been bombed by Italian planes.

Grayle realized, then, why the face of the woman reminded him of Toma. He turned away, following Youssef and tugging the donkey's lead-rope.

The news picture he had seen had been reproduced in magazines and newspapers around the world. It was one of the first from a photographer who had managed to slip around Mussolini's forces and reach the Ethiopian side of that uneven struggle: spears and ancient muskets against tanks and planes. It had been taken by Nora Cesari.

But Grayle knew only that it was from another war, on the other side of Africa. It could have been from another planet. He concentrated on the immediate dangers of his own war as they began the long return trek into the mountains through enemy territory.

23

Two days after Grayle and Youssef returned from Marra-kesh, Salah made one of his periodic reports to Abd-el-Rahman. During much of the time Grayle had been with the Berbers, Salah had been away, watching the progress of the road the French were hacking into the mountains. Grayle had twice gone with Salah to make detail maps of the immediate area through which the road had so far been pushed, and the area it would reach in the near future.

The most detailed were more than maps. They were scale drawings of certain sections in these areas. Every hill, ravine, cliff, and goat track was shown: the relative heights, depths, widths and points of access and cover.

Salah used one of these to indicate the exact point which the road-builders had reached, and the disposition of French troops and native irregulars guarding approaches to it. At intervals along the stretch of road cleared so far, the French had built small forts to hold it. Salah used one of Grayle's larger-scale maps to show the one nearest to the point the road had reached; and another now being con-structed ahead at that point, along the route the road was intended to continue.

Abd-el-Rahman switched his attention back and forth between this map and the more detailed drawing. He took from Grayle two other drawings: one of the area below the point the road had reached, another of the route ahead of it. He spread them out, to either side of the first drawing, scanning them in conjunction with the map.

Youssef, hunched forward beside his father, indicated one point on the map. "This would be a good spot to use the dynamite taken at Ouarzazate."

Abd-el-Rahman nodded, but gave no answer, continuing his study of Grayle's map and drawings. Bou Idriss remained in the background, saying nothing. He confined his advice to assessments of individuals and tribal problems. Military strategy was Abd-el-Rahman's department. If Bou Idriss had any opinions of his own on battle tactics, he gave them in private.

The new road had been allowed to progress so far without a single attempt being made to halt or slow it. Pinprick attacks were not what Abd-el-Rahman had in mind. These could only harass the road-builders, and delay their progress for a few days at a time. And at too great a cost to Abd-el-Rahman's manpower. The forces held in readiness at the French base of operations, where the road began, were too formidable, in terrain too easy to defend.

Abd-el-Rahman had continued to wait for over a year, while the road was pushed deeper into these mountains, ever closer to his own area of power. The farther the road progressed, the longer its single precarious supply line became; and the thinner its defenses had to be stretched to cover its increasing length.

Grayle could detect neither anxiety nor anticipation in Abd-el-Rahman's placid face as he studied the map and drawings. And there was no change in that expression when he finally gave his decision, in a calm, judicious tone.

"Yes. The time has come."

At this stage of Abd-el-Rahman's fight against subjugation, his most dangerous enemies were not the troops, mountain artillery and armed vehicles of the French army. Until the road was completed, these could not be brought to bear on him inside his own area. There were two other enemies more difficult to deal with.

The less dangerous of these two was T'hami El Glaoui, leader of the powerful Berber tribes controlling one of the three passes across the High Atlas chain: the Tizi n'Tichka. In return for allowing the recently finished road from Marrakesh to Ouarzazate to use this pass, he had been given enormous rewards. A fortune in cash. The title of Pasha of Marrakesh. Acknowledged prestige and power almost equal to the Sultan and the military commander of the French Protectorate.

His Berber warriors knew all the ways into the adjacent territory of Abd-el-Rahman. That they had so far failed to penetrate these ways was due to Abd-el-Rahman's spies, sentinels and mobility of counterattack. And, also, to the Pasha's lack of a strong incentive to wager and risk being beaten. Until the French managed to drive their new road into Abd-el-Rahman's territory, and could support the Pasha's warriors with heavy guns and armored cars, an invasion in force remained an invitation to disaster.

The other of the two enemies was the more dangerous: a group of French officers whose major weapons were their abilities to listen, analyze and persuade. They were part of the Bureau des Renseignements. Their job was to discover and exploit dissensions which could be used to divide rebel forces against each other.

Captain Labrune was one of these officers. He had been concentrating for some time on Abd-el-Rahman's *harka*: the confederation of tribes he controlled. Captain Labrune's ears were certain Berbers who had already been won over, and who had contacts with the edges of the *harka*. It was long after Grayle had joined Abd-el-Rahman that one of these Berber ears brought Captain Labrune news of an incident.

The incident had begun as a trivial thing. At the weekly souk in El Kelaa des Mgouna, a Berber village south of the Atlas, a vendor of amber had caught a man stealing from his wares. The thief was known to be mentally retarded. But the vendor had nevertheless beaten him with a stick. Relatives of the beaten man had flocked to his protection, and left the vendor senseless on the ground.

The families of the vendor and the thief belonged to different tribes. Anger triggered by the incident was gradually spreading between them.

Both tribes were allied to Abd-el-Rahman's *harka*.

Captain Labrune began by making secret contacts with both sides. Such simmering hostility had been used effectively in the past to split one tribe away from another. But that was not Captain Labrune's intention.

The major problem facing the French, as he saw it, was this: If they did manage, at last, to force entry into Abd-el-Rahman's territory, where were they to strike first? Abd-el-Rahman might be at his main fortress, or one of several lesser ones; or in any of a series of hidden cave systems within his domain. He might even be away from his home territory at the time of the strike.

Finding out where Abd-el-Rahman was at any specific time inside his area—or catching him when he ventured outside it—was Captain Labrune's concern.

Certain individuals in the two feuding tribes were approached. Substantial rewards were promised. What Captain Labrune was after was advance information on movements planned by Abd-el-Rahman. Having planted his seeds, Labrune sat back to wait for them to grow and bear their fruit.

He was still waiting when Abd-el-Rahman struck his first, long-delayed blow at the new road.

Abd-el-Rahman reached his first observation post: a narrow ledge just below the rim of a high cliff. There was an hour left before sunset. Detachments of his army were moving into their separate positions, miles away.

Three days ago he had gotten word from Hassan in Marrakesh: the hidden arms from the Riff rebellion had been located. But it would be a month or two before that supply of artillery, mortars, machine guns, shells and grenades could be assembled and delivered. For his first strike at the French road, Abd-el-Rahman would have to depend on intelligent deployment of manpower.

There were three prongs to his planned assault. The first was commanded by Youssef and three tribal chieftains allied to the *harka*. The second and largest force was composed of warriors from five other allied tribes; Abd-el-Rahman himself would take command of this one, shortly before the end of the coming night. The third force, which would spring the opening move of the rebel leader's gambit, was the smallest. It was commanded by Salah and Grayle.

The risking of the stranger whom Abd-el-Rahman knew

as Ishmael was deliberate. If the man survived, it would be one more indication that the interpretation of the dream was correct. If he failed to survive, it would prove that it was false.

From his perch on the cliff, Abd-el-Rahman could just make out, in the distance, the deepest point of penetration achieved by the French in the building of their new road. He held out a hand, palm up. The warrior beside him placed the binoculars in it. He raised them and focused on the area where the road ended and troopers were at work on its continuation.

The completed part of the road ran back toward the south from this area, cutting and snaking its way through the rugged mountains. It clung to steep slopes, climbed through clefts, dipped into canyons, twisted along gorges. For most of its length it followed trails used for centuries by caravans and herders of sheep and goats, widening and leveling these ways to allow passage for trucks and armored cars.

The work on the road was slow and arduous, accomplished by troopers with pick and shovel, sledge hammer and chisel. Dynamite was seldom used. Manpower was cheaper, and safer: in most places there was the danger of bringing down an entire mountainside.

Forts had been built at widely separated intervals to guard the road. They were little more than blockhouses, protected by low stone walls and barbed wire. Their garrisons were small: the minimum number of troops needed to patrol their own stretch of road, and hold the fort if attacked. Vital to the defense of each was its ability to signal for help, via wireless radio, to the other forts and the strongpoints at either end of the road.

One of these strongpoints was the supply base in the south, where the road began. The other was here, where the work of road-building continued. Abd-el-Rahman observed this strongpoint through his binoculars as that day drew toward its close.

The fort there had been built on top of a hill overlooking the road. A thick wall of stones piled to shoulder height enclosed the entire hilltop. Below it tangles of barbed wire ran completely around the steep slopes. Within the enclosure at the top were tent-shelters under which the work crews and patrols spent the nights—and a stone blockhouse with a corrugated iron roof, topped by a searchlight on a swivel mounting. There were three heavy machine guns and two pieces of mountain artillery.

Abd-el-Rahman shifted his binoculars away from the fort, to study the forces with which he would be engaged by late the following morning.

Beyond the bend, the gorge widened again. He made an estimate of three hundred troopers at work there. Most of them were hauling stones from the streambed; piling them against the side of a trail above, to widen it enough to serve as a road. Each worked with a rifle slung over his shoulder and grenades hung on his ammo belt.

Other troopers scouted the slopes at irregular intervals, to prevent infiltrators from reaching sniping positions behind the boulders. Abd-el-Rahman counted thirty-one men assigned to these foot patrols. He raised the binoculars to the heights above the gorge, patrolled by armed horsemen. Ten French cavalrymen. Almost forty mounted native partisans, provided by the Pasha of Marrakesh.

Abd-el-Rahman tilted the binoculars downward and focused on the most effective part of the protective setup: two armored cars, one on a partially completed stretch of road, the other atop a low hill. Each had a Hotchkiss machine gun that could be swung in any direction, poking out of the steel plating that protected it and its crew. Their range was over two thousand yards. Sufficient to stem any surprise attack by rebel cavalry; at least long enough for the work crews to scramble to cover, unsling their rifles and join in their own defense.

But Abd-el-Rahman had no intention of engaging them here. He had chosen his own field of battle, and his strategy was aimed at drawing them to it.

Lowering the binoculars, he rubbed his eyes and leaned against the cliffwall, waiting for night. There was no possibility of his being spotted there, even by an enemy using binoculars: the overhang of the cliff's rim above him cast a solid shadow over his ledge, impenetrable from a distance.

He watched the setting sun bathe the cliffs across the gorge, changing them into hazy curtains of pale gold and dark crimson, in which long splinters of white flashed like jagged mirrors. The shadows cast by rock formations lengthened across the bottom of the gorge, and began melting together. In the distance, a bugle sounded, and was heard by Abd-el-Rahman as a faint echo.

The work crews in the gorge formed up to tramp back to the fort. The foot patrols descended the slopes to join their weary march. The two armored cars and the mounted patrols swung away to reach the protection of the fort before dark.

And there they would all remain until the next dawn. No commander was crazy enough to send out patrols at night in these mountains. Until dawn, the land outside the little forts along the new road belonged to the rebels.

Abd-el-Rahman watched the sun disappear. The shadows in the bottom of the gorge joined to form a murky lake. In the cliffs opposite him the white streaks disappeared first. Then the colors went, swallowed by the rising darkness. Rock formations and broken cliffs appeared to swell as they blended into each other, becoming featureless black masses rising out of invisible depths, their looming heights indistinct against the night sky.

Turning, Abd-el-Rahman led the way back along the ledge, trailing one hand against the cliffwall as a guide. After some fifteen yards the ledge rose steeply. When he reached the top the fifteen warriors who'd been hidden through the day were already there, waiting with the ponies.

The warrior who'd been with Abd-el-Rahman on the ledge stayed behind, crawling between two leaning boulders to shelter through the increasing cold of night. The rest followed their leader, single file, as he rode a circuitous route to the last stretch of completed road. They mounted it at a point beyond the fort's probing searchlight.

Abd-el-Rahman took the road in the direction of the next French fort, back down the line. He pushed his mount hard, to check the timing. The pony was trembling, its chest heaving as it gulped air, when he finally reined to a halt.

The road snaked around a massive shoulder of mountainside. Unseen on the other side of that shoulder was the nearest fort to the strongpoint at the road's end. Abd-el-Rahman dismounted, gave his reins to the nearest warrior. The ride had taken him almost three hours. Now he knew what to expect the following morning.

He climbed the slope on the near side of the mountain shoulder, moving with caution. Moonlight showed him the way up, but at ground level the darkness was too solid to make out his feet moving through it. Twice he stumbled on loose stones, and once tripped over an invisible projection. Each time he recovered balance quickly, before the two men following close behind could reach out to steady him.

As he reached the top of the mountain shoulder a warrior materialized in front of him, rising out of the ground darkness. When he recognized Abd-el-Rahman he turned and led the way along a rising ledge. It ended at the top of a cliff. Grayle and Salah were sitting on the rim, with seven other men, gazing down at the road at the bottom of the sheer drop. They rose to their feet as Abd-el-Rahman reached them.

He moved to stand between Grayle and Salah, looking down toward the fort some five hundred yards beyond the mountain shoulder. Its blockhouse was darkly outlined by the moon and stars. Its slowly circling searchlight revealed glimpses of tent shelters and the outer defenseworks of piled stones and barbed wire. The fort was almost identical to the one at the road's end. But its manpower was considerably smaller.

"Have any reinforcements come along the road?"

"None," Salah informed him.

Abd-el-Rahman nodded with satisfaction. Lack of movement along the road meant that the movements of his forces had not been detected. He gestured at the fort. "What is its garrison now?"

"Sixty-two men, twenty-one horses, and one armored car." Salah grinned. "Enough to give us a hot morning."

Abd-el-Rahman placed a hand on Salah's shoulder, his other on Grayle's. "Fight well, tomorrow. Remember, death is a poison all must drink, and the grave a room all must enter. But only Allah decides each man's day of doom."

"I don't mind," Grayle said quietly, "if He decides to postpone it beyond tomorrow."

Abd-el-Rahman turned his head and looked at him closely. But he saw nothing in Grayle's face but an eagerness that matched Salah's. His own smile was gentle. *"Inch' Allah."*

"Inch' Allah," Grayle agreed.

Abd-el-Rahman left them, returning to his waiting pony. He rode back along the road, to the place, halfway between this fort and the one at road's end, where he would take up his command post.

When he was gone Salah said to Grayle, "You always speak as though afraid. Why, when you are not? You think as I do: life is an evil dream, and its end an awakening. Am I right?"

"Ask me again, if we awake together." Grayle turned away from the edge of the cliff. Salah and the others followed, leaving a signalman atop the cliff to observe the fort. They separated on the other side of the mountain shoulder, spreading out to take up their positions and await the coming day.

24

The signalman that Salah had left to watch the fort lay flat, peering down over the rim of the cliff in the early morning light. He watched as the single gate in the stone barricade was opened and two men hurried out to open a gap in the barbed wire beyond the wall. The signalman counted twenty mounted men riding single file out of the fort.

Ten riders wore the uniforms of the Foreign Legion's cavalry. The other ten were partisan warriors attached to the French army: they wore homespun brown djellabas, with red patches signifying their allegiance to the Pasha of Marrakesh. They rode down the slope and onto the road, heading for the place where the road disappeared around the mountain shoulder.

Pulling back from the edge of the cliff, the signalman rolled on his side and drew a small piece of mirror from inside his robe. Holding it in the palm of his hand, he let the sunlight catch the reflecting surface, directing the flashes toward a point above the mountain shoulder. Salah had a man waiting there to relay the signal.

Finished, the signalman slipped the mirror inside his robe, rolled on his stomach, and inched forward just enough to peer once more over the rim of the cliff. The last of the cavalry column was just moving past his position.

Lieutenant Tavernier was uneasy as he led the column. The morning was too silent, without even the cry of a bird. His eyes flicked up to the tops of the cliffs on either side, and returned to Corporal Vronski, riding well in advance as scout.

Vronski vanished around the bend ahead. Tavernier listened for a warning shot from the scout. None came. Increasing the pace of his mount, the lieutenant led his column around the bend.

There the terrain flanking the road gradually opened out. The left flank was unusable for cavalry: a short, sharp rise, littered with loose rocks at the base, ending abruptly against broken cliffs. But fifty yards farther on, the right flank became a series of disordered slopes. Though steep and broken by gullies, boulders and eroded formations, horses could negotiate it.

Vronski had reached the point where the column would begin the climb and had drawn up, waiting. He scanned the higher slopes on the right flank as the column trotted along the road to join him.

Grayle watched it ride past, just below him. He was tucked into a low, narrow space walled and roofed by slabs of stone, above the left flank of the road. On the other side of the road, where the column would make its climb, were the hidden forces commanded by Salah. Grayle's first job was on this side; with fifteen warriors hidden in holes all around him, and one crammed into Grayle's tight shelter with him.

This one's name was Hamid, and he was only seventeen, but already proved in battle. They were stretched out on the ground, their sides pressed together, their feet against the back of the hole, their heads just inside the opening overlooking the road. There was an opened tin of matches in Hamid's left hand. His right held one match, ready to strike. Grayle's hands rested lightly on two packs of explosives. Each had four sticks of dynamite tied together, along with a small stone for extra weight. Part of the dynamite looted from Ouarzazate.

Youssef would be using the rest of it, later that morning. Each of the packs under Grayle's hands was fixed with a very short fuse. It would be Hamid's job to light them, and Grayle's to throw. Abd-el-Rahman had considered no other man for this particular job. Grayle had learned to ride well enough, but would never match the average Berber horseman who'd been at it since childhood. He was a good shot with a rifle, but Abd-el-Rahman had several marksmen who were better. None of them, however, could throw with Grayle's accuracy. That had been determined in competition with hurled stones.

He dug his elbows into the ground and eased himself forward a bit, turning his head to watch Tavernier's column join the forward scout waiting on the other flank of the road.

The column started up the first slope with Corporal Vronski once more scouting well ahead. Legionnaires spread out to watch the flanks. The route they were taking avoided ridges and cluster-formations that might hide large numbers of rebel fighters.

Tavernier wanted to get to high ground before dealing with an enemy force of any size—if there turned out to be any to be dealt with. There never had been, so far, in all the months he had led these daily patrols. But he never grew careless; never took unnecessary chances. And this morning he was more alert than usual. The feeling of uneasiness was still there. He could find no cause for it, as they mounted higher, achieving the crest of one slope, and then another. Perhaps it *was* only the heavy stillness of the air, irritating his nerves. There was not a trace of breeze, even this high above the road.

They were half an hour above it when the route Lieutenant Tavernier had chosen brought them to a stretch so steep they had to dismount and climb on foot, dragging the horses after them. Tavernier was perspiring profusely when he reached the top: a long hump strewn with rock rubble. He did a careful scan of the surrounding terrain before mounting again. They were now too far up to get back down quickly if attacked. But he could detect no sign of anything moving in any direction, not even a wisp of dust.

Swinging back into his saddle, Lieutenant Tavernier led the column up the next slope. They were almost to the high ground he intended to use for the rest of the patrol. He checked the positions of his outriders. They were where they should be, surveying their assigned flanks. He looked up, and saw Corporal Vronski riding ahead, almost to the top of the last slope.

The first rifle shots blasted in that moment, from among the rocks on the crest above. Tavernier estimated five shots, blending together. Corporal Vronski was flung from his saddle. He struck the ground with the back of his head and shoulders, his left foot caught in the stirrup. His horse shied away, dragging the corporal until the foot was pulled free. His leg dropped stiffly, the broken branch of a dead tree.

Tavernier had drawn his pistol as he yelled the orders. He spurred his mount up the slope, swinging to the left. Behind him came the pounding of his Legionnaires' horses. They raced after him, strung out so each man became a separate, fast-moving target, difficult to hit. The native chief, Mustafa, was swinging his partisans up in the opposite direction. They would circle to close in on the snipers' position from two sides.

Tavernier glanced down at Vronski's body in passing: the side of the corporal's head was pulped. Tavernier topped the rise, bent low over his horse and instantly shifted direction to avoid being a predictable target. But no shots were fired at him. He took in the terrain with a swift turn of his head as his Legionnaires came up beside him. The position from which the snipers had killed Vronski was to their right, but the snipers were no longer there. They were sprinting away, dodging from one bit of cover to the next. Six of them.

Tavernier went after them, his Legionnaires spreading out to either side of him. But the pursuit of the fleeing snipers was abruptly interrupted. There was a heavy barrage of gunfire off to the right. Tavernier looked in that direction and saw Mustafa's irregulars racing toward him. There were only seven of them now, and they were being pursued by a dozen rebel horsemen.

Tavernier shouted to his men and changed direction,

racing to join Mustafa's dwindled force and take on their pursuers. But other rebel riders came into sight behind the first dozen: at least twenty more. Too many for Tavernier to take on. He changed direction again, to lead the way back down the slopes toward the road.

Rifles cracked below him, from behind widely separated rocks. A bullet burned across Tavernier's left thigh. He felt his horse break stride, and kicked both feet free of the stirrups before it sagged under him. He hurled himself away, landing on both feet as the horse fell beside him, narrowly missing his leg.

Shifting the pistol to his left hand, Tavernier drew his sword with the right. The way back down would be slow going, against too many well-entrenched snipers and with the rebel cavalry coming down behind them. He spun from the crest and shouted to his men, pointing with his sword at a low hill with a flat top strewn with rocks. The nearest bit of high ground to make a stand. His mounted Legionnaires spurred their horses toward it as Tavernier sprinted after them.

Rifles fired down at them from the top of the hill. There were snipers there, too. Tavernier kept going toward it. The hill was the only available point that could be held against superior forces. It had to be taken.

Ahead of him a Legionnaire fell backward off his horse. He hit the ground and came to a rest in an inert heap. Tavernier ran around him and kept going. Two of his mounted men had reached the hill and were spurring their mounts up its slopes from two sides. Each rider was working the reins with one hand and had a grenade ready in the other.

Halfway up, one of the horses collapsed with a scream of agony. Its rider threw himself free just in time to avoid being pinned under it. He fell on one shoulder, did a fast roll and came up on his knees yanking the grenade pin with his teeth. He threw it up into the rocks on top of the hill, a split second after the mounted Legionnaire on the other side hurled his.

The double explosion threw broken rocks and men from

the hilltop. And that was the end of the sniper fire from there.

Tavernier was the last to reach the top. His surviving Legionnaires were already behind the rocks, firing steadily at the rebel cavalry. One by one, Mustafa's warriors reached the hilltop, and their rifles joined in smashing the first ranks of the rebel cavalry.

The rebel charge broke apart, the riders circling to take cover at various points surrounding the hill. Salah had no intention of wasting his men by pressing home a charge against barricaded defenders. He was a hit-and-run fighter. Besides, Abd-el-Rahman's plan was not to wipe out the fort and its defense force. What he wanted was to have them held under threat—for a matter of hours.

The gunfire died away as visible targets disappeared. But it had been enough while it lasted, Lieutenant Tavernier was certain, to have been heard by the fort. Reinforcements would be on their way, soon. All he had to do was hold on here; and the hilltop was easily defendable, even against vastly superior attackers. If the rebels continued to surround it, they were going to be enclosed in a trap of their own.

The gunfire had been heard at the fort, and the fort's commander had already radioed for help.

Reinforcements from the farthest point, the base to the south, would take most of the day to arrive. But those coming from the fort at the road's end could get there in less than three hours. And they were on their way. In the meantime, the commander sent out his armored car and twenty foot soldiers to the aid of Tavernier's besieged force. That left the fort with just enough men to defend itself against direct attack.

The rebel signalman at the top of the cliff watched the armored car leave the fort. It was a formidable weapon, with its heavy machine gun and steel plates. It was followed by a mixed force of Legionnaires and native warriors.

The signalman pulled back from the cliff's rim and used his little mirror to flash the message to the high point above the mountain shoulder. The man waiting there re-layed the message to Grayle's forces below him by rapping a stone against a boulder. The rapping was passed on until each hidden rebel had gotten it.

Four emerged from hiding with iron bars, converging on a boulder that rested precariously on a ledge over the road. They dug the bars in at the base of the boulder, levering until it teetered forward and fell. It rolled down the slope and crashed to a stop in the middle of the road. There was enough room for men or horses to get past it, but not a car.

As the four men disappeared back in their hiding places, Grayle picked up a dynamite pack in each hand and wriggled forward out of his shelter. An armored car had one disadvantage: Its slits and peepholes did not make for good visibility above.

Hamid slid out beside Grayle, holding his matches ready. His eyes were shiny with excitement. He could hear the approaching vehicle.

It sped into sight around the bend seconds later. The driver saw the boulder blocking the road dead ahead of him and jammed on the brakes. The car skidded wildly beneath Grayle's position. It came to a jolting stop with the front bumper touching the boulder.

"Now," Grayle said.

Hamid struck the first match. The driver put the ar-mored car into reverse as the short fuse of the dynamite pack in Grayle's right hand caught fire. Grayle threw.

The dynamite landed on the road just behind the car, exploding as the car began backing over it. The force of the explosion lifted the rear of the car and hurled it to one side, its destroyed left wheel coming to rest on a hump of rock beside the road.

Grayle shifted the remaining dynamite pack from his left hand to his right. One of the car's doors was flung open and a man began dragging himself painfully out of it. Grayle said, "Now." Hamid lit the fuse and Grayle threw.

The man was half out of the door when he saw it falling. He ducked back out of sight inside. The dynamite hit the road beside the car and exploded as it bounced under it.

The blast heaved the car over, toppling it on its side. The opened door, torn from its hinges, landed in the road forty feet away. The opening remained, where the door had been, but there was nobody left alive inside the ruined vehicle to use it.

Grayle and Hamid slid feetfirst back inside their hiding place. They took up their rifles and waited.

The first troopers to come around the bend stopped at the sight of the destroyed armored car. Then, as others came up behind them, they sprinted forward and used the car and boulder as cover while they studied Grayle's slope. But they could spot no one there. The sporadic fire, between Tavernier's men and the rebels, was coming from high up the other side. The troopers moved around the fallen boulder and started up in that direction, spreading out with their rifles ready.

Grayle watched them climb the slopes. They did it right, mounting swiftly but using every bit of cover along the way. When they were far enough up, Grayle wriggled out of his hiding place and stood up. Hamid came out after him, watching the opposite slope as Grayle signaled with his raised rifle. The warriors assigned to him began emerging from their holes on his slope.

Grayle turned and worked down the slope to the road, accompanied by Hamid. They crossed it in a crouched run, and reached the other side without being fired at. So far, none of the troopers climbing above had looked back down. The other warriors crossed the road and spread out as Grayle started up. Then he heard a warning shout from above, and yelled his own warning.

His men sprinted to cover as the troops on the slopes began to turn and fire. Grayle dodged toward a pocket in the rocks to his left. A bullet rang off a boulder as he passed it, and flying splinters of stone tore his cheek. He jumped into the protection of the pocket. Hamid was in with him a split second later. Two other warriors followed him in. Another started to, but stopped abruptly and then fell forward on his face, without putting out his hands to break the fall. The back of his head was gone.

There was a sudden increase in the rifle fire on the slopes above. That would be Salah's hidden snipers, striking at the troopers. Caught between an enemy force above them, and another below, there was little question about which direction they would choose. Grayle raised up on one knee behind a rock, settled the barrel of his rifle across the top of it and waited for them to come.

Grayle's warriors began to fire from behind their widespread sections of cover as the troopers appeared, working their way down the slopes: Legionnaires and Berber partisans, with the Legionnaires in the lead. They came on spread far apart, each dodging from rock to rock. A pause to fire from behind each rock. Then a short dash to the next. Working from side to side; but each time a little closer.

Grayle caught a brief glimpse of a shifting figure and fired; worked the bolt of his Lebel and fired at another fast-shifting target. Legionnaires. His own. He thought he should feel something, about killing and being killed by his own. But all he felt was the need to stop them; to survive them. Grayle had chosen sides, and the Legion was now the enemy.

His rifle was empty. He rammed in a fresh box of five cartridges, worked the bolt and triggered a shot at a Legionnaire dashing from a slab of rock to a boulder. The runner stumbled, then kept going. But his ability to control direction was gone. He rammed against the boulder, bounced away from it and fell backward. Rolled over in the dust and lay still.

Grayle worked the Lebel's bolt-action, ejecting the spent cartridge and slotting a fresh one into the fire-chamber. He switched his sights to follow a figure in a djellaba, shot and missed as the partisan dove behind a rock. Working the bolt, he steadied the sights on the rock and waited. The partisan charged from behind the rock and Grayle shot him off his feet.

Eject, switch, fire. Eject, switch, fire.

Reload.

There was an explosion off to the left of Grayle's

pocket, where some of his warriors had taken cover. Then howls of agony were wiped out by another explosion.

The Legionnaires were tossing grenades now. Some of them had gotten close enough for that. Grayle saw another grenade arc high, spinning toward his pocket. He threw himself facedown in the dirt, arms crossed over his head. The grenade exploded in the air somewhere above him. A fragment ripped through the back of his djellaba and gouged flesh from his ribs.

It burned, but that was all. He was still there.

Allah determines your day of doom.

He came up on his knees, grabbing his rifle. Hamid lay sprawled beside him, bloody pulp where his face had been. On the other side of Hamid's body a warrior was crawling aimlessly, his guts trailing in the dirt under him.

Other grenade blasts, off to the right and left. More dying cries.

Christ, the Legion knew how to fight.

Grayle drew his bayonet and fixed it to his rifle. The pockets had become death traps. Those who survived drew swords and knives and launched themselves out at the enemy. Grayle went with them.

He held the Lebel firmly with both hands the way he'd been taught for the bayonet charge: rifle up and out, the sharp point leading the way.

A rebel warrior ahead of him was engulfed in a cloud of dust as exploding grenades fell beside him. His shredded arm spun out of the blast, the hand still brandishing its sword. The warrior rolled on the ground, rose on one knee and toppled backward. Grayle jumped over him and charged in through the rocks hiding the enemy.

But those enemies, Legionnaires and partisans, were having to divide their attention now. Salah's cavalry had reached the fight and closed on their rear. Rifles and grenades sought the bigger targets: explosions shredded ponies and riders together. Shot ponies went down, smashing their riders under them. But other rebel cavalrymen managed to fling free as they fell, landing on their feet with their swords slashing.

Grayle dropped to one knee as a partisan rifleman twisted to fire at him from three yards away. The bullet whipped past his eyes, plucking the hood of his djellaba. Grayle fired from the knee. The man's head was kicked to one side and the rest of him followed it. Grayle launched himself off the ground and dodged around the next rock.

A rifle blast deafened his right ear and scorched his cheek. He spun to the right, hacking awkwardly with the bayonet. A partisan stumbled away from him, rifle spilling from his hands as they groped at his torn throat.

Grayle vaulted a fallen pony and charged a Legionnaire unhooking a grenade from his belt. He drove the bayonet into the man's side before he could pull the pin. The Legionnaire's legs buckled and the bayonet was dragged down with him. Grayle yanked it free and dropped to his knees beside the dying man.

He grabbed at the Legionnaire's unused grenades with his left hand, stuffing them into a food sack tied to a rope around his waist. An enemy partisan came around a boulder to his right with a blood-streaked sword, saw him and twisted, drawing back the sword for the slash. Grayle tilted the Lebel one-handed and triggered the shot. The blast and recoil jerked his arm back. The slug rammed the swordsman's chest, slamming him backward. He fell stiffly, as a cut tree falls. Grayle rose to his feet, his hands automatically working the bolt of the Lebel while his eyes and mind registered the shifting situation in his immediate area.

What was left of the enemy was scattering now, discipline disintegrated by the rebel cavalrymen hacking at them from three sides. Grayle put his back to a boulder and dealt with any who came at him. Off to his right several of the enemy scrambled behind a pile of rocks. A rebel cavalryman charged the position, swinging to get behind it. He was met by a three-rifle barrage. The shots thudded into the pony's chest and neck. It went down headfirst, throwing its rider through the air.

Grayle snatched a grenade from his food sack, pulled the pin with his teeth, counted aloud and then lobbed it. The grenade dropped behind the rockpile and exploded before any of the three could get away.

The thrown rider was shoving to his hands and knees, shaking his head groggily. Grayle saw then that it was Salah, and started for him. But something struck the calf of his left leg, ripping it out from under him. He sprawled on his face, spat out dirt and rolled over. Pushing himself up to a sitting position, he ran his left hand over the place where he'd been hit.

The shinbone was snapped, the broken ends poking up through the skin. Grayle found he was breathing harshly through clenched teeth. But the pain was not terrible. Mainly, the leg seemed unusually heavy, not quite part of him. He let go of the rifle and used both hands to deal with his leg. Pulling with all his strength at the separated sections of bone, he managed to tug the broken ends apart. He shoved down hard, trying to force them back together in proper position, and passed out cold.

He came to leaning back against a hump of rock with his legs stretched out on the ground in front of him. There was no noise. The first thing he saw was that the lower part of his left leg had been set and tied with crude wooden splints. He raised his head and saw Salah squatting before him. Beyond Salah rebel warriors moved among the corpses, gathering weapons, ammunition, grenades, boots, clothing. He had slept through the end of the fighting.

Salah grinned at him. "I thought at first that you had awakened from this evil dream without me. But then I saw you only had this." He gestured at the broken leg.

"It is enough," Grayle said. "I won't be of much use for a while."

"A long while," Salah agreed blandly. "Shall I shoot you like a crippled pony? Or tie you on a donkey so you won't fall off if you faint from the pain on the way home?"

"It is an inglorious way for a warrior to leave a battle."

"Our part in the battle is finished, anyway. It is time to leave."

Grayle nodded. They had served as a lure to draw the forces at the road's end in this direction—to the point where Abd-el-Rahman, Youssef and the other chieftains were waiting to deal with them. That was the place where the real battle would take place. And by now it had probably begun.

By that night, Grayle figured, he would probably be hearing the result.

He did hear of it, and often, in the two months it took for him to walk properly again. The story of Abd-el-Rahman's great victory at the road was told and retold by the Berbers, embroidered on and woven into legend.

The strongpoint at the road's end had sent everything it could in answer to the radioed call for help, but its trucks and armored cars speeding to the rescue had been blown off the road—together with a stretch of the road itself by the dynamite looted from Ouarzazate. The French cavalry and the Pasha's mounted partisans had arrived in time to spot Youssef's group carrying off arms and ammunition from the fallen vehicles. Pursuing Youssef, they'd been led into a dead-end canyon, with hundreds of rebel marksmen entrenched on both sides of them. Turning to get out, they'd found Abd-el-Rahman himself behind them.

It was said, later, that less than a dozen of those who'd entered that trap escaped alive.

By the time the massive reinforcements from the French base in the south arrived, it was dusk, and the rebel forces had vanished. Night made pursuit impossible, and by the next dawn it was too late. Abd-el-Rahman's warriors were back inside his stronghold, with its narrow, easily defended entrance passages. The French high command, and the Pasha, could only count their losses—and the loss of face. Accompanied by the increase in Abd-el-Rahman's prestige and power.

An even heavier loss, from the French viewpoint, and the most important gain, from Abd-el-Rahman's: the road could not be extended by another inch that year.

The new work force had first to repair the part that had been blown up. And there was nothing left for a road to cling to, along the cliffside where the dynamited one had been. A longer stretch of road had to be built: descending into the canyon, and up to the other side of the gap. It took three weeks to finish. By then the first snows of winter were hitting the Atlas Mountains. There could be no further road-building until the following spring.

And Abd-el-Rahman was looking forward to that spring. By then he anticipated that his attacking power would have been strengthened tenfold, by the arrival of Hassan's heavy weapons.

25

But if the French road-building was halted by that winter, the activities of Captain Labrune for the Bureau des Renseignements were not. Labrune continued to exploit the feud between the two tribes allied to Abd-el-Rahman's *harka*, using it to extend his network of Berber spies. This infiltration finally netted him informers in the very heart of the Berber stronghold. Winter was close to its end when one of these passed on the kind of information that Captain Labrune had been working for.

Abd-el-Rahman was preparing to lead a large caravan out of his area, east to the undefined desert frontier between Morocco and Algeria. The informer did not know the purpose of this trek, except for a rumor that it was to meet another caravan. Nor did he know precisely where this meeting was to take place. But he did know when Abd-el-Rahman intended to start out, and part of the route that would be used, once he was a good distance east of the mountains.

Grayle was able to walk almost normally by the time the caravan set out to take over the heavy arms from Hassan at the meeting place in the Jebel Bechar. Though he still limped, daily hikes had restored the leg muscles which had withered while the broken bone had mended. But when the caravan set off for the east he was not part of it. He was kept behind as part of the fortress defense force, along with Abd-el-Rahman.

It was an expedition which Abd-el-Rahman had expected to lead. But he had been struck down by a lung ailment, and was still bedridden with a fever when the time came for the caravan to leave. The meeting in the Jebel Bechar could not be postponed. So it was Youssef who took out the caravan.

After it had gone, Grayle continued his daily hikes. The limp improved steadily. But the place where the bone had broken and mended ached like a sore tooth when he became overtired or there were drastic weather changes. Another reason to remember Victor Royan.

The long inactivity of that winter chafed on him as spring drew near. But he had found ways to relieve that, even while he'd still been moving around with the aid of crutches: exchanging banter with the women working along the stream, coaxing stories from Toma about her childhood on the other side of Africa, attending village wedding celebrations that went on for days. Many of his evenings he spent in the village below the fortress, trading stories over glasses of tea. These people knew how to enjoy the small, passing pleasures of their short, hard lives. They had a strong sense of play, and loved stories, telling them with elaborate detail and listening to new ones with excitement.

A favorite tea-drinking companion was the Dream Master. The old man explained the lore of Berber myth and magic, and the ways it gave life and death a meaning. In return Grayle came up with Dante's various hells and purgatories. Others crowded close when he spoke, for they loved to hear of strange matters, and Grayle's special knowledge was stranger to them than the Dream Master's.

Before long Grayle had a position among the villagers as their new spinner of tales. He described lands and cities that were more distant than the moon for them, and told of his adventures on the sea few of them had ever seen. But their favorite tales were those he retold from Shakespeare and Plutarch. These were stories that fitted their own concepts of life, greed, lust, struggle, glory and death. Grayle found himself an eagerly awaited guest at village gatherings, and he fed himself on their zest.

The other change for him had begun well before the battle at the road. He'd begun to summon his slave, Toma, to his chamber less often. Her pride was hurt, and she showed it with increasing flashes of resentment, which Grayle ignored. It was simply that, with time, his desire for her had died, as though she were a toy he'd played with too long.

That didn't surprise him. He had experienced the same, often enough, in the years before Nora: sex without a genuine passion soon lost its stimulation for him. Lacking that, it was variety he required; but he was forbidden to tamper with the village women. In the Legion he'd slaked the demands of the flesh with an occasional prostitute. What he needed here, Grayle decided, was a new slave girl—and for that he'd have to be patient until an opportune trip took him to one of the secret slave markets.

Grayle was still hobbling about on makeshift crutches on the day he chanced to catch Toma flirting with a handsome young warrior named Ali. They faced him with a mixture of defiance and fear. Toma shared many of the rights of Berber women, the right to own property and the right to demand separation from her man. But as a slave she was Grayle's property; until she was sold or freed, sexual betrayal could be punished with death by stoning.

When Grayle gave Toma away in marriage to Ali, and did not replace her with a young boy, the Berbers drew their own conclusion. They had known such men, and such actions, before.

"Celibacy," the Dream Master explained to him, "is often the first step along the path. Regard the Moon, who beds with his bride, the Sun, only once each month: when he is full, and at his strongest. Even that once, her ravenous appetite for his flesh leaves him so thin and weak it requires another month to recover his strength. So too did *I*, who once delighted in fleshly pleasure, depart from women for the life of mind and spirit."

"At what age?" Grayle asked him.

"I was—oh, perhaps fifty."

"I am only thirty-six."

"Ah? I thought you much older."

For the rest of the Berber village, also, Grayle's celibacy

combined with the rumor that he was among them because of a dream of their chief—and belief in his holiness became commonplace. Even for Toma. She had mocked him at first, but no longer did. When they met now, she bowed with respect, even awe.

Grayle smiled and kept the truth to himself. He expected they'd be disillusioned soon enough.

Three weeks after Youssef had left with the caravan, Grayle made a journey with Salah, who continued to come and go as Abd-el-Rahman's best gatherer of intelligence. They slipped southwest to Taroudant, the great walled city below the Atlas Mountains. Grayle posed as Salah's deaf-mute assistant as they settled in as sellers of sheepskins and Berber rugs they'd brought along on two donkeys.

They spent three days and nights there, listening to the rumors that filtered through the labyrinthine passages of Taroudant's ancient souk. Grayle was preparing to visit its hidden slave mart with Salah on their third night when they heard a tale that sent them hurrying home.

But the news had reached there before them.

For more than a month, Abd-el-Rahman had been waiting with increasing tension for word from the east. It had come, at last, brought back by survivors of the ambushed caravan. Though his wounds were severe; Youssef had led their stealthy retreat until the last few days. Then it had become necessary to carry him. He was no longer conscious when they reached the fortress.

The reception chamber had been stripped bare of cushions, divan mattresses, carpets. A heavy candle burned at each corner of the room. The droning voice of the Dream Master, rising and falling without pause as he read aloud from the Koran, seemed muffled in the drifting smoke of agal-wood and gum-lemon incense. Youssef lay on a palmetto mat in the middle of the room, with his head turned so he faced toward Mecca. The Dream Master, sitting cross-legged on the floor against one wall, did not alter the cadence of his reading when Grayle entered.

The recital of the Koran would continue uninterrupted

until the coming of dawn, in three hours. Then it would cease, when Youssef would be carried out, headfirst, to the waiting coffin that had been painted with saffron. But the four candles in this room would be left alight, to burn themselves out during the day that followed. Long before then Youssef would have been swiftly buried. For the dead, the Prophet had said, long for their grave, so they may reach happiness and put wickedness behind.

Youssef had died only an hour before Grayle and Salah had returned. In conformation with the words of the Prophet the preparations for burial had been finished in that hour. The body had been ritually washed, and dressed in its seven items of burial clothes. The needles and leftover thread from the sewing of the clothes had been cast in fire. Youssef's big toes had been bound together so his legs would not spread apart. His thumbs were tied together on his chest and his mouth bound shut with a fold of his burial turban. The shroud in which he was wrapped, the seventh item of burial attire, was knotted shut at both ends. Salt had been sprinkled about the room against evil spirits. An unsheathed dagger lay on his abdomen for the same purpose. For evil ones, it was known, feared five things: salt, sharp iron, incense, light and holy words. All were there in the room, to protect the corpse that was to have become heir to Abd-el-Rahman.

As Salah had done before him, Grayle squatted beside the mat, touched the shroud with three fingers of his right hand and raised them to his lips. As Salah had, he intoned, "May God be merciful to you, noble warrior."

Out in the open court, women groveled in the powdery snow that covered the paving tiles, howling and weeping, scratching their dung smeared faces and bared breasts till they bled. It was forbidden by Islamic law, for death was a visitation from God; but the custom was older than Islam, and persisted. No man cried, however. That would have been unseemly, undermining the dignity of the death.

Even the women ceased crying when they entered the room to pay their last respects to Youssef, for each tear would give pain to the dead. Within that room only children could weep. Children's tears extinguished the fires of hell, long enough for the dead to pass through unscathed.

Grayle remained squatting beside Youssef for a time, his eyes fixed on the glint of candlelight along the blade of the dagger resting in a fold of the shroud. Then he rose and left the dead man and the droning voice behind.

He went out past the wailing women and silent men fitfully illuminated by two torches. The sharp cold of the mountain night made him close the front of his heavy sheepskin cloak and pull its hood over his head, around his face. Bou Idriss waited beyond the torchlight, a squat, shapeless mass in a similar cloak. In the deep shadow it was impossible to make out the expression of his fat, black face. They mounted the narrow, enclosed stairway, to the roof terrace.

Each star glistened like a bright bit of ice in the night sky. Each snow peak of the surrounding mountains was distinct, glowing with reflecting moonlight. The tangy odor of charcoal-and-dung fires rose in the frosty air from the smoking chimneys of the village under the fortress. Abd-el-Rahman stood at the low wall, watching the constellation of the Great Bear rise above the peaks.

What grief he carried within him was concealed under layers of stoic concentration. His face might have been part of an ancient olive tree, gnarled and furrowed, standing without movement against the power of a storm.

"It has come," he said matter-of-factly. "The time of my dream; the time of wild dogs and ravens."

"And the black olive remaining on the tree?" Grayle added. Puffs of steam issued from their mouths when they spoke, fanned past their faces by a light breeze.

Abd-el-Rahman gave him a sharp look. "Have you understood the significance of the dream, then?"

Grayle shook his head. "Only that you've been waiting for something it foretold. And that the black olive could signify your youngest son."

"You have guessed well. The olive is Ahmed."

"But I don't understand my part in it."

"You are the snake that struck at the birds."

Grayle considered the details of the dream. "To keep them from eating him . . ."

Abd-el-Rahman nodded. "Your time has come, also."

"To do what?"

"Youssef's caravan was ambushed as it passed south of Ain Chair and north of Talzaza, through the land of the Bani Gil nomads. A great force was waiting there: French troops, warriors of the Pasha, tribesmen of the Bani Gil."

"So I have been told."

"They were waiting," Abd-el-Rahman repeated. "They had advance knowledge of the route the caravan would take. There are spies within my *harka*. Not a whole tribe, or my own spies would have detected it. Only some individual men. Who they are, and how many they are, I do not know yet. But it means the rot has begun. It will grow, unless I can stop and cleanse it. If it grows it will end in killing me."

"That was what they intended with the ambush. Until the last moment you were to have led it, not Youssef."

"That was the first attempt. There will be others. And if I die, who will take up my fallen sword? That is a question my enemies ask, even as I do. I have already sent word to my sons in Europe, warning them to see to their own safety. And telling them that my black olive—the one remaining fruit on the tree of my dream—will succeed me."

"Ahmed is only ten years old."

"The babies of dead scorpions can grow to sting, in time. As I did. My dream tells me that it is Ahmed who will one day carry on for me. And you are the one who will take him to safety, so he can live to do so. Bou Idriss will be your guide. I have chosen warriors to go with you; each a man I am sure of. They will be your protection, and Bou Idriss your adviser. But *you* will be the leader. Any decision you make will be obeyed by them, always. Everything has been prepared. You will leave now, before the dawn."

"Your enemies will be watching at all passages out of this area."

"Tonight you will not go so far as to be detected. You will go to a place known to Bou Idriss, and there you will wait, hidden. After we bury Youssef in the morning I will lead my forces out, in another direction. This will draw my enemies after me. By tomorrow night it will be safe for you to continue your journey."

"You told me once," Grayle reminded him slowly, "that one must always fight *with* the odds, never against them. If you lead your men out now you are violating that. They are expecting you to avenge the ambush. They'll be waiting for you to come."

"But where? I have told no one what I intend. So their spies cannot give advance warning. Where will I strike? No one mounts an assault in these mountains while the snow still lies in the passes. But there is the desert, and the Bani Gil, who must be punished for their part in the ambush. Perhaps I will strike first at them. It would be logical, do you not agree?"

Grayle didn't like the undertone. "As you have said, no one can launch a mountain assault through the snows."

"So it is believed," Abd-el-Rahman said blandly. "In any case, I must strike—somewhere. The loss of the caravan, and my son Youssef, causes some to believe Allah has withdrawn His blessing from my destiny. Already there are deserters: the warriors of the Ait Umnasf and the Bani Mohammad. There will be more, unless I can restore faith in my *baraka*. For this I must achieve a terrible victory. It must be attempted immediately."

It came to Grayle, with a rush of shock, that the Berber leader's need to test his *baraka* meant that he, himself, feared it was gone. Abd-el-Rahman had counted too much on the arrival of Hassan's heavy weapons. The failure had confused him. What he intended now, Grayle realized, was a deliberate against-the-odds challenge; a weighing of his fate on a supernatural balancing scale. Because only an improbable victory could restore his own faith in himself.

Though it didn't show in the Berber's face, Grayle knew he was looking at a crumbling will—and he was bitter. He had given his own fate to this man; a man too ready to accept disaster fatalistically. A man who was already abdicating to a future foretold in a dream.

As if reading Grayle's thoughts, Abd-el-Rahman shrugged his heavy shoulders. But his expression did not change. "A horseman has always an open grave before him. But if that or victory lies before me is no longer your concern. You will take my youngest son to safety; and gain what you have been waiting for."

"If you know what that is," Grayle told him, "you know what I do not."

"You have been waiting to regain your past, that has always been obvious. Wealth will buy back your own destiny. That wealth lies ready for you, in the place where Ahmed will reach safety. A fortune in gems has been hidden there for you, in the cliffs of Rhoubi, near Biskra. Ahmed knows the hiding place. Only he, no one else. Not even Bou Idriss. So the life of my youngest is now in your hands; and your future in his."

"My future has nothing to do with my past. That cannot be regained, as I have explained." Grayle was startled by the strength with which he'd come to believe what he said next: "Any destiny I have left is with you."

"You are wrong, on both these points. First, you underestimate the alchemy of wealth. Second, you are not a true follower. Others follow me because they need someone to follow; even if they are led to the grave. But you—you are a man who must finally cast your own dice. That is your character, and your fate. And my dream." Abd-el-Rahman removed his cloak, and held it out, waiting.

Grayle knew the ritual. He held back for a moment, and then angrily took off his own cloak, exchanging it for that of the Berber chief. Each put on the other's cloak. It was the first part of the swearing of an oath between two men.

Abd-el-Rahman extended his right hand. Grayle took it in his, linking his fingers through the other's thick, stubby ones. Abd-el-Rahman tightened the grip: "By these ten joined fingers, you shall take my youngest son to his place of refuge."

Grayle said the words required of him: "By these ten I swear this oath, even to the grave of the Prophet."

Abd-el-Rahman released his hand. "Go with Bou Idriss. Go now." He turned to the old black eunuch who had been his guardian, teacher and adviser. Even then his expression did not change, though the two men looked at each other for some time.

It was Bou Idriss who finally spoke, and his voice was strained: "This world is honey mixed with poison."

"So it is said . . ." Abd-el-Rahman turned and walked away from them.

That was the last Grayle saw him: as he passed between his slave bodyguards and disappeared into his chambers where no light showed.

26

A gazelle's skull rested on a shallow shelf near the top of the low lava hill. Delicate and pitted by erosion, its whiteness was almost luminescent against the black of the rock. Grit scraped under Grayle as he approached. A horned viper slithered out from behind the skull, and swiftly vanished into a fissure. Grayle climbed past the skull, and there, just above it, the quarter-moon was framed by a notch at the top of the hill, growing transparent in the dawn sky.

A snake, a skull, a slice of curved moon.

Grayle wondered what the Dream Master would have made of such a conjunction of omens.

East of him a furrowed volcanic plug thrust into the sky, towering above the lava hills that rolled away from it in every direction, coiling into sensual shapes that gleamed like dark flowing oil. Beyond that solitary, eroding tower, gold streaked the lavender flush along the horizon, preceding the coming of the sun.

Grayle shivered in the bitter night-cold rising out of rocks and turned to look back the way they'd come. The dawn light was spreading quickly across the gravel flats beyond the hills of lava, reaching for the night that still shrouded the western horizon. Raising his binoculars, Grayle studied the plain they'd finished crossing last night. There was no sign of anyone coming after them; which could be good or bad. Unless a message came to them today, or tomorrow at the latest, they would have to go the rest of the way without knowing if their danger was extreme or no more than usual.

So far their evasion route had been a compromise be-

tween the two. They were fifteen days southeast of the Atlas Mountains. A long swing away from both their starting
point, and their ultimate goal, which lay east and north. But
to have headed that way directly would have been too great
a risk. This was a time of shifting alliances. They could not
be sure which tribes might have become enemies; or might
betray their direction to enemies.

So they had swung south, avoiding oases, settlements,
military patrols, nomad grazing lands and normal caravan
routes. Whether they had swung far enough south now depended on the success or failure of whatever it was that
Abd-el-Rahman had attempted. This area of dark hills was
the last place a message might come to tell them of this.

From here there were several directions to choose from.
Which they took would be dictated by the contents of the
message; or the lack of one.

Grayle lowered the glasses and started back down to
where the others were breaking camp, loading and saddling
the couched camels.

He had ten warriors, all of one family; desert veterans
from the south, closely related by blood to Abd-el-Rahman.
Bou Idriss and the boy, Ahmed, made it twelve. And there
were sixteen camels: powerful, long-legged bulls that had
been bred and trained for speed, strength and endurance.
The extra four carried some baggage, including the disassembled parts of the two tents, but mostly heavy loads of
filled waterskins. A camel might survive as long as fourteen days without water. A man, for perhaps one day.

A snake, a skull, and a slice of curved moon. Grayle
conjectured again on the possible significance of the three
portents in one place.

He had the answer shortly before dusk.

They picked their way all that morning between the hills
of black lava-rock. The cloudless desert sky was a vague,
pale blue, merging into yellowish white around the huge
golden disk of the sun. Everything under that sky was
black: the hills, the sand, the dust their slow progress
stirred up.

The one who led the way was always Umar ben Hamid

al-Hadj. He was father, brother, uncle or first-cousin to each of the other warriors, and their chief. He kept a scout out some distance on either flank. The rest followed him single file.

Grayle usually brought up the rear, turning regularly to scan their back trail. Umar al-Hadj had come to depend on him to carry out this duty with the aid of the binoculars.

Bou Idriss stayed halfway between them, in the middle of the file, together with Ahmed. On the move or at rest, they were always together. Bou Idriss even slept with the boy, a revolver and dagger close to hand. Ahmed had a dagger of his own, and a Lebel repeater; and he was already skilled with both. A slim boy, tall for his age. His black features, once full of mischief, no longer cracked a smile. It was not anxiety, Grayle knew; it was the gravity of the boy's acceptance of the responsibility his father had placed upon him. He seldom spoke, except to Bou Idriss.

Umar al-Hadj would confer with Bou Idriss and Grayle, when the need arose; and consider their opinions seriously. He would even defer to Grayle's, if held strongly enough against argument. Bou Idriss was a wise man, whose thoughts were to be respected; and Grayle had a tinge of magic about him. But Umar al-Hadj was their guide on this journey. He knew this desert, and much of the Saharan wastelands farther south, as few men did.

He was a stocky, harsh-tempered man of about forty, with short, strong legs and wrinkled, leathery skin. His movements were lazy, energy-hoarding, and he thought and spoke slowly; but his squinty eyes never ceased roaming the horizons. Most of his adult life had been spent leading slave caravans across the Sahara for sale to the Arab dealers. Until the French had won their victory down at Tindouf, and put an official end to the slave trade, overlooking the fact that their most important ally, the Pasha of Marrakesh, owned more slaves than any other single person in Morocco. The trade had become a furtive one, profitable for only a few dealers. Umar al-Hadj had switched to smuggling other goods, supplementing that income with loot acquired fighting for Abd-el-Rahman. But it was lean pickings, compared with his past.

He intended to go into another business, with the reward waiting for him when Ahmed was delivered safely. Abd-el-Rahman depended on his blood loyalty, but had been practical enough to add the incentive of material gain much greater than could be obtained through betrayal.

They broke camp each day just before the sun came up and rode through the lava hills for two hours, then walked for the next two, leading the camels by their headropes. Along the way they picked up the dry twigs and roots of any plants they spotted in passing, together with the droppings of their camels. Mixed, these provided the only fuel for fires to be found in the desert. Walking or riding, Umar al-Hadj kept the group to the same slow and steady hiking pace, calculated to reserve the stamina of men and animals over many weeks of desert travel.

It had taken Grayle four days to learn to control his camel, mount it with ease and ride it for hours with a minimum of discomfort to buttocks and spine. But once he had become accustomed to staying aboard the sheepskin-padded wooden saddle, the steady rocking became pleasurable, lulling him into dreaminess.

It was the same for the others. They dozed much of the time as they rode; jerking awake briefly if their camel stumbled, or to scan the surrounding distances. Even when walking, it was in a half-doze. Their conscious minds were dulled by the virtually featureless monotony of the desert; and by their slow crawl across its dwarfing immensity, their stopping places seldom different from their starting points.

Grayle's mind drifted to what might be done after he delivered Ahmed to his destination. There would be no going back to Abd-el-Rahman, he knew. That was not influenced by whether the Berber leader achieved victory or defeat. Neither, as Abd-el-Rahman had made plain, was any longer his concern.

His time with the Berber rebels was finished, and he had to adjust his thinking to fit that. He reminded himself fiercely that his original purpose in joining the rebels had been to find a way out. That had been all but forgotten as he'd linked his life with the Berbers and found a new purpose in their cause. To fight and achieve something among these people; and be remembered for it by them when he died. It would have filled a void.

But now Abd-el-Rahman was offering him a way out again—and no way back.

He did not share Abd-el-Rahman's faith in the alchemy of wealth. But he was going to have to find what could be done with it, if he survived. He considered the possible ways, as he rocked half-asleep on the plodding camel, and as he trudged on foot leading the animal, his mind driven inward by the crawling monotony of the pace and scenery.

The lava hills petered out into low, isolated mounds drowning in washes of black pebbles. The line of camels and men crunched past the last of them onto a brownish-gray plain that spread without a break to a dead-level horizon.

Grayle pulled his hood over the turban wrapped around his head and lower face, tugged it forward to shield his slitted eyes from the sun's glare and stopped chewing on problems so remote. The future narrowed down to the next source of water, the next bit of shade.

It was eleven that morning when they made their midday camp, setting up the tents for protection from the sun. Though it was too early in the year, and they were not far enough south, to experience the full weight of heat that the Sahara could deliver, they did not move on again until three in the afternoon. It had not been more than eighty degrees at noon, Grayle judged; but it had felt hotter, after the thirty degrees of the previous night and dawn. And the sun's rays, with no air moisture or vegetation to filter them, struck at living tissues with an intensity that could do damage, even in the spring.

Also, it was good to establish sound habits. The farther south they went, or the deeper they got into summer, or the more reason they had to suspect the nearness of enemies, the more they would travel by night and less by day. The sun, men of the Sahara said, was always on the side of the hunters; for it enabled them to see their quarry across a vast area.

"Four things the open desert cannot hide by day," Umar

al-Hadj quoted darkly, "a walking man, a camel, smoke and passion."

It was an hour before dusk when one of their outriders spotted something coming after them. Umar al-Hadj halted their column and walked away from the dust it had stirred up to have a look. Grayle took the binoculars and followed.

Umar al-Hadj squinted in the direction his scout was pointing. "A man with three racing camels."

All Grayle could see back there was a low cloud of dust in movement. He used the binoculars: three camels, one rider, coming from the direction of the lava hills they'd left behind that morning. As he sharpened the focus of the lenses they drew to a halt. The rider forced his mount to its knees and slid off, couched one of the other camels and swung onto it. Then came on again, moving faster.

One man; so it was not pursuit but a messenger. Umar al-Hadj went back to the column to prepare tea. Grayle stayed where he was and continued to watch through the binoculars. When he joined the others they were grouped around a small fire on which a kettle was coming to the boil.

"It's Kaddour ben Salah," he told them.

They made camp for the night where Salah had caught up to them; there was a decision to be made before they went any farther.

Ahmed did not cry. His small, thin face hardened when he took the news. His voice trembled with the only words he spoke: "Then I *must* live—to drink their blood someday." But he did not cry.

He stood a little apart, watching silently, while the others sat around the small fire and Salah told them how Abd-el-Rahman had died. Grayle looked at the boy and didn't like what he saw. The face was too young for such lack of expression under such a weight of emotion.

Bou Idriss showed more than the boy. He seemed shriveled inside his eunuch's fat. The old face had crumpled, the eyes lost in mourning. But his voice had been harsh, as he looked first at Umar al-Hadj, and then Grayle: "One thing this does not change. The wealth promised you when Ahmed is brought to safety. That was arranged long ago. Betrayal would earn you a small reward. Very small, compared with what is hidden in Biskra, waiting for you to fulfill your oath."

When he had been sure they understood this, he had fallen into a private silence. He sat staring into the fire, only half-listening to Salah's account, communing with his sorrow.

Salah told the first part with relish. The revenge strike Abd-el-Rahman had mobilized had achieved a stunning victory for him, and a crushing defeat for the Pasha. Incredibly, he had managed to get his force through the snows of the high passes and reach, without being detected, the Pasha's ancestral Atlas fortress of Telouet. Launching a surprise dawn attack, they had fought their way inside its defense walls in less than two hours.

Since the Pasha's winters were spent in his palace in Marrakesh, the revenge could not be executed directly on his person. But the rebels had killed every man among Telouet's defenders, including an uncle of the Pasha, two cousins and a nephew. Everything breakable had been destroyed; everything that would burn had been put to the torch. The treasure vaults had been looted. Over ninety prisoners had been delivered out of the Pasha's dungeons. And the village belonging to the fortress had been left in flames when the rebels departed.

But the spies within Abd-el-Rahman's *harka*, though they'd been unable to tell the French where he intended to strike, had been able to report that he was going *somewhere*. The French had not attempted to anticipate the direction of Abd-el-Rahman's assault. Instead, the Legion had been sent through the mountain snows, on a trek as daring and unexpected as the rebel leader's had been. Dragging along mules loaded with machine guns and disassembled mountain artillery, the Legion forces had reached the most likely entrances to Abd-el-Rahman's domain, and settled in to await his return.

The victorious rebel force had appeared the next day,

winding its way back home. Entering one of the prepared traps, it had been smashed apart by the artillery fire from both sides. Even then, Abd-el-Rahman had been magnificent. Rallying the survivors, he had almost succeeded in breaking through the ambush.

"And then," Salah said heavily, "the hand of God opened, and Abd-el-Rahman fell from it."

The artillery fire started an avalanche. The snow slide blocked their exit. Abd-el-Rahman's men had panicked as they fought their way in the other direction. It was then that a cannon shell had torn both of Abd-el-Rahman's legs away.

Salah had been close behind him when it happened. "He died quickly. Without pain."

Bou Idriss raised his head, and some of his own pain lifted.

"Before he died," Salah went on, "he told me to race to the lava hills back there, and tell you what happened. He said you should know that now every tribe will be making its submission to the French. And eager to curry favor with them. None can be trusted any longer. He said that your only safety now lies in not being seen. By anyone."

Umar al-Hadj made an unpleasant sound, deep in his throat.

Salah looked at Grayle. "Abd-el-Rahman also told me, before he died, that if I succeeded in bringing this message you would reward me with four stones of great value. A diamond, a ruby, a sapphire, an emerald. He said you could give these, and have enough left for your own needs."

"You will have them," Grayle said. "When we deliver Ahmed at the appointed place. That is where the gems are."

Salah frowned. "I thought you had this treasure with you."

"No."

"This the old fox did not tell me." Salah sighed. "Well, it seems, then, that I must help you get the boy there."

"When you do, you get the stones. You have my word."

Salah smiled at him, and the scar that ran down his face crawled with it. "I will help you keep your word, be sure of it."

Bou Idriss spoke finally, his eyes on Salah. "Did others hear Abd-el-Rahman tell you where to find us?"

Salah shrugged. "There were others near us. Perhaps some heard."

Umar al-Hadj growled, "If they did, they will have told the French when they surrendered. To prove sincerity."

"I am the only one who came," Salah pointed out. "And none were coming after me. I checked my back trail, with care."

"The danger," Bou Idriss said, "lies ahead of us."

"No one could have come faster than I did. Certainly none could have passed me."

"Every military post has a radio," Grayle said. "If they know our direction, by now all the posts ahead will have recruited the tribes, with bribes and promises, to spread out and watch for our coming. Wherever we go, we have to go to water, eventually. That is where they'll wait for us. At every waterhole, east and north of here."

"If we have to fight for water," Umar al-Hadj said, "we are too small a force. You should not have come alone, Salah—just because you wished to keep the reward for yourself. We could use some of your warriors."

"They all are dead, slave trader. Or fled. Or making their submission. To the Pasha, the Sultan, the French."

Grayle studied Salah without appearing to. "But not you."

Salah smiled again. "I am a practical man, as you know, Ishmael. Abd-el-Rahman is no longer a power, and one must make terms with a changed situation. But he mentioned this wealth to be had if I brought the message. I can make my submission later, after I have the stones."

Grayle nodded, satisfied. He turned to Umar al-Hadj. "Some days ago you spoke of a well you know, down in the Erg Occidental."

Umar al-Hadj nodded, but his expression tightened with worry. "Due south from this point. Twelve days. It is in the great sand dunes."

"Along an old caravan route that is no longer used, you said."

"That is so. It is used now only by raiders and smugglers; those anxious not to be detected in their movements. There are no settlements, forts or military patrols, anywhere in the area. An empty place."

Salah made a hissing noise. "A place of drought. There has been no rain there for six years."

"But there is this well," Umar al-Hadj said. "And there was water in it, the last time I passed that way."

"And when was that?"

Umar al-Hadj hesitated, his worry growing. "Two years ago."

Salah shook his head. "Two years without a drop of rain falling. The well may be dry now. *Probably* it is dry."

"It is the only way we can go," Grayle told them. "East and north, the odds are that they're waiting for us. We have to go south to that well. And *then* east again; and north when we're east of the line where they'd expect us."

"I would rather fight men," Salah said. "One might survive a fight. No one survives a well without water, so far from any other source."

"If the well is empty, there'll be just enough left in our waterskins to get back to the well due east of this point."

"To the fight you are avoiding now," Salah pointed out. "And then we and the camels will be too weak to fight properly."

"Even if there is water in the well," Umar al-Hadj worried, "there are the raiders who use it. If we meet any of those, these camels of mine are worth their fighting for."

"*Inch'Allah*," Grayle reminded.

"As God wills it, certainly," Salah agreed. "But to go that far south is to act with an arrogance that may strain His indulgence."

"We have to chance it." Grayle looked to Bou Idriss for support.

But it was the youngest son of Abd-el-Rahman who spoke first, his tone firm: "We will go south."

Bou Idriss looked at the boy sharply, appeared about to

speak and then held his silence, studying Ahmed thoughtfully.

But Umar al-Hadj rounded on the boy furiously. "This
is a discussion between men. When your father lived,
Ahmed, you were armed by the shadow of his greatness.
Now you are only a child. You must speak as a child, mod-
estly, and only when asked to speak."

"I forgive that," Ahmed said gravely. "Because it is true
I am a child; though it will not always be true."

"Umar," Grayle reminded quietly, "it was you who first
spoke of this well in the south."

"True. And now we speak of the dangers involved."

"Danger lies in any direction we take."

"It is a matter of picking the one where the danger is
least."

"South," Grayle said.

Ahmed said, "I will change my words, since they caused
offense. *I* will go south. Or wherever Ishmael chooses to
go."

Salah was more amused than offended. "You think this
foreigner knows more than I? Or than this old slave trader
who was born to the desert and has made the pilgrimage to
Mecca?"

"No," the boy told him, "I think only that I must go
where Ishmael thinks best, in order to live."

"Dreams, boy—they may turn out true or false."

"My father dreamed of his destruction in the fullness of
his power. Was that false? In the dream his power passed
to me, because this foreigner insured my survival. I go with
him. You others must go where you will. As was said, I am
but an insignificant child now."

Bou Idriss broke his silence at last: "I go with my master's son—and Ishmael."

This left no choice for the others. Ahmed *was* only a
child, but a golden one. For the others, the promised rewards depended on reaching safety *with* him. Salah gave
Grayle his hideous grin. "You win without proving yourself
right. The boy's faith is your power."

Umar al-Hadj nodded irritably. "Enough. We go south."

"Don't worry," Salah mocked, "Ishmael knows best."

"I know nothing. It is a gamble."

"But," Bou Idriss said softly, "there is a reason for your choice, even if you do not know it." He stood up stiffly, his age asserting itself into his weakness. He turned to Ahmed, placing a hand gently on his shoulder.

Just as gently, the boy took hold of the old man's wrist and removed the hand. He touched the cheek of Bou Idriss with his fingertips, and then went inside a tent to lie down alone.

Salah slapped Grayle's knee and climbed to his feet. "Whichever way we go, it is a guess and a gamble. One with a dream behind it is at least something."

When it was Grayle's turn for sentry duty that night, he crawled out of the tent and saw Bou Idriss sitting in the open, wrapped in his sheepskins. He sat with his back to the camp, watching the subtle reshaping of the night's landscape by the infinitely slow moving of the moon.

A swirl of night wind stung Grayle's cheek with cold grains of sand as he walked to the huddled figure. After a moment he repeated the words Bou Idriss had spoken to Abd-el-Rahman.

"The world is honey mixed with poison."

Softly, not looking up, Bou Idriss answered as Abd-el-Rahman had:

"So it is said."

They broke camp with the coming of dawn. As they started south, Umar al-Hadj scowled at Grayle:

"You will not like it down where we go, I tell you that."

27

The twelve days south to the well stretched to sixteen. Much of the southern end of the journey was through dunes, which slowed progress. The deep sands had spread farther in two years.

Also, it got hotter. And the air became drier, with the slightest vestige of moisture sucked out of it. Their skin cracked and precious sweat was robbed from it even though they wrapped themselves in head cloths and long, hooded robes.

The amount they drank increased alarmingly. Yet to ration water intake was to court certain death. What was lost had to be replaced. Dehydration sapped body efficiency and thickened the blood. And beyond a certain point came the descent into dizziness, muscle spasms, dimming vision and delirium. They drank what they had to. It increased to more than a gallon a day for each.

Finally they traveled only by night. The moon was swelling to fullness, and the stars seemed to expand and lower. The nights no longer contained real darkness. Moonlight showed the way clearly; and the shadows were less dense than those thrown by the sun during the day. They made camp shortly after dawn; those not on sentry duty stayed inside the tents, with the flaps open for air. They moved on again only at the approach of sunset.

But even by night the air was as dry as the inside of a vacuum. And their water consumption was still enough to cause a steady shrinkage of the goatskin waterbags.

It was the worsening condition of their camels that became the real cause of anxiety. Camels could go a very long time without drinking if they had fresh brush and grass for grazing. There was none here. On their scant, dry rations two weeks was close to their limit, even for these specially bred bulls that had started out in prime condition. They grew gaunt; their jellylike humps dwindled and became flabby. By the fourteenth day Grayle knew they'd never get to the next source of water if there wasn't enough in this one to restore the animals and refill the goatskins.

Great outcroppings of rock surged out of the sands in the distance ahead, tilting in diagonal rows, their blunted snouts and splintered spines silver and black in the starlight. Umar al-Hadj quickened the pace and sent a couple scouts racing in advance, with two camels each.

One of the scouts returned to meet them as they entered between the rows of outcroppings, and reported the way ahead clear. Umar al-Hadj sent him forward again, and led the others in after him.

The separate outcrops gradually merged into parallel escarpments. The prevailing desert winds had swept the ground between them clean. They were moving now over a walled avenue of hard-packed pebbles. In places the cliffs lowered, and the sands from outside lapped over them. But as Umar al-Hadj took them in deeper the walls on either side rose higher, the masses of rock behind them spreading out.

Their avenue descended steadily and merged into the floor of a wide canyon, carved through the heart of an undersea mountain barrier by surging currents back when the Sahara had been the bottom of an ocean greater than existed now anywhere in the world.

That dawn they did not make camp. They stopped only long enough for the daybreak prayers and a brief meal, then pushed on. Their gaunt, weary mounts moved faster, smelling what they needed ahead.

An hour before noon they reached a short, dead-end side canyon. Posting a lookout past the opening, and another on their back trail, Umar al-Hadj turned into it, sending a third lookout climbing to the heights above.

The place they entered was like an amphitheater, and there was blessed shade across much of it. Brown grasses and camel-thorn thrust up out of a mixture of sand and rock-rubble.

Their mounts immediately spread out to graze as the riders slid to the ground. The enclosure was littered with old camel dung, and some not so old. The place had been used steadily over a long period, and also quite recently. Which meant the almost certain presence of water—and danger. Salah caught Grayle's look and nodded, glancing upward to make sure the sentry above was in position.

The greatest concentration of camel droppings was around a flat rock the size of a large tabletop. Two of Umar al-Hadj's nephews dragged the rock aside, revealing the mouth of the vertical shaft it had protected. One of his cousins unhooked a weighted leather bucket from his camel and tied it to the end of a two-hundred-foot coil of rope. The bucket was lowered into the hole.

There was less than fifty feet of the rope left to unravel when the bucket finally hit water. Salah gave a low hiss of relief. But not complete relief. Sometimes good wells became unusable because of the seepage of mineral poisons into the water.

The filled bucket was drawn up. Umar al-Hadj scooped water from it with a tea glass, and examined it critically. The water was clouded; but that could be just rock-sand and dust. Umar al-Hadj sipped it into his mouth. He swished it around his tongue, tasting thoughtfully. Finally, he swallowed. Then he waited, looking at the others as though half-expecting to be struck dead. It was perhaps fifteen seconds before he nodded curtly. "Not delicious, but drinkable."

The camels were watered first. It took hours, pouring one bucket at a time into a rock hollow that formed a natural tub, then lowering the bucket for more. The animals slurped it up as fast as it was poured. Just as their capacity for going long periods without water was incredible, so was the enormous quantity they could absorb at one time when they finally got to it. Grayle estimated that each drank at least two hundred pints before Umar al-Hadj decided they'd had enough for the time, and began the refilling of the goatskins. By evening the bodies of the camels had already converted the water they'd consumed; they were once more sleek, fat and strong, their humps firm.

And that evening, when the time came for the last of the day's five sessions of prayer, the men did the ritual washing of hands and faces with water, instead of the sand they'd been using for weeks.

So much water taken from the well, and still there was no indication they'd reached the end of its supply. The source, Salah told Grayle as they set up the tents, had to be the Wadi Zousfana, the river that emerged from the mountains of the Ksour and then disappeared under the ground, resurfacing for ten miles at the oasis of Taghit before sinking again beneath the sands.

"I think," Umar al-Hadj announced contentedly as they lolled on the ground against their saddles and packs when the night meal was ending, "that we will rest here some days."

"Not too many, slaver." Salah gestured at the mounds of camel droppings around the well. "This place is too popular. The only men who would move through this kind of land are those with reason to hide from government patrols."

"Like us," Ahmed said.

Salah turned his head and eyed the boy without affection. "Like us. But that will not make them our friends."

On their third morning at the well, the lookout above reported about twenty mounted camels approaching from the northwest.

While the others struck camp, Umar al-Hadj took Grayle's binoculars and went up for a look. When he came down he hurried the loading and saddling of their camels.

"They are not soldiers," he told them. "But not merchants, either. No baggage or cargo carriers, only riding camels. And each rider carries a rifle. A pack of raiders, beyond doubt."

He led them out of the canyon, and turned east where the dunes resumed. The camels snarled and roared with anger as they were taken into the ferocity of the lifting sun.

Some turned their necks to try biting the legs of their riders; they had to be slapped back with camel-sticks.

"How far to the next water?" Grayle asked the caravan leader as they dismounted to pull the camels up the hard slope of the windward side of a great crescent dune.

"Ten days, unless the dunes have spread farther in that direction, too."

Bou Idriss looked back with a frown. "We leave a trail easy to follow."

Umar al-Hadj gave a scornful grimace. "Those camels that pack of raiders have don't look to be a match for mine. And ours are rested and well watered, while theirs are worn out and drained by thirst. They have no chance of catching up to us."

So it proved. They reached the next waterhole with no sign of pursuit. Even so, they stayed at this waterhole only twenty-four hours before pushing on. Still going eastward, but tacking according to the location of probable water ahead.

There were changes in the monotony of the landscape, but each change became a new monotony. They finally ascended out of the dunes, onto a denuded plain strewn with eroding rocks. For twelve days they crawled over it, stuck in the exact center of an immense, perfect circle, the horizon a curved level line in every direction. Part of Grayle's brain stayed with his eyes, attuned to danger signs. Another part began ransacking museums and old churches, and feeding on their art treasures. Memories he had shut out for almost eight years. Now, with nothing but the endless broken rocks for his attention to cope with, the vivid, detailed images flooded in to fill the vacuum.

The camel under him plodded on steadily. His body rocked from side to side, while he wandered galleries of the mind.

They crossed a desert of red sand; another paved with fistlike stones of black oxide. He saw Ambrogio Lorenzetti's Sienna mural of Evil.

Three days crunching over brittle fragments, the scree of shattered cliff-remnants that were all that was left of mountains wind-blasted to sand and blown away.

Cimabue's *Virgin with Angels*.

Nine days through mixed dunes, salt pans and sandy basins.

The blazing colors of Van Gogh's small bedroom.

Four days across a table of hard-packed, multicolored pebbles, polished flat and smooth by the grinding of wind-hurled sands. A vast mosaic which cast millions of weird reflections under moonlight, and by day became tiny dazzling mirrors impossible for the eyes to endure.

Munch's lovers.

Nora Cesari . . .

They turned due north, into an area which the government map Grayle carried showed as a vacant space, with a few dots representing oases and a couple of meandering, broken lines indicating uncertain dry wadis. There was nothing to show wells or natural waterholes.

Umar al-Hadj had marked the locations of those he knew about. Printed dots and penciled crosses: on the emptiness of the map they looked like nothing. In the actual emptiness of this dead world they were everything.

They had gone a long, long time without encountering other travelers, but the signs of recent passage were there: small groups—and one numbering perhaps forty camels.

Salah studied the tracks, and the signs around the ashes of campfires. "Not a caravan. Too many riders, not enough cargo carriers."

Forces from the northwest, still searching for them this far south? Or raiders, hunting for prey among caravans carrying illegal and thus valuable loads?

Umar al-Hadj inclined to the latter. "The big group and the smaller ones could be the same. A big raiding party, splitting into small hunting packs, ready to summon the others if the quarry is too well defended for one to deal with."

His opinion was confirmed when they came upon the leftovers of a battle that had been fought around a waterhole along a dune approach to another waterhole.

Human and camel corpses, slowly being buried by breeze-carried sand, were shriveled but not yet polished skeletons. It had been recent. The human bodies had been robbed of their clothing. Some were women; and all of these, like some of the men, had the features of races that lived below the Sahara.

"Slaves," Salah growled. "On their way to market."

Umar al-Hadj nodded, and found a brand that could still be made out on the neck of a dead camel. "The mark of Ali Awlad Sidi Shaykh. Many times I worked with him, bringing slave caravans over this desert. An old Arab, born into the trade. He would not give up the old ways."

He moved among the camel corpses searching, until he found one with a different brand. "Aieee . . . this is the mark of the Asasa branch of the Awlad Jarir, famous as warriors and raiders. But I have never known them to raid this deep in the southeast."

"Too many French patrols in the north lately," Grayle pointed out. "That could be forcing them south for their loot."

One of Umar al-Hadj's nephews, a young man named Mustafa, gestured at the corpses. "This could be a good thing for us. These Asasa raiders will have left to sell their loot to the buyers from Arabia."

His uncle threw him a look of contempt. "You know nothing of transporting slaves. Only a few armed warriors would be necessary to escort the slaves they took here. In this dry land these slaves will walk in any direction their guides say the next water is waiting."

He scanned the great circle of horizon anxiously. "Believe my word, most of this Asasa raiding party are still close, encouraged by this success to seek another."

Bou Idriss was squatting over the corpse of a small child. Ahmed stood watching as the old eunuch scooped away sand covering the dead child from the waist down.

It was a boy, and he had been castrated.

"This one," Bou Idriss said in an odd voice that was almost nostalgic, "was worth more than any of the others, male or female. A eunuch of the correct age to begin his training in his duties."

He stood up slowly, gazing down at the small corpse. "So, too, did I come over the desert, after my wound was healed. I was five years of age."

"Did it hurt terribly?" Ahmed asked him softly. "To be castrated?"

"Very little. They gave us drugs to make us sleepy, and the pain seemed small, and far away. And they nursed us carefully, afterward. For we were worth much. Even so, we were nine boys, and after the operation five died within a few weeks. I was stronger."

They moved on with even greater wariness than before, their scouts sent far in advance.

They were well inside the Algerian frontier, though there had been nothing to mark the crossing. The land continued with the same varieties of disintegration. The sky, too, remained the same: a clamped-down lid of white glare by day, a star-littered cover of frightening beauty at night. And between land and sky, the same drifting mists of dust and heat-haze, trapped between layers of different air densities, through which distant views became distorted optical illusions.

Two days of interminable flatness gave way to the visual relief of isolated monuments lifting abruptly out of arid steppes: naked hills and crags, blunt-topped buttes, spires rising to sharp steeple-points. Between them dust devils swirled around smaller sentinels of stone that had been sand-blasted into grotesque forms.

Umar al-Hadj led the way among them into the beginning of a dry wadi. It meandered north, in the general direction of the next source of water. As they followed its course the bed deepened, until the banks were higher than the head of a mounted man, providing the protection they sought. It hid them from distant watchers. Dust churned up by their passage through the wadi could be mistaken for wind-drifts or shifting heat-haze. The wadi also gave them shade: close to the east banks in the early morning, the west banks in late afternoon. During the direct overhead sun-glare through the middle of the day, they sheltered in caves eaten out of the base of the banks by water that had rushed through the wadi when rains fell once every number of years.

Toward dusk, Ali, who'd been scouting ahead, rode back to meet them with the bad news.

"The trail of many camels and men," he told them. "They crossed this wadi, going in the direction of our waterhole."

"How recently?" Umar al-Hadj demanded.

"I think . . . that it was not long ago."

They looked at each other. Their eyes had become sun-inflamed holes in masks of caked dust and dried sweat. Even Salah's scar was almost invisible.

"A caravan?" Bou Idriss asked in a voice that had become weak and raspy. "Or a raiding pack?"

Ali spread his hands in a helpless gesture. "I . . . am not sure. I hurried back as soon as I saw . . ."

His uncle cut him short with a vicious curse.

Salah said softly, "We must know." It was he who led as they moved on.

An hour later they came to the place where the tracks and camel droppings crossed the wadi, coming down the west bank and climbing over the east bank. Salah examined the tracks briefly. "This is no caravan. Only riding camels." He began to climb the east bank. Grayle and Umar al-Hadj went after him.

They paused as they neared the top, then raised their heads cautiously. East of the wadi spread a wide flat of clay webbed with deep cracks. It ended against a low, broken ridge of dark gray limestone. The trail of the unknown camel-riders led across the webbed flat to the ridge.

Grayle used the binoculars but could see nothing moving there. "Where is the waterhole?" he asked Umar al-Hadj.

"On the other side of the ridge."

They worked their way back down to the bed of the wadi. Salah squatted and picked up a piece of dried dung. He broke it in half and held it close to his remaining eye to examine the inside in the fading daylight. He smelled it, pinched out a small piece and crumbled it between his fingers, tasted it with the tip of his tongue.

"They crossed here early this morning, perhaps. Certainly no longer ago than late last night."

"Then they are still there," Umar al-Hadj said bitterly. "At our waterhole."

"They have had a whole day there," Bou Idriss pointed out. "Time enough to rest themselves, water their camels, fill their waterbags. They may be preparing to continue on their way, at this moment. If they are raiders, they will ride by night."

"*If* they move on," Umar al-Hadj growled. "They may intend to stay, as long as there is water to be drawn on. It is a perfect place for raiders to wait. Any caravan through this area will come there."

"Guessing is wasted thought," Salah said. "We have to know." He held out a hand, and Grayle gave him the binoculars.

Salah set out through the first darkness of night, before the full strength of the starlight. Grayle, crouched at the top of the wadi, watched him move across the clay flat on foot. There were many night shadows at ground level, and they altered with the movement of the moon. A man of Salah's talent and experience knew how to use them. Even knowing where he was, Grayle soon lost sight of him.

Returning to the wadi bed, Grayle sat on the ground and opened the area map on his crossed legs. Striking a match, he studied the locations of the nearest crosses that Umar al-Hadj had penciled in.

There were still several hours to go before dawn when Salah returned to them. Umar al-Hadj's younger brother, Moulay, was on lookout at the top of the east bank. He was as desert-wise and vigilant as any among them, but he failed to detect Salah's approach until his voice called softly from a patch of night-shadow a short distance away. Moulay muttered something about Salah being more ghost than human as his figure appeared from the shadow.

Salah gave him a patronizing pat on the head in passing, and descended to the others waiting inside the wadi. He was tired and hungry, and would not speak until he had eaten some salted goat's meat and raisins. Then he told them what he had found out.

"There are more than twenty of them. Asasa raiders. I traced the brand on one of their camels."

Ali looked at him in awe. "You got so close?"

"The camel was grazing a distance from their camp. Even so, it was close enough to shrink my heart. Their lookouts are well-placed. Also, they are well-armed and in an easily defended position. There is no hope that we can take them by surprise. And without surprise, no way to seize the waterhole from them."

"Perhaps," Umar al-Hadj said, "they will be gone tomorrow."

"I do not think so. They seem to me to have settled down there. In my opinion they intend to stay, and wait. Until fortune brings them a caravan to loot, or they drain the waterhole dry."

"Umar," Grayle said, "you marked two waterholes south of the point where we entered this wadi, and another due east from there. Which is nearest?"

"The one east. But it is at least six days."

"We've got enough water to last us that long."

"But the camels do not. And they are already suffering from thirst."

"We have no other choice. They'll have scouts out, come day, looking for an approaching caravan. This wadi is a natural approach. If they find our tracks while we're still here, we'll be caught in a trap."

"They *will* find our trail," Salah said quietly. "Even if we have left. And come after us."

"And this time," Bou Idriss pointed out, "it is *their* camels that are watered and rested, and ours that are not."

"Pray for wind," Grayle told them flatly, "to wipe out our tracks before they catch up or know which of the three waterholes we're trying for."

"You speak," Umar al-Hadj said angrily, "as though we had already decided. Most of these men and camels are mine, so do not speak as if you command."

"But I do," Grayle told him.

Salah squinted at him, startled by the implacable sound of his voice.

"I remind you," Grayle went on in the same tone, "that

only Ahmed can take you to the reward you were promised. And he will not do so unless I tell him to." Without
looking at the boy, Grayle stabbed a finger in his direction.
"*Will* you?"

"No," Ahmed said, "I will not."

Salah put a restraining hand on Umar al-Hadj's arm. "In
any case, he is right. We must go."

"Now," Grayle said. "While there's still some night left."
Moving his camel, he took its headrope and led the way,
back south through the wadi.

28

They were still pushing south along the bed of the wadi at dawn. Salah took over the rearguard position, dropping back a full mile to watch for pursuit. A blood-red rim of sun appeared on the eastern horizon, and the full moon became a great pearl shot with crimson. As the sun rose it changed to burning gold. The moon faded into ghostly transparency, and was blotted out as the sky turned yellow, clamping down on the land.

It turned into the hottest morning Grayle had so far encountered. Even hugging the shade under the wadi's east bank, the heat was so heavy that only the driving fear of the Asasa raiders behind them kept them moving. Light particles of dust, sucked up by the heat, began forming into listlessly drifting patches of dry mist. Grayle closed the flap of the goatskin sheath that protected his rifle, to keep the dust from sifting in and clogging it.

By noon there was neither shade nor sunlight left. The floating dust around them had congealed into a desert fog as solid as any Grayle had known at sea. Its density changed the sun into a distant blur of indistinct light, like the glow of a receding electric bulb. Soon even this blur was lost, and with it the sun's exact position.

Salah materialized out of the dust-fog behind them, beating his camel to catch up.

The jolt of terror his reappearance caused was allayed a bit by his first words. "If any Asasa scouts came across the trail we left before this fog closed in, I don't know about it. But they could have been right behind me and I wouldn't be able to see them coming."

"A problem which has its good side," Umar al-Hadj

said. "Visibility is just as bad for them. And it will become worse. I have known such dust-fogs to last for days, until a wind comes to blow it away. If the Asasa are after us, it will become impossible to read our trail, unless they stop every few minutes to get down on their hands and knees."

Bou Idriss looked ahead. "As long as we stay in this wadi they don't have to read our trail."

"That much is obvious, eunuch. We leave the wadi. From here we could be striking toward any one of the three other wells. If they are determined to have us, they will be forced to split into three groups and try each direction." Umar al-Hadj looked to Grayle, and this time there was neither anger nor scorn in his manner: "You agree?"

Grayle nodded. "That way, if one of their groups does find us, at least we'll have fewer of them to fight. Let's go."

Ten minutes later they found their way out of the wadi by way of a collapsed section of the east bank and headed east, angling a bit south. There was only Umar al-Hadj's compass to keep them on the right course. And as he had predicted, the fog grew thicker as the day progressed and the raging power of the invisible sun somewhere above sucked more and more dust particles into the air. Visibility shrank to a few yards.

Flankers and scouts were pulled in, and they moved ahead in a tight pack to prevent their becoming separated in the murk. Grayle could barely make out Salah and Umar al-Hadj, riding in the lead just ahead of him. On his right, Bou Idriss and Ahmed rode close enough for him to reach out and touch. So did the man on his left: the lean young warrior named Mustafa.

Salah turned his camel and rode back to them. "Umar says there are three high, sharp peaks close together, due east about a day and a half away." His voice was muffled by the headcloth he had wrapped around his face. There was only a slit for his single eye to squint through. "These triple peaks form a landmark like no others. If we become separated for any reason, we will regroup there."

"And how do we find this due-east direction," Mustafa

demanded with thin sarcasm, "if we become separated from Umar and his compass?"

"You wait, warrior. Until a wind from God blows this dust away, and you can once more read direction from the sun and stars."

"And by then, will anybody still be waiting at these three peaks?"

"Those who get there first will wait—as long as the situation allows." Salah's tone held its own brand of cynicism as he added: "As God wills it." He moved on to pass the word to those behind them.

Late in the afternoon, when they made one of their prayer halts, it was extended for an hour of rest. They ate dried meat and dates, and finished off the meal with water. No tea; even a small fire was too great a risk, even in this dust fog.

It was entirely a matter of chance now. Had Asasa scouts found their tracks in the wadi before the fog thickened? If so, had the raiding pack persisted, even when it became impossible to follow a trail? If they had, they would be split in three now, trying for the three separate wells; and whichever group located its quarry would send word for the others to join it. The group aiming for the well to the east would be following roughly the same route as Grayle's party. That raiding pack could be very close by now; right behind them, or on either side, or perhaps just ahead.

At the end of the hour they moved on, directed by Umar al-Hadj with his compass. They alternated riding and trudging ahead on foot, pulling the camels after them. With the sunset came the swift darkening of the fog, until even the ground under them was invisible and they had to pick their way along by feel. At the next rest-halt they debated staying put until morning if the fog was not blown away before then. But everything argued against it. The longer they waited the weaker the camels would become. If the fog was blown away it would leave them with no cover in open terrain. They had to reach some kind of protective cover before settling down for a real rest.

They went on. The fog began to thin a bit as some of the dust settled to the ground with the cold of the night. But there was still no hint of moon or stars, and the ground was barely discernible. Grayle walked his camel for over an hour, and then forced it to its knees and climbed back onto the saddle. As the animal surged reluctantly to its feet Grayle noticed a darkening area in the fog off to the left.

His first thought was that it could be an outcrop of rock; the kind of shelter they sought.

But then he realized that the darker area was in movement. And the movement was toward them.

He shouted the warning as he dragged his Lebel from its sheath.

Rifles blasted from the approaching patch of darkness, and then there was no doubt left of their bad luck: their route had converged with that of an Asasa hunting pack. Grayle fired into the center of the attacking darkness; worked the bolt fast and fired again as other rifles ahead and behind joined with his.

A barrage of enemy rifle-fire struck at them as the closing patch of darkness spread out, became indistinct figures of swift-moving mounted camels. How many, it was impossible to tell. By Grayle's left side, bullets smashed Mustafa's camel off its feet. Its death scream mingled with that of Mustafa as he was crushed to the ground under its falling weight. Grayle's camel jerked and screamed as though hit, and then swung away to the right, charging between Bou Idriss and Ahmed, knocking their mounts out of its way as it raced off in terror.

Grayle yanked savagely at its headrope, fighting to bring the animal back under control. But the camel abruptly went down, headfirst. Its front knees struck the ground with a jarring impact that flung Grayle from the saddle, somersaulting over the high front pommel. Instinctively, he curled in a ball as he fell. He hit the ground with his right shoulder, absorbing some of the force of the fall by rolling with its momentum.

He came to rest on his side, and found that the Lebel was still clutched tightly in his right fist. Training paid off.

He got his legs under him, waited for his head to clear and stood up. His camel was back up on its feet, stumbling away; already too far to catch. As it was swallowed by the darkness, Grayle turned back in the direction of thundering rifles and screaming camels.

A wild bullet struck across his forehead, leaving a whiplash of fire behind. The force of the blow slammed him back to the ground. Dizziness swirled in his brain, and then ebbed. He rolled over, got his hands under him and realized both were empty. He'd lost his rifle this time. Shoving against the ground, he pushed up on his knees. And froze that way; horror surging in him and bringing bile to his throat and mouth.

He couldn't see. Not anything. Not even the fog.

His hands groped for his eyes. And found bloody pulp. Clenching his teeth, he fought down the vomiting reaction. Carefully, his fingertips probed through a mixture of dust and blood, and found his eyes. They were there. Intact.

He wiped at them, savagely, clawing the soggy mess away. The spasm of laughter was as much hysteria as the panic had been. He stopped it, as he had the other. His vision was blurred, but it was there. It was only blocked by the blood, caking with dust as it ran down from his wound.

His fingers groped higher. The bullet had slashed clear across his forehead, from one side to the other. It had gouged wide and deep, but hadn't broken his skull.

He began unwinding his torn and bloodied headcloth. He heard again the sounds of battle: the gunfire and the screams of hurt animals and men. But much farther away. It had become a running fight, leaving him behind.

Grayle ripped a strip from the end of the headcloth, tied it tightly around his forehead to stem the bleeding. He rewound the rest in a tight turban to hold the bandage in place, and used what was left of the tattered end to wrap across his lower face. He rubbed at his eyes again. The blurring became less, but his vision was still not entirely clear. What he needed was water, to clean out his eyes. And his water was gone with his stampeding camel.

He had a terrible headache and his neck hurt from the twisting impact of the bullet. But his mind was quite clear.

He knew his needs, and the order in which they must be seen to. First, he groped around him along the ground, turning on his knees in a circle until he found his fallen rifle. He picked it up, hoping it was not too clogged with dust to function if he needed it in a hurry.

The sound of the fight was far off now. And the shots had become sporadic. At the moment, that was not his concern. Spreading his feet, he rose in a low crouch and peered around him. What he needed was a dead camel. A lot had been killed. One must still have an intact waterbag attached to its saddle.

Reaching inside his robes, Grayle drew the bayonet from his belt. With that in one hand, and the Lebel in the other, his finger tensed across the trigger, he advanced toward the place from which he guessed his camel had carried him. He almost walked into what he was seeking: a camel sprawled on its side.

Grayle squatted by its saddle and found it: a waterbag, still half full. He untied it, opened it, poured water directly from its spout over his eyes. Wiping the water from his eyes with the tattered end of his facecloth, he repeated the cleansing process. The blurring washed away, and he saw other still forms on the ground around him.

It came to him that he could see better than before the fight. In a moment, he understood why. Breeze fanned his face and hands. A wind was building, beginning to disperse the cloud of low-hanging dust.

Taking a long swallow of water, Grayle closed the waterbag and hung it over his shoulder. He was about to rise when he heard a man groan, off to his right. Instantly, he went flat to the ground, squinting in that direction. In a few moments he made out the figure of a man, crawling on hands and knees, head hanging.

Staying flat, Grayle called softly: "Here . . ." His voice had a thick rasp, impossible to identify.

The man stopped crawling, his head coming up groggily. "Where . . .?"

It was not a voice Grayle knew. He remained still, watching as the figure crawled again, coming nearer. When he was quite close, the head came up again, turning, searching. It was not a man Grayle knew. As the figure crawled past him, Grayle reached under with the bayonet and cut his throat.

He waited for a time, listening and hearing nothing more around him. Even the distant firing had stopped.

If the raiders had won the fight, they'd be coming back here to look for their wounded and strip the dead camels. Grayle got to his feet and started away through shredding curtains of cold, billowing dust.

Stars appeared and disappeared among scattering fans of driven dust-cloud.

Grayle judged that he had been walking for a couple hours. The only certainty was that he had not traveled in a straight line. There was no way that could be accomplished without landmarks to direct him. The only point he could be satisfied with was that he had somehow managed to avoid walking in a circle, back toward the place where they'd tangled with the raiding party. The terrain was changing.

He had entered an area where the ground was flat hard sand, so thickly studded with fist-sized stones that he was forced to concentrate on each step as he picked his way through them. Squinting at the ground most of the time, he stopped occasionally for a glance at the sky. He was searching for a glimpse of the Pole Star; or the Belt of Orion just before it set. But the stops slowed his progress, and what he sought in the sky never happened to be in sight when he glanced overhead.

His first need had been to put distance between himself and any Asasa hunters. In roughly two hours he had neither seen nor heard anyone else, friend or enemy. The time had come now to get himself moving in the correct direction for the rendezvous point Umar al-Hadj had set: the triple peaks that lay somewhere due east.

Squatting, Grayle cleared a small area of the stones. The ground felt ice-cold to his touch. He scooped a shallow depression out of the hard sand. The layer below the surface was warmer. Settling down in the depression he'd created, Grayle attended first to his rifle. He broke it down, and cleaned each part with a strip of cloth ripped from his robe. Reassembling the Lebel, he checked to make sure he had a live cartridge in the firechamber, before wrapping the weapon in a fold of his robe to keep out the blowing dust.

Close around him small patches of loose sand were in movement, crawling along the surface. But there was no warning of trouble in that: the wind stirring it was not increasing in force. It remained just strong enough to continue breaking up the clouds of fine dust; not strong enough to lift much of the heavier sand grains more than an inch above the ground. Leaning back on one elbow, Grayle gave all his attention to the sky.

The highest dust clouds were disintegrating now, into tendrils of wispy mist riding away on the wind. More stars showed, steadily gleaming brighter. Grayle located the Pole Star among them. That gave him north; he was no longer lost. He looked west, searching for the constellation of Orion. But it was still hidden. Rising to his feet, Grayle put his left shoulder to the Pole Star.

Almost directly ahead of him was the vague shape of a low hill. If he directed his line of march to pass just to the right of it, he should be heading pretty close to due east. Grayle began walking again, this time with a direction and in a straight line. It required only brief checks on the hill ahead. The rest of the time he gave his attention to picking his way between the loose stones littering the ground.

When he passed the hill he stopped and looked back the way he'd come. This time Orion was visible, low over the horizon. With the constellation setting, the topmost of the three stars forming its belt told Grayle the exact position of due west. He turned his back to it, squarely, made sure the Pole Star was on his left shoulder, and scanned the area directly ahead of him.

Beyond the first hill there were others. In the strengthening light of the stars each took on a distinct shape. Grayle picked two as his markers and resumed his march along a line that would take him between them. When he passed that point he picked his next marker and kept going.

The ground was rising gradually. He was entering a range of truncated stone hills with fragmented peaks. With dawn not far off, Grayle checked his direction again and picked the most distant landmark that gave him due east: a high double peak shaped like twin corkscrews. As he hiked toward it the hills became more numerous, and the stones littering the ground became fewer. It became less necessary to watch the ground. But when he did, he saw something he didn't like.

There was more loose sand flowing across the surface, some of it snaking as high as his ankles. The wind was strengthening. If it continued to build, he was going to have to climb to high ground to wait it out.

He had continued to hike toward his distant landmark for perhaps fifteen minutes when it happened, with startling abruptness. Gusts slapped at him and ripped the hood from his head. He became sharply aware of the wound across his forehead again, as the makeshift bandage plastered to it by the dried blood was tugged painfully. Sand grains stung his face, penetrated his eyes, ears and nostrils.

Grabbing his hood and pulling it back in place, he held it almost closed across his face. When he looked down he could no longer see his legs below the knees. Turning sharply to his right, Grayle began climbing the scarred and pitted slope of the nearest stone hill. The gusts of wind merged into a steady, battering force. But the level of blowing sand was quickly left beneath him.

The hill was about twenty feet high. More than high enough. At the top Grayle found a niche in the rock and pressed himself inside it. Instantly, he was cut off from the main force of the wind.

Below, the sandstorm flowed past in an unending, hissing mass. The surface of the blown sand was almost level, and nothing at all could be seen through it. Above, the moon and stars were brilliant in a clear violet sky. Around Grayle the tops of other hills rose abruptly out of the wind-borne sand as though from a solid floor.

For the first time, he let his mind dwell on what might have become of the others: Salah, Bou Idriss and the boy; Umar al-Hadj and his warriors. He wondered which were dead by now. One thing was certain. Those still alive were doing what he was doing now: sheltering from the sandstorm. Any raiders hunting them would be doing the same.

As long as the storm lasted, there was no danger. And nothing else to do but wait until it was past.

Grayle drank from the waterbag, curled himself and went to sleep.

29

The air was dead still, and so dry that the membranes of his nostrils and lungs shrank from breathing it. In the spread of rosy-golden light before the rise of the sun, the land between Grayle's hilltop and the circle of horizon bore no trace of life. No man, no camel; nothing moved, and there was no sign that anything ever had.

If anyone had passed this way before the storm, the tracks had been obliterated. And no fresh tracks marred the smoothness of sand that had settled between the end of the storm and Grayle's awakening in the predawn. He was alone in a barren circle of dead planet. He could feel the immensity of the encompassing emptiness.

His head and neck still ached. The open wound across his forehead throbbed and burned, and the makeshift bandage was glued fast to it. He knew he should soak the cloth loose and wash out the wound. But he couldn't spare that much water. It would have to wait. Drinking deeply from what was left in the waterbag, he closed it and slung it over his left shoulder. Holding it in place with one hand and carrying the Lebel ready in his other, Grayle descended the hillslope and struck out for the double peaks he had previously selected as his guide to due-east. They were a long way ahead.

The settled sand under him was like flour. Each step he took sank a few inches into the surface. The sun came up and struck at him. His eyes narrowed to slits against the glare. At intervals he scanned the terrain around him, and turned to look back. He was still alone. Only his own dragging tracks disturbed the death-trance of this land.

He trudged on steadily, not varying from the pace he had set at the start. The twin peaks detached from their escarpment as he closed the distance. The low line of cliffs was some distance beyond his landmark. How far, it was impossible to estimate through the mirage-effect of growing heat-haze.

The sky had become a metallic yellowish-white. Under it the land undulated like molten mother-of-pearl. It was time to find shelter from the sun and stay put until dusk. But he couldn't wait for dusk. Somewhere ahead of him, beyond that long, low escarpment, were the triple peaks that Umar al-Hadj had set as the rendezvous point. Any of his group still living would be converging on that point. Those who had camels were probably already there. They wouldn't wait long for stragglers afoot. Every hour they remained lowered their own chance of reaching the next waterhole.

He drank deeply from the waterbag, and kept going.

The hills petered out; there were only far-scattered stumps of stone. Now and then, a puff of wind twirled a small dust devil into the brassy air. Otherwise, there was a terrible stillness, in which air and heat were as solid as the gritty earth, and the light tasted of old copper.

He knew now what the Devil was: a satin-black sun, burning a hole in a shimmering sky devoid of color. Its radiation was a beating hammer. The world was its anvil. And between the two: a tiny figure moving like a one ant through an emptiness that had no beginning or end.

Off to his right a cracked spire of rock cast a splinter of shade. It was off his route, perhaps a mile away, though the blurring deceptiveness of the light made the distance unsure. But there was nothing nearer. Grayle detoured.

By the time he got there, the sun was almost directly overhead, and the spire no longer cast its shadow. But there were deep cracks in its base. Grayle circled to its east side and found one just big enough for him. It was partially blocked with trapped sand. He knelt and began scooping it out. A sandfish, suddenly exposed to light, swiftly burrowed deeper and vanished. Grayle kept digging, until there was enough room to force himself inside the crevice, sitting down.

It gave him what he required: a measure of protective shadow. He stayed there and waited, dazed and panting for the air that dried out his lungs. His chest hurt and his head was so swollen he could no longer feel the wound. In time, the rock spire began to cast a shadow from its east face, outside Grayle's cramped shelter.

When there was enough of it, Grayle stretched out wearily on his back, part of him inside the crevice, the rest of him sprawled outside it in the slim, short patch of shade. He let his scorched eyes close, and drifted in and out of sleep. It was more than four hours before he got to his feet and resumed walking.

A crimson flower bloomed from a thornbush in a cranny at the base of the twin-peaked landmark. Around it there was nothing but the dust and weathered stones. Grayle knelt before the flower, staring at it. Never, in his entire life, had he seen a single object so precious, so important.

He reached out to touch it, and then stopped his hand. Still kneeling, he drank from the waterbag. Wiping his lips, he reached out again, and let a drop fall from his fingertip into the living center of the flower. A gesture; an offering. Rising to his feet, he turned from the flower and marched toward the escarpment to the east.

At sunset, color seeped back into the sky: a brilliant blue smeared with gold. The sands acquired a mauve tint, with low purple-black reefs of rock breaking its surface. The dull-red escarpment ahead stretched north and south from one horizon to the other. He had to try finding a way through or over it.

Night settled in. When Orion rose Grayle angled toward the high star of its belt. Beneath it there was a notch in the top of the escarpment wall. Using the notch as his goal, he continued his advance through a cold blue moonlight that changed the sands into white drifts of snow.

It was past midnight when he climbed one of the dunes

lapping at the dark mass of the escarpment. Close up, the wall separated into a series of eroded cliffs, broken by deep gullies and narrow canyons.

Grayle stopped just inside one of the dark openings, squinting ahead and listening. He hadn't seen any tracks but his own all day. But that didn't guarantee that these cliffs were empty. His eyes adjusted to the gloom. Starlight filtered in and showed vague masses of looming rock, with darker patches between them. Nothing else. The silence was solid.

Raising the Lebel, pointing the way with it, he moved in among the cliffs. His passage forked. He followed the left fork. It became a gully, leading him down into a basin. He tried one way out of the basin. Abruptly, the stars were blacked out over him and there was impenetrable darkness ahead. The mouth of a cavern, perhaps. Retracing his steps, Grayle tried another direction.

He found a narrow passage and followed it, passing a number of dark openings before coming to a dead end. Returning to one of the openings. he turned into it. Another narrow passage; this one turning, then making a sharp bend, then another.

All sense of direction was lost. And the deeper he penetrated inside the cliffs the darker it got. The masses of stone all around him rose higher, cutting away the stars. A loose stone tripped him and he almost fell. Groping forward through shadows within shadows, his hand came against a ridged slope. He began climbing it, feeling his way carefully.

When he reached a high knoll, Grayle located the North Star and looked east. The broken cliffs continued for some miles in that direction, slashed by twisting pools of blackness. There was no way he could get through that as long as the night lasted. If he didn't fall and break his neck, he'd just waste his strength getting himself lost.

Easing himself back down to a ledge that undercut the knoll, Grayle stretched out and slept the few hours left to dawn.

* * *

Stone entrails curled and interwove around him. They grew haphazardly, soaring and collapsing, splitting into separate configurations and diverging. He was regularly forced to detour. But at least he could see what was immediately around him when he worked his way through the depths.

The maze inside the cliffs, he saw now, was not solely the result of violent weathering and slides. An underground upheaval had broken through the surface here, heaving up gigantic slabs of rock, cracked and splintered, tilted askew and leaning against each other.

It was like a stone jungle. He had to climb over, under, around. There were narrow passages that turned back on themselves, crumbling bridges and partially blocked under-passes, tight canyons choked with tilting slabs and cracking boulders, openings that became tunnels and others that dead-ended inside caves.

He was traversing a short curve of trench in the middle of this maze when he came upon the dead camel.

A bullet had smashed the skull above its right ear. The animal had been stripped of everything: saddle, blankets, waterskins, saddlebags, sheepskins. Grayle crouched and examined the stretched neck. It bore the brand of Umar al-Hadj.

Grayle tied his goatskin waterbag in place across his shoulders and raised the rifle in both hands, his finger sliding across the trigger, just touching it. His head turned; looking, listening, smelling the air.

A thin sound reached him. His flesh crawled.

Sand bottomed the trench. Footprints led away through it. Grayle placed each step with deliberate care as he moved past the dead camel and followed the tracks, making no sound at all in the soft sand. The trench entered a gully. The gully led to a pocket where a lot of sand had become trapped, forming a dune rising high between cracked walls of rock.

The head of a man stuck out of the sand on the crest, staring at the sun.

Grayle studied the rocks around the trapped dune, giving patient attention to shadowed areas. Then he climbed the sand slope, to the top, and squatted low before the face that grew out of the dune.

It was Umar al-Hadj.

The thin sound leaking from him could have been the mewling of a gutted cat. His eyelids had been neatly sliced away, and the sun of the previous afternoon had burned the eyes to blindness. His genitals were stuffed into his wide-open mouth. Whatever else had been done to the rest of him buried deep inside the sand, Grayle didn't want to learn.

He drew his bayonet with his free hand and drove the point deep into Umar al-Hadj's jugular, wrenching the blade sideways. The head flopped back as though the neck had broken. Blood spurted, spattering Grayle's knife hand and robe. He didn't draw away to avoid it. The mewling sound had ended. Soon the blood ceased its flow.

Grayle sheathed the bayonet inside his robe without wiping it clean. He crawled back down the sand slope. His mouth was open and he was panting. His eyes were wild as they darted to every opening and patch of shadow while he descended.

He was almost to the bottom when a rifle shot echoed among the rock faces around the dune. Grayle rolled the rest of the way down, holding the Lebel high to prevent its becoming clogged with the dust he churned up. When he came to rest he was in a pocket of shade on his back, squinting and aiming upward, scanning the ledges and fissures.

But the shot, he knew, had not been meant for him. The sound had come from another part of this jungle of stone. Not far, however.

Grayle rolled to his knees and came up onto his feet in a tight crouch. The enemy was close. Maybe they didn't know that he was, too.

He went hunting for them. It was not a decision made with conscious calculation. What had to be done was any action that would wipe out the image burned into his brain: how Umar al-Hadj had looked and sounded before he died.

He threaded his way through the decaying entrails of the broken cliffs and tilting slabs, past other pockets of trapped sandhills. Then he was climbing, working toward a high vantage point.

He reached a short ledge in the dark shadow of an overhang. From that point he found himself suddenly overlooking the eastern limits of the cliff maze.

Far off, across a flat of sand and stones, three sharp peaks showed on the curve of the eastern horizon, grouped tightly together.

Camel tracks led away in that direction. Others angled in toward the cliffs under Grayle. And there, close to the debris from the cliffs and heaped against their base, sprawled two other dead camels. These had not been stripped. Their saddles were shaped differently than those Umar al-Hadj had supplied. The pattern of their saddle blankets were unfamiliar to Grayle.

Some of the enemy—perhaps all that was left of the pack they'd tangled with—were still here. And at least one of Grayle's people was still here. Whoever he was, the raiders were still stalking him, hunting him down before going on.

A rifle cracked again: below Grayle and off to his left. He ducked low while the noise still echoed. But again, the shot was not aimed in his direction. He peered down from his shadowed perch, seeking its source.

30

Directly below Grayle's shadowed vantage point, a cliff dropped into a parched gorge. It had been gashed and split by sandstorms, flash floods and freezing nights. Rock-rubble and collapsed sections of cliffwall bigger than houses formed a jumbled mass spreading out and down from its base.

Near the lowest point of this rubble, a man with a rifle was hunched down inside a pocket surrounded by low, broken rocks. All that Grayle could distinguish about the man was that the hooded robe he wore was dun-colored. Like his own.

A rifle cracked again. This time Grayle spotted the source: a cave of darkness under a rock slab that leaned against the top of a boulder. It was some distance on the other side of the man hunched down in the pocket—beyond range of Grayle's rifle. The shooter was not trying to hit the man in the pocket; he couldn't possibly see him from that point. His bullet could have only one purpose: to keep the man inside the pocket pinned down.

Methodically, Grayle surveyed the tangle of rocks and fallen cliff-sections around the pocket containing the pinned man. His eyes narrowing to slits against the sun-glare and heat-haze, he finally located what he was searching for, below him: something had changed inside a slash of darkness among the rocks there.

Grayle steadied his attention on that point. It was repeated: a shadowy movement within the deep shade. Grayle quietly slid his Lebel forward, tucked the stock into his right shoulder. The shadow emerged into a patch of light atop a boulder and acquired solidity. A figure swathed in dark-indigo hood and robe, with swatches of light blue.

None of Grayle's group was dressed like that. It was an Asasa raider.

Another rifle shot from the dark cave in the distance. Again, the bullet merely chopped dust from one of the rocks above the man trapped in the pocket. Just keeping him pinned down there, while the raider almost directly under Grayle worked into a position from which he would have a clear angle of fire down inside the pocket.

Grayle watched the dark figure go down on one knee atop the boulder and raise a rifle, aiming downward. The Lebel roared in Grayle's hands. The shot struck the dark, kneeling figure exactly between the shoulder blades and bucked him forward, off the boulder. He fell onto a ledge below, rolled over and shoved up on his hands and knees, head dangling. Grayle watched him crawl blindly and topple off the ledge, landing face-down across the top of another boulder, arms and legs hanging limply. The figure did not move again.

From the dark cave, the rifle blasted again, this time in Grayle's direction. A wasted shot, at that distance. Unless it was intended to pinpoint his position for others.

A swift scan of the area failed to reveal anyone else. Grayle looked back to the pocket among the rocks. The man there had twisted over on his back to stare up past the fallen body, in Grayle's direction.

There was no mistaking that scar-distorted face.

The dark shade of the overhang across Grayle's ledge made him invisible to Salah. But at least he knew somebody was up there who was on his side. Salah raised a hand slightly and pointed in the direction of the sniper who had him pinned down. Then he made a circling gesture and pointed again—twice—in the direction between him and the cliff under Grayle.

The meaning was obvious. Grayle did a slower scan of the rocks below, narrowing his field this time to the piles of scree backed against the base of his cliff. The first scan revealed nothing. Grayle repeated it, slowly and thoroughly, checking out each likely bit of concealment.

Something moved within a slice of darkness that cut between two jagged ground formations. Just a glimpse was all Grayle caught, and then it was gone. It seemed to him that the movement had been in the direction of the cliff base under him. Grayle trained the Lebel on the point where the slice of darkness ended in that direction. But no one emerged into the light there. They knew, now, that he was around. The rest wasn't going to be that easy.

When he spotted movement again, it was a shadow within a shadow, some yards above the point where his rifle was aimed. The glimpse was too brief, too vague, for him to try for a lucky shot. And Salah had indicated two men in his direction. Grayle couldn't be sure if the two movements he'd glimpsed had been made by two different men. If both had been the same man, there was another somewhere Grayle didn't know about.

That worried him. But it was what they intended to do that was important, and that was fairly predictable. The movements he'd spotted had been angling toward a fissure in the base of his cliff. Almost certainly both of them would be coordinating to get at him. Salah was pinned down for the moment. Grayle was not. Stalking someone who had freedom of movement was a two-man job. They'd try to get behind the ridge above Grayle and come at him from behind, and from two directions, to squeeze him in a trap.

Grayle shot another glance down at the pocket in the rocks. Salah lay on his back, holding his rifle pointed upward. He flapped it in Grayle's direction. A message easy to read: Go away.

While there were three Asasa raiders down there, Salah was unable to wriggle out of his trap. But if two of them were drawn away by Grayle, Salah would find a way to deal with the single enemy left behind to keep him pinned.

Grayle wriggled backward, off the ledge and through a notch behind it. When he was down behind the ridge he got to his feet. Whatever route the Asasa stalkers used in their climb of the other face of the cliff, Grayle was, for a time, cut off from their sight. Time enough, he judged, to get where he wanted to go before they could see him and use their rifles.

He went down a slope into a tight, shallow canyon choked with boulders. His descent was swift, and he kicked stones loose, sending them clattering down ahead of him. The noise echoed loudly in the confines of the canyon. It would carry to the ears of his pursuers.

That was fine. It exerted a measure of control over the direction they followed in hunting him down.

He reached the bottom and ran, threading between the looming boulders. The canyon narrowed. The boulders thinned out as the walls pressed in close on either side. Dead ahead of him was a barrier of broken slabs and fallen rock. Grayle came to a halt, breathing harshly, looking back. His hunters could be inside the canyon by now, coming up behind him.

There was only one way past the barrier ahead: up and over. He would be completely exposed for a second or two. But the climb was an easy one. He'd have surprise and speed going for him, if they did spot him.

He scrambled up the barrier. Rifles fired from the boulders behind him as he reached the top. Two of them, sounding almost in unison. Bullets slapped the stone wall on Grayle's right and spun away, chipping rock-dust from an outcrop shouldering massively from the wall on his left. Grayle went down the other side of the barrier on the jump, fell the last part of the way down, sprawled in the dust, rolled instantly to his left and came up on his knees.

With the barrier shielding him, he crawled into a shallow trench that undercut the outcropping on his left. Snaking through the trench, he came to his feet with the outcropping behind him, panting and gripping the Lebel tightly in both hands. He had what he needed: he was hidden again from the pair stalking him.

A gully twisted up a steeped-back cliff. Grayle climbed through it, bent low. The sides of the gully continued to protect him. But swirls of dust churned up by his climb would betray his route, and continue to exercise some control over that of his stalkers.

The gully bent around a rock shoulder, into the lower

end of a ravine. Grayle cornered it, and then stopped and squinted back down the way he'd come. There was no sign of the two trailing him. They knew this kind of work. Not even a wisp of dust betrayed their movements. Grayle listened for gravel slippage. What he heard was the distant crack of a rifle. It was followed, seconds later, by two shots fired in rapid succession.

That would be Salah and the third Asasa raider, stalking each other. Salah's problem. Grayle's was much nearer, and getting closer with each second he stayed put.

He headed up the ravine, pushing as fast as he could, driving himself with powerful thrusts of his legs. Reaching the top, he dropped flat to the ground, gulping air into his lungs as he twisted around to look back down.

There were two dark-robed and hooded figures below, just within range. But before Grayle could level his rifle and take aim, one slipped to the left, behind a boulder, and the other vanished under a natural bridge of stone to the right.

Grayle steadied the Lebel's barrel on a flat slab of slate in front of him. His eyes switched back and forth, waiting for one of them to reappear.

The first movement was down to the right. Grayle shifted to catch the raider in his sights. But the movement had been a feint. The figure spun and darted back to cover as Grayle fired. The bullet chopped dirt where he had been.

Grayle worked the bolt as he switched his aim to the left. But he was too late. The other figure, sprinting from cover down there, reached the safety of another boulder and vanished behind it. Grayle put a clamp on his nerves and waited.

After some time, he detected movement on the dark side of the natural bridge. He lined his sights on the spot, finger tensing across the trigger. A rifle blasted from the darkness there. The bullet ricocheted off a stone shelf twenty feet from Grayle. He did not fire back, because there was no real target down there. Only the dark area. Grayle waited for the shooter to shift for a better line of fire. He didn't.

Instead, there was another wild shot. This one kicked up dust some yards below Grayle.

He swung his attention back to the boulder where the other Asasa raider had vanished. No movement at all there; and there'd been no shots fired from that point. But there were a great number of other boulders behind that one. What his two stalkers were doing was obvious.

The one in the shelter of the stone bridge was firing to hold Grayle's attention. The second would be crawling back through the other boulders, angling for a route he could use to circle and reach a point behind Grayle. This was their kind of terrain; they'd had plenty of experience stalking quarry through it.

Grayle wasted one bullet into the dark patch beside the stone bridge, just to let them know he was still there. He got a fresh five-cartridge box from his belt pouch and reloaded. Then he slithered backward. When he reached a point where he could not be seen from below, he rose in a crouch, turned and moved on through the ravine.

His retreat was not aimless. He had come this way earlier that morning, working through the entrails of the broken cliffs in the opposite direction. He knew where he was going, and what he would find when he got there.

Near the top of the ravine there was a long, deep trench angling off to Grayle's right. It cut straight through solid rock, and was bottomed by a thick layer of sand and dust. He ran through it, dragging his feet. The dust he churned up clogged his nostrils and ate at his narrowed eyes. It swirled higher, forming a continuous cloud in the dead air above the trench, revealing the direction of his flight. Wherever his pursuers were, at least one of them was certain to spot it.

The trench ended abruptly, opening out into a tight little canyon in which a trapped dune was banked against one side. Grayle didn't go on into the canyon. Instead, he turned and made his way back through the trench. This time he placed each step with care, stirring up as little dust as possible. The little that did rise from his footsteps would be invisible in the heavy clouds that still hung from his first passage through.

Reaching the ravine again, he squatted just inside the trench and leaned forward a bit to peer down through it. There was no sign of his pursuers down there. As he'd expected. They'd be climbing after him by different routes. To follow exactly the same route he had used would be an invitation for him to ambush them. And by now they'd be angling away from the ravine, in the direction of the dust he'd raised. Moving separately in an attempt to get ahead of him in that direction and catch him in a pincerlike movement.

Stepping out of the trench, Grayle went swiftly up the rest of the ravine, moving quietly and keeping to shadows, working his way higher. Turning a rock shoulder, he crossed a shallow basin, and pushed through a break in the wall on the other side. It was partially blocked by rock-rubble. Grayle moved up over it carefully.

On the other side of the blockage a shallow gully funneled upward. He hauled himself into it and crawled through, slivers of shale digging into his hands and knees. The gully twisted, and the climb became steeper. When he came out of the top of it, his goal was directly in front of him.

It was a short, narrow shelf, darkly shadowed by a furrowed overhang. Grayle climbed onto the shelf and crawled under the overhang. Swinging to a sitting position with his back pressed against ridged rock, he looked down.

Below him sprawled the area through which he would have been moving if he had continued out of the trench and across the small canyon with its trapped sandhill. There were three likely routes through that area. Grayle scanned them, and the spaces between. His stalkers hadn't arrived yet. He rested the Lebel across his raised knees and watched.

Sun, shadows, silence. His nerves were coiled tight. He made himself relax, just a notch. His mouth was bone-dry, his throat parched. There was still water in the goatskin bag he carried. He didn't reach for it. Immobile in the shadow of the overhang, he listened, observed and waited it out.

Something seemed to change slightly at the base of a cliff on the other side of the stone jungle down there. Grayle thought he'd detected a flicker of movement near the bottom end of the cliff's ledge.

There was no movement now. Only a still shadow. But there was nothing to cast that particular shadow; and Grayle was almost certain it hadn't been there before. He fixed his attention on it.

After a time, the shadow moved. It became a dark-robed figure, starting cautiously up the ledge. Sunshine glinted off the rifle the figure held ready.

Grayle had one of them. He looked for the other. But he was unable to spot anything else moving. He gave it more time. Still nothing. He returned his attention to the one he did have.

The dark figure was halfway up the cliff now. A long shot. But it could be done, exercising proper care. Again Grayle lowered his gaze, searching for the second stalker. Again, he failed to locate him. It wasn't good. He wanted to know where both of them were before he started. But if he waited much longer, he wouldn't have either. The man climbing the ledge would reach the top and vanish.

Grayle raised his head and hefted the Lebel, tucking it against his shoulder. He brought his knees in a bit closer and leaned forward, resting his elbows on them to steady the rifle barrel. The dark figure was almost to the top of the cliff.

Lining his sights on the dark hood that concealed the head and face, Grayle led the man a fraction and very gently squeezed the trigger. Blast and recoil. He was already working the bolt action when the shot hit. It got the raider low in the body, sagging him against the cliffwall. He half-turned, trying to bring his rifle around and up.

Grayle steadied his aim and fired.

The bullet smashed into the dark figure's chest. Dead center. He was slammed against the cliff and bounced away from it, going loosely over the edge of the high ledge and spinning down. Grayle didn't watch his fall. He worked the bolt as he scanned again for the other stalker.

Still no sign of that one. Grayle cursed softly, rolled on his stomach and snaked through the shade of the overhang, back toward the jumbled formations from which he'd come. Wherever the second stalker was, he knew now the position from which Grayle had fired. The first necessity was to put distance between himself and that position.

When he was well inside the protection of the formations, Grayle got to his feet and headed back downward; angling to reach Salah and join him. By now Salah would have found a way to eliminate the Asasa raider who had kept him pinned inside the pocket. If the surviving stalker was stubborn enough to continue his pursuit of Grayle, he was the one who was going to wind up having to deal with two enemies at the same time.

Grayle reached the top of the ravine, but did not enter it. He moved past it, and found another way down. A much more difficult way, but one with cover on all sides. He worked his way down between boulders and broken slabs and outcroppings, changing direction to keep inside protected shadows, halting frequently to listen and study all approaches around him. If the surviving stalker was anywhere near, he couldn't be seen or heard.

He came to the top of a cliff and went to ground. Easing forward on his stomach, he peered over the edge. The cliff dropped below him into a tight pocket. It was half-filled with a hill of sand, out of which projected spires of black stone. Grayle surveyed the ridges surrounding the pocket. He had the immediate area to himself.

Pushing off the ground but keeping low, he moved along the clifftop, circling the pocket. His head and eyes continued their own movement, searching.

Across the pocket, there was a shift inside the shadow of a ridge cleft. Grayle twisted and triggered a snap shot. Its sound blended with the rifle shot from the shadow. Grayle's shot slashed chips from one side of the cleft. The enemy bullet punched through the flesh of his side, between the lowest rib and his hip. It spun him around, tilting him over the edge, and suddenly there was nothing but air under his right foot.

Grayle wrenched himself around at the last second,

holding the Lebel high away from him with both hands. His back struck the sand slope, hard, between two of the black spires. He spread his legs wide apart as he started to slide, stopping himself halfway down the slope.

Loose sand cascaded over his hooded head, fanned past his face. He didn't try to pull away from it. The man who'd shot him had been on the other side of the dune. He'd have to circle the pocket to get another shot at him. Grayle wriggled himself back and forth, digging his back deeper into the slope as he worked the Lebel's bolt. He couldn't feel the puncture wound in his side, where the slug had gone in and out taking his flesh and blood with it. His nervous system was too preoccupied for the moment with staying alive to send him pain messages about something he already knew.

He stopped digging himself into the slope when there was sand protecting him on both sides and above. He had the stock of the Lebel tucked into his right shoulder and was looking along the length of its shiny barrel, twitching it back and forth, waiting for his target to appear. There was no way the Asasa stalker could try for his killing shot without showing himself, however briefly.

But the waiting time stretched. And his nerves began to stretch with it. He fought against it, so he wouldn't be frozen in the vital split second when the time came. But it didn't come. Instead, he heard and felt, finally, the thump of something landing on the dune, somewhere above and behind him.

Grayle knew then that he'd committed the ultimate stupidity: underestimating his opponent's mind. The raider hadn't considered creeping around for a direct downward shot at him. He'd jumped down to the top of the sandhill.

Moments later, sand began to slide down Grayle's side of the dune. A little at first; and then much more.

Unless he jumped away, he was going to be buried under the sandslide started by the man on top of the dune. The man up there was waiting for him to jump free, into his rifle sights. Grayle had to try it, anyway.

There was a single plus-factor: the downrush of sand was throwing off a billowing dust cloud.

Grayle drew his legs up under him, braced his feet and launched himself through the downpour of sand, out into the rising cloud of dust. He didn't go straight out, but cut to the left, throwing himself down the slope as he went. There was a rifle shot from the top of the dune. It missed him. He turned his fall into a fast single roll, and came up on spread feet with eyes and rifle raised toward the top of the dune.

Through the spreading cloud the figure up there was too vague a target. Grayle fired anyway, and missed, as the raider's answering shot missed him.

A third rifle cracked from one of the ridges above. The vague figure was flung from the dune top. He fell loosely, turning in midair. He struck an upthrusting prong of rock with his back, and was broken like a snapped stick.

31

Grayle's legs suddenly became too weak to hold him. He sat down on the sand slope, and let the Lebel fall beside him.

Salah called down: "Where is the other one?"

His voice came from a ridge up to Grayle's right. But when Grayle looked he couldn't see him.

"I got him," he called back. "You got yours?"

For answer, Salah rose into view and lowered his rifle in one hand.

Grayle pulled open his clothing to investigate the place where the bullet had gone in and out of his side. The wound was shallow, but ugly. He opened his waterbag and drank deeply; then used more water to wash out the wound as best he could.

Salah had jumped to the top of the dune and was trudging down the slope to him. Grayle ripped a strip of cloth from his shirt and tied it tightly around his waist.

Salah squatted in front of him and looked at the blood that began staining the cloth where it was drawn over the wound. "How bad?"

"A small hole. But unpleasant."

Salah grunted and indicated the blood-caked bandage across Grayle's forehead. "And that?"

"It doesn't hurt much. But I should clean it."

Salah took the waterbag from him, and began soaking the bandage where it was stuck fast to Grayle's head wound. Feeling a deep lethargy, Grayle leaned his torso forward and braced his crossed arms on his knees. Salah tugged carefully at the soaked bandage. Grayle winced and steadied himself, holding his head still while Salah finished peeling the bandage away and dropped it.

Salah looked at the exposed wound and gave a soft whistle, impressed. "Now you will be almost as pretty as I am." Tipping water into the palm of his right hand, he began washing the crusted dirt from the wound. His touch was delicate, and expert.

Rivulets of water and blood ran down Grayle's face. He wiped it from his eyes with the back of his hand. "They got Umar."

"I know." Salah continued with his delicate cleaning of the wound across Grayle's forehead. "We must have killed many of their own the other night. It was no longer loot they were after, here. The sought blood revenge." He gestured to the dead raider lying broken at the base of the dark spur of rock. "But that, I think, was the last of their pack."

"They'll have sent a rider back, to bring the others."

"But that will take much time. We will be well ahead of them. I know where they left their camels hobbled. Two of them; one for each of us."

"What about our people?" Grayle asked him. "How many left?"

Salah shrugged. "We will find out, when we get to the three peaks to the east. Do you still have the map with the waterholes marked by Umar?"

Grayle tapped the belt-pouch under his robes. "I have it."

"And I have Umar's compass. It was on the Asasa I killed back there. So, we will find the next water. Till then, the waterbags on their two camels are still more than half full. Enough to get us there."

"We can't be the only ones left."

"One hopes." Salah unwound his headcloth and tore a strip from it. He tied it around Grayle's head to protect the wound. Rising, he lowered a hand to help Grayle to his feet. "Let us go and find out."

From the small assortment of medicines which Bou Idriss carried in his saddlebags, he chose a salve and mixed certain powdered herbs into it. He smeared the mixture into Grayle's head wound and tied a fresh strip of cloth over it.

Ahmed stood close, his dark eyes hard and observant. The rifle the boy held looked massive in his small hands.

Higher up the slope under the three peaks, watching the west for signs of pursuit, were the rest of the survivors: Salah and two others. Only two—Umar al-Hadj's younger brother, Moulay, and his nephew, Ali. What had happened to the other men none of them knew. The only certainty was that they had not reached this rendezvous point, and that they could be waited for no longer.

The sun was setting. They must move on, through the coming night, if they were to have a chance of reaching the next waterhole on time.

With the addition of the recently filled Asasa waterbags brought by Grayle and Salah, there would be enough to carry the five men and the boy for several more days. But the camels were in trouble. Not the two Asasa animals: those had been rested and watered by the raiders at the well Grayle's group had been forced to bypass. The problem was the other four, those of Bou Idriss, Ahmed, Moulay and Ali. If they didn't get to a waterhole very soon, they would be finished.

Bou Idriss used a handful of their precious water to soak loose the cloth stuck to Grayle's side. He frowned and prodded the puffed, discolored flesh around the puncture wounds. He raised a hand to Grayle's head.

"I don't have a fever," Grayle told him.

"No. But it will come, I think." Bou Idriss poured a bit more water and cleaned out the wound with it. "You may become very ill. But you will not die."

"Your scientific opinion? Or the dream?"

Bou Idriss looked at him thoughtfully. "Do not mock. I am an old man and have seen many things that boil the blood, things that chill the soul. And I tell you that you will live—to deliver Ahmed to Biskra." He turned away to prepare a mixture of ointments and herbs for the wound. "But that—I do not think that I will see."

* * *

Through the night the terrain they crossed gave way to a level plain of stone, swept clear of loose sand. Around midnight this flat began to undulate. In the moonlight the swells and waves of stone appeared to move with insidious stealth. There was some sand again; small rivulets and pools of it, caught in clefts and tight basins. It was there, in one of the sand pools, that Moulay's camel lay down and would not get up. That was the first.

Its saddlebags and other gear, including the almost empty goatskins were distributed among the other animals before its throat was slit. Some meat was hacked from it to provide fresh food over the next couple days. There was no time to spend on a complete butchering job; and anyway the meat would soon go bad.

Since the Asasa camels were in much stronger condition, Moulay doubled up with Grayle when they moved on. Much of the time, however, they walked and led the camels, to lessen the drain on their last reserves.

By dawn the terrain was changing again. The surface of solid stone ran out among ever-larger spreads of clay packed with small rock fragments. Monoliths of red sandstone appeared, rising nakedly from the yellow-brown flats on either side. They grew larger as the morning wore on, expanding to low, deeply grooved buttes. Some merged together, casting shadows it took more than half an hour to pass through. It was in one of these stretches of relatively cool shadow that Grayle became aware that it wasn't only the sun that was hot.

The skin of his face and hands were beginning to radiate a heat of their own. Bou Idriss had been right. The fever was rising in him. Not much, as yet. But he could feel it, running in his blood. Before long, he was drinking more water than usual.

The course they followed, by map and compass, led down into a vast depression. Increasingly large areas of it bore a thick skin of hard salt-crust webbed with deep cracks. By ten in the morning the white glare off the salt crystals was blinding. They turned into a narrow cove in the base of a butte, slumping exhausted in its sheltering shade to wait out the sun's passage overhead.

Their prayers were from the heart, intoned in gasps and whispers. Their sleep was oblivion. At four in the afternoon it was only the lure of water, very close now, that dragged them to their feet.

The camel Bou Idriss had been riding wouldn't get up. Tugs and kicks and blows were unavailing. The worn-out animal rolled its eyes in mute appeal and moved its legs weakly. It could not rise, couldn't even snarl when it was beaten.

They stripped it, killed it and moved on.

Bou Idriss took Ahmed's camel. The boy shared Salah's. Grayle and Moulay took turns walking and riding their shared camel. Ali brought up the rear, turning often to look back. But if they were still being pursued, there was no sign of it.

They moved on at a steady pace, restored by the six hours of shade and rest, and drawn by the lure of water waiting ahead. Grayle still had a touch of fever, but it seemed no worse; not enough to slow him.

At dusk Ali's camel lay down and tried to stay down. But with a few minutes of kicking and whipping they got it back on its feet and dragged it on with them. The water was very close; the camel could still recover if they could get it there.

They reached it shortly after midnight. There was a group of buttes bunched together. A narrow break between two of them led into the interior. According to the map of Umar al-Hadj, the waterhole was there. They spread out, searching for it. Finally, as their eyes adjusted to the dimmer starlight in the enclosure of looming buttes, they made out mounds of camel dung.

They began digging into the dust near these mounds, until they uncovered the stone lid. As the dust was swept from it, Grayle picked up a wad of dung. It disintegrated in his fingers, falling as powder dust. His chest constricted with premonition. If the rest of the dung was that ancient . . .

The stone lid was rolled away, uncovering the hole. Scenting the water, the camels surged forward. They had

to be beaten back, roaring with rage. Ali lowered the
bucket. It hid water less than thirty feet down.

The constriction in Grayle's chest grew tighter at the ac-
rid odor that came up with the filled bucket. Grave-faced,
Bou Idriss dipped a finger in the water and touched it to
his tongue. His arm fell limply.

"Poisoned." His voice trembled and he looked to Grayle.
"Chlorine and magnesium have seeped into it. Too much.
It is undrinkable."

Moulay shoved him aside and seized the leather bucket.
He took a swallow, and abruptly threw the bucket aside,
sinking to his knees and retching. He stayed there on his
knees, head hanging.

"We are dead men," he sobbed.

A small fire was lit. Tea was brewed. No one spoke
again until they were drinking it. The light of the tiny
flames flickered across their shadowed faces; the tightly
hobbled camels rumbled and shuffled in misery behind
them. When they did speak, the words were few. What
they had come to crushed any desire for discussion, and
robbed it of any purpose.

There was very little water left in the goatskins for them.
Nothing for the camels. According to the map, the next
source of water lay six to eight days to the north. The two
Asasa camels might survive that long. The other two would
not. Nor could the five men and the boy. The last drop of
the skins would be drunk before they covered half that distance.

"Moulay has said it," Ali rasped. "We are dead."

"Unless," Salah put in slowly, "we come across a caravan. Or another raiding pack comes this way after us. One
small enough for us to cut down. They would have water.
Enough, added to ours."

His words held out the slim hope—but not his tone.

Grayle looked toward the narrow passage between the
buttes. "Only the one way in. And if they don't know the
well is poisoned, they'll come through it." He raised his
eyes to the fissured and pitted butte walls. "We *could* turn

it into a trap for them, even if they were double our number."

"They would have to come soon," Bou Idriss said quietly. He looked at the silent Ahmed.

Salah nodded. "Very soon."

Ali and Moulay curled themselves on the ground and dropped into sleep. They had no faith in this miracle, and preferred to enter their fate in the easiest manner.

Grayle motioned to Salah as he picked up his rifle and got to his feet. "Let's go up for a look."

Salah followed him as he started up a dark slope that seemed to present the least difficult climb. None of the buttes surrounding the enclosure was very high. They reached the top in less than ten minutes. Under the stars the land spread far on all sides. The flat depression, the stone towers, the long shadows. Nothing in movement, anywhere.

Salah made a harsh sound. There was in it a suggestion of a drained laugh; an acceptance. Then, after a moment, he said carelessly: "But they might come. They might even come in time."

Grayle considered the odds against it. "It's possible," he granted.

"If God wills it so, eh?" Salah grinned at him. "All right, Ishmael, just in case He does, I will look for the best covering positions below. Take the first watch up here. I'll relieve you later."

He hefted his rifle and scrambled away down the dark slope. When he disappeared, Grayle sat down facing the direction from which any pursuers were likely to come. If they came.

He rested the Lebel on his crossed legs and growled softly, "Come on, you bastards . . ." And laughed at the foolishness of it.

No chance. Not a chance in Hell. This was where it ended, and what did that matter? It had to end somewhere and nobody ever thought it was the right place. Nor the right time. That life surge inside always had its piece to say: not yet, wait a bit—another year, say? What about a week then? Foolishness.

But he kept watching, though there was nothing out there and he knew there wasn't going to be. Nothing but the emptiness, the silence and the implacable bidding of time.

He stopped thinking about it. Made his head a dark, empty warehouse. And suddenly the voice of his aunt echoed through it, telling him the one about the wolf and the deer:

"Man hungers and prowls and savages like the one, and longs to enter the paradise of the other."

Now why did he remember that one, particularly, after so very many lifetimes?

A rifle boomed in the enclosure below. The noise of it was magnified, reverberating among the butte walls as it rose to him. Grayle spun to his feet, bringing up the Lebel with him. He peered into the darkness below, but could see nothing.

There were no further shots. That puzzled him. His first jolting suspicion centered on Salah. But there would have been more than that single shot.

Cautiously and quietly, he made his way down the butte. Halfway down he detoured, using a different route than he had on the way up.

Bou Idriss sat by the ashes of the fire, his rifle discarded, his head bowed.

Ahmed stood stiffly to one side of him, watching Grayle's slow approach. Bou Idriss did not raise his head. Moulay and Ali were on the other side of him, sprawled on their backs, open eyes staring sightlessly at the stars. Their throats had been slashed.

Grayle almost tripped over Salah. He lay face-down. The side of his head was wet pulp.

Bou Idriss heard the sound Grayle made, but still did not look up at him. "It was the only way," he said heavily. "There was not enough water to take six of us to the next source. Now it will be enough—for two."

Grayle shot him. The bullet rammed into the eunuch's chest and bowled him over backward. He came to rest crumpled on his side, one arm folded under him, the other outflung. He struggled to raise his head.

Slowly, mechanically, Grayle closed in on him. Small electric charges kept sparking his nerve ends, just under the surface of the skin. There was neither anger nor pity left in him; only the need to finish what both knew had to be done. The condemned man had ordered his own execution.

Bou Idriss turned his head painfully for a last look at the boy, standing there staring down at him, the small face gone utterly blank.

"You see . . ." Bou Idriss whispered, "now there is enough water . . ."

Grayle fired the next bullet into his head.

32

The sky and earth reeled, and he marveled at his ability to walk upright between the two. He didn't think he was delirious, but bubbles of laughter kept bursting in his throat. The midday sun felt as cool as midnight moon on his fever-swollen face. It reduced the contrast between his over-heated skin and the ice running in his veins.

The boy kept tugging at him, trying to pull him back into the patch of shade. Grayle flung an irritated backhand at him. It missed and tipped him over. He spat dust and tried to get up, but the black imp kicked his leg and dumped him. Then he was crawling, anger in his laughter now, trying to get at the boy. Ahmed kept backing and beckoning, until they were once more under the rock over-hang whose shadow provided thin protection from the palpitating glare of noon. Grayle slumped forward at the boy's feet, his cheek scraping the hard earth, and slid into sleep.

It wasn't always that bad. The poison in his bloodstream worked at him without letup, but in different ways. There were hours at a stretch when he was lucid: able to use map and compass, to keep going along the shortest route to the northern point where the next water waited, up there inside the hills which had still not appeared. But he was never entirely awake, though most of the time he managed to walk steadily, one foot in front of the other. And when he rode, he was usually capable of controlling his camel.

They had only the two Asasa camels. The other two had slowed them too much, and it had become necessary to kill them. Only the essentials had been transferred to the Asasa camels: food, blankets, the waterskins. Even so, the two remaining animals deteriorated visibly with each day's march.

Grayle and Ahmed rode them as little as possible, to make them last. But there were occasions when Grayle lost the knack of walking properly. When he fell too often and got up too slowly. Until Ahmed helped him drag himself aboard his camel. At these times he slumped in the saddle, no longer a rider but a fever-raging weight of baggage, carried by a weakening animal being dragged onward by the boy.

Late one morning Grayle became aware that the camel carrying him was the only one left to them. It startled him, and he fought through the mist in his brain until it cleared. But he still couldn't remember the other camel dying.

That noon, while they rested in the shade against the base of a low mound, Grayle instructed the boy with the map and compass: "This point marked in the hills here, that is your goal." With his lips dry-cracked and his tongue fever-swollen, each word was a separate problem. "And this line, this is the route you must take to it, if I cannot."

Ahmed shook his head, a rare betrayal of fear in his expression. "No, it can only be with you. You must take me there."

"I intend to. But if I can't—this is the way you will go. The water, first. That is this cross, here on the map." Grayle trailed a finger down from the marked hills. "And here, roughly, is where we are now. The compass direction . . ."

But the boy shrugged, and looked away.

Grayle cuffed him. He watched the boy sprawl in the dirt, and cursed himself weakly. This boy was the only one left to him now.

Ahmed sat up, touching the side of his head where Grayle had struck him. There hadn't been enough strength left in Grayle for the blow to do any damage. The boy pointed upward. "Look!"

All morning heavy clouds had been gathering, and now they hung darkly overhead. Rain had begun to fall from them. Grayle and the boy sat panting in the shade, staring up to the rain, waiting for it to strike them.

They could see it with absolute clarity. It poured straight down at them. But not a drop of it touched them. The rain simply vanished, above their heads.

It wasn't a mirage, Grayle knew. It was the heat of the ground surface, rising up to meet the falling water and turning it to steam. He'd heard accounts of this, but never seen it before. Desert nomads called such occurrences "the Devil's Rain."

Grayle watched in a half-daze as the clouds drifted away to the east, still dropping the rain that failed to reach the earth. They were gone from sight when he and the boy and the camel resumed their slow march to the north.

He kept seeing their faces as he shuffled forward with Ahmed and the camel. The face of Umar al-Hadj, sticking out of the sand dune in which the rest of him had been buried. The face of Bou Idriss, when the bullet smashed through his temple. The face of Salah, hideously distorted by the diagonal scar and mocking grin.

All dead. Grayle's dazed mind wandered over the enormity of it: all of the men who had started out across the desert with him—every one of them had died. And he had survived. Only he—and the boy. A dead man's dream had come true. He was living in it.

He saw the hills, growing higher and closer together as they moved among them. But these hills they had finally reached, and the thornbush in the dry wadis between the slopes, seemed as real and unreal as the faces. A semidelirium was upon Grayle now, though somehow he continued to move through it, like a sleepwalker.

It was, he realized, when they settled down to rest, the growing thirst that was doing it: adding its havoc to the ravages of his fever. He reached automatically for one of the waterskins, and then remembered and let his hand fall. The skins were empty. They had drunk the last drop from them. Grayle and Ahmed stared dumbly at each other, their mouths glued shut. When they sprawled out to sleep, Grayle wondered if they would ever awake. Only the dream of Abd-el-Rahman gave any hope, and when Grayle entered his own dream he found it was the same one. Born in a brain the worms would have digested by now, in the great mountains so far away to the west.

When he did come awake, in the cooling of evening, Grayle felt both surprise and irritation. The heat of his fever generated a last spasm of energy that got him to his feet. He kicked Ahmed awake, and seized the camel's headrope. The animal refused to get up, though Grayle hauled on the rope and Ahmed slashed its hindquarters and legs with the camel-stick.

Grayle bent down awkwardly, hooked his fingers inside the camel's nostrils, and yanked upward with all the strength left to him. The beast rolled and came up ponderously on its legs, roaring with pain and rage. Grayle turned immediately and trudged forward, dragging the camel by the headrope. Ahmed plodded beside it, hanging on to a rope attached under its saddle.

After a time they traded places: Ahmed leading the camel and Grayle hanging on to the saddle-rope. Darkness came, and then was dispersed by the light of stars. Great black cliffs pressed in from either side, broken at intervals by narrow entrances into side gorges and canyons. The clumps of thornbush increased in size, and long patches of dry grasses made their appearance. Grayle forced his head up and scanned the peaks, searching for the landmarks Umar al-Hadj had spoken of as guides to the water.

He had spoken of it with awe: not a man-made well this time, but a natural pool. Remnants of an ancient lake that had been covered for thousands of years—perhaps millions—by folds of rock thrown over it by convulsions of the earth's surface. Exposed again, finally, after eons of winds had sandblasted that covering away. Protected from the evaporating suction of the sun by the high cliffs that loomed over it.

But Grayle failed to spot the promised landmarks that would reveal the way to it through these cliffs.

He stumbled, and saved himself from falling by clutching the saddle-rope. At first he thought it was his own weakness, making it more difficult to keep up with the camel's plodding gait. Then he understood: the beast was increasing its pace, moving more briskly. Its neck no longer hung forward but had arched upward, head held high, nostrils flaring.

The significance hit Grayle, and he tried to communicate it to Ahmed. But he couldn't get his mouth open; all that he managed was a meaningless croaking noise. Suddenly the camel broke into a grotesque, shambling trot.

Grayle lost his grip and fell to one knee. He saw Ahmed trying desperately to hang on, dragged by the rush of the camel, then flung aside, rolling into the stone-littered dust of a shallow wadi. The beast turned and headed for a break in the cliffs to the right. Grayle shoved himself up from the ground and stumbled past Ahmed, following it.

The break led into a deep, narrow passage between sheer walls. In its darkness, Grayle could not see the camel up ahead of him. But he could hear it, and he followed the sound. He tripped over loose stones, fell, heaved to his feet and stumbled on. The passage forked, and Grayle came to a halt. It took him several moments to decide that the noise of the camel's staggering run came from the left fork. He entered it, moving as swiftly as he could.

The passage widened a bit, and more light filtered down, making it possible to see where he was going. But suddenly he could no longer hear anything. Freezing in place, panting, he turned his head, listening for some sound of the camel's movements. There was only silence. But the passage continued on ahead of him, absolutely straight. Grayle pushed on, his desperate need bringing an extra spurt of energy to him.

The passage ended abruptly, opening out into a wide, flat-bottomed bowl. All around it were tall cliffs, with side passages cutting away between them. It was like an open village square, but surrounded by blind skyscrapers. The camel was not there. But something else was. Grayle stared at it, stunned.

It was a massive, gnarled cypress tree. Most of it was long dead, but there were several young branches from which fresh foliage grew. Its age had to go back thousands of years, to an age when this land had been watered and fruitful, and many such trees had grown. Now only this one remained, born out of another world.

Grayle moved toward it, and then stopped.

There was a man seated on the ground before the great tree, gazing at it fixedly, his scrawny hands lying empty on his bony knees, palms up. He wore a tattered black turban and a ragged robe through which parts of a skinny naked body could be seen. His feet were bare, and encrusted with dust. It was impossible to judge his age; but there was no doubt about what he was.

A holy man; a would-be prophet, following the example of Mohammed: going off alone into the heart of the desert in search of his own special religious revelation. One found many such around the fringes of the Sahara. Some returned to civilization after many years, bringing their desert visions with them. Others never returned. One thing Grayle was sure of: this holy man might be their salvation.

He must have seen the camel run past; he had to be aware of Grayle's presence. But he continued to contemplate the ancient cypress, as immobile as the tree, uniting himself to its link between past and future. Grayle advanced on him, trying to make his lips and tongue work, to force the single word through his teeth: "Water . . ."

What came out was a noise, not a word. But the holy man responded to it, in a way, rising from the ground. He was taller than Grayle, gaunt as a stick. Without a word, and without looking directly at Grayle, he turned and motioned for Grayle to follow. He walked with long, measured strides toward the entrance to one of the alleys leading off between the surrounding cliffs. Grayle moved after him, unsteadily.

They were some twenty yards inside this side passage when Grayle heard the camel again, up ahead. It was not the sound of its running, which he had been following before. It was a different sound, unmistakable; and what it meant gave strength to Grayle's legs.

Farther on, the passage expanded, and the holy man came to a halt. Grayle kept going, past him, straight toward what was revealed to him: starlight gleamed from the surface of a wide pool of water, trapped between smoothly rounded humps of solid rock. The camel wallowed in the middle of it, noisily guzzling like an inexhaustible suction machine.

Grayle was almost to it when he saw another, smaller rock pool, off to the right. He diverted to it, wading straight into the water until it was up to his thighs, and then throwing himself facedown into it and letting himself sink entirely beneath the surface.

The cold water soaked into his fevered flesh, bathed his eyes, filled his dust-clogged ears and nostrils. His mouth came unstuck and he opened it wide, sucking in water with his head submerged. He broke surface abruptly, strangling and sputtering.

The instant his nostrils were clear enough for him to breathe again, Grayle crouched and began gulping water. His knees sank until they touched bottom and the surface was just under his armpits. He stayed that way, drinking and drinking. His belly swelled and his head began to experience a clarity he had almost forgotten was possible. A renewed life filled his body as the moisture entered his blood and bones.

Finally, he could drink no more. His insides were churning, his heart pounding painfully, his chest heaving. He straightened his head and looked around him. The camel was still wallowing and guzzling in the other pool. The holy man still stood, watching.

But Ahmed was not there.

Alarm jolted Grayle. Suddenly, the boy seemed the most important human being on earth to him. Wading out of his pool, he started back through the rock passages, hunting.

He found Ahmed where he had left him, still sprawled in the shallow wadi, his eyes closed. Grayle bent to him swiftly. There was a lump on the boy's forehead where it had struck a large stone when he fell. But his breathing was steady. Grayle pressed a palm to the boy's thin chest. The heartbeat was normal.

Scooping Ahmed up in his arms, cradling him against his chest, Grayle carried him through the passages to his pool of water. The holy man stood there, observing without expression as Grayle waded into the pool with his burden, until Ahmed's legs, body and arms were submerged.

Squeezing the boy against him with one arm to keep his head above the surface, Grayle scooped water with his free hand and splashed Ahmed's face with it. He scooped more water and tried to force it between the boy's lips. Ahmed stirred a bit, but his eyes didn't open. Finally, Grayle shoved the boy's face under water.

Ahmed's body spasmed in his grip, his head jerking wildly. Grayle raised him, letting his twisting face come up clear of the water. The boy was choking and coughing, his eyes wide open and terrified, not understanding what was happening to him. Grayle carried him out of the pool and laid him down at its edge. Ahmed stared at him, then raised both hands and looked at the water dripping from them.

Grayle rolled him on his side, facing the pool. A second later Ahmed was dragging himself into the water, drinking greedily. Grayle smiled weakly and sat down. Suddenly all the strings holding him together let go. He fell back, and stared up at the stars. His eyes closed and he drifted into a half-sleep.

He drifted out of it with awareness of cold water soaking the bandages stuck to his wounds. His eyes sprang open with the pain of the bandage being ripped from his forehead. The holy man was crouched over him, outlined by the stars above.

Grayle spoke as the scrawny hands washed his forehead. "I have bad fever. The wound in my side. It is infected . . ."

The holy man continued cleaning the head wound, saying nothing. Grayle repeated it in another Berber dialect, then tried Arabic and finally French. None of it brought a word of response. But the holy man nodded, and began the task of peeling the bandage from Grayle's side wound.

A shock of agony made Grayle clamp his teeth and eyes shut, groaning. His head spun. When he opened his eyes again, he saw the glint of starlight on the curved blade jutting from the holy man's fist.

The knife was lowered to his injured side. Grayle braced himself. Felt cold steel slice deep inside the engorged wound. His life seemed to gush from the opening. Consciousness poured out with it.

The fattest and juiciest dates produced in Algeria came from the palm groves surrounding the town of Biskra. It was to transport these dates to the world that the French had built the railroad line northwest to the distant port of Algiers, turning Biskra into the most thriving center on the northern fringe of the Sahara. Before that it had been a small village of mud-walled houses and dusty lanes, a native shopping market for local desert and mountain tribes.

It was in a border area between the old town and the new that the luxurious house of Aisha, Ahmed's grandmother, was located.

A large aquarium covered most of one wall in the tower room assigned to Grayle. Inside it brilliantly colored tropical fish swam between chunks of coral and fronds of seaweed. From his divan in an alcove, Grayle watched their darting colors as he allowed himself to wake with delicious slowness from his afternoon nap.

These lazy naps, and long nights of sleep, had taken up much of his time since he and the boy had reached the safety and comfort of this home. He was still recovering from the journey, though the fever had left him in the eight days they had remained with the holy man in his desert sanctuary.

The holy man had not uttered a single word during those eight days, though he shared meat with them when Grayle had shot and cooked a gazelle, and later a prowling jackal. And in the end they had left him as Grayle had found him: seated before the ancient cypress, communing with its immortality.

It had been three weeks more, north to Biskra; but by easy stages. Through hilly areas where water had no longer been a rarity; where no one hunted them, and where the caravan drivers they met were not overly inquisitive about the purpose of their journey.

Since their arrival in Aisha's home, Grayle had seen less and less of Ahmed. He knew that the boy was being prepared for what lay ahead of him; Grayle's own part had ended when they'd reached here. For a time their lives had been linked by a dream, and the dream was over.

Grayle heard the bugle and drums from the nearby parade ground of the French-Sengalese barracks, and roused himself from the divan. He removed his sleeping gown and washed from the bowl of water just inside his doorway. Drying himself, he put on the freshly laundered robe that had been laid out for him while he slept. It was of soft linen, embroidered with red satin and blue silk. As he slipped his feet into velvet-lined slippers, one of the servants, a burly Arab bodyguard, appeared at the doorway. Aisha wished to see Grayle.

He followed the man from his room, down the tower stairs. They crossed the courtyard garden around which the house was built. Peacocks strutted under the shade of sweet-lemon trees. A tame gazelle was munching fresh-cut grass from a stone bowl. The bodyguard stopped at the entrance to Aisha's reception chamber. Grayle kicked off his slippers and stepped inside.

Ahmed's grandmother sat waiting for him on a short divan in an arched alcove before a low table of bronze. She was a thin, dark woman in her fifties, with a deeply wrinkled, tattooed face. Her black eyes were watchful, her manner quietly assured and guarded.

She was one of the Hatari, a black slave-caste of the Tuaregs. Her small branch of that group lived in cliff dwellings and caves in the Aurès Mountains; and it had been there that Bou Idriss had bought her daughter. No one hereabouts knew that the daughter had given a son to a Berber chief called Abd-el-Rahman, far off in the High Atlas of Morocco. They knew only that Aisha had become the richest of her tribe, and that the source of her wealth remained a mystery.

Grayle lowered himself cross-legged to a floor cushion, looking up at her across the low bronze table.

"Ahmed has gone," she told him in softly accented French. "His half-brother, Tahar, came and took him away in the night."

To Algiers, Grayle thought; and thence by ship to some part of Europe: to grow up as his father had planned, making himself ready to fulfill his destiny. Grayle wondered what it would come to, and guessed that he would never know.

"My grandson wished to bid you farewell," Aisha said. "But we thought it best not to disturb your sleep, and there was no time to wait."

She removed a black velvet covering from a small box and spread it flat on the table between them. The box was of ebony, inlaid with yellowed ivory and rusty coral, held together with bands of dull gold studded with pearls and opals. She opened the lid and took out a satin bag, closed by a drawstring of silk braid.

"You are welcome to stay here as long as you wish," she told Grayle, "and you are free to go whenever you desire. Ahmed asked me to say that you will always be an honored guest in his home—and to give you this."

She opened the satin bag and poured its stones across the black velvet: a glittering mixture of ice, blood and sea.

Part 3:
MONSIEUR HUGONNET

"I paint not what I see,
but what I saw."
                    —Edvard Munch

"Life is an explosive, see?
Bang, and a man is born and then,
Bang, he falls to pieces And
we think it lasts some years."
                    —Karel Capek

33

She waded through the tall grass below the village and around the low dry-stone wall of the old cemetery, hunting among the profusion of wildflowers. The dense tangles of green that covered the undulating slopes were full of them: purple toadflax and yellow archangel, cowslip and bird's-eye primrose, sandwort and hawkweed, larkspur and columbine. But she gathered only those with specific practical uses.

She was eleven years old in that spring of 1939, and her grandmother had long since taught her which to select. Borage, especially: its hairy leaves were good in soups and salads, and its bright blue flowers made an ointment that healed cuts and eased her grandmother's arthritis. Vervain, for brewing a tea that calmed the nerves. Thyme, delicious in cooking sauces and excellent for the skin when crushed into hot bathwater.

There was a man in the little cemetery. It was the old stranger she'd seen before. He was unmistakable, with that short, gray-flecked beard. None of the men of the valley had a beard. The other two times she'd seen him, he'd been having a coffee at one of the two tables outside the cafe, under the big tree in the village square. The second time, he had returned her look, in a peculiar way. Given her a straight, appraising look, with thought behind it.

Carrying the gathered wildflowers in her tucked-up apron, she moved down between the blooming mimosa and cherry trees, to a place where the slope banked up against the cemetery wall. There the top of the wall was little higher than her waist. The man was standing before one of the graves, seeming unaware of her approach. She took off her apron and pulled the corners together to form a sack, setting it on the wall as she studied him.

Everyone was curious about him. The village wasn't accustomed to the presence of strangers. It was tucked out of the way in a valley of small farms and vineyards, east of the Rhône River just under the low mountain chain of the Alpilles. Sometimes tourists stopped at the cafe for a snack or cigarettes, on their way west to Avignon or Arles, or southeast to Marseilles and the Côte d'Azur. But none stayed longer than an hour; there was nothing in the village to hold them.

But the stranger had showed up almost a week ago, and he was still there. Her grandmother had heard from a villager that he was staying at the ruin of the ancient chateau, a mile away across the valley. Jumeau, the leather craftsman, lived in a work-shed he'd fixed up in part of the ruin. It was possible that the stranger was visiting with him. Possible, but unlikely. Jumeau, who was not right in the head, kept to himself and had no friend or relative that anyone knew of.

What made the girl even more curious was the gravestone that he was looking at.

As she watched him, he turned his head and looked at her—not in surprise but as if he had known she was there, all along.

She realized now that he was not as old as she'd thought, in spite of all the gray in his beard. His eyes were young, and sharply observant.

Actually, she decided, he would be rather handsome, if it weren't for the beard and that horrible scar across his broad forehead—its ridges dead-white against his tan. She tried a smile on him. He didn't smile back.

"That is my grandfather's grave you were looking at," she told him.

"Is it?" His voice was quiet, but deep and strong. She liked the sound of it.

"Yes. I never knew him. He died before I was born. But he used to be a famous artist."

He nodded, his eyes fixed on her. "I recognized the name."

That surprised and pleased her. Nobody around the village seemed impressed with her grandfather's name. "We have a lot of his old pictures in our house. My grandmother says they'll be worth money again, someday."

"Do you like them?"

"Oh, yes. Some of them are strange, though."

He looked again at the gravestone of Claude Cesari. "He was a damn good painter. Not one of the big masters. But—he had something."

"I have the same name as him," she said, and let the pride show. "My family name. Pascale Cesari."

He looked away from the grave, his eyes returning to hers. "Mine," he said, "is Jean Hugonnet."

With a proper formality, they reached across the cemetery wall and shook hands.

Her hand was small and thin in his. The hand of a child. But the long gray eyes that regarded him with the measuring interest of a critical mind—those eyes were Nora's.

In her sixties, Madame Cesari was a lean, vigorous woman whose days were full. She was never bored, except by people incapable of being awakened to the profusion of natural phenomena around them. She had never liked city life, preferring the excitement of an ever-varying countryside. She could become absorbed in the progress of an insect through the leaves of a plant, had a keen eye for changing weather-signs, checked regularly on birds nesting in the trees shading her vegetable garden; and she found enchantment in long hikes around the valley and surrounding hills, seeking out forgotten paths, gathering snails and mushrooms, keeping a sharp lookout for rare herbs.

She had observed the changing of her granddaughter with the same judicious interest. Pascale had revealed early a logical, acquisitive mind. At seven she could be trusted to do much of the food shopping. Since eight she had been her grandmother's kitchen apprentice, helping cook their meals. With Nora away so much it was Madame Cesari

who had raised the child; and she regarded Pascale possessively, as an extension of herself.

But lately she had become aware that the girl's intelligence was beginning to wander off along paths of its own.
Probably influenced by the greedy appetite she had developed for romantic novels: Dumas, Hugo, Scott. So she was
merely a bit amused, over their dinner that evening, by the
romanticism with which Pascale described her encounter
with the strange Monsieur Hugonnet.

Pascale went upstairs to finish her homework and write
in her secret diary before going to bed. Her small room was
in the upper floor of the narrow stone house that had belonged to her grandfather's family for generations. Most of
the room was filled by the wide bed which Pascale's
mother shared with her when she was there. It left barely
enough room for the other furniture: a narrow bureau, and
a table and chair against the window that overlooked the
slate roofs of this side of the village slope.

The two dresses Pascale wasn't wearing hung from a
wire nailed to the wall. On the bureau was her mother's
photograph, in a standing frame. Pascale had taken it two
months ago with her grandmother's box camera: her mother's camera had been smashed by a bullet during her escape from Spain, over the Pyrenees.

Above the bureau, beside the framed mirror, Pascale had
tacked three of her mother's last pictures to the wall. They
were from the already famous series she had brought out
with her: of the buildings and people of Guernica being
destroyed by the Italian and German dive bombers that
had been sent to help Franco's fascist army win the Spanish civil war.

Pascale sat down at the table, facing the window. She
had a view to the north, past the bell tower of the church.
The village was part of the humped shoulder of a hill. Beyond it the valley with its small farms rose in folds to steep
slopes and low cliffs overgrown with evergreens.

By craning her head to one side, Pascale could make out
the slope which held the old chateau. It had been uninhab-

ited for so long that trees and bushes almost concealed it. All she could see was the top of a collapsing tower.

She opened her diary to a fresh page. Usually it was her homework she did first, leaving the diary for when the light began to fade. But this evening, she had real news for her diary. Something nobody else in the village knew about, yet.

Pascale unscrewed the cap of her ink bottle, dipped in the pen and began writing:

> *Monsieur Hugonnet* owns *the old chateau! And all the grounds around it. He has bought it from the family it belonged to, down in Montpellier. He intends to fix up part of it so he can live there permanently. Of course it is just a ruin now, but by the end of this summer he hopes to have some rooms with roofs solid enough to keep out the rain.*
>
> *Jumeau is going to help him with the work. And on Tuesdays and Sundays, when there is no school, I'm going over to help out, too. He has offered to pay me for any work I do, by the hour, the same amount he would pay an adult worker. That will surprise people.*
>
> *I am sure Monsieur Hugonnet is hiding something. Some awful tragedy in his life he can't stand to talk about. Or some terrible thing he has done, that he is afraid will be discovered. But he will learn—his secret would be safe with me. I like him. Very much. I know that he likes me, too. I could see it, even that first time he looked at me, when he was having a coffee out on the Place Clemenceau.*

It began raining in Manhattan shortly after nine that spring night. A torrential downpour. It was still coming down at three in the morning, when Nora left the party at the townhouse of Arnold Rudofsky, the public-relations man who specialized in big businesses and big politicians. This was Nora's first time in New York, and she was shocked by the relentlessness of the storm that slashed the stone towers of the island city.

She was with Harry O'Neil, who had brought her to the party, in one of the chauffeur-driven limousines Rudofsky had provided for his guests. Sheets of water ran down the outside of the car windows, as the limousine crept along the bottom of a drowned canyon, following the vague blobs of its headlights. Nora saw a geyser of steam issuing from a manhole cover turned a diabolic crimson-yellow by the neon of an all-night diner. The most modern city in the world beset by tropical storms and undermined by warnings from the fires of hell.

She could sense no connection at all between this place and her part of Europe. New York was a real city. Spain and France were myths: one convulsed in its death agony, the other decaying into senility.

As the limousine passed Harry O'Neil's apartment, he put a hand on her knee and asked, "Sure you won't drop into my place first, for a last drink?"

Nora shook her head. "No, Harry, I'm sorry—I'm just too exhausted."

"Okay," O'Neil said with good-humored resignation; "so you're not in a romantic mood. My hard luck. So let's talk business. It's about time you replaced that camera you lost when you were escaping from Spain. I just bought a new Leica. But my old one's still in good shape. I'll sell it to you, cheap."

"I'm not in the market for another camera, Harry. Not now. I didn't come here to shoot pictures."

Harry O'Neil was *Look* magazine's top photographer. He and Nora had met briefly when they had both been covering the fighting in Madrid—before the roof fell in there. He'd gotten out, long before she did, and he'd been one of the first to meet her on her arrival in New York. And because he understood why she'd come, he had given unstintingly of his time. He had introduced her to the sort of people it was important for her to meet: important columnists, the picture editors of *Look, Time,* and *Life,* the foreign editor of *The New York Times,* Arnold Rudofsky and his influential crowd. Through them, she had gotten her introductions to prominent politicians in Washington, her next stop. Contacts that were more important for her purpose than those given her by the Spanish refugee committees in Paris.

She had come to raise money for Spanish exiles in France; and to help others still trying to escape from Franco's murder squads. The pictures she had taken in Spain had been given lavish display in *Life*, and they'd been picked up by American newspapers coast to coast. That gave her the entry, authority and glamor to carry out her mission here. As far as she was concerned, the time for taking pictures of people dying was past. What was needed now was to save those who were not yet dead.

The limousine came to a stop in front of the Algonquin Hotel. Nora kissed Harry before climbing out. She *was* fond of him. As she hurried under the hotel canopy into the lobby she glanced back, and he blew her another kiss.

She'd been out of the hotel since the previous morning, and there was a letter waiting in her room slot. The night clerk handed it over with her key. Nora looked at it as the elevator creaked up to the third floor. It was from Paris, and the handwriting was Victor Royan's.

As soon as she was inside her room, she stripped off her clothing and started a hot bath. While the tub was filling, she dried her hands and opened the letter.

It was depressing reading: partly because of what it told, but also because of the sarcasm with which Victor told it. The first part was about matters she already knew, too well: the plight of the Spanish refugees was increasingly desperate, and the need to obtain aid for them increasingly urgent. The French politicians were a confused pack of corrupt cowards. Another world war was coming; anyone with senses could feel it in the air. Hitler and Mussolini had merely sharpened their teeth on Spain. Now they were ready to chew up the rest of Europe.

The rest was much worse: the wavering intent of the French government was finally settling into a policy of kissing Franco's ass—and Hitler's boots—by treating the exiles as criminals. There was a clear indication that very soon they were going to be shoved into prison camps, or shipped back to certain death in Spain. Those who had connections in Cuba and other countries in South America were already trying to raise money for their passage across the Atlantic. How bad were the chances that the United States could be persuaded to take in this new batch of Europe's poor and hungry outcasts, yearning to breathe free? She didn't have to tell him.

Nora could *hear* his tone, as she crumpled the letter and fought down her own despair. And she could see what Victor's face had looked like as he'd written it. He was slipping back into the character he'd been in those first years she'd known him. *Lack* of character, with that mask of sardonic lethargy.

He'd been another man entirely in Spain—with no sign left of the year he'd spent recovering from his fall from the horse, except for his white hair. He'd become charged with energy, using his experience as an officer in World War I to train and lead the inept foreign idealists who arrived from all over the world to fight against fascism. He had been magnificent then: bigger than life, excited, determined, purposeful, cunning—and irresistible. They had become lovers for two months, during the fighting outside Barcelona. Before the fighters there had broken into rival factions, the communists and anarchists so intent on wiping out each other and anyone else not bound to them, that they almost forgot about holding off the fascists who were their common enemy.

It had become necessary for Victor and Nora to get out, along with a lot of others who'd merely believed in trying to save democracy, before they were hunted down and executed by one or another of the roaming bands of rival fanatics. They had been too well-known by then to escape by train or roads. Hunted, they'd finally made it across some of the worst parts of the Pyrenees into France.

Victor had been magnificent there, too, through all of that hard, dangeross trek. But his deterioration had set in as soon as they were back in Paris. Arguing at save-the-Spanish meetings was not the same as fighting bullets and bombs. Cursing opposition politicians and newspapers was not like sabotaging enemy bridges and railroad tracks. Victor was a man who needed the imminent danger of death to bring him to life.

The tub was full. She took her hot bath; and then took a pill to help her get to sleep. Her train to Washington left early that afternoon, and she didn't want to arrive exhausted. There was too much to be done there; and hardly any time left for it to be of use to anyone.

34

The villagers decided early that Monsieur Hugonnet was in some ways not normal. The first sign was the fact that someone like Jumeau was apparently content to share "his" chateau with him. The second came with the discovery that Hugonnet had actually bought the place, though its buildings were in such ruin that he had to live in what was once its storage barn while he undertook the enormous job of restoring the rest.

Another abnormality of Monsieur Hugonnet's was his habit of taking long walks in the rain. While sensible people stayed indoors, there he'd be: striding past through the wet in his boots and corduroy cap, the collar of his farmer's jacket turned up and water dripping from the beard that concealed much of his face.

As the spring wore on, they began to learn other bits and pieces about him. His pleasure in rainy weather became understandable: he had spent his entire life in the hot, dry climate of Algeria, where he'd been born to French parents in Constantine. This information came from the two places where Monsieur Hugonnet had showed his papers and registered his presence in the area, as required by law. First with the mayor of the village, Pierre-Baptiste Chabot, who owned the largest farm in the valley. Then with the gendarmerie in Arles, which was responsible for this area, and whose young adjutant, Alain Nugon, now lived with his bride of a year in nearby Fontvielle.

It was from Adjutant Nugon's wife, Katie, a nurse whose duties often brought her to the village, that the villagers learned he'd made the money on which he'd decided to retire from exporting Algerian textiles.

Then he bought a small truck to transport building materials to the chateau, and the way he handled it at first revealed that he was new at driving anything.

Other things about him came from Pascale Cesari, passed on through her schoolfriends to their parents. And still more from craftsmen and their assistants, hired to work on the chateau. Some stopped at the village cafe before heading home at night: the carpenter and roofer from Arles, the plumber from St. Remy, the stonemason who lived up in the Alpilles at the entrance to the ancient underground quarries near Les Baux.

The story was that Monsieur Hugonnet's scarred forehead was a result of an attack by an insurgent tribe while he was purchasing Arab rugs at a remote village. He had no family, his parents having died and he never having married. He intended to restore only part of the chateau, leaving the rest in ruins and allowing Jumeau to stay on without paying rent. He was not afraid of hard work and learned quickly, doing much of the basic labor himself, with the help of Jumeau and, occasionally, little Pascale. Both of whom he paid as fairly as he did the specialists he hired. A man with money to squander, obviously.

An odd man but decent, some said. Others professed to detect a potential danger in him that one sometimes sensed in shepherds who spent too long talking only to animals and themselves.

He remained "the stranger"—but that became merely a label that fixed his position in their society. By summer he was an accepted part of the human scenery of the village area, together with his gossip-provoking eccentricities and remnants of mystery.

The land Grayle now owned had once been clearly defined by outer defense ramparts running completely around it. Most of it had disintegrated to low mounds of rubble covered with earth and weeds. The grounds within were composed of slopes and hollows, except for the relatively level area which held the complex of buildings and ruins. Where once had been neat groves of trimmed trees, graceful pathways and terraced gardens, there was now a wilderness. It pressed against the walls of the buildings, even penetrating them in places.

What the village called "the chateau" had been many things over the previous six centuries. Originally it had been an abbey. Later it had been rebuilt as a fortified farm; still later it had been converted into a country mansion for a wealthy merchant. It had been abandoned long ago, and been gutted by a fire that had made many of the additions of the previous century as unusable as the ruins dating back hundreds of years.

Grayle had bought this place because it was the only one available that would give him the privacy he wanted— where he wanted it: close to the village where Pascale lived, and to which Nora would return.

The enormity of the job ahead of him here was also what he wanted, and needed: to expend his energy creating something, instead of destroying—it had been a very long time since he'd done that.

Most of the buildings that were left were grouped around a big courtyard containing a blocked-up well that dated back to the cloister of the original abbey. The chateau proper, which the wealthy merchant had developed by extending a two-story farmhouse, loomed across the rear of the courtyard. Its stone walls stood solid, but much of the roof had collapsed in the fire that had made its interior unliveable.

Linked to the right corner of the chateau was a squarish building that had probably been a monks' chapter-room. Here, too, though the walls remained, the roof had caved in.

But stretching from it along the right side of the courtyard was a long, low building with a curved roof of trimmed stone, most of it intact. Attached to the outside was a vaulted arcade, its exterior arches still supported by thick columns. The interior had contained a dormitory for the abbey's lay brethren, and had been used later as a supplementary barn. There was a large fireplace at one end. At the other was a narrow doorway to a washroom with a large stone basin, topped by a fountain that no longer worked when Grayle moved in.

The window openings of the long room were crumbling and there were cracks in the walls and roof vaulting. But it could be patched up and made habitable in a reasonably short time. Grayle concentrated on this first, before beginning his work on the chateau.

It took Grayle two weeks to finish the basic work on the abbey building that was his first living quarters. The clearing of the wild bushes and vines around the buildings was still going on when he began the job of restoring the part of the chateau he had chosen for his future home.

He filled in the gaps in the walls with fallen stones from other buildings, strengthened bulging sections with metal clamps and tie-rods. Next came the replacing of rafters and beams, the repairing of timber ceilings, the laying down of new flooring. For the roofing, old tiles were best: Grayle and Jumeau gathered up all they found still intact among the debris.

The fireplaces and chimneys were still serviceable. All that was required was cleaning them out and adding to the upper portions. No electrical installation was needed: the fireplaces would provide sufficient heat, a wood-and-coal-burning stove would do for cooking, oil lamps and candles would supply the kind of night light Grayle wanted.

Plumbing was a greater problem. Pipes had to be laid from the spring out back to the chateau; and from it down to a new cesspool dug in the slope below. Water heaters fueled by bottled gas had to be installed.

In all, Grayle reckoned that more than a year of work lay ahead of him. But once he had the basics done—the rooms cleared, the fireplaces operating, the floors solid and the roofs completed to keep out the rain—he could proceed with the rest at an unhurried pace.

To Pascale he assigned, first, the job of clearing out the main courtyard; he oversaw her work until he was sure she could handle the cutting and digging tools without hurting herself. At times she told him what her mother, who was now traveling toward California on a lecture and fundraising tour, had written about America. Grayle listened with quiet interest, but made no comment.

She learned the work quickly, and soon became quite expert at it. Even so, with all that thornbrush to deal with, she always left with a new assortment of scratches on her arms and with her eyes smarting from the smoke of burning what she had cleared that day. The second time she came, her grandmother came with her.

Grayle stiffened when he saw them enter the courtyard through the open gateway in the low wall out front. Madame Cesari's hair had gone all white and her wrinkles had deepened; otherwise she hadn't changed in over a decade since he'd last seen her. Forcing his tensed muscles to relax, he advanced through the rubble and brush to meet them. He knew that *he* had changed, a great deal. Not just the beard and the scar. He looked ten years older than he was. Even his voice was not the same; there was no trace left of the American accent. It should be enough.

"She wanted to see the work we're doing," Pascale explained as she introduced them. But it was obvious that Madame Cesari had come to see what kind of man her granddaughter's new "friend" was; and to decide if she approved of their spending so much time together.

He shook her hand. "I hope you don't mind my employing Pascale to help out?"

"Some experience of working for wages never harmed any child," she answered crisply. "But I'm afraid you're spoiling her a bit, giving her the same pay you'd give a grown-up."

Grayle indicated the overgrown courtyard. "She's doing a grown-up's work."

She liked his manner, the way he spoke, the way he met her penetrating gaze.

For his part, Grayle detected no sign of recognition in her.

"Would you like to see what I plan to do inside?" he asked her.

Pascale headed toward the back of the courtyard, to begin clearing another patch, as he led Madame Cesari into the arcade. A table and chairs and a camp bed had been set up under its stone vaulting.

"I'm already living inside," he told her. "But this is a cool, shady place to eat or rest in the heat of day." He took her through an archway from the arcade into the long abbey room. It had been cleared of rubble, and there was plenty of sunlight, streaming in through a line of narrow window openings. A wide bed with a brass headboard had been installed, and a long table with many chairs around it.

"When the work crews are around they usually eat in here with me," Grayle explained. "I cook in the fireplace there. It works perfectly; has from the start."

"That's one thing they've always built well in this country," Madame Cesari said. "I've seen ruins where the *only* thing left standing was the fireplace. Still functioning."

He took her out through the courtyard into the chateau, using the new oak door he had put in. Taking her through the place slowly, he explained in detail what he intended with each room.

"You are very house proud," she commented at one point.

He thought about it. "Perhaps. It feels good, to *make* something."

She considered that and observed him shrewdly as he took her through the place, outlining his plans in that quiet, unhurried manner. There was a directed energy about him, apparent even in his way of standing still—controlled and contained. A man who'd had a deeply troubled life, she decided; and who obviously lived with some of that still. But—a man of solid nerves.

"I don't see Jumeau around," she mentioned. "Pascale said he was helping do the restoration."

"He's in his shed, at his leather work. He only helps with the house when I work together with him. Otherwise it's not fun for him."

"Fun? I thought you paid him."

"He doesn't do it for the pay, really. I tell him stories while we work together, you see."

Madame Cesari eyed him with growing curiosity. "What kind of stories?"

"Anything. About Africa. Or from books. Or legends I learned from an old Berber called the Dream Master."

"Dream Master . . ." she repeated slowly, investigating the alien sound of it.

He didn't explain it further. "What the stories are don't matter much, as long as he feels my own interest in them. Like with children. He's a sponge. They fill him with new images to think about."

There were facets to this man which she did not fully comprehend. She examined what it was that she felt, as they went back out to the vaulted walkway. Pascale was chopping at the thick base of a vine, handling the axe with a newly acquired sureness. Madame Cesari sat at the table beside a pointed arch, resting herself a bit, while Monsieur Hugonnet got a pitcher of cold spring water and filled a glass for her.

As she drank it, she studied the way he watched her granddaughter at work. There was no danger in him, she determined finally; not where Pascale was concerned. He was just a lonely man, becoming elderly and needing the nearness of youth; with no children of his own to give him that necessary feeling of future.

"Would you care to join us for dinner this Friday?" she asked him.

"Thank you. I'd like that."

"Good." She stood up and called to Pascale: "Don't come home too late."

"I won't."

"Until Friday evening, then," she said as she shook his hand in parting. "Around seven."

She left the courtyard and strode away along a newly cleared path between twin ranks of tall pines. What he had revealed of himself intrigued her, as did the sense that there were aspects he withheld. Somewhat like a forest animal: not hostile, but wary. Altogether, the most interesting man she had met in a very long time.

* * *

That afternoon, after Pascale had gone, Grayle wandered down to a hidden place in the tangle of woods below the chateau. It was a lovely, slender stream, running between steep banks choked with bushes and young trees, deep grass and wildflowers. Seated against the trunk of an old tree above it, he listened to the concealed birds, watched the way the sun pierced through the foliage above him.

He loved the sheltered secrecy of this place. He could see her here, taking off her clothes to bathe in the stream.

She would return by early August, at the latest, she had promised Pascale in her last letter.

A decade, it had been—but in this secret place it seemed that he had merely turned his head and looked away from her for a moment, retaining the look and sound of her, savoring her feel and taste. The dapples of sunlight would lick at her skin, as it did on the flowing water.

On the opposite bank, a small black rabbit eased out of the gnarled roots of a kermes oak, and shook itself, airing its sleek, thick fur. A twig cracked nearby, and the rabbit vanished back inside its hiding place. A savage woods cat, scrawny and tiger-striped, with a missing ear, slunk past the roots, seeking something farther on.

Grayle stayed until no sunlight penetrated the enclosure, and only the damp, musky odor remained, rising from the deepening shadow between the banks.

Jumeau had their supper waiting, outside his shed in a curve of ruined wall. Bread and cheese, black olives and the gray wine of the Camargue. By the time Grayle returned to his courtyard, the night had a solid presence. The big olive tree he had left standing near the old well was visible only as a darker blur in a dark surrounding.

The sky had become overcast, and there was a damp, chill wind blowing. Grayle went in through the arcade and entered the long abbey room. He knew it too well, by now, to have to grope his way. Lighting a candle, he gathered kindling and arranged it in the deep fireplace. When it was burning well, he added split logs, setting each in exactly the right position. They caught quickly. A well-made fire in a well-made fireplace: one of the oldest pleasures.

He backed off a bit and sat on the floor, drawing up his knees and folding his arms on them. All his senses seemed to have become acutely aware, savoring the variety of stimuli: the smells of earth, vegetation and woodsmoke, the sounds of frogs and nightingales and the crackling logs. He watched the play of the flames.

By August, she would come.

35

That June morning when Pascale climbed the path through the woods to the chateau, she saw before she reached it that he was away. The truck wasn't parked in its accustomed spot outside the front wall of the courtyard. But wherever he was, he'd be back; in the meantime, there was work waiting for her. She pushed open the low swinging gate he'd put in the wall opening, stepped into the courtyard and surveyed it with some pride.

It was cleared of debris and wild brush now, and she had the scabs, bruises and calluses to show for it. Her new job was laying down brick tiles to form paths that had been marked out with string. But after an hour at it she began to suffer from the heat—and boredom. She was as hopeless as Jumeau, she told herself: unable to enjoy the work unless Monsieur Hugonnet was there. Finally she gave up and went off through the ancient ruins to the left of the courtyard, in search of Jumeau.

Circling the old defense tower, Pascale headed toward a curved wall that was the only thing left of a large church, the rest having been carted off long ago to build the chateau and houses in the village. The shed in which Jumeau lived and worked was built against this wall, out of fallen stones, planks and tin sheeting.

He was inside it, at his workbench, punching holes in a belt he'd just finished cutting. A stocky, stolid man in his forties, with guarded, injured eyes, and tangles of yellowish hair sprouting out from under the checkered cloth cap he always wore.

"He's gone to the stonemason," he told her curtly.

Pascale knew by now that the sharp tone didn't mean anything. He never spoke to anyone unless a few spare words became absolutely necessary; even when he came into the village for an occasional drink. That was why he'd been given the nickname, more than a decade ago— Pascale's grandmother had told her the story:

One night after finishing his drink at the bar, he'd suddenly begun making a speech. It had concerned the relative merits of the orderly life of bees and the chaotic existence of humans; and it had gone on for almost half an hour. Then he'd paid for his pastis and walked out. One stunned listener had joked that it *couldn't* have been the man they knew—he must have a twin brother. And the name had stuck: Jumeau—the Twin.

Leaning against the wall, Pascale watched him take a shears and a strip of leather, and begin cutting out another belt. He didn't acknowledge her presence; but neither did he voice any objection to it. While she watched him work she told him bits of gossip from the village and school, and stories from her history lessons. He didn't offer any response to this, either; but she was pretty sure he enjoyed her stories almost as much as he did those of Monsieur Hugonnet.

When Jumeau stopped for lunch, he shared it with her, silently; and then stretched out on his bunk for a nap. Pascale walked back to the courtyard feeling lethargic and a bit dizzy from her wine, and decided she would take a nap, too. Monsieur Hugonnet had left the camp bed outside under the vaulted arcade. Pascale sprawled on it and fell asleep.

That was how Grayle found her. He stood there in the courtyard for some time, watching her sleep, framed by the crumbling stone columns and the arch they supported. She didn't wake when he finally went past her into the house. He came out with a pencil and the copybook he used in planning the work on the buildings and grounds.

Back in the courtyard, he settled on one knee, and looked again at the sleeping girl in the frame of old stone. Opening the copybook, he rested it on his raised knee and began to draw.

It was the first time in more than ten years.

It required an effort not to think about it; to let his hand discover what it could remember by itself. When the drawing was finished he shut the book immediately and took it back inside the house.

He didn't look at the drawing again until late that afternoon, when Pascale had left for home. Then he looked at it for a long time.

The next morning he drove down to Arles, and went into the art-supply shop on the Place du Forum. It was exceptionally well-stocked for a town that size. The explanation for that hung on one wall: a copy of Van Gogh's painting of his bedroom in Arles. They didn't forget that he had worked here.

When he returned to the chateau, he told Jumeau he was taking off the rest of the day. Jumeau went back to his shed, and Grayle set up the easel in the arcade, put the stretched canvas on it. He spread out the rest of his purchases on the table next to the easel, and put the drawing of Pascale beside them. Using a stick of charcoal, he lightly sketched the main lines of the drawing on the canvas. Again, it required effort not to think critically of what he was doing; just to let it happen.

There was a faint queaziness in his guts as he began to mix his paints. But it was gone when he'd finished preparing his palette. He looked at the drawing, and saw again what it had told him before: his eyes and hand had not forgotten.

Then he selected a brush, looked at the waiting canvas and began to live again.

As the summer wore on, the village had another eccentricity to add to what it knew of Monsieur Hugonnet: he would sit, sometimes, on the Place Clemenceau, making sketches of the women washing clothes at the long stone basin attached to the fountain, of the children playing around the great plane tree, of the old farmers competing at boules on the patch of leveled earth between the butcher shop and the side of the dilapidated Romanesque church.

He didn't seem to mind when people stood behind him and watched what he was doing. The village verdict, finally, was that his drawings weren't at all bad.

But they didn't see his paintings. These he worked on at the chateau, in hours he could take from the work of restoration. Gradually more of these hours became available, as the roofs of the chateau were completed, and one by one its rooms became habitable.

Once enough had been done so that he could shift his living quarters into the chateau, the long abbey room became his studio. That was where his paintings were done; and that was where they stayed.

From then on, on, he allowed the work on the chateau to take its time: supervising it for a few hours a day, at most. The rest of his daylight hours became devoted to sketching treks, and the painting. In good weather he painted outside under the shade of the arcade. When there was too much wind or rain, he used the interior of the abbey room.

When he finished the painting of Pascale he began another. This time it was memory he turned to: he could see the Berbers again—and when he finished, one of the memories was on canvas.

Immediately, he began the next painting. Driving himself relentlessly. Increasingly, there were days when he neglected the work on the buildings entirely. Mornings when he woke with the first light and went immediately to the canvas waiting on his easel; sticking with it through the rest of the day, snatching bites of whatever cold food happened to be available and falling into an exhausted sleep when the coming of darkness forced him to quit.

There was a lost decade to be filled in—and an urgent premonition of limited time left. Like many in Europe during that year, he knew the approach of a second world war. Just how its coming would affect him he could not predict. But he was aware of its presence; a vague barrier that rose across the path of his future.

Grayle was certain of one thing: if this war came, he wanted no part of it. He'd had enough of fighting and killing and watching the dying. All those years with the Legion and then with the Berbers had burned the last vestige of need for it out of him. Even the remembered anger of childhood was gone. And, he had his painting again. What he wanted from life was what he was building here: a place to work in peace and live with those he loved.

There was in his painting during this period none of the remembered paralyzing hunt for the right subjects, for an underlying theme. He was not the same man, and he had found something, out of all those years he had lost.

He tried, when Pascale became curious, to explain it to her. "There is a difference between a leaf and a fragment of stone. A leaf is born and it dies. Its time is short. That invests it with a mystery, a significance, that even a beautiful stone doesn't share."

He was squinting at the picture they stood before; his eyes nearly closed, to filter out the colors and see only the lights and darks, to make certain they held together. "And human beings have even more of it than a leaf, because they also have memories, and fear."

"But—that's simply obvious, isn't it?"

He laughed and looked at her. "Yes. Very obvious. But it wasn't always; not to me, anyway. Maybe that's why it matters so much, now that I know."

Pascale was not certain she understood what he meant, and she looked from him to the painting, scowling as she tried to see what he saw. Grayle hoped she could find the answer there. She would, if he had done what he'd set out to.

He remembered Hassan, the arms smuggler, saying that ambition should be limited. Well, life was limited: a journey that ended. That gave it emotional meaning.

But Grayle allowed himself no preconceived notions that would influence or confine the direction his work was taking. He was learning from what emerged as each painting took shape. Sometimes he didn't know until it was completed, why he had chosen that particular subject. The doing of the work itself told him what it was about.

* * *

The old men playing cards in the shade of the tree out-side the village cafe were of a type: short legs and long, thick torsos; tough, sagging faces with weathered skin webbed like heat-cracked clay. Their conversation, that August afternoon in 1939, was about the war that was cer-tain to come soon.

Jacques Boulat, whose son worked for the postal depart-ment in Avignon, said the government was sure of it: Ger-many was asking to be taught another hard lesson in hu-mility. Hitler, and his partner Mussolini, had been allowed to get away with too much, and it was making them inso-lent. Germany had taken over Czechoslovakia and Lithu-ania; Italy had invaded Albania. There were rumors in the newspapers of an impending pact between Hitler and Sta-lin, to allow Germany to invade Poland and give the rest of Eastern Europe to Russia. But at least England, which had so far crawled on its belly before Hitler, was now warning that a German invasion of Poland would mean an immedi-ate declaration of war.

There was a much more reliable indication that war was very close: the doctor from St. Remy reported that two out of every three babies born lately were boys. A well-known fact, documented by the past: in peaceful times, more girls were born; in wartime, more boys.

The other men agreed with Yves Gloaguen, who owned vineyards in the valley, that if France was sucked into the war, it would not affect any of their lives much; except for the better, by raising the prices of all farm products. And they all agreed with the newspapers and politicians that France was in no danger of an attack by Germany: Hitler was not stupid enough to break his teeth on the impregna-ble Maginot Line.

None of them realized that the start of the war they were discussing was less than three weeks away. So they were easily diverted to another subject when Nora Cesari climbed out of the taxicab that had brought her from the train station in Arles.

Her mother, Madame Cesari, was an established part of the village life. Nora, because her visits had been infrequent, and usually brief, was in a way almost as much of a stranger to them as Monsieur Hugonnet. But at least her history was well-known, giving them sufficient material for satisfying sessions of gossip. Including the fact that her lover had murdered her husband; and that one could not be certain if her daughter was from the husband or the vanished lover.

No one was scandalized by these facets of Nora Cesari. In a country of peasants such stories were not uncommon. The best baker up in St. Remy had murdered his shrewish wife and sawed her into pieces which he'd tried unsuccessfully to hide. Arrested, he had been released awaiting trial. That had been six years ago, and everyone knew the trial would never take place: the baker was a popular man who made excellent bread and pastries, and his wife had been disliked by everybody.

Everyone was certain that Madame Lorenzi, the shepherdess on the other side of the valley, had poisoned her late husband when he'd stopped beating her with his hands and began using a stick. Nothing would ever be done about it, because it was an accepted fact that shepherds were odd, lonely people given to occasional gusts of passion. And Serge Brion, the local beekeeper whose honey had the flavor of the wildflowers of the Alpilles: his household included his wife, and his late brother's widow and teenaged daughter, and he was quite obviously husband and lover for all three of them.

The villagers had a kind of gratitude for such people, for providing them with interesting subjects to talk about. And Nora Cesari was another of them. The old men at the outdoor tables greeted her respectfully as she crossed the Place carrying her suitcase and a shoulder bag. She returned their greeting politely. They watched her go off through the passage between the bakery and the little general store, and begin to climb the stepped lane to her mother's house.

* * *

Nora Cesari had spent only two days in Paris on her return to France: just long enough to give her report to the Spanish Refugee Committee. The money she had raised on her American tour was in the hands of the committee's representatives in Washington. The American politicians she had seen were flatly opposed to any official interest in the problem of the Spanish refugees—because that would be an affront to Franco, and through him to Hitler and Mussolini. Even the few politicians who secretly sympathized were afraid of their American voters.

Her discouraged weariness after the months in America hadn't been helped by seeing Victor Royan while in Paris. He had sunk deeper than ever into a sour lethargy, and had become increasingly solitary. Jill hadn't returned to him, and he had made no effort to get her back. She lived with his wife on his Normandy estate now; he never visited them, and lacked the energy or the desire to find anyone else.

When Victor had seen her off at the Gare de Lyon, Nora had told him she had no idea when she would return. She was unable to contemplate anything beyond a long rest—for her body, mind and nerves. The time had come for her to devote herself to something that her photography and her work for the refugees had caused her to neglect far too long: being a normal, responsible mother to her daughter.

She was disappointed not to find Pascale at home. "She's probably nowhere in the village," her mother told her. "Now that it's school vacation, Pascale spends most of her days up there at the old chateau." Madame Cesari explained about Monsieur Hugonnet showing up as the new owner of the place, and his hiring of Pascale to help with the restoration.

"I think," she added with a small smile, "that it is an infatuation between the two of them. Pascale's very first."

Nora frowned at her mother's indulgent acceptance. "You think it's a good idea, to allow her to spend so much time up there alone with this man?"

"Don't worry. There's no harm in it. An interesting man. You'll like him. I do."

After Nora had bathed and changed to slacks, shirt and hiking shoes, she decided to go up to see for herself.

The valley, at that time of summer, was full of sunflowers: pools and rivers of them, flowing among the vineyards, farms and fruit groves. Nora crossed the dirt track along which a car could reach the chateau by corkscrewing up and around the slopes of several hills. But on foot there was a shortcut: a path that climbed out of the valley through a deep, wide ravine so thickly wooded and choked with underbrush that it was otherwise virtually impenetrable.

Nora knew this route from the hikes she'd taken with her mother, and later with Pascale. The foliage that intermeshed overhead turned the twisting pathway into the shadowed tunnel she remembered. But the tangles of ground-creepers and brush no longer impeded her climb. The path had obviously been used a lot that spring and summer.

She climbed the side of the ravine to a bulging shoulder at the bottom of the chateau's slope. Above her, she saw, the woods had been cut back and trimmed. The crumbling defense tower rose clear. The path Nora was using curved past it and turned in under an archway that remained from the ancient ramparts. A new lantern had been hung under its peak.

The front wall of the courtyard still had vines growing over it; but only enough now to decorate, without overwhelming it. The facade of the chateau had been patched up, windows with blue-painted shutters had been set in place in their deep openings. It still looked very old, but solid and serviceable; and the tiled roofs crowned it with muted beauty.

The wild, high bushes Nora remembered as blocking the approach to the courtyard had been pruned to low hedges which revealed fruit trees. She went through the wall's gateway, into the main courtyard, once an overgrown rubbish dump. Graceful brick walls now coiled across it, between green plots of shrubs and beds of ivy. Young willows had been planted and orange-clay urns sprouted dahlias, geraniums and asters. A rough-hewn table and several

wicker armchairs sat on a patch of grass under the big olive tree, next to the ancient well.

There was no one around. Only the bees droning past
her, a golden-blue lizard climbing a stone column support-
ing an arcade arch, birds twittering in nests under the over-
hangs of the new roofs. The cool shadows across the courtyard were a relief from the thick weight of the summer
sunshine. The place seemed to spread sheltering arms
around her, inviting her in.

As she followed a brick walk to the small entry court of
the chateau, all the birds fell abruptly silent. Nora was
country-wise enough to look to the sky for the reason. A
falcon was gliding over the ruins. It went on, rising toward
the Alpilles.

Nora tried the heavy iron knocker on the solid oak entrance door. It resounded inside the building. She waited,
but no one came. Finally she walked to an open-shuttered
window to her left. The window was open, too.

She called through it: "Monsieur Hugonnet? Pascale?"

There was no response. Nora moved closer, peering inside. It was a large kitchen, with a wood-burning stove for
cooking, and a long, massive table of beautifully grained
olive wood, with straight-backed chairs around it. The interior walls had been plastered and whitewashed, but the
heavy ceiling beams remained exposed.

The next window was shuttered, but the one beyond that
was open. Nora moved on to it and looked into the long
main living room. The ceiling and walls were as in the
kitchen: rough but solid. The middle of the room was dominated by a huge aquarium swarming with tiny tropical
fish.

There was a huge sofa and a number of comfortable
looking wing chairs. A tall grandfather's clock stood in one
corner, its brass pendulum ticking resonantly back and
forth. On the wall near it hung an unframed painting; but
the room's shadows made it impossible for Nora to see it
clearly.

She called out again; and again there was no answer.
Turning, she looked toward the abbey arcade and the long
building to which it was attached. Obviously, it too had

been restored for use; someone might be inside. The long wall of the building had an old-fashioned two-section door. The lower section, as high as her waist, was shut; but the upper part was wide open. Nora crossed to it and looked inside.

It took a moment for her eyes to adjust to the relative dimness of the interior. Then she saw what the room was: an artist's studio. Nora squinted at the unframed paintings on the opposite wall. Then she pushed open the lower door.

The painting directly across from the doorway drew her to it: a vast sweep of empty, drab land where nothing grew, and another sweep above it: a sterile sky, barely distinguishable from the land. Only when she was closer could she identify the small daubs of brighter paint near the lower corner: three half-seen people. Nothing explicit; impossible to guess what they were doing there. Yet these human specks, in that vastness, focused the attention and gave impact to the canvas.

There were three other canvases hung on the same rough wall. In each the angle of perception, the contrast, was the same: the shock of difference between what lived and what merely existed.

A tree that was dying, against a wall that had never been born.

Her sleeping daughter, framed by an arch and columns of stone that could never awake.

An orange-red flower, blooming out of a desert of dead-blue sand under a metallic purple sky.

None of the pictures was signed.

Nora turned from them. A painting hung on the opposite wall: the ruins behind the courtyard—and the tiny, barely identifiable figure of a girl in a red dress and straw hat, running off through them.

Ranging to one side of the painting were a number of large charcoal drawings: a gallery of faces, some of which she knew from the village. Faces lit by inner passions: avarice, anxiety, grief, humor, tenderness. Each perishably human.

And dreadful faces that were alien to her: a fat, soft

black face, caught in the moment of death, tipping forward with the side of the head exploding. A swarthy face that seemed to grow out of the ground, its eyes without lids and something she did not want to identify crammed in the open mouth. A face scarred as though by a bolt of lightning, gazing out of the picture at her with a cheerful, horrible grin.

At the far end of this gallery of faces, color leaped from the wall again: a watercolor of women washing clothes at the village fountain. A pastel of her mother, bent over a steaming stew pot, with Pascale standing close, watching attentively.

The constriction around her heart was becoming painful.

There was an easel at the end of the room, with a half-finished painting on it. Nora moved toward it, feeling the trembling of her legs. A ragged, dirty African sat on the ground, regarding a cypress tree so old that the fresh leaves growing from some of its branches was difficult to believe. The tree, in turn, seemed to be regarding the man. And around them, there was nothing but naked and splintered rock.

Nora turned from it in panic, hurrying to get out of the long room. The lower part of the door leading out to the arcade had swung shut behind her. She stopped when she reached it, staring out. Through the columned arches, she saw a man entering the courtyard, coming in her direction.

A big man, his face shadowed by the brim of the straw farmer's hat he wore. There was white in his beard, but his figure was powerful, his walk vital.

Nora gripped the top of the lower door tightly, with both hands. "I'm sorry . . ." she heard her voice say. "I was looking for my daughter. Pascale . . ."

The man stopped where he was. He squinted in her direction, and took off the straw hat. All she could register at first was the terrible way his forehead was scarred. She was aware that her fingers were hurting from their grip on the wood of the door.

He spoke finally: "She's gone to hunt for wild strawberries."

Nora didn't grasp the words. There was only the voice. She felt her hands, pushing at the door, opening it. She took an uncertain step, out into the arcade toward him; and then another.

And then she was running.

36

Victor Royan
Paris—November 3, 1939

My dear Nora:

I was surprised, naturally, by your letter informing me of your marriage. A retired businessman who has settled down to vegetate with the peasants does not quite fit my image of your style, or your needs. However, you are probably right: let the world destroy itself without you, since nothing one does can stop the folly.

You have at times accused me of being too cynical. But if I were not, if I allowed myself to care too much about the idiocy of mankind, I would have killed myself long ago, out of sheer nausea. As it is, I can wait until others try to accomplish that for me, secure in the faith that it will not be a long wait. Paris now lulls itself with a belief that this limbo of military inactivity will continue forever—but a rude awakening is coming.

In September, when we declared war on Germany, Paris panicked and sent its children away to the country to escape the gas bombs that were expected to start falling on the city. Nothing happened, Hitler being too busy consolidating his conquest of the east to turn his attention in our direction as yet, and now all the children are back—because Paris has convinced itself that nothing will ever happen.

People here are grumbling that the only enemies in sight are the British soldiers who were shipped over to help defend our frontiers, and who now have nothing *else to do but marry French girls who should be waiting for their drafted French boyfriends to return home. And those young Frenchmen write letters assuring their parents that the only thing they are in danger of being killed by is boredom.*

My wife took Jill off to England, and I have warned them to stay there. Jill writes that London now calls what is going on the Phony War. Here in Paris they call it the Joke War. The joke will be on them—on all of us—and we will deserve it, for our arrogance.

At least the communists, despicable as ever, are more realistic. They know what is coming, and they are preparing for it by sabotaging France's desultory efforts to be ready to cope with it. Their press denounces any attempt to strengthen our military defenses as "war mongering and profiteering." Their factory workers make sure that weapons and vehicles being manufactured won't work when they are needed.

The few uneasy friends I have left among them have the grace to be embarrassed by the "necessity" for this, caused by the pact signed by Hitler and Stalin to divide up Europe between them. But even these friends cling desperately to a Jesuit-like faith that whatever serves Moscow will ultimately benefit all mankind—or whatever is left of it. Moscow is due for its own rude awakening, and I anticipate that with bitter pleasure.

You have accused me, in the past, of being truly alive only when violent death is hammering at my door. In that case, I shall become exceedingly alive again, before too long. Violent death, on a scale even greater than you and I knew in Spain, will soon be kicking down the doors of the entire world.

So, again, perhaps you are right to relax through this waiting period and ignore the disgusting antics of the real world. Give my love to your delightful Pascale. I'm glad that she is so fond of her new "father."

*That he has adopted her as his legal daughter and heir
indicates that he is at least a decent man. If I guess
that he is also a bit dull and limited, you can put it
down to my scorn for humanity in general, and in
particular toward new-rich businessmen who retire to
premature old age in an uneventful countryside. Just
don't let yourself become too dulled. You will be
needed. I am the one who sinks into lethargy, remember? Not you.*

*I remain, aging cynic though I may be, your affec-
tionate friend,*

                        Victor

Nora woke slowly in the dim morning light that filtered
through the shutters of the chateau's master bedroom. She
rolled over on her side with luxurious laziness, reaching out
with both hands for Grayle. But the space beside her in the
wide, comfortable bed was empty. The smells of woodsmoke, hot coffee and warmed bread drifted to her from
the floor below, mingling with the wet odors of earth and
vegetation outside.

For several minutes longer, Nora continued to huddle in
the warmth of the blankets and quilt, her breath making
puffs of steam in the damp cold of the December air. Then
she flung the covers aside and leaped from the bed, plung-
ing her feet into felt slippers. Striding to the corner fireplace, whose bricks still radiated warmth from last night's
fire, she took her fleece-lined sheepskin coat down from
the cherrywood coatstand beside it and put it on quickly
before opening the window shutters.

Pale morning light flooded in and spread a gloss over
the polished oak panels of the room's walls. The sky was
overcast with a soggy gray. Darker and lighter grays
churned within it, and as Nora watched, a roundish spot of
cold white appeared: the sun fighting to burn a hole
through the massed clouds. But it failed; the dripping
shroud shifted its grays to the weak point, sealing up the
hole.

Moisture ran down the recently finished russet-tiled roof

of the low chapter-house below the tower bedroom. There were still its door and windows to be finished, but there'd be no work on it this day; that was done in dry weather. When completed, it would become Pascale's bedroom. Until then, on nights when there was no school the next morning, Pascale slept on the huge sofa in the main living room downstairs. Other nights she spent with her grandmother in the village.

Madame Cesari, herself, seldom came to the chateau anymore.

Nora remembered that August morning when she'd gone back down to the village from the chateau; the oddly uncertain way her mother had confronted her. "Pascale thinks . . ." her mother had begun hesitantly, ". . . she has a notion that you've fallen in love with Monsieur Hugonnet. I told her . . . it is a bit too quick, for that."

Nora had looked at her for a moment, and then decided the time had come for the truth between them: "It's him, Maman. It's Nicholas."

The way it had hit her mother: the shock—and then the frightened hopelessness. "Oh, my God . . ."

"I don't know if it is God's doing," Nora had told her. "But he is back."

Her mother had pressed trembling fingers together. "Be careful, Nora," she had whispered finally, knowing herself helpless to interfere. "You were lucky, with Pascale. She's a healthy girl, with a sound mind. God was merciful, that time." She looked down at her clenched hands. "Be very careful . . ."

Nora had tried often since then to reassure her mother—without success: her mother could still only think of him as Nora's half-brother. But to Nora, he was her husband and lover—the strange tie of the past no longer relevant. For her they had met anew, their relationship now sprung from very different roots.

Her mother need not worry: there would be no other children. But there would be nothing and no one to separate her from Grayle again.

Yet her mother had continued to avoid Grayle, as though the sight of him renewed the fear she was unable to control. Tonight would be the first time she had invited Grayle to join them for dinner in her house in the village. This time she could not avoid it, without the estrangement becoming obvious to Pascale. Tonight was Pascale's twelfth birthday celebration.

Nora crossed the bedroom and threw open the other shutters, to let in a cross-breeze and air the bedclothes. This window gave her a view through the ruins behind the courtyard, of smoke rising from the slender tin chimney of Jumeau's shed behind the curve of ancient wall. Jumeau had accepted her presence at the chateau without comment, but with no hint of hostility or annoyance in his silence. It was merely that he spoke to her no more, and no less, than he did to Pascale or even Grayle.

Nora had watched Grayle work with Jumeau and the mason early that fall to finish a new fireplace for Jumeau. She liked the contentment she saw in Grayle when he did that kind of work: laying heavy stones in their proper place, or sawing fallen trees and chopping them into firewood.

She saw the same kind of satisfaction in his face when he looked at anything that grew. He had been intimate with Hell, and his mind sometimes went back there still—and he was more alert than most to any vestige of Paradise.

Nora went through the dressing room into the bathroom, and then down the curving stairway. In the dining area two logs blazed in the fireplace. Grayle had left coffee simmering on the stove, and bread still warm in the oven. The rest was waiting for her on the long olive-wood table. Nora cut several crusty slices from the loaf, and layered them thickly with butter and honey.

Through the mullioned windows she could see smoke rising from the chimney of the abbey building across the courtyard. He was already in his studio there, working at the easel. Nora's gaze shifted to the wall beside the window. The painting he had begun at the end of August hung there.

It was a nude of her, bathing in the sheltered stream at his hidden nook in the forest below the chateau. There was a Dionysian exultation in the mingling of her sun-dappled skin and hair with the warm-damp foliage and flowing water.

Her figure was flagrantly erotic as he portrayed it. She hoped he was going to see her that way for a long time to come. A pulsing heat spread in her loins as she remembered his hard hands on her flesh, and her own fingers delicately exploring the terrible scars in his.

Nora washed the dishes and went back upstairs to dress for the cold of the outside world: heavy wool slacks, turtleneck pullover, socks and cap; rubber boots and the sheepskin coat. She went out through the courtyard to the truck, without disturbing him to say she was going.

When he awoke like this, with the painting already at work in him, he could remain with it all day, unaware of anything else. Increasingly, it was Nora who managed the practical activities of the chateau and supervised the further restoration. It was his money that had bought shares in the produce of local farmers, but Nora was the one who kept a regular check on the return from these investments. Jumeau was now in charge of the chickens raised in pens behind the ruined defense tower, while she took care of the shipment of their eggs to the markets in Arles.

If Grayle was still at his easel when she returned, she would leave lunch for him on a tray.

Nora once had been as immersed in her photography as he was now in his painting. But not since she had escaped from Spain. Grayle had suggested that it was time for them to buy her a new camera and set up a darkroom at the chateau. But she was not ready, yet. It was as if the desire had been eroded in her by all the death and destruction she had recorded; it would take time for it to grow back.

Jumeau had already stacked the egg crates in the back of the truck when Nora got there. She climbed up in front and drove down through the valley to the Arles market. Twice, the truck had been used for a more secretive purpose—when Victor had sent a small group of Spanish exiles for her to help.

There were still some two hundred thousand refugees from Franco's Spain inside France, where the government was making life increasingly difficult for them. A ship had been obtained in the United States, with the funds raised by Nora and others, to transport large numbers of them to Latin American countries which had agreed to accept them. But legal and political difficulties in Washington were keeping the ship from sailing. For the exiles unable to buy passage to safety there was only one alternative: scatter throughout France and somehow earn enough to eat while avoiding police notice.

Nora and Grayle had taken Victor's two groups to Marseilles. There, they had obtained false French identity and working papers from the same man who had provided Grayle with his forged identity. That gave the Spaniards at least a chance to spread out and get factory and farm jobs.

It had been expensive. Victor knew that her husband had supplied the necessary money; but he was under the impression it was Nora who located the vital forger-contact.

Victor still didn't know the truth about the man Nora had married. Eventually, he was bound to come down here—and then he would know. But Nora was not going to trust to the mails the information that her husband was an escaped prisoner, still wanted for murder by the police.

On a dry, clear Sunday at the end of the first month of 1940, Grayle took Nora and Pascale with him in the truck when he drove up into the Alpilles to pick up the blocks of cut stone he'd ordered from the mason for the framing of the window openings and doorway of what was to be their daughter's private room. The dirt road cut up through a tight, twisting passage among the upper crags of the low mountain range. It was called the Valley of Hell, because many of the eroded formations of chalky limestone that protruded from the heavy scrub brush and pines on both sides of the road looked like gargoyles poised to pounce on passing travelers. But these stone monsters were frightening only at night. By day Pascale found them funny.

The cutoff to the underground quarries was a short distance below the ruined fortress village of Les Baux, originally built by invading Saracens. The stone underlying this range was of a soft quality that allowed it to be easily cut to exact measure, and quarrymen had been digging deep into the heart of it for more than two thousand years.

The removal of so much stone over the centuries had left literally hundreds of mammoth interconnecting subterranean chambers. The entrance Grayle wanted was reached by a path just wide enough for his truck to slip through. Sylvio Trimarco, Grayle's stonemason, had his small house and work shack just inside the mouth of one quarry chamber, where it was protected from the Alpilles' winds and rains.

Trimarco was only twenty-five, but he had been at his profession since he was four, when he had been apprenticed to his father, one of the best stonemasons in Tuscany. His father had also been an active communist, until Mussolini had outlawed the party in Italy. Arrested, he had escaped and fled with his wife and son to France.

He had taken up his trade again at the quarries in the Alpillas when his apprentice-son was twelve. But four years ago, his wife dead and his lungs eaten and clogged by decades of breathing the chalky stone-dust, he had retired to a room in the village. He would sometimes lend his son a hand, when required. But most of his time he spent at the village cafe and playing boules with the other old men.

As Grayle climbed down from the truck with Nora and Pascale, Sylvio Trimarco came out to greet them, covered with the white dust of his work. He was a handsome, easygoing man with a husky build, and a wracking cough that indicated his own lungs were going the way of his father's. "They're all finished and ready for you," he said, indicating the neatly squared-off stones stacked together just outside his quarry entrance.

With Trimarco's measuring tape, Grayle began checking each of the cut stones against the figures in his notebook. He knew Trimarco always cut exactly to measure, never a fraction off; but the checking was part of an accepted ritual. Nobody but a careless fool paid good money without making certain he was getting exactly what he had commissioned.

Nora peered curiously into the quarry entrance. She had never been here before. Pascale, who had come before with

Grayle, led her mother into the interior to show her around. Grayle and Trimarco began the heavy labor of lifting one stone at a time from the stack, and loading them into the truck. When the job was done they were both sweating in spite of the cold wind. Trimarco took Grayle inside to share a towel and some wine.

"Don't start setting the stones in place until I am there," Trimarco warned.

"I know how to set them properly, by now."

"Yes, you do it well. But it is *my* profession. If something goes wrong, if they should start to separate or sag, perhaps ten years from now, people will say that *I* did the work badly."

"All right," Grayle conceded. "When can you come?"

"The day after tomorrow. In the morning. Early."

"Good enough." Grayle finished his wine and headed inside the quarries in search of Nora and Pascale. A square-cut tunnel led into a vast underground cavern whose dead-straight walls bore ridges that marked clearly where great blocks of the stone had been removed. The bottom was covered with stone-dust and rubble, and there were several hacked-out passages leading off in different directions. Grayle crossed the room and proceeded deeper into the labyrinth of interior galleries, rooms, corridors and giant steps. There were great cracks in the walls and overhead, letting in enough sunlight to see by. But when he called out, the echoing of his voice mingled with the echoes of their mocking replies, making their direction difficult to determine.

He located them, finally, when he climbed through a hole onto a ledge high on one wall of a deep quarry-chamber. They were below him, in a corner of the bottom, using a clasp knife to cut their initials in the soft stone. Grayle sat down on the ledge and watched them at play, their hair cascading from under identical cloth caps, Nora in dark green, Pascale in her red dress. Getting out a pencil and notebook, he began to sketch them and their surroundings.

Pascale glanced up and spotted him first. She nudged her mother, and then they were both looking, laughing.

Grayle turned to a fresh page. His pencil moved even more rapidly. As they turned from the corner and began to climb to him, Grayle opened the small box of pastels he always carried, and made notes of the colors. But when they were near he closed the box, and just watched the way Nora moved: still like a dancer, supple and provocative. But there was a toughened resilience to her now.

Pascale reached him first. He stood up and put his arm around her, drawing her close. She rested her head against his arm, and Grayle felt again the poignancy of the deep affection that had grown between them though she didn't know they were father and daughter.

She did know the story of her father—Nora had begun explaining it to her quite early, before others could do so more harshly. Pascale had understood the feeling behind her mother's words before she could fully grasp their meaning. By the time she did grasp the meaning, it had suited her growing romanticism; perhaps fed it.

But she did not know that Monsieur Hugonnet was Nicholas Grayle—and perhaps would never know; Grayle was not sure. For him the relationship was there, and the feeling between them confirmed it. For him, too, Pascale was further proof that Nora was wife and not sister. Nevertheless this child was more of his blood than any other could have been.

Grayle continued to hold his daughter to him as he and Nora looked at each other. The years they'd been apart had changed Nora's eyes, he saw. They looked at people with the same observant keenness they always had, but now they also let others look in.

That afternoon, when they were back at the chateau, he began the painting inspired by his sketches in the quarry. It was to become one of Grayle's most stirring pictures. The shaft of light fell through the chamber roof upon Nora and Pascale, and the warm tones of their colors contrasted with the cold tones of the geometrically cut, chalky corner behind them. Their figures seemed to be *growing* in that corner, exuberantly defying entombment within that mineral sterility.

And their faces, finally, became indistinct; so they no longer seemed mother and daughter, but the same woman in two stages of a single life, younger and older.

He finished it early in March and, as always, he did not sign it—though Nora pointed out that he could keep it in his studio, where there was little danger of anyone else seeing it.

"There is always the chance," he told her. "And there is no point in taking it. My painting can't be exhibited with my name on it anyway, until after I'm dead. Meanwhile I have them, and I know they're mine. And that's enough. It has to be."

But as Grayle studied the considerable body of work he had accomplished at the chateau, the need to feed himself again from great paintings of the past grew sharper, until finally the hunger became intolerable. Paris was unsafe: too many people had known him there, and the danger that someone might recognize him in spite of his changed appearance could not be ignored. There was no such risk for him in Florence. Late in March he drove to Avignon and boarded the train for Italy, taking Nora and Pascale with him for a three-day visit.

Nora Cesari would not have been a welcome visitor in Mussolini's Italy. Her name was known to the authorities from her early antifascist photographs of Rome and her documentation of the fascist army's atrocities in Ethiopia. But the frontier guards who checked her passport found nothing in the name Madame Hugonnet to make them think twice. She was passed through without hesitation.

They lodged in a hotel in the heart of Florence, close to the Piazza della Signoria, and early the next morning they entered the Uffizi. While Pascale wandered through the linked galleries, Nora watched the changes in Grayle's face as he remained for a long time before Botticelli's *Primavera*. It had been so very long since he had last seen it. Grayle sucked it in.

They left the Uffizi for the church of Santa Trinita, to stand before the orchestrated strangeness and harmony of

Ghirlandao's *Resuscitation of a Child.* And then across the
Arno to the Brancacci Chapel where Grayle experienced
again the excitement of Masaccio's *Expulsion of Adam and
Eve from Paradise.*

Masaccio had died before reaching the age of thirty. But
his paintings were still there. Still alive. Still talking to people more than five hundred years later.

Pascale was sleepily weary when they headed back to
their hotel. Grayle hoistered her up onto his shoulders, her
legs astride his head, and carried her across the Ponte Vec-
chio. Halfway across, she nudged his chest with her heels
and pointed excitedly: "Look!"

Nora stopped with them, seeing how the line of buildings
above the bank of the Arno was reflected in the river. The
surface of the water was dead flat, and every detail of each
building was repeated with absolute clarity, upside down.
As they looked, a rowboat came out from under the bridge,
and cut across the reflection, shattering it into thousands of
separated patches. But each patch retained its own image
of a piece of a building—wavering for a time, and then
steadying as the boat passed on and the reflections began to
reunite.

Pascale leaned forward eagerly, with her hands clutching
the sides of Grayle's head, enchanted. "That's the prettiest
picture I've seen all day."

Grayle laughed. But Pascale turned her head and looked
at her mother with something like resentment in her expression. "I wish *I* was a great photographer. I wouldn't be
walking around here without a camera."

At the hotel, Nora and Pascale settled down for a nap.
But Grayle went out to walk the streets of the city. It was
late when he came back. He was carrying a wrapped package.

"An extra birthday present," he told Pascale. "A bit delayed in arriving."

Pascale tore it open. It contained a new Leica camera,
and three rolls of film. With a screech of joy, she leaped
from her chair and threw her arms around him, kissing
him passionately. Grayle felt the fragility of the bones in

that slim, vibrant body. It had taken him a while to accept that it was not the fragility of an eggshell. He hugged her, hard.

Nora was smiling at him, with a touch of mocking sadness. "You figure it must be in her blood, is that it?"

"She's old enough to begin finding out what she's capable of, don't you think?" His tone was offhand. "The darkroom equipment we can get in Arles. I'll fix up a place in the chateau, so you can show her about developing and enlarging, too."

Nora reached for his hand. What he really wanted, she knew, was that in teaching Pascale, she would rediscover her own lost enthusiasm for photography.

When they returned to France, Grayle set to work under the chateau, converting a cellar vault into a darkroom. Nora installed the equipment she bought in Arles for it.

Pascale's diary was soon largely neglected. Now it was camera images she sought and thought about, with growing awareness that she was good at it.

Once Nora was sure she had the basics of handling the camera, she let Pascale find her own style of seeing, and concentrated on working with her in the darkroom. Nora didn't find in it what Grayle had hoped for, but she found something else: a deeper relationship with her daughter, a sharing that had been missing before.

Pascale soon learned not to waste film, to take each shot with a final product firmly in mind. She learned, too, how to search each print for an unexpected lucky fragment, how to crop away what was superfluous in order to bring it out. Before long she was launched into a documentary project, inspired by the gallery of faces in Grayle's studio. She began to take close-ups of every member of her village.

But it wasn't one of these that Grayle pinned to the wall of his studio. It was a shot Pascale had taken while experimenting with the Leica's highest speed: a raven, its glossy feathers aglow with sunlight, frozen in flight as it dipped past the headstone of Claude Cesari.

Two weeks after their return from Florence, the German army smashed into Denmark and Norway. The jokes about a fake war suddenly died. France began to wait for the war to turn against its own frontiers.

The waiting became more uneasy with every day that it failed to come. The suspense made Madame Cesari afraid, and from her fear came an invitation for Nora to bring Grayle to the village to have dinner with her and Pascale. What she wanted to discuss was whether there was danger that the war could ever reach this far south.

"There is the Maginot Line," she said. "The people who are supposed to know such things swear that the Germans can't possibly break through it."

"They'll go over it with their planes," Nora stated flatly. "And around it with their tanks. I saw the German tactics in Spain. Our generals have no idea of what they'll be up against. The Nazis will have taken Paris and the Maginot Line will still be sitting there, far behind, still being impregnable."

"I don't care that much about Paris," her mother snapped. She put a hand on Pascale's, resting on the table beside her dinner plate. "What I care about is will the war come *here*."

Grayle said mildly: "No one can predict that. There's nothing to do about it but wait and see."

Nora shot him a flash of irritation she couldn't quite conceal. "Just wait—because in the meantime your house and work are more important."

He smiled at her. "To me, yes. And since there's nothing I can do about whether the war will come or not come."

Madame Cesari told him tartly, "I'm afraid I find it difficult to adopt such a fatalistic attitude."

Nora was still studying Grayle, but the anger was gone now. "And when the war does come?" Unconsciously, she used Victor's words: "When it is suddenly kicking down your door?"

"I'll do whatever there is that can be done, like everybody else. When the time comes. *Inch' Allah*."

Pascale frowned at him. "What does that mean?"

"It means," he told her, "that there are some things a man can't stop."

* * *

The waiting for war continued into early May, and though the tension continued with it, people began to get used to the waiting. One day when Nora and Jumeau were helping Grayle clear rubble out of an ancient cistern in the cellars under the chateau, they discovered something unexpected.

The cistern had been built by the monks of the abbey, and it went down into a part of a cellar that had been filled with earth over the centuries. Grayle wanted to get it back in condition to store water that would be piped in from the spring out back. What they discovered, when they had cleared out much of it, was an opening in the back wall of the cistern.

It was just big enough for a man to crawl into. But he couldn't crawl far, the passage having become blocked by stones and the roots of vines.

"It must have been a hiding place for the monks," Nora said, "from the days of the religious wars."

"Or the start of a tunnel for them to slip away through," Grayle said.

"I wonder where it leads?"

Grayle shrugged. They continued with the work of clearing out the cistern.

That night, after supper, when he was alone with Nora in the bedroom, Grayle lit four candles and undressed her. Then he had her stroll back and forth while he sat on the bed making a pastel sketch of her figure in movement; of the way the reflected flames licked the curves and hollows of her flesh.

Nora abandoned herself to it until, glancing his way, she saw that he was no longer drawing. He had put the sketchbook aside and was just watching her. With a slow smile, she moved close to the bed, looking down at him. They remained that way, looking at each other, for what seemed a very long time. She made an unintelligible sound, deep in her throat, as his hands took hold of her, pulling her down to him.

* * *

They were having a late breakfast downstairs in the dining area the next morning, when Jumeau rushed in, startling them.

Grayle had changed Jumeau's life by buying him a battery-operated radio like his own. Since then Jumeau listened to it all the time—and had stories of his own to tell.

He was shaking with excitement at the story he had this morning. And he continued with his confused recital of it, following them as they hurried into the living room to turn on the radio there.

Germany had launched a blitzkrieg into Holland, Belgium and Luxembourg, and was slashing through their disintegrating defenses toward France, beyond the point where the Maginot Line ended.

37

From the variety of canes in the entry foyer of his Paris house, Victor Royan chose the stoutest: a thick staff of knobby, polished elm, with a lead-weighted handle that would make a useful weapon if needed. The other end of the cane was tipped with a steel point, as an aid to climbing in rough country; it would also increase the cane's defensive potential, if it came to that.

He climbed the stairway to his study, where the clothing he had chosen was spread out on the couch beside the knapsack. Spares for what he was wearing: sensible, serviceable clothes for a cross-country hike. Through the window he saw the pall of black smoke still discoloring the cloudless sky over Paris: drifting from the gasoline dumps at Rouen, more than a hundred miles to the west, which the French army had blown up just before fleeing south from the crushing onslaught of German armor and warplanes.

Victor unlocked the small safe in the wall of his study, after putting aside the picture that had concealed it: a Grayle pastel, bought long ago from Pauline Renard. He took from the safe the gold coins he had stored there for such an emergency. A few he slipped in his pocket, to be used during his escape to the south. The rest he stuffed inside thick hiking stockings, and placed them at the bottom of his knapsack under the spare clothes.

Everything else in his Paris home, all the valuable items inherited and collected over the years, he was leaving behind. Without regret. Divesting oneself of the accumulations of a lifetime was one way to become young again, starting over from scratch. Besides, he couldn't carry more

than the knapsack on his back. Though he would be starting out in the automobile of a friend who was also fleeing
Paris, Victor had no illusion about how far the car would
get in the mass exodux out of Paris. And there was likely
to be little gasoline left for it in the pumps along the roads
outside the city. Another lesson from Spain: what to expect
when a surrendered city abruptly emptied itself before the
entry of the victorious enemy.

Victor remembered Grayle's sarcastic advice, delivered
in this very study more than a decade ago, that he should
get rid of all he owned if he wanted to find a purpose in
life. Well, Victor thought with a wry smile, he was finally
doing so.

It was Wednesday, the twelfth of June: almost exactly
one month since Hitler's blitzkrieg had struck; and already
France's last despairing gestures of defending itself were
almost done with.

Scattered French forces were still trying to fight back as
they retreated south. The bulk of the French army, however, had been trapped in position by the incredible speed
of the German advance. Along the northeastern frontiers,
troops were surrendering by the thousands without firing a
shot, on orders from the demoralized French high command.

The government had fled to Tours, and was preparing to
flee farther. Paris had been declared an open city, to save
her from being bombed. This allowed the Germans free
entry, without resistance. By now the advance troops of the
Wehrmacht were approaching from the north, only hours
away. And French Nazis were hurrying out to greet them.

Victor Royan knew that his name was on the extermination lists prepared by these traitors. His antifascist activities
in Spain and then here on behalf of the refugees from
Franco had marked him as a dangerous man. It was time
to get out.

Much of Paris had already done so. For days and nights
the crowds had been pouring through the streets around
Victor's house, heading for the southern exits out of Paris.
People in cars, trucks, horse-drawn wagons. People walking, carrying suitcases, pushing baby carriages loaded with

their possessions, dragging handcarts piled with trunks and mattresses.

They all had had the same stunned look: unable to comprehend how France could have come to the brink of final defeat in a mere matter of weeks. But radio broadcasts by the French government, confirming what was contained in propaganda leaflets dropped from German planes, had begun to give them a scapegoat to blame it on: the British.

The main thrusts of the Nazi attack had been west and then south: to seize control of the coastline and swing in toward Paris. Most of the British army had been caught in a German vise there: on the coast of France near Dunkirk. Those British troops that had survived the first slaughter and evaded capture had managed a mass escape across the Channel to England—in every kind of vessel that could get through Hitler's dive-bombers. They had taken along with them what French troops they could. But the German leaflets presented a different interpretation, and the French government repeated it: the British had treacherously deserted France, and that was the cause of the defeat.

Victor was not surprised by the eagerness with which his countrymen swallowed this excuse. It meant they didn't have to look elsewhere for an explanation of what had happened: into their own blind stupidity, arrogance, cowardice, inefficiency. With a grimace, Victor picked up his knapsack and carried it to his bathroom. Where he intended to go, once out of Paris, he did not know. Such plans could wait until he had a chance to see the direction of future events. Until then, it was only important that he take himself somewhere else: anywhere where his name would mean nothing to anybody.

In the bathroom, Victor prepared a basic toilet kit and added it to his knapsack. He paused to look at himself in the mirror over the sink, seeing again how old he looked. Well, he *was* getting old; but not *that* old. His hair had gone entirely white. That was not from age; it had happened during his long recovery in the hospital after that stallion had thrown him, up in the hills above Menton. And the trenches in his gaunt cheeks, the networks of wrinkles around his eyes: those were from Spain.

He didn't like that elderly reflection in the mirror. But it might, he reflected, have its advantages in what was coming to France.

A car's horn sounded in the court outside his house. Victor went down to the kitchen and added a final item to his knapsack: a package of food he'd prepared—sausage, cheese and rolls. Carrying the knapsack and the cane he'd selected outside, he turned and locked his front door. He laughed as the futility of that automatic act struck him: within a matter of days, German officers would undoubtedly have taken over his house.

The waiting car was a black Citroen. A streamer trunk was tied on its roof, and the back seat was crammed with suitcases. The wizened, bald-headed man behind the wheel was Don Ferguson, a retired British surgeon who had settled in Paris seven years earlier. His wife, Eve, sat next to him holding their cocker spaniel on her lap. She was a plump, gray-haired woman, whose resilient humor Victor had always liked: mocking, but carefully restrained.

He squeezed in beside her and settled the knapsack on his knees. As he shut the car door, Eve said in a perky voice, "Well, here's wishing us luck . . ."

"We'll need it," grumbled Ferguson, and looked past his wife at Victor. "Have you heard the latest? Italy, after waiting this long to make sure the Germans got most of it over with, has declared war on us and invaded the southeast of France."

Victor nodded blandly. "It was on the radio."

"Stab in the back, from an old ally. Really lovely." Ferguson began backing the car out of the courtyard. Victor gave his house a final glance and leaned back, his eyes half-closed.

Ferguson turned the Citroen into the Boulevard St. Germain and sped along it, heading for the Porte d'Orléans, the main route south out of Paris. The boulevard was almost deserted, all the shops closed, houses shuttered and locked by residents who had fled the city. The car caught up to a straggling group of about ten French soldiers, trudging in the same direction. Victor turned his head to observe them as the Citroen raced past. Their uniforms were filthy, their faces sullen with exhaustion. Only two of them still carried their weapons.

"Got separated from their units, I suppose," Eve murmured. "And now all they want to do is try to get to their home villages and throw away the uniform."

"Might as well," Ferguson growled. "They've the same alternatives as we. Get out, or get shipped to Germany as prisoners of war."

He spun the Citroen into the Boulevard Raspail, the tires squealing with the speed of the turn.

"There is a third alternative," Eve observed quietly. "Getting oursleves killed in a car crash."

But soon, Ferguson was forced to slow down. A car appeared ahead of them, and then an army ambulance, and moments later they were into heavy traffic: vehicles and pedestrians, civilian and military. All flowing in the same direction. No one was going the other way, not today. And with no train service operating, from any of the Paris stations, the only way out was by road. Before long Ferguson's Citroen was creeping along in a bottleneck converging on the Porte d'Orléans. All of Paris seemed to have tilted to the south, trying to empty itself before the Germans marched in from the north.

It was night before Ferguson got his car through this jam-up, onto the Route National 20. The scene there, in the glare of headlights, with people screaming at each other in their efforts to keep families together, was nightmarish. Thousands of people on foot: weary lines of troops; civilians carrying heavy suitcases, or pushing or pulling their belongings in a bizarre variety of wheeled carriers. Others in cars, trucks, ammunition wagons. Some riding mules and horses; others on bicycles.

From the city they'd left behind came the booming of explosions: ammunition dumps and fuel supplies being blown up. Along the crammed highway, vehicles began to stall or run out of gas, adding to the congestion and confusion. Ferguson's car groaned forward in low gear, was forced to stop, eased forward again, was blocked again.

"Let me drive for a while," Victor offered.

But Ferguson shook his head. "Gives me something to do. I'm too nervous to just sit."

The dog on Eve's lap began to whine. Victor glanced at the dashboard's distance indicator. In four hours on the highway, they'd gotten less than six miles below Paris.

It was what Victor had expected; and he knew the time had come to get out of the car and start walking: through the wheatfields beside the highway. He'd go a lot farther and faster on foot. But the Fergusons had delayed to pick him up, and he was reluctant to leave until they, too, realized it would be better to abandon the car with its luggage, and go with him. Tipping his head back on the top of the seat, Victor forced himself into sleep.

When he awoke, stiff from hours in the same uncomfortable position, the first morning light was spreading across a pure, clear sky—and the Citroen was still caught inside a barely-moving mass of vehicles and refugees on foot. He looked immediately at the dashboard. The car had progressed another nine miles.

Victor rolled his head to ease a cramp in his neck, and prepared to present the Fergusons with the alternatives of coming with him or letting him hike on alone. Then he heard a sound from the north: a sound he knew well from Spain, and understood before the others. The drone of planes approaching, coming in very low.

"Get out!" he yelled at the Fergusons. He rammed open the door on his side and leaped from the car.

His bad leg had gone to sleep, and it collapsed under him. Victor fell on one knee in the road, and threw himself down the rest of the way, rolling quickly underneath a stalled truck. And then the scream of the incoming warplanes became very loud just above the highway, accompanied by the staccato bursts of their machine guns and the clanging of bullets ripping into the metal of vehicles.

Victor did another fast roll, out from under the truck, into a hedge growing along the side of the road. He crawled through the hedge and hurled himself into a ditch. Hitting the bottom he sprawled facedown, pressing himself flat in the dirt. More German planes were swooping down, machine guns strafing the crowded highway. People fell on top of Victor as they fled the death slashing down at them out of the beautiful June sky.

Then, abruptly, the noise of the planes and machine guns was gone—and the human sounds could be heard: screaming, crying, moaning. Victor forced himself up through the people still huddling on top of him. The German planes were winging away, gracefully swinging to the southwest. But there would be more planes, he knew, that would come during that clear day to continue the work these first ones had begun.

He climbed out of the ditch. An old woman was sprawled across the hedge, snared in its foliage, blood dripping from her smashed face onto the green leaves.

Victor shoved through the hedge. The noise of human agony, shock and grief filled the jammed highway. A bullet-gutted baby was huddled against the tire of a truck. Victor limped around the truck, and found his way blocked by a dying horse that lay on its side, still attached to the cart it had been pulling, its legs kicking feebly. A young man crouched beside it, cursing softly and steadily. The cart was piled with cheap household furniture, and a very elderly couple sat close together on a mattress, staring without comprehension at the horse's death throes.

Circling behind the cart, Victor approached the black Citroen. The windshield was shattered. Ferguson's head rested against the steering wheel, the area around his temple torn away. Eve sprawled against the back of the seat, her chest bloody, her head tipped back and her open eyes staring emptily at the car roof. The dog across her lap was also dead.

Victor's knapsack lay in the road beside the door he'd rammed open in jumping out. He bent and picked it up, got his arms through the loops and settled them on his shoulders, the bulk of its weight against his back. He took his cane from the floor of the car. In the rear seat, among the bullet-ripped luggage, was a dripping case of smashed wine bottles. Victor spotted one bottle still whole, reached in and dragged it loose.

People were climbing back from the roadside hedges and ditches: climbing back into vehicles, gathering up dropped luggage. It was the same as far ahead as Victor could see along the refugee-jammed highway. Disabled vehicles, slaughtered people and animals, were being dragged aside. Gradually, the survivors began to resume their crowded, crawling trek south—sticking to the highway. Victor opened his mouth to shout, and then with a grimace shut it without a word. Useless to argue the stupidity of what they were doing. People who couldn't learn from such a lesson as they'd just been dealt, couldn't be persuaded to rethink what they were doing.

He didn't look at the Fergusons again. Leaning with one hand on the stout walking stick, dangling the bottle of wine in his other hand, Victor started hiking across the fields between the ranks of growing wheat, away from the highway.

When he came upon empty dirt roads, Victor used them as long as they led south. When they diverged, he left them and again marched across fields and through wooded areas. The day grew hot, and he had to take off his jacket, tying it to the knapsack on his back. He was not certain exactly where, or how far, he intended to go. Sometimes he thought about the area where Nora lived. The war would probably be over before it reached that deep to the south. Perhaps he would go there. But there was another possibility, not quite clearly defined as yet, that his mind toyed with as he walked on.

At noon he sat down to rest and eat lunch in the shade of an old elm tree, beside a narrow lane. He opened the wine bottle with the corkscrew attachment of his jackknife, and drank some with slices of sausage and cheese. The rolls were already going stale, but he bit into the hardness of one and chewed it down. A bit more strength for his trek.

Three bicycles came along the lane toward him: a husky middle-aged man in the lead, followed by a girl of about ten, with a pretty woman in her early thirties bringing up the rear. Suitcases were tied on racks attached to the handlebars and behind the seat of each bike. The girl waved cheerfully to Victor as they passed him. He watched with envy as they sped away to the south. It was a lot faster than walking, and they could still avoid main roads. But the knee-articulation of Victor's bad leg couldn't handle pedaling a bike.

He had finished his lunch and was corking the bottle when an army platform-truck came along, crowding the lane. The platform was for hauling a cannon; but now it was crowded with refugees and their baggage. Victor made no attempt to stop and join them. Soon the truck would have to turn onto a main road, and even out here it was too obvious a target for German planes.

That night he slept under a hedge, grateful that it was the warmest June France had known in years. He woke the next morning with his leg gone so stiff he could hardly stand up. For five minutes he forced himself to march back and forth, working the stiffness out. Then he break-fasted on the sausage, cheese and last stale roll, washed down with wine, and continued his walk to the south.

At ten in the morning he came upon a wide paved road leading south. It was almost as packed with vehicles and humanity as Route National 20 had been. Victor crossed the road, threading through the crowds, and went on across the fields on the other side. He was about a mile from the road when he heard the planes behind him. Turning quickly, he saw there were four of them. They dropped very low, following the road, their guns spitting steady streams of death into the massed ranks of refugees. Victor plunged ahead into a stretch of forest.

It was late evening when he reached the town of Dour-dan. The grass of the small park in front of the city hall was covered with sleeping figures, and there were more on mattresses· lining the sidewalks wherever Victor looked. People wandered anxiously among them, searching and calling out the names of children and aged parents who'd become separated from them during the chaos of the mass rush to the south.

Part of the ground floor of the town castle facing the park had been converted into a kitchen for refugees. Victor went inside and got a bowl of hot soup, with a chunk of fresh bread, to add to the last of his sausage and cheese.

From the radio inside, he heard the latest war news: all

bad. The Germans had entered Paris in force, and now were in total command of it. The German armies were driving south, below Paris and along the coast, virtually unopposed. The French government had fled farther south, to Bordeaux.

Victor went out to the park, and found a patch of grass to sleep on.

In the morning, after exercising the stiffness from his leg, he had coffee with bread for breakfast. He squirreled an extra piece of bread into his knapsack and walked down a narrow street until he came to a food shop.

Its iron shutters were down and locked. He walked around to the back of the house and banged on the door there. A tall, fat woman with a permanent scowl opened the door a bit and gave him a suspicious glare.

"Nothing left," she snapped before he could speak. "Everything has been sold. Everything."

Victor jammed the steel point of his stick into the floorboards inside in time to prevent her shutting the door in his face. He reached into his pocket and drew out a gold coin. The woman stared at it. Victor moved it a bit, so sunlight glinted off it. The woman reached out and took the coin, studied it, bit into it. Then she opened the door wider and whispered, "Come inside, quick."

He left with a chunk of salted beef, a package of olives, a square of cheese and a bottle of wine. At the town's railroad station, a crowd of refugees was camped, waiting for the next train south. There hadn't been a train going in any direction for five days. The stationmaster had put up a notice that there wouldn't be one in the foreseeable future. But the crowd around the station continued to grow, and wait. Only a small number who came there had enough initiative to accept the situation for what it was, and head farther south on foot, as Victor did.

That noon he shared his food and wine with a corporal of the French air force—who had deserted his post at a military airfield after German bombing and strafing had destroyed all the French fighters while they were still on the ground.

"By the time I crawled out of my hole there wasn't an

officer left in sight." He shot Victor an angry look. "Well, you can't expect the men to stay put if the officers run away, can you?"

"Hardly."

The corporal had stolen a military motorcycle and was fleeing south on it to Orléans, where he could hide with his parents until the hostilities were over. In exchange for the shared meal, he took Victor south with him on the motorcycle. Victor rode comfortably enough on the back of the seat behind the corporal, who stuck to empty country lanes all the way.

It was late in the day when they neared Orléans. Experience had taught Victor that congested cities could prove as dangerous as crowded highways at this stage of a battle. He got off the motorcycle at a small farm eight miles east of Orléans, and struck a bargain with the farmer and his wife: one gold coin for each week that they gave him bed and board. He had come far enough at this point, Victor decided. His first objective had been achieved: getting out of Paris. Now he could wait out the storm and then calculate what there was for him in the debris that would be left over.

His first night at the farmhouse was spent in the cellar with the couple that owned it, listening while waves of German bombers roared over them on their way to pound the city of Orléans. They dragged down mattresses with them, but none of them slept much. The bombing of Orléans continued through most of the night; and there was always the risk of a drop falling wide of target and hitting the farm.

By dawn, when they climbed out of the cellar, there had been silence for two hours. Through the farmhouse windows, they watched the black smoke rolling from the city west of them.

The news on the radio was even worse than expected. Not only Orléans had been transformed to flaming ruins. Tours and Rouen, too, had been smashed. New waves of German bombers were already devastating other cities, and even villages.

As they finished breakfast, columns of German motorcycle troops and armored cars appeared from the north.

Hurrying to the windows with the farmer and his wife, Victor watched them speed south along the dirt road leading past the farm. Hundreds of them. They were followed by heavy trucks carrying infantry troops and arms. Then the first German tanks came into sight, churning straight across the fields.

"Right over my crops," the farmer muttered bitterly.

"Just pray God," his wife whispered, "that they don't stop here to harm *us*."

When the last of the trucks and tanks vanished to the south, Victor returned with the others to the table. He sat down slowly, considering the situation. His decision to stay put, he decided, had been correct. With the Germans already below him, there was no point in continuing in that direction. Nor in any direction, for a time.

The German army continued to roll past the farm, in spaced units, over the days and nights that followed. Victor stayed inside the farmhouse, most of the time close to the radio, listening with oddly mixed emotions to the finality of France's downfall.

When that downfall was completed, one possibility for him would be to move into what was left of Orléans. His name meant nothing to anyone there; and nobody would have any reason to interfere with him. He would be quite safe.

On the seventeenth of June, Victor listened to Marshal Pétain, the eighty-five-year-old new premier of France, announcing over the radio that he had asked the Germans for an armistice. He heard the trembling in the aged voice of what had once been a French hero:

"At this sad hour my thoughts go out to the hapless refugees streaming down the roads of France in utmost destitution. . . . It is with an aching heart that I say to you today that the fighting must stop."

Victor felt his contempt for the human species confirmed by the jubilation with which the farm couple, like the French radio commentators, seized on this swallowing of a shameful peace.

The next day there was another French general on the

radio. This time it was Charles de Gaulle, who had fled to England, speaking over the BBC from London:

"France has lost a battle, but France has not lost a war! Believe me! France is not alone! She is not alone! This is a world war. There are in the world the means for destroying the enemy one day. Unite with me! The flame of French resistance will not be extinguished!"

De Gaulle's message that the time had come for a real resistance to begin was considered plainly riduculous by the farmer and his wife. And by all who spoke of it on the radio that day. England, too, was certain to fall before a German invasion within weeks. Pétain had said the war was over; and he above all should know.

Victor, too, regarded General de Gaulle's call with deep skepticism. Could such a people ever be expected to stand up on their hind legs and act with courage? Victor knew better.

Nevertheless—there *were* certain distinct possibilities in that call to resist the conquerors of France. A few habitually rebellious souls could always be found, for a start. And what he knew of Nazi methods was bound to stir up others.

Four days later the armistice was signed between France and Germany. It divided France into two zones, almost two foreign countries, with a Demarcation Line between them. The Germans would occupy and directly govern more than half of France: the north and the entire Atlantic coastline, from their headquarters in Paris. South and east of the Line was to be considered an Unoccupied Zone, governed by Pétain from the city of Vichy—with help and advice from the Germans.

Radio broadcasts from Paris, backed by assurances from Vichy, urged everybody who had fled south to return to their homes. The war was over. Pétain promised that there was no further danger for anyone who was law-abiding. An end to chaos would help the Germans to establish their administration, and they wanted everybody to go back where they belonged.

Victor thought of the Paris he had left behind, now under German rule. He could risk it now—not to his own house, of course. But he had some friends without embarrassing political backgrounds, who might take him in while he sniffed out what could be done to discomfit his old enemies.

A German motorcyclist appeared along the road outside the farm. The farmer tensed when he saw the soldier stop at the lane leading to the farmhouse. But he did not enter it. Instead, the soldier took a poster from a pack, and nailed it to a tree alongside the road. Then he sped on.

Victor went out to look at the poster. It showed a handsome German soldier with a benevolent smile holding ragged French children who were beginning to return his smile. Accompanying this picture were the words: "Abandoned population, have confidence in the German soldier!"

Victor went back inside and packed his knapsack. Bidding farewell to the farm, he set out on the road to the nearest railroad station—to ask the Germans there to assist him in getting on a train that would carry him "back where he belonged": Paris.

Back into the tiger's teeth. Nora had been quite right about his peculiar character, he reflected, as he left the farm behind. He had not felt so young in a very long time. The excitement burned pleasurably in his veins.

A German patrol approached him, coming along the road in the opposite direction, with a group of dispirited French military prisoners in tow. The Germans paid scant attention to Victor as they marched past him. There was no danger in a white-haired old man, hobbling along with the aid of his cane.

Victor's retrurn voyage to Paris was again part of a mass movement. Most of the refugees who had fled south from the German advance were slowly beginning to turn around, now that the war was officially over, and return to their homes in the north.

Only small, separated groups, and certain isolated individuals continued to work their way secretively toward the south; sneaking past guards and patrols at the Demarcation Line into the Unoccupiee Zone where, in spite of the Vichy government's police, there was still some hope of escape. Some were people who knew there was no hope at all for

them where the Germans ruled directly: political and Jewish refugees from Germany, who had settled briefly in
France, which had now turned into another death-trap for
them. Others were a small number of French soldiers and
officers who refused to accept the ignominious surrender
of their country. And thousands were British troops who
had failed to escape at Dunkirk, but had so far managed to
evade capture and were now wandering through France in
search of a way out to England.

It was on the fifth of July that Victor left the farm to
make his way back to Paris.

It was later in that month that Nora Cesari began organ-
izing and operating what came to be code-named in her
honor by a British officer in a war room in London: the
Jeanne d'Arc escape line.

But it was actually Pascale who started it.

38

Pascale had spent the previous night at the chateau, and she awoke that July morning in the little house that had been rebuilt for her. She loved it: her very own house, between a corner of the chateau and the rear end of the abbey's arcade. One large but cozy room, with closets and a big bureau for her things, shelves for her growing stacks of photographic enlargements, a wide desk.

There was even a curved canopy over her bed: something she had dreamed of having ever since she'd read of such things in a novel about the Middle Ages. And an extra bed, for nights when she invited a girlfriend from the village to stay over with her. On the paneled walls were two framed paintings by her grandfather. And certain favorites from among the photographs she'd taken of village faces. There were also two special presents: an enlarged picture taken by her mother of a beautiful young Ethiopian mother holding her baby as she cowered under a bombardment by Italian warplanes. And a watercolor by her stepfather of the tropical fish swimming inside the great tank in the main living room of the chateau.

Pascale swung off her bed and dressed quickly. It was little more than an hour past dawn. She had set her mental alarm clock early, and as usual it had not failed her. There were things she wanted to accomplish before this morning grew much older. She hurried through a covered walkway into the ancient washroom of the abbey. Its fountain functioned now, musically trickling cold spring water into the low, massive stone bowl under it. Sprinkling a bit of the water on her face, Pascale dried herself with one of the towels that hung near the fountain and went out across the courtyard.

Nobody else was up yet. Pascale entered the chateau kitchen and made herself a breakfast of hot chocolate with buttered rolls. Wolfing it down, she hurried back to her own little house to pick up her camera and an extra roll of film. Jumeau had made her a special strap of soft suede for the Leica. Looping it over the back of her neck, with the camera hanging against her chest, Pascale strode off through the old ruins beyond the other end of the chateau.

Her project for this morning was to get pastoral shots of the valley and her village, while the sun was still low enough for the trees and buildings to cast long, dark shadows. She had already chosen the vantage point for taking the pictures: the battered defense tower.

Though much of its upper structure had fallen, the base of the square tower remained massive and solid. To one side of it were the cages and run for the chickens, partially roofed with planks to provide shade and shelter from rain, the rest fenced and covered with wire mesh to keep out foxes and woods cats. Against the opposite side of the tower, Grayle, Nora and Jumeau had constructed a shelter for the truck out of timbers and tin sheets.

Pascale entered the base of the tower through a gaping break in a third wall.

The bottom of the tower's interior had recently been roofed over with planks and tin to form a shelter for tools and storage. Part of what was stored there were three extra drums of gasoline that Grayle had bought through the black market during his last trip to Marseilles.

The flooring of what had been the tower's several upper levels had long ago rotted and burned away, along with the joists of the support timbers. But the stone steps were anchored solidly into the inner faces of the main walls, and most were still there.

When she reached the truncated heights, Pascale swung herself into a sitting position on a crumbly wall, her feet dangling outside the tower. From her perch she had a wide view of the entire valley below, with the crags of the Alpilles rising out of the forests to the left and her village straight ahead on the other side.

The shadows were exactly what she'd wanted: long and black, sharply defined. Pascale snapped three pictures of the valley, with the distant village creating a background focal point. Then she looked toward the Alpilles, examining the clarity with which the morning light defined each separate tree and outcrop of pock-marked stone, even each clump of low scrub brush.

Adjusting the lens opening, Pascale took a shot of this. She changed the shutter speed and prepared to take another shot of the same scene. That was when she spotted the man.

He was coming down from the low mountain chain, toward her valley, walking slowly along one side of the road that cut across the Alpilles from St. Remy. He was very small, that far away, but even so Pascale could see that he was not acting naturally. He stopped when he reached a point where the road topped a rise, and spent a very long time examining the terrain ahead of him.

First he studied the village. Then, slowly, he scanned the valley. Finally, he looked toward the chateau. Pascale was quite certain he could not see her, because the perch on which she sat was shaded by a prong of the tower wall behind her. But he looked in her direction for some time, before scanning the rest of the valley again. At last he resumed walking, following the road as it led down through the forested slopes toward the bottom of the valley.

Pascale narrowed her eyes in order to make him out more sharply. He was tall and thin. Sunlight glinted in his carroty-red hair. She knew no one with hair like that. And there was something else that was not natural: He wore some kind of long coat. It reached to his knees, and it was entirely buttoned in front.

Even this early in the morning, the midsummer heat was too strong for anyone to wear a coat—and all buttoned up, at that.

Suddenly, the man darted off the road, diving into the wild bushes beside it. He scrambled in deeper on his hands and knees, until the bushes concealed him.

It was several moments before Pascale saw what had alarmed him: An automobile appeared, coming along the road from the direction of St. Remy. A long, black car, with two people in front. It sped down toward the valley, past the bushes where the man was hidden. Now Pascale began to understand what he must be.

Since the armistice the gasoline shortage had become acute, even here inside what was known variously as the Unoccupied Zone, the Free Zone or Vichy France. Anyone driving a car or truck now was likely to belong to one of the few groups with special access to fuel: the police or other functionaries of Pétain's Vichy government, Germans, or people with businesses that were important to Vichy or the Germans. The man in the bushes must have reason to fear being seen by such people. Pascale considered the few groups he might belong to; who would have to travel south through this area in secret.

None of the battles of the war had reached this area. And since the armistice relatively little had happened here to make people feel they were part of a conquered nation. The German-occupied zone was too far north and west. Though Pascale's mother was certain that Pétain's government would soon be copying the restrictions of its German masters, so far there was little indication of it.

But there had been several side occurrences of the war and its aftermath.

First there had been the matter of Sylvio Trimarco, the stonemason, and his father. Since the start of the war it had been the policy of the French government to round up enemy aliens—Germans living in France, including refugees who'd flew there from Germany—and intern them in prison camps. When Italy had declared war, "enemy aliens" had been extended to include Italian residents.

The elder Trimarco had understood what would happen from the moment Italy entered the war. He had left his room in the village and taken his son away from the quarry with him before the local gendarmes could get to them.

The Trimarcos had hidden in the chateau. And Sylvio Trimarco had occupied himself during their time there by beginning to excavate the ancient escape tunnel that led from the cistern in the cellars. He'd gotten only partway through it when the war had ended. Two weeks later Sylvio had returned to the quarry and his father to the village. Italians were no longer regarded by France as enemies, but as conquerors who could be hated but had to be treated respectfully. The fact that the Trimarcos were antifascists didn't affect anyone in the village.

The Trimarcos were part of the village, and no one in it had any intention of denouncing them to the authorities. As for the local gendarmes, they didn't come searching again. They had done their duty the first time: a duty few of them liked.

But though Sylvio Trimarco was back at work at the quarries, he agreed with his father that the dagner could come again: from other sources, for other reasons. So from time to time he returned to the chateau to continue his project of removing obstructions inside the ancient escape tunnel. Occasionally, Pascale helped with it. She was intrigued with the mystery of where it would finally lead.

There had been other incidents since the armistice. First, there'd been the arrival at the village of a weary, hungry French solider who had thrown away his uniform and put on stolen civilian clothes. His unit had surrendered to the Germans. The soldier had evaded the German guards at night, and run away. He was on his way to his home in Marseilles, hoping to slip unnoticed back into his former job as a dock worker.

Madame Cesari had taken him in for the night, sharing their dinner with him, and giving him her own bed while she slept with Pascale. Before leaving the next morning Pierre Brion had given her grandmother his address in Marseilles, in case he could ever return her hospitality.

And more recently, there had been the arrival at the village of five French people of Jewish ancestry. A middle-aged couple, and a younger couple with a boy of five. They had escaped together across the Demarcation Line out of German-occupied France, and had trudged south through Vichy France for weeks in search of safe shelter.

The young couple with their child had been taken in by Marcel Reynaud, who had a small farm outside the village and whose wife was half-Jewish. They were still there, with little likelihood that anyone would betray their presence. The first loyalty of the people of this area was to their village and valley; the Reynaud family was as permanent a part of this as the buildings and crops.

But the middle-aged couple no longer believed any part of France would remain safe for Jews. So Grayle had used up the last of his gasoline to drive them to Marseilles. Through the harbor contacts of Pierre Brion, passage had been obtained for the couple on a cargo ship bound for Algeria.

To obtain fuel for his return trip to the chateau, and the three extra drums for emergencies. Grayle had used his forger to make contact with a gangster active in the black market of Marseilles. Legal allotments of gasoline were soon supposed to be issued by the Vichy government to people engaged in farming activities. So far, however, the promised rations had not begun to be distributed.

So the man Pascale had seen dodge into hiding, if he was the fugitive she guessed him to be, was wise to be frightened of any vehicle on the road.

She watched the long black car speed off across the bottom of the valley. It passed the turnoff road that led to the village, and continued toward the southwest in the direction of Arles. Pascale switched her attention back to the place where the red-haired man in the buttoned-up coat had vanished. He was crawling out of the bushes. Standing up, he brushed himself off as he looked around, as though undecided about his next move. Finally he continued the way he had been going: along the side of the road, down to the valley.

When he reached the bottom of the valley, he followed the road past the end of the forested ravine below Pascale. At a lane cutting toward the village, he stopped again, undecided. Then he turned into the lane. He'd taken only a few steps when he was frozen by the noise of another approaching engine.

In the distance to the south, a motorcycle had appeared,

speeding along the road into the valley. The man Pascale was watching spun around and sprinted back out of the lane, dodging across the road and into the underbrush of the ravine.

Pascale swung herself off the top of the wall, and began making her way down through the interior of the tower.

Lieutenant Russell Cawthorne crouched behind the bushes at the base of the ravine, squinting through the foliage as the motorcycle went past his hiding place. The rider of the motorcycle was a uniformed policeman.

Cawthorne stayed where he was, listening to the motorcycle race off to the north. He was perspiring profusely, and the old raincoat he'd stolen from a barn didn't help. He wore it buttoned to conceal the Australian uniform jacket underneath; but he was ready to rip it open at a moment's notice. If he were caught out of uniform they might shoot him for a spy. With the uniform jacket, there was a chance he'd just be turned over to the Germans as a prisoner of war.

But even that was not certain. He had come upon notices nailed to trees in the Jura forest by the German army, warning escaped prisoners to give themselves up: that any caught trying to get away would be shot on the spot.

But Cawthorne was still trying to get away. To him, it wasn't an act of bravery. He just couldn't stand the idea of being locked up somewhere until the end of a war that might go on for years. He wanted to get to England, where if not safe he would at least not be a prisoner. There were two possible ways to accomplish this objective: reach Marseilles and try to find some kind of vessel to carry him to Gibraltar. Or cross into Spain, and report to the British consulate in Barcelona.

He cursed the bad luck that had gotten him stuck on France's eastern frontier, instead of along the Channel coast where he'd have had a chance of getting away in the Dunkirk evacuation. All because he and his superior had been assigned to the French army north of the Jura as liaison officers.

The noise of the police motorcycle had died out in the distance. Cawthorne straightened and pushed through the bushes out onto the side of the road. He was hot and tired, and wanted to lie down in the shade and rest a while. But he was also famished, and hoping to find something to eat before much longer. Perhaps he would have to chance the village. Cawthorne started across the road, to take the lane that led toward it.

Pascale emerged from the bushes at the bottom of the ravine, off to his right, and called out: "Are you looking for a place to hide?"

Cawthorne twisted toward her in a spasm of panic. Then he saw it was a very young girl, and made himself relax a notch. He hadn't understood her words; but her tone had been deliberately reassuring, and her smile was friendly—even understanding.

"Do you speak any English?" he asked her tensely. He repeated it in French, and he did it well enough to she understood.

Pascale shook her head. "But my parents do." It had been a source of some irritation for her in the past when they had used it to say something to each other that they didn't want her to understand. She motioned to Cawthorne. "Come, I'll take you to them."

He failed to understand her words. But he understood that she wanted to help him. When Pascale turned to go back up the path through the ravine, Cawthorne went after her. He unbuttoned the raincoat and took it off as they climbed through the woods.

Lieutenant Cawthorne devoured every morsel of food they set before him, washing down chewed mouthfuls with wine. "I hope I don't get drunk on this tasty stuff," he told Grayle. "If I do, please excuse me in advance. It's been quite a while since I've been able to relax enough to drink this much."

"Finish the bottle," Grayle said. "You're safe here."

Pascale sat at the long dining table between him and Nora, gazing possessively at the Australian officer. He was hers; she had found and saved him. She didn't understand what was being said, but her mother had whispered a promise to translate it all, later. For the moment, Pascale was contented with merely assessing the character of the rugged face under that ridiculous carroty hair.

Cawthorne couldn't stop his gaze from straying to the painting of the nude woman at the stream that hung on the wall at the end of the long table. He glanced from it to Nora's face and then quickly took another sip of wine and looked back to Grayle, forcing his expression to remain impassive.

He told about his trek through the Jura. "Picked up other British troops along the way," he said. "By ones and twos, all trying to get away, like I was. By the time we were south of the Jura, there were eleven of us. And then some French troops who'd deserted their units began joining up with us, heading for home. They were a great help. Took us along little paths where we weren't likely to run into Germans. Put us up at their homes when we reached them. The last two lived close to the Demarcation Line, and they slipped us across between the German patrols. After that we were on our own. No French guides. But they'd given us a map of the area down here. And at least we were inside the Unoccupied Zone. No more German troops to worry about."

"There are some Vichy cops," Grayle remarked, "who're eager to prove they can be as efficent as the Germans. And your presence here is against Vichy's latest laws."

"So we discovered," Cawthorne told him bitterly. And then: "You know, with that accent of yours, you could almost pass as a Yank."

"I spent some years in America. You ran into trouble with the French police?"

"Did we ever." Cawthorne sighed unhappily. "We got to a village, late in the evening. While the rest of us looked around for a barn to spend the night in, five of the men headed for the cafe to try their luck. See if they could scrounge some decent food and drink. When we went looking for them, they were being shoved into a police van by gendarmes waving pistols. I managed to shove off with the five men I had left, before we were spotted."

Nora asked him, "What happened to the five men you had left?"

"Well, we were understandably suspicious of anybody after that experience. The rest of the way we avoided people. Stuck to the woods, traveled by night, slept in the bushes, ate what we could steal from farms we passed in the dark. Finally, we had another bit of luck. Walked smack into a farmer, a day north of here, and he turned out to be all right. One of my men spoke enough French to talk with him. Seems he has two sons that were drafted into the army. And now they're in a POW camp somewhere in Germany. So this farmer was inclined to help anybody ready to go on fighting the Germans."

Cawthorne forked another portion of food into his mouth and chewed it slowly. "We stayed with him three days. No way of knowing if we could find another safe haven like that, farther south. The other five men are still up there."

"But you came down alone," Nora said.

"Well, we couldn't stay there forever, could we? Somebody had to see what could be found down here. No sense in all of us trying it together—and maybe getting caught together. And since I'm the senior officer . . ." Cawthorne shrugged, a bit embarrassed. "I said I'd go back up and get them if I found more friends down this way. And I have, thanks to your little girl, here."

He gave Pascale a grin, and she grinned back at him, delighted. His rugged face, she had decided, was really quite handsome, in an unusual way.

Nora said quietly, "It will be safer if *I* go up and bring the rest of your men down. I know the best way to travel. And if I leave tomorrow morning, I can get there by late in the day. And lead them down in the night."

Grayle looked at her and started to say something, then stopped himself.

Cawthorne looked at her with surprised gratitude; and avoided glancing again at the nude painting of her on the wall. "That's very decent of you. If you're quite sure it will be safe for you."

"It will be," Nora assured him flatly.

"Then all that'll be left for us is the last stretch to Marseilles." Cawthorne looked at Grayle. "We're hoping to find a boat there; steal one if we have to . . ."

Grayle shook his head. "The security around the port has tightened considerably. Too many plainclothes police, and Vichy informers, on the lookout for people trying to get out that way. Some still make it; but the chances are getting slimmer."

Cawthorne frowned over this. "The other thing I thought about is trying for Spain. But there's the Pyrenees mountains blocking the way, and I don't know anything about the ways across."

"I do," Nora said.

Grayle shot her another look. She met his gaze firmly. Again, he said nothing. Still looking at him, Nora went on: "From here there are routes where no one would spot us. West and south through the Cévennes. Or by train, partway. There is a safe-house we can use, in Perpignan. I used it before, when I was bringing Spanish refugees north. And another, west of there: a farm where the people can be trusted to help. Below there, I know two Basque shepherds, either of whom I can get to take people over the Pyrenees."

Cawthorne looked uncertainly from Nora to Grayle. "This is very kind of your wife. And extremely brave. But I'm not sure I can allow a woman to put herself in that kind of danger for my sake."

Grayle kept a stony silence, holding what he had to say to Nora until later.

"You're not likely to make it without me," Nora told Cawthorne. "Another thing—a woman can move about where she's not known, and scout the way ahead, without arousing the kind of suspicion a man would. A woman isn't necessarily anchored in place by a job. She can give many reasons, even silly reasons, for going off somewhere. A visit to friends or relatives. A shopping trip to the city."

She spoke judiciously, from experience. "And, in France at least, a woman is still primarily a woman, before anything else she might be. Even to a policeman, if she uses charm and humor." Nora smiled at the lieutenant. "There

is always that slight air of flirtation, to make him forget it
is his profession to be suspicious."

Cawthorne felt himself begin to blush, and was very
careful not to look at the nude.

Grayle glanced at his empty plate. "I imagine you're
tired. If you've had enough to eat, there's a bed for you."

Cawthorne laughed and patted his stomach. "I'd say I
ate like a hog, and I hope you could spare it. I *could* use a
nap. Walked all night."

Grayle stood up. Without looking at Nora again, he led
the way out to the main corridor. Nora stayed behind with
Pascale, telling her everything that had been said in English. Taking Cawthorne into the downstairs library, Grayle
indicated the two couches that had been used by the Trimarcos during their stay in the chateau. "Take either one,
close the shutters and you'll find sheets and pillows in that
closet. But if we get unwelcome visitors while you're here,
this is where you disappear to." He crouched and opened a
trapdoor in the flooring.

Below were wooden steps leading under the chateau.
Grayle lit a lantern and carried it down with them. Cawthorne followed him through the cellar vaults to the cistern.

The pipe Grayle had run from the spring out back was
connected to it now, and the cistern was half-filled with
water. Taking off his shoes, stockings and trousers, Grayle
lowered himself into the cistern. When he was standing on
one of the rocks he'd left at the bottom, the surface of the
water was more than halfway up his thighs.

Cawthorne had shucked his own trousers, stockings and
boots. When he was down in the water, Grayle handed him
the lantern and turned to the rear wall of the cistern. It
was of old blocks of stone, with deep cracks between them.
Grayle dug his fingers into the cracks around one of the
stones, just above the surface of the water.

"When you're going in to hide," he told Cawthorne, "you
shove it in ahead of you. And then push it back in place
once you're inside. Make sure you set it right; flush with
the other stones around it." He dragged the stone out. It
was heavy, and he leaned it against the cistern wall to help
him hold it.

The opening, Cawthorne saw, was just big enough for a man to wriggle through. He shone the lantern inside, and saw the low, narrow tunnel leading away, with a slight incline downward. "Lovely. Where does that go?"

"We're not sure yet. Haven't finished clearing the other end of it. Just get inside if there's danger, and stay put until one of us comes for you." Grayle shoved the stone back into the opening, sealing it shut. He pressed his hands at the sides until the stone was level with the others. Then he climbed out of the cistern and led the way back to the library.

He showed Cawthorne the bathroom next to it, and they used the towels to dry their legs. Grayle put his trousers, stockings and shoes back on. Cawthorne was getting the sheet from the closet, with a pillow and blanket.

"Shove these back in the closet if you have to do a disappearing act," Grayle told him, and went back through the corridor, leaving Cawthorne to get his sleep.

Nora was in the main living room with Pascale, sitting on one of the carpets, spreading open a number of Michelin maps on the floor around them. She looked up at Grayle, and her voice was steady: "When our lieutenant wakes up, I want him to show me the exact route he followed, coming down from the north. Every place they were able to find shelter. The names of everyone who was willing to help them."

Grayle sat in one of the leather wing chairs, looking down at Nora and their daughter, his face drained of expression, his mouth hard.

Nora drew a breath. "Look, there will be others. Political exiles from Germany. Jews. British soldiers. Even French soldiers. Trying to find their way through. Trying to get out."

"Lieutenant Cawthorne made it this far on his own."

"He was very lucky. And Vichy hasn't really gotten down yet to the business of finding and catching escapees. But it will. And then none of them will be able to get through. Unless somebody sets up the routes for them, finds the safe-houses for them to stay in, locates guides willing to show them the way."

Grayle said flatly: "It doesn't have to be you."

"I won't be the only one. You know that. By now there must be others, starting to do the same thing. But I know certain things most of them don't: how to get safely from here to the Pyrenees, and how to cross them into Spain. All that's left is to find contacts, to the north." Nora forced a smile. "You did want me to stop being a drone, to become active again."

In spite of himself, Grayle felt his own smile start. But it was bitter; not at her, but at what was pressing in on them, and could not be stopped. "I was thinking of photography."

Nora shook her head. "That's over, for the time being."

She reached up and took one of Grayle's hands in hers, tightening her grip on it. "You're driven by your needs. You can't stop me from being driven by my own. Not even out of love."

His eyes narrowed, but not enough to conceal that pain. "I know."

They had been speaking in French. Allowing Pascale to absorb what they were saying; and she registered not only the words, but the strength of feeling between them. She said, softly, "In school, the last month, we were studying the history of the French Revolution—the time of the Terror. What's happening now is something like that, isn't it?"

Still holding Grayle's hand tightly, Nora put her free hand on Pascale's head, caressing it. "Not quite yet. But I think it will come to that, eventually."

"What do you think about Charlotte Corday?" Pascale asked. "Was she right to murder Marat? He *was* a monster, wasn't he?"

"He enjoyed having people executed," Nora said. "People not even connected with the politics of the day. People he didn't like, or just didn't care about. He enjoyed it. Yes, a man like that is a monster."

"Then she was right to kill him?"

Grayle asked quietly: "Did it change anything?"

It was Nora who answered: "No, not really. The Terror

got worse. The number of executions increased. There were other monsters to take Marat's place."

"There always will be," Grayle said deliberately. He looked down at his daughter. "So your Charlotte Corday didn't achieve anything by what she did."

"But she was so beautiful," Pascale said. "Everything about her. Do you know what she said before they guillotined her?"

He shook his head.

"She said, 'I killed one man to save my country. I don't have the slightest fear of death. Because I have never had the slightest regard for my life, except as a means of being useful.'"

Nora was watching his reaction to that. Grayle looked at the big fish tank in the middle of the room, watching the tiny, brilliantly colored bits of life dart around inside it. He remembered Abd-el-Rahman: where do you find the end of a man's fate? When he conquered? When later he lost all? When he won success again? When he died? Or when he was remembered?

Late that night, when Nora fell asleep in his arms, Grayle continued to lie awake, holding her close to him, squinting at the darkness above him.

There were some things a man could not stop, he told himself again. He could only avoid them—or go with them and strive for a measure of control: to bend their direction.

39

In addition to the black market gas that Grayle had brought back from Marseilles, he had bought bicycles for Nora and himself. Pascale, like many of the village children, already had her own for riding to school in Fontvielle. But the gas shortage was making them the common mode of travel for adults, too.

Nora took her bike when she set out after breakfast for the farm where Lieutenant Cawthorne's men were waiting.

After she had gone, Grayle took Jumeau and Cawthorne down to the cellars. He posted Pascale atop the tower, where she could see anyone approaching in time to get down and warn them. The three men crawled into the tunnel, one by one. It was an aspect of the decisions Grayle had come to in the night: if the chateau was to become a safe-house along Nora's escape route, it was time to discover, finally, exactly where the secret exit came out.

Sylvio Trimarco had cleared several hundred yards of the tunnel. By now its direction was apparent. Some distance behind the chateau an overgrown cliff dropped into a ravine even more densely wooded than the one leading into the valley. This one was also narrower, and deeper. The tunnel was angling toward this ravine.

Grayle crawled in first. When he was as far as he could go, he put down his lantern and attacked the debris blocking further passage. Most of it was earth and fragments of stone. He used a hammer and chisel to split larger rocks into manageable chunks. When he had filled a bucket, he shoved it behind him. Cawthorne dragged it back to Jumeau, who emptied it into a wheelbarrow above the edge of the cistern. Each time the wheelbarrow was full, it was pushed to a deep recess of the cellars and dumped.

Grayle had begun to feel a draft of cool air, seeping in through the debris ahead, when they quit to rest and have lunch. Pascale was called down to join them in the kitchen. She had been on lookout all morning, without a sign of anyone approaching; but she was not bored. The importance of her part in this excited her almost beyond bearing. When the meal was finished, she went back up to the tower, and the men returned to the tunnel.

An hour later Grayle broke through, into a small, natural cave. He climbed inside and found it was high enough for him to stand erect. The floor showed signs of once having been leveled by hand. Now it was covered with squat mounds of stalagmites, upon which liquid dripped from delicate stalactites that dangled from the cave's irregular roof.

Cawthorne climbed in after him and glanced around the cave appreciatively. "You could put up ten men here, easily. More, in a pinch. Clean it up a bit, bring in mattresses and the necessary facilities, enough food and drink, and they could stay holed up for quite a while. All cozy and neatly hidden. You even have fresh air."

Grayle lowered the lantern and looked at the place the air was coming from: a break in the cave wall. There was some daylight filtering in through it, too. But not much, because of a screen of evergreen boughs across the outside of the opening.

He handed the lantern to Cawthorne and crouched before the opening. It was large enough. He crawled through, gently parted the thick boughs of the evergreen bushes and looked out. Below him the cliff fell into the forest-choked ravine behind the chateau. Grayle turned his head and looked up. The opening was about halfway down the cliff.

Pulling inside, Grayle told Cawthorne: "Go back through and have Jumeau help you scatter what we've excavated, so it won't be noticeable."

Crawling into the opening again, Grayle edged out into the open. Being careful not to break any of the boughs that screened the hole, he began the downward climb. From above or across the ravine, the cliff looked sheer. But he found plenty of footholds: spurs of rock concealed under the curtain of brush covering the cliff. And the bushes themselves, with their roots gripping deeply inside the porous stone, provided secure handholds. In less than half an hour, he was at the bottom.

From there, he looked up. It hadn't been an easy climb down, but at no point had it been dangerous. He doubted, however, that anyone was likely to try climbing up that cliff, without knowing of a specific reason.

Turning his back on the cliff, Grayle started working his way across the bottom of the ravine. The foliage overhead concealed him all the way. There were no pathways: he had to work himself through low branches, climb over exposed roots and ground vines, go flat and slither under bushes too closely packed to force through. When he reached a slope on the other side, the climb up was difficult at first. But then the underbrush began to thin out; and finally he was atop the crest of a hill. He looked back at the cliff from that point.

It was impossible to see the opening to the cave and tunnel. All that was there was another of thousands of similar patches of shadow.

Pascale helped Grayle make an early supper for the four of them. Then he walked her down to the village, to leave her with her grandmother. She didn't like it, and Grayle quietly explained why it was necessary now.

"By dawn tomorrow morning, we'll have six British soldiers hiding in the chateau. That's against the law. While they're there, it could be a dangerous place for you to be."

"I don't care."

"But I do. And your mother will. Listen, Pascale: if the lieutenant and his men manage to get back to England, it will be because you made it possible for them. But the rest of this is going to have to be done very carefully. If we're worried about you, we won't be able to give it our absolute attention. And then we might make a mistake. You understand."

Pascale's "yes" was reluctant.

Grayle explained it again to Nora's mother, when they reached her house. He told her exactly what had happened, and what was likely to happen in the next few days. Madame Cesari heard him out tensely, and her fear as she brooded over it was obvious.

But her voice was firm when she finally spoke: "Nora is right. Someone has to do it. Someone has to begin acting with human feeling for people who are in trouble."

Grayle gave her a bemused smile. Then he kissed Pascale and turned to leave. Madame Cesari's thin hand shot out and caught his arm, stopping him.

"Be careful," she said. "Take care of Nora."

Grayle looked at her. "I'm going to do what I can."

"Yes . . ." Her fingers continued to grip his arm as she searched his face. And then, for the first time, she kissed him on the cheek.

On his way back across the valley, Grayle detoured into a lane leading to the farmhouse of Pierre-Baptiste Chabot, the village's mayor. Chabot was a short, squat man, with huge hands and a broad, pockmarked face that could frighten people when he was angry. His wife had died three years before, his daughter had moved away to Dijon to marry a dentist, and his son, who'd been caught with the British near Dunkirk, hadn't been heard from since. He worked his large farm now with hired help; and he was alone in his kitchen, listening to a BBC broadcast from London, when Grayle came in.

Chabot motioned him to a chair, heard out the last of the broadcast and then snapped off the radio with a hard smile. "The Germans are bombing the hell out of England. But you know what Churchill has done? He's refused Hitler's offer to discuss peace terms. That old bulldog! I wonder what they'll say now, the people who were so sure he'd have to be *sensible* in the end, like Pétain."

"They'll say Churchill isn't a logical politician. And that Pétain is."

"Exactly," Chabot sneered. "We are such a practical people. Look how well we're doing."

He heaved to his feet and lumbered off to get a bottle of

his own wine. He put it on the table with two tall glasses of intricate design and delicate color. Mementos from his honeymoon in Venice. Plumping down in a chair facing Grayle, he filled both glasses to the brim, and raised his own without spilling a drop. "Your health."

"And yours." Grayle took a sip, considered the taste, smiled approvingly and took a longer sip.

Chabot sipped from his glass and smacked his lips. "My best batch this year. I won't sell a drop of it. Just for myself and my friends."

Grayle drank again. "This buys you my vote."

"Perhaps I won't run in the next election. I've been mayor long enough."

"It's not much work; and there's the honor."

"Let God give the honor to someone else—and give me my son back."

"Gilbert is probably in England—with de Gaulle."

Chabot rapped the wood of the radio with his scarred knuckles. "I listen for a message from him. I even pray for it. *Me*—who hasn't been inside a church since my Communion when I was twelve." He sighed, finished off his glass and eyed Grayle, waiting.

"I talked the other day to some of the farmers. Hervé Frenay, Marcel Reynauld, others who don't have their own trucks," Grayle said. "Of course they have their horses and wagons, but it's slow for long hauls. I've agreed to take their produce to the markets in mine, along with my eggs and poultry; and haul in equipment and fertilizer for them. I think that entitles me to an official paper stating that my movements are important for the agriculture of this area."

"No problem. You can have your paper. Why not? But gasoline for your truck—that I still can't help you to get. Shit, I need fuel myself. I keep phoning; and the government keeps assuring me the gas rations for farmers will soon be available. Soon." Chabot shrugged. "I guess they will be, eventually. Germany wants us to produce food, and so does Vichy."

He refilled their glasses as he assembled the remainder

of his speech. "Religion, big families and agriculture: the three legs Pétain says he wants what is left of our France to stand on. Well, the first two require faith and balls. The last . . ."

"Can do without gas," Grayle finished for him. "But gas does help—and it hasn't come yet."

"That is the situation, at the moment. Drink your wine."

"I have some gas," Grayle told him. "I put a bit aside, before the shortage."

Chabot's little eyes narrowed on Grayle shrewdly. "*Did* you. Clever."

"We'll see if I was clever enough. Depends on whether the amount of fuel I stored lasts until the rations arrive."

"But in the meanwhile, you have no problem. You have the fuel to drive your truck. So far, I haven't heard of the police stopping anyone to check on their reason for traveling. They're afraid they'll find they're annoying someone connected with the Germans."

"So far," Grayle agreed. "But they'll be getting their orders to make spot checks, sooner or later. I don't want trouble when Vichy tightens security regulations." He finished off his wine and set the glass down carefully. "I'd like to have that legal authorization. Just in case."

Chabot was still regarding him thoughtfully. Finally he nodded. "Come to the village tomorrow. I'll be at my office around noon. You'll have your paper, complete with my official stamp and signature."

It was still dark, two hours before dawn, when Nora returned to the chateau with the five British troopers. Some of them still wore remnants of their uniforms. Grayle took these from them, and replaced them with items from his own spare clothing. For the future, he decided, he was going to have to stock up on French civilian clothes, used and new. He asked if any of them still had weapons on them. Two of them did, and Grayle took these, too: a Browning FN 9-mm automatic pistol, and an Enfield .380 revolver.

After a solid breakfast, Nora and the men she'd brought

back with her settled down to catch up on their sleep. In
the morning light, Grayle took Lieutenant Cawthorne with
him out to the defense tower. Jumeau was outside, feeding
the chickens. He gave Grayle his habitual hurt look.

"We have some more guests in the chateau," Grayle told
him.

"I saw," Jumeau said, and looked a bit less hurt. He
liked it when Grayle included him in what was going on,
though he was not curious to know details or reasons.

"They won't stay long," Grayle informed him. "Then
you'll have the place to yourself for a few days. Nora and I
are going to visit some friends near Toulouse."

Jumeau nodded disinterestedly, and began gathering
newly hatched eggs for the market. Cawthorne helped
Grayle roll one of the gasoline drums out of the tower's
storage shed, and fill the tank of the truck. Back inside the
tower, Grayle sent Cawthorne up to stand watch. Then he
dumped a keg of nails on the dirt floor. Wrapping in oil-
cloth the two weapons he'd taken from the troopers, he
placed the package at the bottom of the keg. He refilled
the keg with the dumped nails, and then tipped it over on
its side so that some of the nails spilled out again. Anyone
searching for hiding places would be less likely to pay attention to something handled so carelessly.

Grayle found himself thinking about the hidden weapons
again when he drove the truck down to the village. Mayor
Chabot had his paper prepared: an official authorization
for travel on agricultural business. As they shook hands,
Chabot said an odd thing: "Good luck, Monsieur Hugonnet."

"For what, Monsieur Chabot? I'm only taking food to
the market in Arles."

"Of course."

Grayle drove along the valley to the various farmers
with whom he had made the arrangement. The amount
each had agreed to pay him was quite small. But between
all of them, it added up to enough to pay for the gas he
used up. A reasonable arrangement for all parties; with
nothing about it to arouse questions about Grayle's motives.

The truck was half-filled with their produce when he drove it back to the chateau. Jumeau had left the egg crates and three cages of poultry beside the truck shelter. Grayle was not ready to load them yet. He was still thinking about the weapons.

Going to Jumeau's little house, Grayle got three strips of leather and took them back with him. He attached them under the truck dashboard to form a snug sling. What it would hold would be out of sight, yet in position to be snatched out quickly. He went into the storage shed, emptied the nails from the keg again and removed the Browning automatic from the oilskin package. The magazine was fully loaded: all thirteen rounds in place. Grayle scooped most of the nails back inside the tipped-over keg, to hide the Enfield revolver.

Nora was coming from the chateau when he stepped out of the tower carrying the Browning. She watched him open the door of the truck's cab, and lean in to slide the automatic into the hidden sling under the dashboard. As he pulled out and turned to her, she shook her head.

"That won't be necessary. Anyway, I don't know how to use it."

"I do," Grayle told her. "And I'll be driving."

"I know how to drive the truck," she reminded him gently. "And I know the rest of the way, which you don't. You can't always go along to watch over me, you know. You'd just be an extra person for me to get through."

"If I go along this time," Grayle pointed out, reasonably, "then there'll be two of us who know how to get people from here to Spain. Suppose you're sick, or off somewhere, the next time a group of them have to be guided south?"

Nora had to agree that it made sense. When they left for Arles, Grayle was driving, with Nora up front beside him. Cawthorne and the other five men were in back behind the stacked produce, hidden under old burlap sacking. They had instructions to jump out the back and dodge into the bushes beside the road, if the truck stopped along the way and Nora rapped a signal on the panel behind her. But they reached Arles without incident.

*   *   *

Arles was having its open market that day. Both sides of the Boulevard des Lices were lined with vendors' stands and carts; crowds from the town and country milled back and forth between them. Each of the farmers had long-standing agreements with certain of the vendors, just as Grayle did for his eggs and poultry. The six British soldiers remained hidden, half-suffocating under the burlap sacking, while Grayle and Nora off-loaded the produce at the various stands. Then the truck was driven to the quay behind the ruins of the ancient Roman baths.

The narrow roadway along the bank of the Rhône was deserted. Grayle stood watch beside the truck while Nora climbed inside and pulled the sacking off the hidden men, allowing them some fresh air and a cold meal: hard-boiled eggs and broiled chicken Nora had prepared at the chateau, with bread bought at the market. There was more for the trip to Toulouse, in a canvas pack in the cab of the truck.

They drove to the railroad station and parked beside a freight shed, while Grayle stuffed the Browning deep inside the food pack. It was unlikely that they'd be searched during the train trip. But if it turned out that the government *was* starting checks of passengers, the weapon would be needed. Only one of their British escapees spoke any French; and none had proper identification papers.

Nora bought four tickets. Several minutes later Grayle entered the station and bought four more. It was quarter after six in the evening when their train pulled in. Nora made sure no one was around before she called the six men out of the truck. She boarded the train immediately with two of the men. Cawthorne followed her aboard seconds later with two others. Grayle boarded after them with the remaining one.

The train wasn't scheduled to depart for Perpignan for another half hour. But with the Germans taking so many French trains north for their own use, the ones left for civilian travel were always full. By boarding immediately, Nora's party was able to secure an entire second-class compartment. Since they took up all eight seats, there'd be no strangers in the compartment with them.

The train was ten minutes late in pulling out. Except for when they shared a meal later that night, they all slept on and off through the entire trip. There were no security checks for identification. The Vichy government hadn't gotten around to that this far from the Demarcation Line and the Spanish frontier. The only official who disturbed them was a railroad conductor checking their tickets. The disguised soldiers handed theirs over without a word.

It was two in the morning when they reached Perpignan. Nora led them away from the south end of the station to a narrow canal flowing under low bridges connecting dark, empty streets. They turned left on Quai de Hanovre, and left again into Rue de Venise. The safe-house was half a block from the city canal, three short blocks from the railroad station: a third-floor apartment owned by Madame Simone, an elderly widow who had helped Nora in the past with antifascist Spanish refugees. Nora had phoned her from Arles, and Madame Simone was prepared for them.

There was only one bed in the apartment. Nora slept on the living room sofa, while the men crowded the floor. In the morning Madame Simone went out and came back with rolls and milk for all of them, to go with the coffee Grayle brewed in her tiny kitchen. Immediately after breakfast Nora left to take a train west. The next safe-house was a farm that had no telephone, and it was necessary to check the situation there before descending on it in such a large group.

While she was gone, Grayle and the other men remained in the apartment, their shoes off so they wouldn't be heard in the apartment below. They kept away from windows and spoke in whispers. Madame Simone was more fascinated than frightened to be part of their escape. "What can they do to an old woman like me?" she explained. "A bit more excitement before I die is a welcome surprise, at my time of life. The only people I know around here are as old as me, and their only subjects of conversation are their ailments and grandchildren."

Nora returned late that afternoon. The farm was still safe, and the couple who had it were ready to cooperate. The train they would take was departing at ten that night.

Madame Simone made a rich stew for all of them before
they left. and she accepted Grayle's generous payment for
the meal with dignity: "I want to help, and I would prefer
to do it without being paid. But the prices of food in this
city are rising every day. And my husband didn't leave me
much, other than this apartment." She kissed each of them
in turn as they went out into the night.

The trip from Perpignan was as untroubled as the one
from Arles; and considerably shorter, though the train
stopped at every village.

It was still night when they got off at the town of Olette,
fifteen hundred feet up on the banks of the Tet River.
Nora led them directly south into the countryside. Farms,
vineyards and olive groves became less frequent, separated
by rising expanses of pine forest. The altitude increased
steadily, and their breathing became labored as they
climbed. Miles ahead of them the range of the Pyrenees
lifted abruptly: an endless, towering wall of blackness, its
jagged heights stabbing into the stars. Even in mid-summer
there was snow gleaming on the highest peaks.

Nora's route followed narrow pathways forming a shortcut that occasionally crossed the single dirt road that made
wide bends through the area. An hour after dawn they
rounded a hill of wild scrub and entered a rutted lane. It
led through a grove of fig trees, past a barn of split logs
and rough-hewn drying sheds, to a small stone farmhouse.

Gaspard Brault, the lean middle-aged farmer who
owned the place, greeted them nervously, and hurried them
inside. His wife, Eulalia, had a cheerful smile and an ample hot breakfast waiting for them. She was considerably
younger than her husband; plump and pretty, with black
eyes. Half-Spanish and half-Gypsy, Eulalia was the reason
this farm was a safe refuge. Her two small children were
by her former husband, who'd been killed by Franco's police. And she was aware that Gypsies were second only to
Jews in the extinction policy of the conquering Germans.

While Gaspard stood guard outside, and the others slept
through the day on straw inside the barn, Eulalia bicycled
south to contact the Basque shepherds Nora hoped would
still be willing to guide escapees over the mountain into

Spain. Both shepherds were antifascists because of Franco's harsh measures against the Basques' traditional independence. But both were also poor men, who expected to be paid for any work they did.

Eulalia returned triumphantly before sunset. She'd found one of the shepherds, José Dominguiz, and he was ready to do the job for the price Nora had offered. Eulalia gave them food to eat on the way, and stood outside, waving, as they left in the horse-drawn cart driven by her husband.

The dirt road he followed mounted steadily between ever-higher mountains. It was well before morning when they entered a twisting, rising gorge, and neared the rendezvous: a tiny, windswept stone hamlet atop a rocky slope above the timberline. Beyond it there were no more roads.

This stretch of the mountain chain was infrequently patrolled. Grayle could see why. The mountains forming the division between France and Spain seemed to present an impassable barrier here. He could spot no trace of a pass across. But Nora assured him there were ways to get over: not easily negotiated, but it could be done, with a guide who knew how.

Gaspard stopped his horse-cart well below the Basque hamlet. "I'll wait here," he whispered, looking up uneasily. Nora led the way on foot, up a treacherous path that required climbing from one rock formation to the other. As they left the last tree below, and neared the tight little cluster of stone houses, José Dominguiz stepped out of the darkness on their right.

He was a small man in his sixties, with short thick legs and sparse gray hair straggling out from under his black beret. He stared at them without expression, until Nora turned to him and he recognized her. Then his weathered face creased in a wide smile, and he stuck out a sturdy hand. "It has been a long time."

Nora shook his hand warmly. "I'll be back more often, in the future."

"Ah." The Basque scanned the men with her. "All?"

"Six." Nora took from Grayle the money promised per head. "This is my husband," she informed Dominguiz, and gave him the money.

The Basque saluted Grayle. "My congratulations, sir. You have superb taste—at least in women." He pocketed the cash. "We start now." His tone had become commanding. "We are in poor Spain in three hours. If you keep up with me."

One by one, the British soldiers shook hands with Nora and Grayle before turning to follow their guide. Lieutenant Cawthorne was last, and he held Nora's hand a bit longer than the others had. "I'll never forget you," he told her. "*Now* I believe Joan of Arc was a saint."

And that, after Cawthorne reached England and told the story of how he'd made it, was how her escape line acquired its code name.

Nora gripped Grayle's hand as they watched Dominguiz lead the six men up the cobbled steps of the hamlet's single narrow passageway and on beyond it. As they vanished against the darkness of the high mountain barrier ahead of them, Nora whispered, "He'll get them across all right, I'm sure of it. I only hope they reach the British consul in Barcelona without trouble."

"The rest is up to them," Grayle told her. "Let's go home."

40

The anxiety began to gnaw at Grayle as he watched Nora's train grind out of the Arles station. His mood was not helped by the damp gloom of that late November morning. The smoke of the departing engine vanished into the blanket of fog that spread across the rooftops of the city. The murky air was cold and heavy with moisture, the streets still wet from the rain of the night before.

He reminded himself fiercely that this time Nora wasn't guiding fugitives, was not heading south to the Spanish border. She'd made two more trips like that since the Cawthorne group, and Grayle had gone along on both. He couldn't dissuade her from carrying out what she conceived as her mission; what he *could* do was to be with her, ready to protect her if it became necessary.

But he'd had to concede that where she was going this time, her movements were less likely to be questioned if she was alone. He told himself again that there would be little risk in what Nora would be doing over the next couple weeks. There were no restrictions against a Frenchwoman going where she wished inside the Unoccupied Zone.

Nevertheless, the anxiety continued to work in him when he drove the truck away from the station. He was used to being in charge, and the one thing he did least well was to wait. The past had taught him the tricks for controlling his nerves during tense stretches of waiting. But none of them worked this time.

As he usually did in Arles, Grayle made several purchases: a woman's coat in one shop, a used suitcase in another, a mattress in a third. By scattering the purchases over the months and many different shops, he had seen to it no one would be aware of the quantity of bedding, luggage and assorted clothing now stocked at the chateau.

So far, there had been little need for this stockpile. It had taken Nora only three weeks, back in August, to organize her escape line from the north: people who had sheltered Lieutenant Cawthorne and his men during their trek south, plus additional contacts of her own. But in the months since then only six people had been passed through this line to the chateau, and been taken on from there to Spain.

The reason had become apparent: Nora's stretch of escape line was too isolated. The people to whom each safehouse belonged knew only the location of the next one south of them, and the best route to use in reaching it. There were no sources leading to Nora's escape line. The people who had used it, so far, had come upon it by chance.

Grayle had not been unhappy that the number had been so small. It meant that the normal routine of their lives had been disturbed only twice since the Cawthorne group: when they'd moved the next pair to Spain, and when they'd taken another lot of four. Except for these times, and the visits by German requisition agents expropriating eleven percent of all farm produce for transport to Germany, the life of the region had continued pretty much as before the war. This suited Grayle: all he wanted was to concentrate on his painting now. But it did not suit Nora.

This was the reason for her present journey. Many of the people trying to get out of France—British soldiers, political refugees, families fleeing increasingly vicious anti-Jewish measures by Vichy—would gravitate to large cities with underground organizations known to be sympathetic. Nora intended to reestablish contacts she'd had in the past with antifascists in certain of these cities: Valence, Grenoble, Lyon, Clermont-Ferrand and Vichy itself. Those who could still be located would be able to feed her escape line.

If she succeeded, all the purchases they had secretly stocked in the chateau would soon be needed.

After making a final purchase, a camp bed for the cave

at the end of the hidden tunnel, Grayle parked near the church of Saint Trophime and strolled across the square to calm himself by contemplating its Romanesque sculptures.

He went through to the small, exquisite cloister. The pillars of the arcades on all four sides were not like the heavy, plain columns at the chateau. These were slender, and adorned with lovingly fashioned scenes from the Old and New Testaments. Half an hour spent with the timeless calm of those faces and figures did have a soothing effect. But as he drove away from Arles the anxiety began to reassert itself; and this time none of it could be blamed on the weather.

A stiff wind was blowing across the countryside, breaking apart the cover of fog. There were still rolls of mist blurring the shapes of the Alpilles, but above the roofs of the village there were patches of blue sky of dazzling purity. Yet, by the time Grayle returned to the chateau, he was tormented by nerve-twisting visions involving Nora. There was only one release left for tension so implacable.

He went into his abbey studio and resumed work on a painting he had almost finished.

It was a large canvas, with Mayor Chabot in the foreground, seated at a table on the Place Clemenceau. A simple picture, on first look, with elements that grew the longer one looked at it: the colors that combined and collided like symphonic sounds. The weight of Chabot's strong, aging bulk. The almost impenetrable deep-blue shade under the plane tree behind him. The centuries-old church wall behind that, drenched in sunshine. Chabot's massive hand, cradling the delicate wine glass. The shrewd little eyes in that seamed peasant face, regarding the viewer with harsh insight and a priest's pardon.

There were only the final touches to be done. In the next two days, Grayle completed them. The following day he spent working outdoors with Pascale, down inside the ravine behind the chateau. Wading through wet ferns and fallen leaves and branches smelling of damp rot, they gathered pine cones that would spread a marvelous aroma when they blazed up in the fireplaces, and add delicious flavor to meat cooked over them.

Grayle paused while dropping pine cones into his burlap sack and looked up at the cliff. Though there was less foliage covering it than in the summer, the opening to the hidden cave still remained invisible to his searching eyes. Relieved, he raised his eyes to a line of trees spaced out along the top of the cliff. They looked to him like pilgrims, marching across it to an undiscovered destination.

The sky that day was slate-blue, with a high wispy haze but no clouds. The winter sun was strong enough to make Grayle and Pascale sweat in their woolen clothing. But whenever they stepped into shadow, the downdraft from the mountains cut them with an unexpected coldness.

Occasionally they heard the crash of a shotgun, or the crack of a rifle, echoing down the foothills of the Alpilles. It was hunting season in these parts. When the sacks were filled, and Grayle and Pascale were hauling them up to the chateau, they spotted three of the hunters coming down a slope with the food they'd bagged.

One was Marcel Reynaud, whose farm was halfway across the valley between the chateau and village. He had a hunting rifle slung on one shoulder, and the other two men had shotguns: Sylvio Trimarco and Jacques Manuel, the young Jew who was living at Reynaud's farm with his wife and child. They had pheasants and wild rabbits hung from their belts; between them they were dragging the carcass of a wild boar. For the next week or so, they and their neighbors were going to eat well.

Pascale looked from them to Grayle. "You never hunt."

"No," he said, "I don't."

"Don't you approve of shooting animals, even to eat?"

He smiled down at her. "It's just that I've never been a sportsman. And we have enough to eat. When we don't, I'll go hunting."

Late that afternoon, when Grayle and Pascale took a sack of the pine cones down to Madame Cesari in the village, Mayor Chabot had news for him: new rations of gasoline for agriculture purposes had arrived. Grayle celebrated by driving Pascale and her grandmother up to Avignon that evening to dine at a superb Provençal restaurant facing the palace of the Avignon popes. They spoke of everything except what Nora might be doing at that moment, somewhere in the north—and that night Grayle's nerves were crawling again. The next dawn he began work on another painting.

The painting, when finished, was not given a name. Across the lowest portion: a desert of naked, undulating stone. Above that, filling almost the entire canvas, a star-filled sky of velvet darkness. Only after looking for a time did one identify the two touches of orange in the lower portion as figures moving across it: a man leading a camel, dwarfed by the implacable distances. No goal in sight. Nothing but those three elements: specks of life, pushing across that unyielding surface, under those eternal constellations.

Late on the fourth afternoon of his work on this painting, Grayle heard the approach of an automobile. He walked out into the courtyard as the car came to a stop at the gateway. The man who got out was the adjutant from the gendarmerie in Arles.

Adjutant Nugon was as tall as Grayle, with a lean figure balancing a boxer's solid shoulders. He was thirty-three and had the manner of the conscientious civil servant he was. The severity of his short-cropped hair emphasized the bullet-shaped head and did not fit with the quiet intelligence in his good-natured face.

Grayle had first met him when he had registered at the Arles gendarmerie. They had met again, months later, when Grayle had taken Nora into a restaurant and found Nugon waiting for a table with his wife, Katie. Nugon's wife had been the nurse who'd tended Madame Cesari through a period of illness. She and Nora had become friendly then. The four of them had shared the next table that had become available. It had proved a pleasant evening. Grayle had found Alain Nugon easy to like, and unwise to underestimate.

He wasn't in uniform. The hunting jacket and jaunty fisherman's hat he wore meant he hadn't come on an official matter. But his green eyes were not quite at ease.

He glanced around the courtyard and chateau as they

shook hands. "I haven't seen this place since you began fixing it up. Beautiful. You've put a lot of work and money into it." Without much change of tone, he asked, "Is your wife around?"

"No, she's gone off to visit a friend in Lyon. Come in for a glass of wine?"

"Thank you, I can use it." Nugon followed Grayle to the chateau. "Unpleasant day at the office."

Grayle took him into the smaller living room next to the main one, and gestured him to a leather wing chair with a polished oak coffee table beside it. "Red or white?"

"White, I think."

Grayle went out into the corridor and stood perfectly still for a long moment. Then he went to the wine closet and opened a bottle of Chabot's best white vintage. He carried the bottle and two glasses back with him, and sat down facing Nugon across the table. He poured, and they drank each other's health.

Nugon set his glass down and looked at Grayle. "Is your wife due back from Lyon soon? Tomorrow, perhaps?"

"I've no idea." Grayle gave the words no importance. "She'll probably stay until she gets bored there. Why?"

Nugon looked at his glass, but did not pick it up. "This is a difficult time for France. But we police still have our job to do. Just like a baker. You still go to the baker and he sells you bread. Well, we sell, you order."

He leaned back in his chair with a slight grimace. "Order," he repeated. "The opposite of trouble. But I had a telephone call today from a cop who prefers to sell people trouble. He's a young inspector with the criminal brigade of the Police Judiciaire in Avignon. He is also, it seems, a dirty cunt. An active member of the fascist party run by Joseph Darnand, who as you probably know is very close to Pétain. In charge of his personal bodyguard, for a time. Well, this dirty cunt of an inspector—his name is Floriot, by the way—has been busy for the past five years compiling his own private list of what he calls 'potential trouble-makers' in this part of the country."

Grayle took a sip of wine and watched Adjutant Nugon.

"After his call today," Nugon told him, "I phoned his

chief in Avignon. Commissaire Gaillard. In the commissaire's opinion, this Inspector Floriot is something that should be flushed down a toilet. However, Floriot's connection with Darnand in Vichy gives him a certain dangerous political power. The kind that, in these times, makes even his chief wary of interfering with his activities as a card-carrying fascist. You understand?"

"Why are you telling me this?"

Nugon sighed. "Three of those on Inspector Floriot's list are in this area. He wants to talk with them; to check, as he explained to me, on whether they are still a potential threat to the stability of the Vichy government. In other words, still convinced antifascists. The authority of the Police Judiciaire does not extend outside the city. Here in the country the police authority resides with the gendarmerie. So he was obliged to phone and ask for my cooperation. Which, unfortunately, I am obliged to extend to him."

Grayle's frown was merely puzzled.

"Two of the people Inspector Floriot wants to talk with tomorrow, in my presence, are the Trimarcos. I have already spoken to them, privately. The old man is too sick now to be moved from his bed, and I imagine Mayor Chabot will not allow him to be bothered much. Sylvio will probably get lost somewhere in his quarries for a while. The third person the inspector wishes to interview is Nora Cesari."

"Her name is now Madame Hugonnet."

"But she is better known by her professional name. Too well-known. We have been quite proud of her. A famous photographer, with all those pictures in newspapers all over the world. All those articles written about her: a beautiful, courageous woman, with a talent few men can match—*and* an outspoken antifascist."

Nugon paused to lean forward and pick up his glass. He looked at it, not drinking. "I hope that your wife will not be here when I arrive with this Inspector Floriot tomorrow—and that she is not expected to return for some time to come."

41

Grayle accompanied the three policemen during the tour of the chateau and grounds that Inspector Floriot had insisted on carrying out. They didn't find Nora; nor did they find any of Grayle's paintings and sketches of her. That was one of the matters he had attended to after Adjutant Nugon had left the previous day. The other matter he had discussed with Pascale and Madame Cesari. There'd been no need to discuss anything with Jumeau, who could only tell the inspector the simple truth: He didn't know where Madame Hugonnet was, or when she would return.

The clothes of all four men were damp from the thin November drizzle outside when they finally returned to their starting point: the main living room. Grayle turned and faced them, his manner dismissive. "As I told you, a complete waste of your time and mine. Quite unnecessary. My wife is in Lyon."

Nugon wore his uniform today. The gendarme who had driven their car was also in uniform. Inspector Floriot, a plainclothes detective, was dressed in an ill-fitting suit that looked new. He was built like a young bull, but his face was sharply chiseled and handsome, the features neat and small. His manner was disarmingly relaxed and cheerful; but his cold blue eyes gloated over his newfound power.

"Shall we sit down for a moment?" he said, already lowering himself into one of the chairs.

Grayle strolled over to the big fish tank and began sprinkling some pellets of food into it. Adjutant Nugon walked to a window and gazed out at the rain. His gendarme became absorbed in watching the tiny fish swarm up to the surface and snatch at their meal.

Inspector Floriot crossed one leg over the other and looked toward Nugon's back. "It is curious, Adjutant Nugon. I phone to ask your cooperation in interviewing certain people in your area—and they suddenly disappear."

Nugon turned from the window and gave him an unbending stare. "If you are insinuating some irregularity on my part, you should make the complaint officially, in writing. Along with your evidence to back it up. Two of the people you wanted to see happen not to be at home today. If you wish, I'll check from time to time, and inform you when I learn that they have returned. The third person you wished to interview *was* at home."

"Just the old man," Inspector Floriot said disgustedly. "Too sick and senile to talk sense, even if he wished to." He transferred his attention to Grayle, opening a small notebook on one knee and taking out a pen. "If you can tell me, Monsieur Hugonnet, what is the name and address of this friend your wife is visiting in Lyon?"

"I don't know," Grayle told him carelessly. "The only old friends of my wife whom I've had the occasion to meet are those in this area."

"Ah? But it is strange, don't you agree, that you also don't know when she will return. You are her husband, after all."

Grayle turned from the aquarium, his expression uncomfortable. "As a matter of fact, Inspector, my wife and I had a quarrel, and she felt a bit of separation would be good for both of us."

Inspector Floriot looked properly sympathetic. "I'm sorry to hear that. What did you quarrel about?"

"That is none of your business. A personal problem."

"Not a political quarrel?"

Grayle's frown was puzzled. "Why would we quarrel about politics?"

"Come now, Monsieur Hugonnet. Your wife is well-known to be a supporter of communist causes. Unless you've been able to change her views. After all, you're a wealthy man." Inspector Floriot's gesture took in the room. "You have a beautiful place here. Surely you realize that everything you have would have been taken away from you if the communists had taken over. Which they certainly would have, before long, except for the prompt action taken by Hitler, and our present government, to prevent it."

"I was under the impression that Hitler had made friends with communist Russia."

Inspector Floriot's smile was tolerant. "You are not that naive, Monsieur Hugonnet. One enemy at a time. Our first problem has been to eradicate Western governments controlled by Jewish bankers, Freemasons and their corrupt political lackeys. Soon that will be finished, and then we can turn our wrath on communist Russia."

Nugon regarded him with flat dislike. "We?"

"Germany and France, united by a common purpose and destiny. An unbeatable combination."

Grayle said sharply, "I'm not interested in discussing politics. If you've finished what you came for, I have other things to do, and I'm sure you do, too."

Nugon told Inspector Floriot: "Let's go."

The inspector closed his notebook and rose to his feet. "I believe Nora Cesari's mother and daughter live in that village down there. Perhaps they will have more information about her than her husband does."

"That's possible," Grayle said, and looked to Nugon. "If her mother has any idea of when my wife will be back, or exactly where she's staying, I'd appreciate it if you'll let me know."

Nugon relaxed a bit. Obviously, they would find no further information in the village. He motioned to his gendarme and they led the way out.

Inspector Floriot paused in the doorway as he followed them, and looked back at Grayle with a relaxed smile. "As I said, a beautiful place you have here. With magnificent views of the mountains and valley. I'm a bit of a photographer myself. Perhaps I'll come by again, sometime, with my camera. An *unofficial* visit. Strictly for the pleasure."

Grayle walked outside and stood in the rain, watching the car carry them away. What stayed with him was Inspector Floriot's parting remark. The next time the inspec-

tor came looking for Nora, he would not inform Adjutant
Nugon about it ahead of time.

The second day of December had been dry but very
cold. After one of its warmest summers, France was entering one of its most severe winters. There was a flashy sunset as Grayle drove away from Arles: low clouds shot
through with lavender, red and gold scudded across the horizon before a harsh mistral. But the sky above was abnormally clear, and the stars appearing in it by the time he
reached the chateau came out unnaturally bright.

He had spent most of the day in Arles, going to the railroad station to meet each train. It was nearing the time for
Nora to return; he wanted to be there to get her quickly
out of sight when she did. But he felt sharply the futility of
the day he had spent watching for her.

She might not arrive for another week. He couldn't
spend every day for the next week hanging around the station. There were members of the French Nazi parties in
Arles, too. Not many, but enough to be dangerous. If some
were acting as Inspector Floriot's informers, they'd soon be
watching all the incoming trains with him.

Grimly, he sought for an alternative. He could go up to
Valence, the station above Avignon: jump aboard every
train that came in from the north, and go swiftly through
all its compartments before it pulled out again. An impossible task. And Grayle could not even be sure that Nora
would be coming from that direction.

When Grayle entered the chateau he was startled to find
Madame Cesari there in the kitchen with Pascale, preparing the evening meal for the three of them.

"Jumeau has run off," Madame Cesari told him as soon
as he came in. "That police inspector from Avignon was
here this afternoon, and frightened him."

"I was here," Pascale said quickly. "Down in my darkroom, enlarging a picture. When I came up I saw him—the
detective. He was wandering around the chateau, looking
in windows. And he had a camera with him. As soon as he
saw me, he turned away and began taking pictures of the
valley." Pascale made a scornful face. "He couldn't have
gotten anything much. Too many trees in the way."

"Then he asked Pascale if her mother was back," Madame Cesari added tensely. "And when she said no, he went to talk to Jumeau."

But Pascale was eager to tell it herself: "I followed him in. First he took a picture of Jumeau. Just pretending again; the light wasn't good enough for it to come out. Then he asked Jumeau the same thing he'd asked me. And when Jumeau couldn't tell him anything, the inspector got mad. He asked if it was true that Jumeau is a Gypsy. Jumeau said he didn't know. Well, he doesn't."

Grayle nodded. Jumeau had first arrived in the area as a very young child, brought by a wandering Gypsy leather-worker. It was the Gypsy who had built the first shed in the ruins, and stayed long enough to teach the boy how to work leather, before wandering on and leaving him behind. Whether Jumeau had been some part of the Gypsy's family, or just a lost child he'd come across and taken care of, no one knew. Including Jumeau.

"He told Jumeau," Madame Cesari said angrily, "that there will soon be laws here to kill all Gypsies. And half-wits. Like in Germany. But he said he could save Jumeau, if Jumeau would cooperate with him. Jumeau didn't understand, of course. Only the threat."

"He began to cry," Pascale told Grayle. "And the inspector finally got disgusted and went away. And left poor Jumeau so scared he was afraid to stay here anymore."

"Where has he gone?"

"He said he'd see if Madame Lorenzi could hide him."

Grayle ate quickly and then left them. Putting on a wool scarf and his heavy sheepskin coat, he trudged up the foothills into the Alpilles. He had hiked this area often enough, by day and night, to find his way in the dark. The overbright stars helped, once his eyes had adjusted. But his sense of hearing was a better guide. The stream which curled in relative tranquillity through the ravine between the chateau and valley was a lower branch of a torrent that poured down from the heights of the mountains. The higher Grayle climbed, the steeper the fall of the stream, and the louder its crashing through rock-filled rapids and around tight stone bends.

He kept the rushing sound just to his left through most of his climb, and then angled toward the pounding thunder of two narrow waterfalls that cut down the face of a stepped cliff to feed the stream. Circling around the waterfalls, Grayle climbed to an old stone bridge that arched over the stream above them. He crossed it and found the sheep track that twisted its way toward his destination.

Madame Lorenzi was the shepherdess who had, according to village rumor, poisoned her husband when he became difficult for her to get along with. It took Grayle two hours to reach her place: a small stone cabin with a slant roof of rusty corrugated iron. The shelters and split-rail pens for her sheep fanned out from three sides of it. Light showed through the shutters of the single tiny window, and smoke curled from the chimney. Two sheep dogs began yapping wildly when Grayle approached the house.

The door slammed open suddenly, and Madame Lorenzi filled it, pointing a double-barreled shotgun at him. She was a big, fat woman of about sixty, with a seamed but handsome face. When she recognized Grayle she lowered the shotgun.

"Thought you'd come. He's inside."

She moved aside so Grayle could enter, then shut and locked the door. The cabin interior was a single room. It was filled by the fireplace and a cabinet of kitchen utensils, a round table with two chairs and a large bed with a high trunk at its foot. There was the good smell of a meal just finished, and Jumeau sat at the table, drinking wine from a tin cup.

His eyes blurred with tears when he saw Grayle. "I'm sorry. But that policeman—he said people are going to kill me!"

Madame Lorenzi went over and stroked his head with maternal tenderness. "Don't worry about that anymore. Nobody will find you here."

"Can I stay?" Jumeau begged Grayle.

"It might be best. For a while." Grayle looked at Madame Lorenzi. "If you don't mind."

She shrugged her heavy shoulders. "Why not? He's a

man, and I've been alone here long enough. At least he doesn't talk much. My husband never stopped talking—at the top of his lungs. As if I were deaf."

She got a tin cup for Grayle. Before filling it from the jug on the table, she refilled Jumeau's cup. "Drink it up," she told him firmly. "It'll calm you so you can sleep good tonight."

When Grayle left them he had a hunch Jumeau would not be returning to the chateau, even after the trouble was over.

He examined the shape of that trouble as he hiked down through the darkly timbered slopes. Inspector Floriot had come this time without alerting Adjutant Nugon. He would come again, from time to time. Unpredictably. Unless Nora kept away from the chateau, permanently, eventually the inspector would have what he wanted. And more than he expected, if Nora's mission had been successful.

It was getting dark when Inspector Floriot left his office in Avignon on a Friday evening and made his way home. It was cold and cloudy, with a feel of more rain in the air. He strode through the streets briskly. As he reached Rue Saint-Étienne a man crossed in front of him, hurrying along it in the direction of the river.

The man was bundled in a heavy sheepskin coat and had the peak of a corduroy cap pulled down over his eyes; there was something furtive about the swift way he moved. Inspector Floriot caught only a glimpse of the man as he went past. But there was something about his size, and the beard . . . The inspector turned into Rue Saint-Étienne and followed him.

Inspector Floriot observed the man's stride. And then he was sure who it was. He always paid attention to the way people walked: it was something they seldom thought of disguising.

His quarry turned into a dim passageway. Inspector Floriot reached inside his coat, drew the police revolver from its holster and transferred it to the outside pocket of his coat. He kept his hand in the pocket as he entered the passage. The figure he was after had increased the distance between them. Inspector Floriot quickened his pace. The passage twisted down a steep slope through a shabby section of factories and bleak houses, toward the fourteenth-century city ramparts overlooking the Rhône. His man reached a ceramics factory near the bottom of the passage, and went under a streetlamp. The inspector saw then that he was carrying a package in his right hand: something slender, wrapped in brown paper and tied with string.

The man stopped suddenly, and turned to look behind him. Inspector Floriot dodged into a dark doorway before he could be spotted. When he peeked out he saw the figure hurry alongside the factory and turn out of sight behind it. Inspector Floriot went down after him, reached the rear corner, then stopped and carefully leaned forward to peer around it.

There was a small, unpaved area between the back of the factory and the city ramparts, for trash and delivery vans. His man had gone to the rear of a small truck parked there, pulled aside the canvas flap at its rear and begun shoving the package he carried inside it.

He still had his hand inside with the package when Inspector Floriot stepped up quietly behind him, gripping the gun in his pocket, and said, "What are you up to here, Monsieur Hugonnet?"

Grayle half-turned his head to look over his shoulder at him, shocked. "I . . . this is my own truck. I have some fertilizer in it I bought here for . . ."

"I can smell that," Inspector Floriot cut in cheerfully. "What else is it that you just put in with it?"

"Only a present . . ." Grayle drew out the package and began to turn slowly to show it to him.

The turn was completed abruptly. Inspector Floriot barely had time to register the swing of Grayle's arm, and no time to drag the revolver from his pocket, before the heavy base of the bronze candlestick inside the paper wrapping struck his temple.

* * *

Nora had been back at the chateau for two days when they heard a car coming along the hill road. She went down into the cellars immediately, ready to enter the secret tunnel if it proved necessary. Grayle strolled out into the courtyard as a police car came to a halt outside it.

The gendarme driving remained behind the wheel as Adjutant Nugon climbed out. He was wearing his uniform. Grayle met him at the gateway. "Good day, Alain. Come in for a drink?"

"Not this time. I've got too many other things to get done today."

"What is it?"

"You remember Inspector Floriot, of course. Well, he's disappeared." Nugon watched Grayle's face as he said it.

"What do you mean?" Grayle met Nugon's gaze steadily.

"No one has seen him for three days. Hasn't shown up for duty, hasn't been at his apartment, hasn't been in his usual bar or restaurant."

"I haven't seen him either, if that's what you came to find out."

Nugon nodded, and then asked carefully: "Not since that time he came with me?"

"No. He came once, after that. But not on official business, and I wasn't here at the time. My daughter talked to him. He only wanted to take some photographs of the valley and mountains from this point."

"I see." Nugon glanced up at the Alpilles rising behind the chateau. "Must have made some pretty pictures. There's snow on the peaks. Pretty—but it means we're in for a hard winter." In the same conversational tone, he went on: "Floriot's chief is checking with everyone Floriot saw recently. Naturally, the most obvious explanation for his disappearance is that somebody who didn't like him decided to do something about it."

"I didn't dislike him that much," Grayle said evenly. "Is this something I should be worried about, Alain?"

"No, not really. There are too many people closer to Avignon who hated his guts. With more reason than you. And some who have rough criminal records."

"Not a pleasant character."

"Not very. By the way, that political record he'd made of people in the region—that's disappeared, too. It's been removed from his apartment, if that's where he kept it. He definitely didn't keep it at his office. Never trusted his police colleagues enough for that. With good reason. They loathed him."

Nugon was watching Grayle's expression again. "But that doesn't mean they don't care about what's happened to him. Cops get pretty worked up when something happens to one of them. They'll make a very thorough search for him, of that you can be absolutely sure."

Grayle doubted that their search would ever turn up Inspector Floriot. Even if anyone went deep enough inside the underground quarries of the Alpilles, it was not likely that they'd get around to removing the tons of stone that Sylvio Trimarco had dumped on top of the body with a very small charge of dynamite.

42

Victor Royan began to worry that bright, warm morning in September, when a glance at his pocket watch showed that Colin was six minutes late for their rendezvous. Returning his watch to his pocket, he picked up his coffee cup with the appearance of a man who had nothing on his mind but enjoying the feel of the sun on his face. His slight grimace could be attributed by passersby to what he was sipping. It was made of chicory, and no one liked the taste. But in Paris, by 1941, real coffee could only be obtained in certain top restaurants patronized by officers of the German occupation forces and their French friends.

He continued to wait, seated at the sidewalk table of the bistro, using his cane to brace himself erect in his chair. You always knew you were up on the slope of Montmartre, Victor reflected, when any chair you sat in leaned sharply. Pushing aside the dregs of the coffee substitute, he asked the waiter to bring him a small bottle of spring water. As the waiter went inside the bistro, a French police van came roaring up the steep Rue Lepic toward Victor, followed by an open German military truck loaded with Wehrmacht troops.

Victor's nerves quivered as they swung into Rue des Abbesses in front of him. A black civilian touring car followed the troop carrier. The five men inside it wore civilian suits and hats—and expressions that went with their occupation: they were German Gestapo agents, with some of their Parisian helpers, members of the French Gestapo.

There was no vehicle traffic to slow their progress. Normal civilians not on foot were riding bicycles or horse-drawn carts. Victor watched the three vehicles speed off toward Rue Ravignon. When the waiter brought his water, he paid for it, filled his glass and took a long, slow swallow. Colin would have been coming down Rue Ravignon to keep their rendezvous. He was now more than ten minutes late for it.

Victor took another drink of water and forced himself to wait, just a bit longer. Someone who knew him only from old photographs circulated among the police and their German supervisors might fail to recognize him. At least, it had worked so far: his hair dyed brown and clipped short, the mustache also brown, the steel-rimmed glasses. The false identity papers he carried gave him a new name—his fifth since his return to Paris—and a respectable status as an official of the National Union of Wounded Veterans, which was run by pro-Nazi collaborators and supported by the Germans. But Victor was tensely conscious of the fragility of both his disguise and false identity, should he be seized for interrogation. His first two underground networks had been burned, their members all executed or in prison now. He had survived both disasters to form a third network; but too many of its members were still amateurs, without the skills at secrecy that could come only from training and experience.

Colin was now fifteen minutes late, and Victor knew he must not wait much longer. He drank the last of his water without quenching his thirst, and looked at the black-edged red and yellow poster that had been fixed to a wall across the street sometime during the previous night. The printing was in German on one side, French on the other:

NOTICE: Cowardly murderers in the pay of England and Moscow have killed, by shooting in the back, an officer of the German Military Administration in Paris, on September 21, 1941. As a first measure of reprisal for this crime, I have ordered that fifty hostages be shot. If the murderers are not in custody by September 24, 1941, at midnight, fifty more hostages will be shot.

I offer a reward of fifteen million francs to any citizens who help in the discovery of the guilty parties.

Information can be given to any German or French
police official, and the informant's identity will remain confidential upon request.

THE GERMAN MILITARY COMMANDER IN FRANCE
                                                    von Stülpnagel

Someone had already scrawled, with blue crayon: "The
General of Shit." The scrawl had almost certainly been
done by a child's hand. There were not many adults left in
Paris with the nerve to deface German posters. The punishments for doing so had become severe. Victor knew that
nine of the total of one hundred hostages scheduled to be
executed were men and women who'd been caught attempting to tear down or write on such notices. The rest of
the hostages were almost equally divided between Jews and
communists.

That last, at least, had a certain military logic behind it.
Victor was quite certain that the killer of the German officer had been a communist. Since Hitler had broken his
pact with Stalin by invading Russia in June, the nature of
the resistance in France had been changing drastically—
because the Communist Party had launched its own. Its
policy was simple: The more trouble it could cause the occupation forces, the more German troops that would have
to be diverted from the attack on Russia to control France.
And the more vicious the German reprisals became, the
more French citizens who would become angry enough to
join the Resistance.

Victor had to admit that they were already proving more
effective than the other Resistance groups: the socialists,
the Gaullists, the various intellectual and religious groups,
the unaffiliated hotheads and the loose-knit cabal of police
officials and army officers who couldn't stomach the occupation of their country by a foreign power. It was to this
cabal that Victor Royan belonged, and its hatred of the
Communist Party almost equaled its hatred of the Germans. But the time had come, Victor knew, to put this
aside for the duration of the occupation. The communists

had organization, discipline, prior experience in secret operations and courage backed by absolute faith, that could be used against what was now the common enemy.

Not that Victor's own small network, here in Paris, had been ineffective. Its first purpose was propaganda against the Germans and the French collaborators. Its second was the gathering of military information to be passed on to London. Both had been accomplished well—so far. It was Colin who was supposed to be bringing him the latest batch of information, on the positions of German ammunition and fuel dumps. This he was to have been obtained from a bilingual secretary who worked for the German Todt organization, and lived at the top of Rue Ravignon, in the seedy Hotel Paradis.

But Colin was now more than twenty minutes late, which meant that it had become too dangerous for Victor to wait any longer. If Colin had been taken, he would talk. It might take an hour in a Gestapo torture chamber, or a day, but he *would* break, as everyone did. And then he would tell them, not only about Victor, but about the others in their network.

Still, Victor hesitated, torn between the necessity to warn the others, and a need to be certain whether Colin had been taken or merely delayed.

Two German soldiers, very young and handsome, had wandered down from Rue de Maistre and stopped nearby to consult a sightseeing map, looking uncertainly from it to the street names on the corners. Finally they turned helplessly to a long line of people, waiting with their ration cards for their turn inside the nearby bakery, and asked if anybody spoke German.

None of the people in the line answered them. Few even looked at them.

Victor kept his smile inside, and his face straight. One of the posters his group had spread around Paris had advised: "If you don't know German, be very slow to learn. If you do know, be very quick to forget. To be ignorant is to *refuse* to be subjugated!"

One of the young soldiers approached an old woman at the end of the line and tried his best with slow, broken French: "Please . . . you can show? Where is Sacré-Coeur?"

The women let him have a blast of machine-gun slang, the gist of which was that she couldn't understand a word he'd said. Others in the line were making no attempt to hide their smiles. The two Germans moved on, embarrassed, studying their map again.

Using his cane, Victor heaved to his feet as they reached him, and asked in German, "May I be of assistance to you?"

The gratitude that lighted their faces almost touched his heart. The taller one said with relief, "You speak excellent German!"

"I spent some years in your lovely country. Is it Sacré-Coeur you wish to see?"

"Yes, a beautiful church, we are told."

"It is a monstrosity," Victor said firmly. "But the view of Paris from the terrace is worth the climb. Come, I'll show you the way."

"That is most kind of you," the smaller one told him.

Some of the people in the bread line threw dirty looks in Victor's direction as he led the German pair away. They flanked him, politely slowing their stride to match his limping pace. The shorter one asked him, hesitantly, how he had hurt his leg.

"In the war. The last war. Before you were born."

"Then . . . I hope you hold no anger against us for it?"

"Of course not. I was an officer. Wounds are an expected part of a military career, are they not?"

The two soldiers had automatically straightened their posture, and the taller one asked respectfully: "What was your rank, sir?"

"Captain."

They used "sir" with every sentence from then on. Victor turned into Rue Ravignon and led them up its steep climb. It wasn't the shortest way to their destination, but it was to his. The police van, troop carrier and Gestapo car were parked empty at the bottom of the steps leading up to the Place Emile Goudeau. When they climbed up onto the small square, Victor saw other police and military vehicles parked on the other side of it. There were seven German troopers lined up in the middle of the square, holding submachine guns and facing the Hotel Paradis.

Victor stopped as they reached the sergeant in command. "What is happening here?"

The sergeant responded immediately to the authority in Victor's tone, as well as to the sight of the two soldiers flanking him respectfully: "Two terrorists have been caught inside the hotel. The police are searching for more."

"Ah . . ." Victor limped on across the square with his trooper-tourists. He had no desire to stay and watch Colin brought out with his secretary-informant.

He left the pair he was guiding at the corner of Rue Gabrielle, after pointing out the rest of the way to them. After they had shaken his hand with fervent thanks, and gone on, Victor circled back down the hill, avoiding the area of the Hotel Paradis, to the nearest métro station. He had to reach the others, as quickly as possible.

Two of them had telephones. Victor used the pay phone in the métro station to call them. There was no response from one number, though it was a print shop that should have been open at that time of day.

The other number was a bistro on the Ile Saint-Louis. The voice of the man who answered was unfamiliar to Victor. Victor asked if the owner was there.

"No, he stepped out for a few minutes. Who is calling—I can have him call you back when he returns."

"Well, is his wife, Marie, there?"

"She went out with him. If you'll just leave your name and number . . ."

Victor hung up. The bistro owner's wife was named Suzanne. He took the next train to the métro station at Saint Michel and hurried along the left bank of the Seine to the Quai de la Tournelle. One of the bookstalls along the stone parapet across from the rear of the Cathedral of Notre Dame was a letter-drop for his network. Messages were left in a volume marked "Sold" in the back of the stand. But

Victor saw, as he neared it, that the stand was shut and locked.

The folding chair on which Madame Dobin, its owner, sat while awaiting customers, was still there on the sidewalk, against the chestnut tree. But Madame Dobin was not.

Victor strolled past the stand without asking any of the other booksellers what had happened to her. If she'd been arrested there would be at least one plainclothes detective somewhere around, watching for someone to do just that. Turning away from the river, he hurried toward an apartment building between Rue Galande and Saint Julien-le-Pauvre. There were police roadblocks set up at the corners of the street in front of and behind the apartment building.

A bit more than an hour later Victor was sure of it: Whoever they had caught first had given away the rest. Every member of Victor's group had been taken in a coordinated roundup. He was the last one they were still hunting for.

Henry Fadel's apartment was just off Rue de Rivoli, two buildings behind Smith's English bookshop, which was now a Nazi bookshop, with framed photographs of Hitler and his top aides in its windows.

"You're no more use here in Paris," Fadel told Victor as he handed him a large snifter of cognac. "It's time for you to get out. South, into the Unoccupied Zone. It's going to heat up considerably down there before long. And with all the young Frenchmen that're beginning to slip south across the Line, to evade being drafted for forced labor in Germany, you'll soon have quite a number of potential recruits for a secret army."

Pouring a considerable amount of cognac into his own glass, Fadel sat down, facing Victor across his cluttered desk. The walls of his study were paved with photographs. A huge blow-up of Hitler centered the wall behind the desk. On both sides were pictures of Fadel—posed with Goering, Himmler, Goebbels, Rommel, Mussolini and Franco. The other three walls were covered with photographs of handsome young men and boys.

Henry Fadel himself was scrawny, freckled, ugly. A foreign correspondent for a group of newspapers in the United States, he was in a unique position in occupied Paris. Though Germany was not at war with America, and American journalists were tolerated by the German authorities, a careful watch was kept over them. But Fadel was of German parentage, had been a member of the Nazi Bund in New York and had written articles about the courtesy and kindliness of German troops toward French civilians. As a result he was a welcome guest at parties given by top Nazi officials. Some even, from time to time, brought up the possibility of his doing just a bit of intelligence work for them. Henry Fadel always refused politely. Thought he was sympathetic to Nazi Germany, he explained, he was also a patriotic American.

"London wants more coordination down in that area," he told Victor as they sipped their cognacs. "The elements are there, but isolated from each other. They need to be consolidated; prepared for what's to come. A man of your experience could be an invaluable addition."

"Preparing for *what?*" Victor demanded.

Fadel explained that, in detail. Then he told him of a good contact in the area to start with: a woman near Arles and Avignon, south of the Alpilles. "You introduce yourself to her by saying that Lieutenant Cawthorne sends his regards to Joan of Arc."

He told more about her, without noting the slight narrowing of Victor's eyes. "Her husband," Fadel added, "is a retired businessman from Algeria, quite well-off. He helps, too. Though his main interest seems to be in art."

"Art . . ." Victor said it softly.

Fadel nodded. "An amateur painter, apparently. Quite a good one, according to one of our officers who stayed at their chateau and happens to know a bit about art."

Victor was silent, staring past Fadel's head at the huge portrait of Hitler.

"But it is the woman who is important to you," Fadel went on. "Several of our escape lines have been broken in the past two months, by infiltrating agents posing as escapees. And we've got more and more British airmen being

shot down on missions over France. Those who survive and
evade capture have to be gotten back to England. So the
escape lines that're left become increasingly vital. This
woman is the key to one of them."

Victor's smile was small. "And her code name is Joan of
Arc."

"Shortened to Joan. Of course, you won't have to use her
escape line. I'll have new identity papers ready for you tomorrow. You'll be an official of a legitimate French firm
which supplies Todt with materials for military construction. And you'll have an official permit to pass across the
Demarcation Line by train, first-class. But she is probably
your best contact as a starting point in that area."

They finished their drinks and moved to the bathroom.

Fadel stood in the open doorway, watching Victor use
dye to change his cropped hair from brown to black while
Fadel fed him other contacts in the area south of Avignon:
a priest in the Cévennes, two railroad officials in Marseilles, a businessman and his wife in Toulon, a harbor
worker in Séte, a socialist gangster in Marseilles, a Czech
radio operator hidden near Carcassone, a bistro owner in
Aigues-Mortes, the mayor of Arles, a printer and several
university teachers in Montpellier.

Victor had trained his mind to file and retain such details for as long as they were needed. He concentrated on
doing so as he began shaving off his mustache.

Fadel said, "By the way, I checked on your wife while I
was in London. She's been driving an ambulance through
the bombings. But so far she's okay—though her apartment got demolished by a German blockbuster."

Victor froze with the razor against his upper lip. "And
Jill—the girl who shared my wife's apartment?"

"Unfortunately, she was killed. I'm sorry—was she a
close friend?"

Victor's eyes regarded their reflection in the bathroom
mirror. After a moment he finished shaving off the rest of
the mustache, without drawing blood.

Fadel did not press his question but returned instead to
the subject of contacts in the south: "I know you have

some of your own down there. Army officers, retired and still active in the armistice army."

"Even some police officials."

"Then that leaves only the communists." Fadel sighed. "They could be the most valuable of all, if only we knew how to establish contact and get them to trust us and cooperate with the other groups."

"I'll find them," Victor told him quietly. He dried his face and went into the bedroom. Fadel followed and watched him change into one of the two suits Victor kept ready in a closet.

"Perhaps you should stay here tonight. By now the Gestapo probably knows all your other hiding places."

"No, they don't. I still have one bolt-hole none of my people knew about. It's one I've seldom used."

"Ah, in that case . . ." Fadel left the bedroom. He came back with something in his hand. "If you *are* caught, you have so many secrets in your head—and they'll rip it out of you, after a lot of suffering. Don't expect to be brave. No one is, after a short time with the Gestapo."

"I know that, Henry."

Fadel opened his hand. A small brown pill lay in his palm. "If you're about to get caught—this acts very quickly. At least you'll die without pain."

"And not be able to give anything away."

"That too."

Victor slipped the pill in a pocket of his jacket before he left.

Victor's last bolt-hole was a room he had rented in a private house in the little tucked-away Rue Planquette. It was getting dark when he trudged up from the métro station at Place Blanche. There was a black Citroen parked in front of a bistro across the street from the narrow passage that led into his street. But it was empty. Victor slowed his pace, leaning more than he needed to on his cane as he scanned the area ahead.

He could spot nobody paying special attention to his approach, or the entrance to the passage. But when he turned into the passage he found his way blocked by two French policemen, one in uniform, the other not. It was the plain-clothes detective who demanded brusquely: "Show me your papers, please."

Victor found himself reaching into his jacket pocket, one finger touching the pill Fadel had given him. The calm in his voice surprised him: "What is it? I'm merely taking . . ."

But the detective and the uniformed cop were now look-ing toward something behind him. Victor turned and saw a well-dressed man hurrying across the street toward them, grinning.

"Paul!" the man called out cheerfully to Victor. "You're going the wrong way! I told you I'd wait in the bistro!"

He was almost to them when Victor experienced the shock of recognition. The man was Maurice Fourrest, the impoverished sculptor Grayle had brought to his house so many years ago, sick from his need for drugs. He looked remarkably fit now, and far from impoverished: the hat and shoes he wore were flagrantly expensive, and his new suit exquisitely tailored.

He threw his arms around Victor and hugged him. "I was beginning to be afraid you wouldn't show up!"

The two cops moved to flank them both. The plain-clothesman had pulled open his jacket to put a hand on his pistol, and the one in uniform was opening the flap of his holster. Maurice Fourrest drew back from Victor, looked at them and snapped: "What do you two think you're up to?"

"We'll have a look at *your* papers, too," the detective snapped back. "Immediately."

"Certainly," Maurice sneered, and took out his wallet. He flipped it open to show a yellow identity card issued by the German authorities.

The detective's face twitched as he stared down at it.

Victor held his breath. The card identified Maurice Fourrest as a *Gestapache*, a French security agent for the Gestapo's Section IV. The uniformed cop backed off and almost saluted before he remembered that he didn't have to.

"My friend and I," Maurice growled at the detective, "had an appointment to meet here and go off to a private party. Now, whatever you are supposed to be doing here, I'm sure it doesn't include bothering friends of *mine*." He shut his wallet with an authoritative flourish and put it away. "You can discuss it with the two German gentlemen waiting in the house on Rue Planquette, if you wish. They happen to be friends of mine, too."

The battle of conflicting emotions showed in the detective's face: anger, fear, resentment. The *Gestapache* leaders were a gang of French petty criminals who did jobs the German Gestapo would have found more difficult: finding hidden Jews, resisters and political undesirables. In return the Gestapo let them loot their victims before turning them over—and also gave them an authority that even the French police were forced to respect.

"I'm only carrying out the duty I was assigned to," the detective grumbled uneasily.

"Fine. Good for you." Maurice linked his arm with Victor's and turned away with him. "Come on, or we'll be late."

They crossed to the black Citroen. Not until Maurice had driven four blocks did he speak again. "That was close. I was waiting to grab you before you got there, but I looked away to pay my bar bill and almost missed you."

"How did they find out about my room on Rue Planquette?" Victor asked him.

"I told them about it. Look, I had to. If the Gestapo dug the address out of one of your group, they'd wonder why *I* hadn't told them."

"None of my people knew this address. How did you find out?"

Maurice shrugged. "I spotted you on the street almost a month ago, and started following you around."

So that was it. Now Victor knew: *he* was the one who had led the enemy to each member of his network, one by one.

Maurice shot him an unhappy glance. "Hell, Victor, if I hadn't broken your group, somebody else would have, sooner or later. You've had everybody in Paris hunting you for almost a year."

"By everybody you mean the Gestapo, I suppose. Both the German and French varieties. Nice friends you have these days, Maurice."

"They've treated me a lot better than anybody else ever did," Maurice answered defensively. "I've got a swell apartment now, wait'll you see it. And everything I need: money, women, liquor, dope . . . What did France ever do for me? Nothing but hurt me."

"Some people didn't treat you too badly," Victor said. His tone was exceedingly mild.

"A few," Maurice agreed. "Grayle—well look at what France did to *him*, for God's sake. And you—I just saved your life, Victor. Wouldn't you say that was a pretty fair repayment for a very small kindness long ago?"

The apartment Maurice took Victor to was on the top floor of one of the solid, well-kept buildings facing Place des Vosges. The living room was enormous, with high-decorated ceilings and tall windows, and furnished with expensive antiques. Maurice grinned at the way Victor took it in. "Really something, eh? Belonged to a rich family I caught hiding an escaped prisoner of war."

"What happened to them?" Victor asked, and his tone was still mild.

"The soldier was sent to Germany. The couple that had this place were executed. Well, that's the penalty now, you know. And—that's war."

"Remember my girlfriend, Jill?" Victor asked him.

Maurice's smile was warm with the memory of her. "Of course. Have any idea where she is these days?"

"Dead. Killed in London, by German bombs."

Victor was startled by the tears that welled in Maurice's eyes. Maurice turned away from him, toward the windows. When he spoke again his voice was choked: "Christ, I'm sorry . . . She was so nice to me . . ."

"That's war, too," Victor said blandly.

It was a moment before Maurice wiped his eyes and turned back to him. "Listen, Victor, you've got to make a choice. And soon. Either join us or get out of Paris."

"By *us* you mean the Gestapo, I take it."

Maurice nodded. "Or get out. Tonight. I'll help you. I

. . . just don't want to be the one who gives you over to them."

"I'm grateful for that. Maurice, I could really use a drink at this point."

"Anything you'd like. Champagne?"

"That would be fine." Victor watched Maurice go off through a wide corridor leading from the living room to the rest of the apartment. Walking to one of the tall windows, Victor stood gazing down at the trees in the square, and the children playing under them. He stayed that way, leaning on his cane, one hand thrust in his jacket pocket, and heard the pop of the champagne cork from another room. He turned from the window when Maurice returned, carrying the bottle and two glasses. Maurice sat on a couch facing a low table, and filled both glasses. Victor limped over and lowered himself into a chair facing him.

As Maurice put down the bottle, Victor looked at a bronze nude on a pedestal behind the couch. "Is that one of your sculptures, Maurice?"

Maurice turned around to look at it. "Yes, one of my old ones." He continued to look at his work. "I was damn good, even if nobody admitted it. Maybe someday I'll try it again."

Victor dropped the pill Fadel had given him into Maurice's champagne.

Two minutes later Victor finished his own glass of champagne and stood up. Maurice remained sprawled on the floor between the couch and the table as Victor let himself out of the apartment.

43

It was extremely cold that November in Marseilles, and there was no heating at all in the Saint Charles railroad station. At least on the train from Arles there had been the warmth of others sharing Nora's compartment. She drew on her thick woolen gloves as she climbed down from the train. Tugging up the heavy red scarf until it touched her beret and protected her ears, she joined the other debarking passengers. They were forming long lines, awaiting their turns to be checked, questioned—and in some cases searched—before being permitted to leave the station.

The check was conducted by French police and customs officers, but under the watchful eyes of several Germans wearing leather coats over their civilian suits. They were part of the Armistice Commission which had arrived in Vichy France, ostensibly to facilitate cooperation between the Occupied and Unoccupied zones. But it was a secret from no one that each was a member of the Gestapo.

The inspection of passengers arriving at the Saint Charles station had become routine. It was the reason Grayle now remained in charge at the chateau, whenever it became necessary for one of them to come here. The scar across his forehead made him too memorable, and regular visits to Marseilles would arouse suspicion.

Marseilles had become the end of the line for too many refugees and escapees: It provided, if not a way out, at least more places of concealment than any other city in Vichy France. And their presence there made it a germination oven for resistance activities. The city was also perilously short of food, as well as medicines and coal. Rationing was severe, and severely enforced. All this had turned Marseilles into the worst trouble spot for the Nazis in Vichy France, and contributed reasons for the inspection of arriving passengers: detecting of people with foreign accents, spotting Resistance workers whose identities had been divulged by collaborators and catching country dwellers trying to bring in farm products for sale at high prices through the black market.

But this time, Nora realized with a jolt as she waited in line, the inspection had some additional purpose. She saw several attractive women ahead of her being questioned more thoroughly than usual, though they carried no packages that could have contained contraband. One of them was led away to be searched by a woman employed by the police.

Nora fought her nerves as she waited her turn. All that she carried was a shoulder-strap handbag, and there was nothing incriminating in it. But if she was subjected to a strip-search they'd find the photographs on her: contact prints from the closeups Pascale had shot of five escapees presently hidden at the chateau.

The cop who inspected her identity papers was in his twenties, and darkly handsome. Nora reached for an exactly natural balance of flirtatiousness and impatience as he gave back her papers and took her handbag.

"What do you expect to find in that except my lipstick, and a few other items a woman needs to make herself attractive?"

He grinned as he glanced through her bag. "I'd say beautiful is a more accurate word, in your case, Madame."

Her smile was just a touch arch.

But he didn't wave her through immediately when he handed back her bag. "Are you going to be in Marseilles long?" In part, it was an automatic response to her manner. But there was also an element of interrogation.

"Only long enough to buy a new pair of shoes. If the stores haven't closed by the time you . . ."

She was interrupted by the nearest leather-coated Gestapo agent. He had been looking from her face to a small photograph cupped in the palm of his hand. Thrusting the picture into his pocket, the German stepped over to the cop and snapped, in almost perfect French: "I detect no British accent. Do you?"

The cop gave him a sulky look. "No, Madame is unquestionably French."

"And the woman we are looking for is not. So why do you delay her? Get on with your job."

The cop waved Nora through without meeting her eyes, shamed by his imposed subservience. The Gestapo man gave Nora a polite smile and tipped his hat as she passed him. She shot him the cold glance he would expect and strode away. A Frenchwoman might be attracted to a German's looks, power or extra rations—in private. But if she didn't snub them in public she'd soon have a reputation as a collaborator.

Emerging from the station, Nora paused on the heights of the long stone steps and drew several slow breaths to steady herself. Below the hill on which the station stood, most of Marseilles had vanished inside a milky mass of icy, slow-churning fog. She could see no building more than a block away as she hurried down the steps and along Boulevard d'Athènes to the Canebière. It was like walking through a congealed cloud of freezing white smoke.

Nora moved swiftly down the wide Canebière, the city's principal shopping and entertainment street. It ended at the Old Harbor. Fishing boats rolled sluggishly against the Quai des Belges, their masts appearing and vanishing in the mist. Most of the narrow harbor beyond was invisible. The moan of foghorns, clanging of bells and shrill whistles sounded from unseen vessels moving through it. Nora turned right along the deep end of the harbor and then left along the Quai du Port.

The Vieux Port district spreading out from both sides of the harbor was a rats' maze of grimy interconnecting buildings and narrow, fetid alleyways. It was the city's red-light district and for centuries it had provided a breeding place and concealment for crime. Now it also hid thousands who had fled from the Nazis, along with those who helped or preyed upon them.

Nora made her way through a slippery cobbled passageway and entered a small, dingy bistro at its dead end. The customers crowded into the place wore their coats and hats, and some even their gloves. The only heat these days was provided by the drinks. They were a seedy crew: petty criminals, pimps, sailors and dock workers, a pair of prostitutes, one sadly aging and the other barely into her teens.

She moved among them toward the bar, aware of the curious and interested stares she drew; aware also that among the petty criminals were probably some who earned extra money as informers for the Gestapo and Vichy police. André, the enormously fat patron of the bistro, recognized her and came quickly around the end of the bar to greet her with a happy smile, kissing her on both cheeks.

"How is Uncle Damien?" Nora asked him as he seated her alone at a small table.

"Much better today," he answered her cheerfully. "And looking forward to seeing his favorite niece."

It was said loudly, to insure that none of the men would annoy her. Damien was André's ailing father, and what had been said established that Nora was part of the family: a Corsican family. Anyone who flirted with a woman belonging to a Corsican family, without prior permission, could expect to be found one morning lying in a gutter with his throat cut.

André went back behind the bar to get her a brandy. As he poured it he whispered to his twelve-year-old son, who left off washing the glasses and ducked out the back. André brought Nora her drink, patted her shoulder and returned to tending to his customers. Nora drank down her brandy, savoring its warmth, and waited.

André's son was back at work behind the bar within five minutes. It was almost ten minutes before a short, sickly looking man with a narrow, wrinkled face appeared in the doorway. Fabrice was the only name Nora knew him by: the forger Grayle had obtained to produce false papers needed by her escapees. He glanced around the room, his gaze resting only briefly on Nora. Then, as though he had failed to see whoever he was looking for, Fabrice turned and went out again.

482 MARVIN H. ALBERT

Nora waited a few minutes before getting up, waving to
André and leaving the bistro. The passage outside was
empty. She crossed it and opened a door. Inside, a dim,
dirty stairway led upstairs. Nora climbed to the third floor,
opened another door and crossed a wooden bridge to the
building on the other side of the passage.

Fabrice was waiting for her in a small, windowless room
containing only two kitchen chairs and an old desk with
nothing on it. This was not where the forger worked, only
where he discussed work with potential clients. He locked
the door from the inside and turned to her, his voice nervous and hushed as always: "What do you have this time?"

Nora opened her coat and got the five contact prints
from inside her blouse. He studied the faces: two men, two
women, a little girl. "Which speak French?"

"All of them, this time."

"That makes it easier." Fabrice stuck the photos in his
coat pocket. "I can have their papers ready this evening."

"What about the other two matters you were supposed to
check on for me?"

"I got in touch with certain persons and I was instructed
to make a certain phone call the next time you showed up.
I have already done so." He unlocked the door and motioned to her. "Come, there will be a car to pick you up.
Meme wants to see you."

He used a series of corridors and stairways to lead her to
a different side of the building. As they emerged from an
entrance doorway facing a narrow street, a small Italian
car pulled to a halt in front of them. The driver had the
build of a wrestler and a face as battered as a very old
coin. He opened the door for Nora without a word, and she
got in the car as Fabrice disappeared back inside the building.

She hadn't asked him who she was being taken to, and
she didn't ask the driver. In Marseilles, when people used
the nickname Meme, there was only one man they could be
talking about.

* * *

Bartholemy Guérini helped her take off her coat and put it in a closet with her gloves, scarf and beret. The small sitting room on the second floor of the brothel was furnished with Victorian luxury, and well-heated by a cast-iron stove burning a copious amount of coal that was impossible for most of Marseilles to find at any price. The whole house was heated in the same way, for the comfort of the important customers who patronized the high-priced girls in this establishment.

It was an ordinary-looking three-floor villa on the respectable Rue Paradis. Less than two blocks away there was an almost identical villa with an address that was becoming notorious for quite a different reason: 425 Rue Paradis, headquarters of the Gestapo.

"Several of them are turning into regular customers," Meme told Nora with a charming smile. "Gives us a bit of extra protection, of course."

The leader of the Guérini brothers was Antoine, whom few people got to see. He was a fervent socialist, a power in the Resistance movement and head of one of the two mobs that ran most of the crime in Marseilles. The gangster who ran the other mob was also a Corsican: Paul Carbone. The two had been close friends and it was rumored that they still were, in spite of the fact that Carbone now did work for both Vichy and the Germans, and carried a Gestapo card. It was supposedly part of an agreement between the two gangsters to insure that however the war finally turned out, one of them would be on the winning side, in a position to help the other.

But if Carbone's allegiance to the Nazis was merely a practical move, Antoine Guérini's antifascism was not. His father and grandfather had been socialists. He had inherited the cause and believed in it. His brothers followed him in this, as in everything. So did every member of his various underworld activities.

He had been described to Nora as an utterly unemotional man with a hard face and a voice like ice. His brother Meme was nothing like that. Strongly built and handsome, his eyes were warm and the set of his thick lips good-natured. He was settling Nora into a comfortable chair facing his leather-topped desk when there was a knock at the door. A man brought in coffee service for two on a silver tray, left it on the desk and went out as Meme was asking how much cream and sugar Nora wanted in her cup.

She registered the shock with her first sip. It had been some time since she had tasted genuine coffee.

Meme grinned as he observed her response. "Just a matter of knowing the right people, and having enough cash to pay for it. Always been that way, hasn't it?"

Nora found herself returning his smile. His spirit was impossible to resist. They discussed the terrible weather until the coffee was drunk, and then he got down to business: "It seems you have a couple problems. Fabrice decided we were the ones to pass them on to."

Nora leaned back in her chair. "I think he made exactly the right decision. Can you help us?"

"Tell me a little more about these special papers you want for you and your husband, first."

"Simple enough, Monsieur Guérini. Security checks are getting tighter. I need official passes, complete with police seals, that will enable either of us to move through checkpoints without trouble."

Meme nodded. "Antoine discussed that with me. There's a guy just arrived in town who may be able to help with it. By tomorrow we'll have a better idea about that. But if we *can* come up with these special passes for you and your husband—it's an expensive proposition, you know."

"The matter of expense," Nora said coolly, "brings us to our other problem. I'm sure you know the kind of work I'm doing. I believe you approve of it."

"You've been moving a lot of people lately. Antoine admires the smooth way you've handled it so far."

"It has required us to buy more and more gasoline on the black market. And the price gets higher each time."

"That's only natural. The law of supply and demand."

"I was under the impression," Nora said quietly, "that your people are not always so interested in adhering to any law. I am also under the impression that your brother Antoine has certain principles he cares about, even more than he cares about his profits. Am I wrong?"

Meme laughed softly. "You're a clever woman. Okay, Antoine thinks we can make a deal that'll take care of both your problems. There'll be some things we'll want in exchange. Maybe not right away, but in the future. Set it up for me to talk to your husband about it."

"Talk to me."

Meme's shrug was a shade uncomfortable. "Look, we've got a lot of respect for the way you run your setup. So it's nothing against you, but this is a serious business discussion that's needed now. I can't talk business arrangements with a woman."

"Why not?" But Nora smiled as she asked it.

He smiled too, gently. "I just never have. It's not right—not the way it's supposed to be done. Come on, you understand how it is. Got to be between men."

That was the code, and Nora could find no point in arguing against it at this point. "Can you make it at noon, tomorrow?"

"With your husband?" Meme persisted.

"Do you have a detailed map of the Camargue area?"

He opened a drawer of his desk, took out several maps, selected one of them and spread it open on the desk. Nora took a pen from his desk holder and made a small mark on the map. "He'll meet you here. Can you find it?"

"I buried a few people near there, in the old days. Those papers Fabrice is fixing up with the pictures you just brought him—I'll deliver them at the same time."

"At noon," Nora repeated firmly. "I don't want him waiting there longer than necessary. Be on time."

Meme's appraising gaze acquired a certain element of basic approval. "You worry about your man, the way a good woman is supposed to. Don't worry, I'll be there."

* * *

The taste of the air was from the sea. The smell was frozen decay and brackish water. The only sound was the wind: a breeze barely strong enough to stir the tops of reeds and grass clumps, but magnified in the cold silence of the marsh. The solitude was intensified by heavy mist.

Grayle had bicycled down from Arles, taking one of the few paved roads that cut through the Camargue, that vast spread of salt marshes that reached all the way along the Rhône delta to the Mediterranean. At the point Nora had marked on the map, he had turned off the road onto a dirt track. Much of the year it was an impassable mire of soft mud, but now the mud was hard as rock. It threaded between lagoons and creeks, stretches of dense, tall reeds and patches of slightly higher ground with barebranched trees. He saw only one dwelling as he followed the track: that of one of the *gardiens* who tended the half-wild herds of black bulls and white horses that grazed the Camargue marshes.

When the road was out of sight behind him Grayle stopped and set the bike up on its stand. He opened his box of watercolors and a small jar of water on the seat of the bike. The Camargue was one of his favorite places: for a painter its variety always presented something new. And if a cop chanced to wander in this way, it would explain his presence.

Standing by the bike he went to work with his brush and pad, trying to capture the special quality of the winter colors and obscured light: the lavender-gray mist, with an invisible sun trying to penetrate it, creating swirls of ochre, yellow and smoky blue. The black of the water, the silver shine of exposed mud flats, the withered brown of the reeds and marsh grasses.

In other months the Camargue stretched flat and green to deep-blue horizons, and there were flocks of herons, ducks and flamingos. In March he had sketched a pair of flamingos engaged in their shy mating dance in the bog behind a beaver dam not thirty feet from where he stood. Now most of the birds were gone. There was only an occasional seagull, gliding in and out of the haze above.

There were splashing noises behind the curtain of mist. Cattle or horses, wading across a stretch of water to reach grazing on a sandbar or mud bank. Something began to solidify within the curtain. Grayle watched, and slowly a stocky white horse emerged. Putting down his brush and pad, Grayle took out a pencil and small sketchbook. He worked quickly as the horse advanced toward him, knee-deep in muddy water, as insubstantial at first as the wreaths of mist through which it came, then solidifying as its advance turned into a charge.

Fountains of foam were thrown up to either side by its charge. Grayle's pencil moved faster. The horse came to a jolting halt at the rusty strands of barbed wire fencing at the side of the road: nostrils flaring, bloodshot eyes wide with menace. Grayle continued to sketch, and after several moments the horse turned aside, following the barbed wire, until it dissolved back into the mists.

There was the sound of an automobile coming along the road that ran past the end of the dirt track. Grayle half-turned, listening. The car stopped. Its doors opened and were slammed shut. Grayle put the pencil into his coat pocket and left his hand inside, fingers against the metal of the pistol there.

Two men in heavy city overcoats appeared, coming along the dirt track toward him. Both had their hands in their pockets. They stopped when they saw Grayle. The larger man took his hands from his pockets, and came on. The other one stayed where he'd stopped.

Nora's description of Meme Guérini had been detailed. Grayle's hand left the pistol and came out of his pocket. He put away the sketchbook, was closing the watercolor box and emptying the water from the jar when Meme reached him.

"Monsieur Hugonnet?"

Grayle nodded and looked at his watch. "One minute before noon. My wife was sure you'd be on time."

Meme's warm smile did not quite hide the fact that he was making a quick and expert appraisal of Grayle. "I try to keep my promises." He handed over a thick sealed envelope. "Here are the papers for the five people you want to move, with the pictures your wife gave Fabrice. No charge this time."

Grayle slipped the envelope into his pocket. "How come?"

"A goodwill gesture, to get our relationship started right. Antoine thinks we're going to need some help from you, before long. That's a smooth little operation you're running. One of the few left that they haven't been able to infiltrate and break."

"My wife runs it," Grayle corrected him. "I just help out."

Meme studied him curiously. "That's what I heard, but it's hard to believe. Your wife's a smart woman, but she's still a woman. A man's supposed to control his woman. Things work better if the man makes the decisions, if you don't mind a little advice."

Grayle just looked at him.

Meme recognized something in that look which surprised him. It was something he often saw in the eyes of his older brother, Antoine. "Sorry," he said, in a tone that still demanded respect, but now also returned it. "I spoke out of turn. My apologies."

"Accepted. What is the deal you wanted to talk about?"

Meme smiled slowly. "Your wife was complaining because what we're charging for black market gas keeps going up. Well, it's going to go even higher. And you're going to need more of it, because from what we hear, pretty soon it won't be safe to use the trains to move people that can't pass for French. You'll have to use your truck to move those people to the Spanish border. The deal's this: for you, we keep the gas price where it is now. No more raises in what we charge you."

"In exchange for what?"

"I guess you've heard of Paul Carbone?"

"I know the name. And what he does."

"He's passed a warning to my brother. According to Carbone's friends in the Gestapo, the Germans aren't satisfied with the way Vichy is running things. Too many English airmen that get shot down manage to get back to England to fly again. And there are too many Resistance organizations building down here. The German army is almost sure to move down and take over, sometime in the coming year. Now, *we've* got people we've been slipping in and out of the country, mostly by ship. If the German army takes over the ports, we won't be able to, anymore. We want to know we can move these people through your setup, when that happens. Guarantee that, ahead of time, and we keep what we're charging you for gas where it is now. *And* each time you move somebody for us, in or out, you get a supply for free."

Grayle gave it a moment's consideration, and then nodded. "Agreed. Now, the matter of those special passes for my wife and me. If what your friend Carbone says is true, we'll have even more need for them."

"Yeah, but that's harder than the gas. Passes like that— they'd have to be signed and sealed by the Germans, not just Vichy officials. But a guy just showed up from Paris this morning who has exactly the kind of papers you're talking about. If he checks out, we should be able to get you the same kind, working off his. By the way, this guy claims to know your wife."

Grayle's eyes narrowed a bit. "Who is he?"

"His code name's Masson. Mean anything to you?"

"No."

"Like I said, Antoine's having him checked out. If he's genuine, I guess you'll be hearing from him. If he turns out to be a plant, nobody'll be hearing from him. We'll take care of that."

Meme smiled as he said it, and Grayle experienced an odd jolt of memory. Meme's handsome face was not disfigured by any scars. But there was something in that smile that was exactly like Salah's.

The last traces of the fog that continued to shroud Marseilles and spread west across the southern reaches of the Camargue marshes had been left behind by the time Victor Royan approached the Alpilles. The night air was cold but dry, and the stars were clear. It was late, and no lights showed from the village as he drove past. The headlights of the car Antoine Guérini had lent him pierced the darkness ahead and caught the marker he'd been told to watch for.

Turning off the road that continued on across the Alpilles to St. Remy, Victor followed a dirt road up into the hills on the far side of the valley.

He drove slowly. The road became narrow, with tight turns and switchbacks. It ended, finally, at a great archway that seemed to be all that was left of an ancient rampart. Turning in under it, Victor drove along a straight lane. The chateau loomed ahead as a black blur that blocked out part of the night sky, a half-moon rising over it, wearing a long plume of white cloud.

The lane ended at a closed gate in the wall fronting the chateau's courtyard. Victor stopped the car and set the brake, hitting the horn and then waiting. Nothing happened. No window of the chateau lit up, no one appeared at the gate. Finally Victor cut the motor and lights, and opened the car door. He reached for his cane and used it to help himself climb out. His increasing dependence on the cane irked him, but had to be accepted. He started through the darkness in the direction of the gate.

A flashlight snapped on to his left. Its strong beam caught him squarely in its glare, and glinted off something to his right: the muzzle of a shotgun, aimed at his midsection. Victor halted abruptly, leaning on the cane and squinting at the gun.

Its barrel dipped until it pointed at the ground. The figure holding it stepped out from the shadows: Nora.

"I was instructed," Victor told her with a crooked smile, "to introduce myself by saying that Lieutenant Cawthorne sends his regards to Joan of Arc. A bit pretentious, wouldn't you say?"

She laughed softly. "Just a bit."

He looked to the left, raising his free hand to shield his eyes from the glare. "And this?"

Grayle lowered the flashlight, and the pistol held in his other hand.

"Hello, Victor."

44

"He seems to have turned mystic," Victor told Nora as he studied the work in Grayle's abbey studio. "Strange, from a man who used to have even more anger in him than I."

He shook his head slowly. "So drastic a change—there has to be some streak of madness behind it."

"Victor," Nora answered him, "he is the healthiest person I've ever known. Certainly healthier than you or I."

"In some ways," Victor acknowledged. "But the other is there, too. Whatever it was in his mother, in the aunt who raised him."

"Perhaps, but with an important difference: He has his safety valve." Nora's gesture took in the paintings surrounding them.

Grayle had left the previous afternoon, with the five refugees bound for Spain. Nora's success in drawing increasing numbers to her escape line had finally made it necessary for one of them to stay here, ready for any new fugitive who arrived. Grayle had decided that he would be the one to go, while she remained at the chateau. As he'd pointed out, by now he knew all the routes, and the people she depended on along them, as well as she did.

Nora realized that any time and effort he took away from his painting for this war had one purpose only: to protect her. But she'd had to accept his decision. He'd given her no choice.

Victor was eyeing her appraisingly. "*You* certainly have a look of fulfillment I've never seen in you before. I'm not sure that I'm not envious. Did you ever tell him about us— in Spain?"

MARVIN H. ALBERT

"Yes, I told him."

In spite of himself, Victor was a bit taken aback. "And what was his reaction?"

"Nothing." Nora's smile was almost pitying. "You should know that something like that wouldn't mean much to him. He knows I belong to him. There are a small number of people he cares about, more deeply than most of us care about anybody. Nothing changes what he feels about them."

"And the rest of the world he has no feelings about at all."

Nora shrugged. "Perhaps."

Victor didn't ask which category he was in. "As I said, quite mad. Entirely disconnected from most of reality." But he wasn't certain that was true. He looked around again, at the paintings that had so disturbed something in him. Then he went with Nora, across the cool symmetry of Grayle's courtyard to the cozy warmth of the chateau kitchen. While she made ersatz coffee for them, he told her more about the coordination of now-isolated underground elements he intended to knit together. And he drew from her more information about her immediate area: how to make contacts with its small number of active Resistance fighters, and its larger numbers of *Tranquillots*, the "quiet ones," who under certain circumstances would give whatever help they could.

Though the cold, sardonic manner remained on the surface, it did not hide from Nora the feverish excitement underneath, pushing Victor now in a single direction. And something about it made her uneasy. He was not a different man, as she had thought in Spain. He'd found another war, that was all. His direction was death; for him or for others, that part of it didn't matter much to him.

That was an essential difference between Victor Royan and Nicholas Grayle. Nora studied Victor and thought of what the two men had said to each other on the night Victor had arrived, when the three of them had been discussing what was happening around them.

"There is no point in looking for a pattern to anything in

our world," Victor had said. "No plan to it, no purpose behind it. It's a chaos, without meaning. Man's life, the world, the universe—utterly without coherence. Convinced Catholics and communists are the only ones left who still delude themselves that a meaning exists."

Grayle had shown him a dried leaf. "Look closely. No pattern? No form?"

"And the meaning?" Victor's smile had been tolerant.

"That, everyone has to find for himself. The pattern is there; meaning is only what you search for in the pattern. Each has to find his own; maybe a different one each time."

"Or none."

Grayle had laughed. "Then the lack is in you, not the leaf, Victor. Because the pattern does exist."

"And I fail to interpret it correctly? Perhaps."

It had been Nora who had ended that discussion: "You fail to interpret it at all, Victor. Or even to look for it. There is your failure."

Pascale arrived from the village as they were finishing their coffee. She gave a cry of pleasure when she saw Victor, hugging him ferociously and giving him a kiss on each cheek. He'd come to the village with Nora after Spain, and another time to visit her—and Pascale had acquired an odd liking for him. But then, with Pascale, Victor was never quite like he was with others.

The three of them went out into the woods to hunt dead branches for kindling. But Victor soon tired of his reliance on his walking stick, and left them to it, returning to the chateau alone. He entered the abbey studio again and spent a long time there, trying to analyze what it was about Grayle's work that almost frightened him.

The technical virtues that Grayle's paintings had possessed in the past were still there: the structural stability, the balanced strength of composition, the juxtapositions of opposites. And the uncanny emotional power of the imagery—that was still there, too.

Victor looked at two paintings that hung side by side. One was of an African leader, a monument of a man who stood untouched, unmoved, though wild dogs surrounded

him and ravens flew close over his head. The other was of
Nora and Pascale at the aquarium in the chateau living
room. The subjects were so different, yet Grayle had managed to give both an equal intensity.

It was the same in all the paintings that filled the room:
even seemingly mundane scenes were vibrant with a mysterious energy, a feeling of mystical significance; permeated
by the presence of something unknown and miraculous.
There was a sense, not of looking at a face, a flower, a
hand, but of glimpsing its *reincarnation*.

It was an enchanted world that Grayle lived in; and Victor had to struggle to resist its hypnotic pull. He did not
want to enter that world; and he did not know why.

The unease aroused in Victor by the paintings was confirmed after Grayle returned from the Pyrenees. Grayle
stayed up late with Victor one night, long after Nora had
gone to bed, telling him about North Africa. Victor began
to understand what Grayle's experiences there had used up
in him, and left with him—and wondered how much help
he was going to be to the new Resistance network. Grayle's
course and his own had grown too far apart.

But Grayle did allow him to make use of the chateau.
And with that as his base Victor began to move back and
forth along both sides of the Rhône valley in the months
that followed, making contact with isolated Resistance
groups. His first priority was to establish communication
and trust between them, whatever their political affiliations,
so they would be able to coordinate their actions when the
time came for open attacks.

His first contact after his arrival at the chateau was with
the leader of the group nearest to it: Sylvio Trimarco.
Grayle and Nora brought them together, and Trimarco was
frank: "I don't have enough men to be of much use on our
own. A couple French soldiers who escaped from a
prisoner-of-war camp. Three young Jews who got tired of
running and decided this was as good a place as any to
start fighting back. A socialist school-teacher who managed
to slip out of the internment camp for what Vichy calls

'antipatriots' at Saint Paul d'Evieaux. Two boys from the Occupied Zone who got across the Line and came down here because they didn't want to get shipped off by STO recruiters as forced labor to Germany. And a German sergeant who married a French girl and deserted from the Wehrmacht."

Victor stiffened a bit. "I'd advise you to keep a close watch on that one. Infiltrating false traitors is a favorite Gestapo trick."

It was Grayle who assured him, "Gert can be trusted. I've talked with him. He doesn't consider himself a traitor to Germany. He just can't stomach what the Nazis have done to his country."

Victor considered it, and nodded. There were getting to be more like that, up in the Occupied Zone. He'd seen two German deserters who'd been caught and executed in Paris, along with the man and woman in whose apartment they'd hidden.

"Also," Trimarco put in with a grin, "Gert's wife is good for our morale. Tough—and very pretty. And she happens to have just the right name: France."

"A name to fit the times," Victor agreed. "Especially if she's pretty. What's your situation as regards arms, ammunition, combat training?"

"Training's one thing we're not lacking. There's Gert—and he's a damn good sergeant. Arms—two hunting rifles, a shotgun and one revolver. Very little ammunition, even for those."

Victor registered the needs. "What about explosives?"

Trimarco shot Grayle a faint smile. "We have a bit left: dynamite."

Nora had kept silent until now. When she spoke, her tone was harsh: "Victor, I want this area kept quiet. We've got one of the few escape lines that are still intact. If you attract too much attention to the area, we won't be able to operate."

"I'm not here to agitate for any premature action," he assured her. "At this point your escape line is as important to me as it is to you. I've only one purpose here: to make certain we're *prepared* for action when the time is no longer premature." He turned back to Trimarco. "So in all you've just ten in your group? Including the girl and yourself."

"That's all. So don't expect much of us."

"You'll get others. The draft of STO workers for Germany is becoming more demanding. There'll be more and more young Frenchmen slipping south to evade it. And they'll be looking for groups to attach themselves to."

"I can't take too many more," Trimarco told Victor. "There's enough places to hide in the quarries, but if the Vichy police start combing through the Alpilles, that's the first place they're going to look. Then I'll have to move my people out. There are other places to hide up there, but not enough to conceal a really large force. You've got to remember the Alpilles are just a long, thin spine of high hills."

Grayle said, "If you're thinking of building a large concentration of Resistance fighters, Victor, you need concealment that's hard to get at. The mountains. Over in the Cévennes. Or north of the Alpilles: the Luberon, and the Ventoux Massif. There's a big group up in the Ventoux already, with a good leader. Dr. Cordeau."

"Medical doctor?"

Trimarco nodded. "Which comes in handy. So does what he learned fighting in Spain. His men are well-trained."

"How do I find him?"

"I can take you to him. He's a friend of my father." Trimarco's mouth thinned, and he corrected himself: "*Was*. My father died a few weeks ago."

"When can you arrange this meeting?"

"I'll have to get in touch with him, first. I'll let you know."

"Victor," Nora told him quietly, "if you're still as angry about what happened in Spain as you were, you should know: Dr. Cordeau is a communist."

He smiled at her. "At this point in history I allow myself to feel nothing but love toward *anyone* who doesn't care for the Naxis. I even managed to be quite civil to a Resistance activist in Marseilles who happens to be a Catholic priest."

They met two days later, in a cave in the mountains overlooking the Vaucluse Plateau: Victor, Trimarco and Dr. Cordeau. Victor noted how well-placed the lookouts and guards were along the approach to the cave. He also noted that only three of them were armed.

Cordeau was a husky man in his forties, with a thin, determined mouth and dreamy eyes. Behind his gentle manner, Victor sensed the reserve of force.

"I have twenty-four fighting men and I've trained each of them. Soon I'll have more." Cordeau paused, and then asked politely: "What do you have to offer?"

"For one thing, contact with certain Resistance groups none of your communist cells know about as yet. For another, weapons for your men."

Cordeau regarded Victor shrewdly. "Weapons that you *have*? Or ones you hope to get?"

"Weapons I *expect* to get."

Cordeau smiled. "I expect to get some, too. Shortly. By raiding several police stations."

"You won't get the kind and quality of weapons that will be needed when the Germans move their armies down here. And they will."

"I know they will."

"I'll be in radio contact with London. There will be arms, ammunition and explosives parachuted into this area. There'll be the problem of keeping the enemy from getting hold of them, of hiding them—and then putting them to the proper use in a coordinated effort."

"That is a kind of help I would be pleased to give you," Cordeau said mildly. "How do we arrange to keep in contact?"

"I'll contact you."

"You ask me to trust you, but you don't trust me."

"Perhaps," Victor told him, "I will learn to, after we have had further dealings together. I hope so."

They shook hands courteously before parting.

* * *

Contacting the different Resistance groups, operating as a link that would enable them to coordinate their operations, supplying military officers to those groups that had no one capable of giving them combat training, finding chemists to manufacture explosives with available materials, working to supply the other needs of this loose-knit network—all of this was half of Victor Royan's mission in the south of France. The other half was propaganda.

The nation was now officially called the *State* of France. The word *Republic* was forbidden. The four-page newspaper that was turned out in secret by Victor's printer, and distributed by certain of the groups he had contacted, was named *The Republic*. Its purpose was to serve as an antidote to the Vichy newspapers and radio, ripping away Pétain's claim that what he ruled was indeed a "Free Zone." Victor's illicit newspaper documented in detail Germany's control over the Vichy government, its police, its customs officials; and it revealed how much Germany was milking out of the French industries it also secretly controlled: the iron and steel works, the paper and dye industries, the insurance companies, even the Bank of France. In addition, *The Republic* named active collaborators—and kept readers in touch with the changing nature of the war.

The first change occurred shortly after Victor's arrival in the south of France: the entrance of the United States into the war. *The Republic* pointed out exactly why this made the eventual defeat of Germany inevitable, and used it to encourage more cooperation with the resistance. But it also made for problems.

With Victor's American contact in Paris gone, the false papers he'd supplied, which had been copied for Nora and Grayle, became too dangerous to carry. One of Victor's early contacts in Toulouse was a *Tranquillot* who worked for a firm that supplied steel beams used by the German army for constructing its defense works along the coast of France. He supplied new papers for Victor, Nora and Grayle, bearing German endorsement, that allowed them to pass as traveling representatives for the privileged firm.

The other problem caused by the entrance of the United States into the war grew steadily through the year that followed: there were now more and more downed American airmen who had to be moved through Nora's escape line, in addition to the British ones.

The changing nature of the war continued through 1942. German reverses in Russia forced Germany to send more of its manpower to the Eastern front. Workers were needed to take their place, and the STO program of drafting Frenchmen to Germany for forced labor expanded drastically. The punishment for anyone caught trying to evade this draft was death. Evaders fled to the mountainous areas in the south of France, swelling the ranks of the Resistance forces beyond the dreams of its leaders.

Finally, fulfilling Guérini's prediction, the First German Army and the SS Second Panzerkorps poured south across the Demarcation Line into Vichy France. The takeover of what had formerly been called the Free Zone was accomplished swiftly, while Pétain sent his protest to Hitler but at the same time ordered the French to offer no resistance. Resistance groups managed to ambush several of the invaders' truck convoys and derail some trains carrying their troops into the south. But these amounted to no more than pinprick delays. In a matter of days the German armies had occupied each city and town in the south, disbanded what was left of the French armistice army and seized control of every defense position.

Trimarco, warned just in time, got his group out of the quarries and shifted to another hiding place in the Alpilles. The Wehrmacht moved into the underground quarries and began the work of converting them into a storage place that would be safe from Allied bombers. And they stuffed into them the bulk of the ammunition and fuel that would be needed if the Allies attempted to land on the southern coast of France. The troops and weapons for defending this vast quantity of vital stores were also stationed inside the quarries, and all the entrances except two were sealed, to render the place as invulnerable as possible against attack by land. The hills immediately around it were enclosed in networks of barbed wire and reinforced concrete barriers, and declared a forbidden military zone.

SS units and Gestapo teams spread out from there to

comb the Alpilles, and the countryside below them, in a house-by-house search for Resistance bands, STO evaders, refugees, Allied escapees—and anyone attempting to shelter them.

From this time on, Grayle began allowing Nora to guide her groups of escapees to Spain, while he remained behind. The danger at the chateau, and the area around it, had become greater than on the route south. He wanted to be where he could stay on top of events there—and deal with what was coming.

45

No man stood still while they waited. The night was too cold, and the wind had the cut of ice in it. Like the others, Grayle and Victor paced back and forth, stamping their feet and swinging their arms to stir the blood, steam wafting from their mouths and nostrils. And they looked up, watching for the plane that would dip out of the heavy clouds, if it got this far on its flight from England.

The drop area was inaccessible except by difficult climbing on foot: a high basin covered with juniper bushes and scrub oaks, enclosed by torn cliffs and thrusting mountain folds, topped by undulating ridges and masses of gaunt limestone. It was deep within the interior of the forty-mile-long Luberon range. To the south, across the Durance River, lay the eastern end of the Alpilles, where Trimarco's guerrillas were hidden. To the north, across the Coulon Valley and the Vaucluse Plateau, rose the much higher Ventoux Massif where Dr. Cordeau ruled. Here in the Luberon it was Anatole Gaillard who commanded the Resistance.

All three of the guerrilla bands nearest to Grayle's chateau had grown since the German armies had taken over the south—thanks to the influx of STO evaders, officers from the disbanded French army, underground workers whose city networks had been broken by Gestapo agents and informers, Resistance fighters chased out of other areas. Trimarco now had more than twenty men, Dr. Cordeau more than eighty. Gaillard had nearly fifty.

Ten were spread out below, around the approaches to the high drop area, on lookout for enemy night patrols. The

rest were up in the walled-in basin, ready to gather up the
supplies scheduled to be dropped there that night, according to Victor's radio communications with London.

Gaillard strode over to Victor. "That plane is now one
hour overdue." His voice, as always, was hushed, as though
if he didn't whisper he might scream. He was a tall, thin
man with a severe face and tragic eyes, who had been a
mechanic in Orange until his Jewish wife had been seized
in a Nazi roundup of non-Aryans and shipped off to an
extermination camp in Austria.

"It will come," Victor told him, with more sureness than
he felt. "Be patient a little longer."

"Another hour. Not a second more. We're too vulnerable
up here." That was true; if the drop area was difficult for
the enemy to get at, it was also an easy place in which to
trap Gaillard's men if the enemy managed to reach it.

Gaillard stamped away, swinging his arms for warmth,
one hand gripping a shotgun, the other a powerful flashlight with a red lens. Victor's flashlight had a green lens.
Scattered among the junipers and scrub oaks across the
basin were drums filled with kerosene and kindling, ready
to be set afire when the plane from England appeared. If it
appeared.

Grayle squinted at the clouds above them, straining to
hear the sound of airplane engines through the noise of the
winter wind. He was there because his truck was needed,
and because he owed certain things to Victor in exchange
for the false passes he'd obtained for Nora and himself.
The truck was hidden in a cedar forest at the bottom of the
steep trail up which Gaillard had led them, close to the
nearest road through the area. If the plane did get this far
without being intercepted, the sky-watchers at the nearest
enemy garrisons were certain to spot it when it made the
drop. There wouldn't be much time left to get the dropped
supplies out of the area, before the enemy sealed it off.

Twenty minutes before Gaillard's deadline, an American
Liberator came into sight, banking down out of the clouds
and flying past just under them. Victor and Gaillard aimed
their flashlights at it and blinked the prearranged signals.

But the plane kept going. It was beyond the drop site by the time Gaillard's men finally set the kerosene drums ablaze. Victor began to curse softly. The plane was vanishing into the night behind them.

It was almost gone before it began its turn. Victor stopped cursing. The whole basin was lit up by the kerosene-drum fires. The Liberator's crew would have had to be blind for none of them to spot it. And the enemy lookouts around the Luberon, Victor knew, would also have to be blind not to see the reflection of the blaze in the sky.

It came in very low on its return, doing a series of slow banking turns over the drop area. Large canisters fell from its opened hatch, each swinging from its own parachute. The wind blew some of them too far, but these struck the gnarled stone walls enclosing the drop site, and slid down into it. Gaillard's men were running to pick up the first canisters to hit the ground, four men to each.

The Liberator's hatch closed and its wings fluttered a farewell. It went into a steep climb, and the cloudbanks swallowed it. Victor stuffed his flashlight into his overcoat pocket and turned to Grayle, pivoting on his cane. "Get the truck ready to go." His voice was taut, juggling anxiety and exhilaration.

When he reached the truck Grayle continued past it to three of Gaillard's men standing lookout under the trees beside the road. There were others stationed farther off, but Grayle couldn't see any of them. The road was still dark in either direction.

"Those signal fires lit up the whole sky," one of the lookouts growled nervously. "We could see that plane clear as day."

"So start running," a second man snapped scornfully. "You sound like a rabbit, let's see if you move like one."

"When I run," the first snapped back, "I'll have your tail bouncing in front of me to guide the way."

The third man laughed, but there were strung-tight nerves in it. "Just pray we've all run before they can get here from Apt."

Apt was the nearest town with an enemy garrison. Grayle looked back up the trail. There was only a small glow left up there now, and as he watched it was snuffed out. He went back to the truck, swung up into the cab and started it. Letting out the brake, Grayle eased the truck forward until he had it between two cedars at the very edge of the road. Setting the brake, but leaving the motor running, he went around back to let down the tailgate and pull the canvas flaps aside. He was tying them in place when the first four of Gaillard's men reached him, lugging one of the canisters.

They lifted it inside the truck, and Grayle climbed up beside it. He manhandled the canister forward to make room for the rest to come. It weighed, he estimated, a bit over one hundred pounds. Some of the canisters that followed weighed more, others less. As he hauled each forward in turn Grayle had a brief but very intense memory of long nights at Les Halles.

The interior was more than half full when Victor called in, "That was the last. Quick!"

Grayle jumped down from the back, put up the tailgate and tied the flaps back together. Other than Victor, only Gaillard was left. His men had all gone, including the lookouts: scattering to get as far across the countryside as they could before dawn, to prearranged farm hideouts. From there they would move separately over subsequent nights, to rejoin their leader at his temporary command base, in the Ventoux. A few would remain behind. The enemy searchers might spend anywhere from a week to two weeks combing the Luberon chain before they would get discouraged and quit. When that happened people in the area would know, and the word would be passed along that it was safe for Gaillard's guerrillas to return.

Gaillard and Victor climbed up beside Grayle in the cab of the truck. He let out the brake and drove out onto the road, turning to follow its course through the forests, down into the Coulon valley. He drove fast, with his lights off. In a way it was safer at night, with less chance of turning a sharp bend and finding enemy vehicles suddenly coming at him. The German drivers didn't know the area well enough to drive through the dark with their headlights off, and could be spotted coming a long way off.

The truck was into the valley when they saw the headlights, approaching along a crossroad from the direction of Apt. Grayle swung off the road into the woods. When the truck was out of sight behind a dense growth of birch and chestnut trees, he set the brake and cut the motor. The three of them jumped out to watch, Gaillard holding his shotgun ready, Grayle drawing the Browning automatic from his pocket. Victor held only his cane, but his free hand undid two buttons of his overcoat to give him quick access to the revolver resting in his belt holster.

Minutes later the enemy convoy roared past them: an armored car with a mounted machine gun, followed by a command car and three open trucks filled with troops. The three men beside the hidden truck watched the convoy race off toward the drop site. It was unlikely that the troops would attempt to climb to it in the dark. Their intention would be to surround the area and seal escape routes until dawn, when German planes could drop paratroops into the enclosed basin. Then the paratroops would fan out from the drop site, while the ones below moved up in an encircling movement.

When the convoy was out of sight and beyond hearing range, Grayle climbed back behind the steering wheel and started the truck. Victor and Gaillard squeezed in beside him, and he drove back onto the road. He turned into the next country lane they reached. For the rest of the way north across the valley and up over the Vaucluse Plateau he followed little side roads to lessen the chance of running into trouble. Enemy vehicles tended to stick to the main roads.

There were still two hours left before dawn when the truck mounted the lower reaches of the Ventoux Massif. Grayle climbed the last stretch of passable graveled road, coming to a stop where a drift of frozen snow lay across it. Above that, deep snows blocked the approaches to the higher passes.

He blinked the headlights on and off quickly, just once. Men appeared out of the dark pine forest on either side of the truck, carrying rifles and shotguns. Victor and Gaillard climbed out. When they were identified, Victor signaled Grayle. He turned the truck to the right, into the forest, driving very slowly as he wound his way in and out among the trees, not stopping until he had pushed in as far as the truck could go. Dr. Cordeau appeared as Grayle climbed down. Trimarco was with him, to make sure his group got their share of the dropped supplies.

"The plane came?" Cordeau demanded.

It was Victor who answered, coming up beside Grayle. "I told you I could get the kind of weapons we need. There will be more coming, if you coordinate with me in your use of this load." He turned to Trimarco. "There is a more powerful radio transmitter and power pack in one of your packages, in addition to other items."

Cordeau was issuing swift orders to his men. As they began dragging the canisters from the truck and carrying them up the wooded slope in rope slings, more of his men kept emerging from the shadows to help. They were all needed. The way up became progressively more difficult: mounting timbered terraces of stepped-back cliffs, descending into a gorge, climbing out of it by way of steep slopes through a chaos of broken rocks and tangled brush. Finally they left the trees below, negotiating a path worn originally by wild sheep, through a break between eroded ridges. There was morning light when they entered the deep, remote grotto where the canisters were set down.

Victor pointed out certain of them that were marked with a red V. "These," he told Cordeau, Gaillard and Trimarco, "are not to be opened. Not until I give the word." He was exhausted, and spoke harshly to keep from slurring his words. "There will be more of them coming, and they are intended for a specific use. When we have enough of them, and I say so."

Cordeau let that go for the moment. "According to our agreement, half of the others are for my men."

Victor nodded. "Two-thirds of the rest for Gaillard: the other third for Trimarco."

Cordeau'ss men immediately began opening canisters

that did not bear the red V. Their excitement heightened as they began drawing out what they contained: Sten guns, the coveted submachine gun for guerrilla work, and the thirty-two-round magazines for them; antitank and antipersonnel mines; other special-purpose demolition devices; delayed-action pencil detonators; grenades; four .45 caliber pistols, two long-range sniper rifles and packs of ammunition for both.

But Trimarco kept looking at the forbidden canisters. "I think you should at least tell us what's in them."

Victor considered it. "All right, I don't want anyone opening them out of curiosity. They contain other special-purpose demolition units. Along with mortars and projectiles for them."

Cordeau whistled softly. "Those mortars—those could be very useful."

"London has its own use planned for them," Victor told him coldly. "And they'll send more, until we have enough to carry out that use. I repeat, they are not to be opened, until London signals for us to do so. If they are, there will be no further drops to us, of any kind."

"All right," Cordeau said placatingly. "Don't worry, I'll take personal responsibility for keeping them stored safely here, until you give the word."

Gaillard nodded, watching what was being taken out of the other canisters. "They will do well enough, for a start."

Grayle studied Victor's profile. Later, when they were alone, settling down to sleep through the rest of the day, Grayle asked him: "Do *you* know what London is saving those special canisters of yours for?"

"Yes, I know," Victor told him. He did not expand on that.

An SS search party came to the chateau two days later. There were five men hidden in the chateau at the time, waiting for Nora to take them into Spain. Two were from Guérini: prosperous-looking men who did not volunteer their profession or purpose, and weren't asked. Two were young Americans: a navigator and tailgunner who had escaped south after their bomber crashed near Lyon. The fifth was a British pilot.

There had been three previous searches of the chateau by units of the SS security service. The first time it had been part of the house-by-house sweep of the entire area conducted after the Germans had converted the underground quarries into their main fuel and ammunition depot. That sweep had resulted in three local casualties. A shotgun had been found hidden in the barn of a valley farmer, in violation of the edict that all weapons were to have been surrendered to the authorities. And a Jewish child was discovered hiding in the attic of a woman who lived two doors from Nora's mother.

The woman had driven a carving knife into the back of a trooper dragging the child away, wounding him severely. She had been hanged in the village square. The child had been sent to a concentration camp. The farmer had been deported to Germany as slave labor.

But they had found nothing incriminating at the chateau—not during that first sweep, nor in the two surprise spot checks that had come later. The security system Grayle maintained was never relaxed. When the SS came this time, they were spotted while still a long way off. The lookout posted at the top of the old defense tower was the tailgunner from the crew of the downed American bomber. Using the binoculars Grayle had given him, he observed the SS convoy when it appeared out of the Alpilles along the road leading down into the valley: a weapons carrier with a mounted machine gun and crew, followed by a command car and two troop carriers. He scrambled down the interior of the tower the instant the convoy turned into the hill road leading to the chateau.

By the time the SS arrived, the five escapees, and all weapons, were hidden inside the secret tunnel and cave under the cellars. The courtyard gate was open and Grayle was crouched just inside it, replacing two cracked bricks in a courtyard walk, when the vehicles drew to a halt outside. He straightened and put the trowel aside as an SS sergeant jumped from the back of one truck and swiftly led the troopers from it in an encircling movement to seal off the chateau and search the surrounding grounds. A lieutenant assembled the troopers from the other truck, preparing to enter the chateau. But Grayle's attention was on the command car.

Its driver had run around the front to open the other door. The officer who stepped out was tall and dark-eyed, his left cheek burn-scarred and most of his left arm missing. Grayle noted his insignia of rank as he advanced through the gateway to greet him.

"Good morning, Hauptsturmführer. I am Jean Hugonnet, the proprietor here." Grayle held out his hand.

The hauptsturmführer—the SS equivalent of captain—hesitated, and then shook the offered hand. He was not accustomed to such open politeness from the French.

"My name is Klaus Brandl," he offered.

"I'm pleased to make your acquaintance, sir," Grayle said. "Though I'm surprised we haven't met before. I recognize some of your men from previous visits."

"I was transferred recently from the Russian front. After a period of recuperation leave."

Grayle glanced at the empty sleeve. "The military profession has never been an easy one."

The officer took in Grayle's scarred forehead. "You speak from experience, perhaps?"

"No, I was never a soldier." Grayle explained how he had gotten the wound: during a rebel attack on an Algerian village where he'd been purchasing carpets for his firm.

The lieutenant, in deference to his superior's conversation with Grayle, had been holding his men in waiting beside their truck. Now he snapped a salute and asked, "Shall I begin searching the buildings, Hauptsturmführer?"

Grayle spoke quickly, to the commanding officer: "May I ask, Hauptsturmführer Brandl, that your men be especially careful while searching my studio? Paintings can be damaged so easily."

Brandl frowned at him. "You are an artist? I thought, a businessman."

"Art has always been my hobby. Since my retirement I have been able to indulge it more. I don't claim that my work is valuable, but to me it is, naturally."

"Naturally. If you will take us to your studio, you can be present while that is searched first."

"Thank you." Grayle led the way into the courtyard, with Brandl at his side.

The lieutenant followed with his troopers. Most of them he delegated to search the other buildings. Glancing at his superior, he called after them: "And be careful! You will not break anything!" Then he led three of his men into the abbey studio after Grayle and Brandl. The search there did not take long. When necessary, Grayle moved paintings stacked against the walls, so they could look behind them and test for secret compartments or trapdoors.

Brandl strolled about, looking at Grayle's pictures. When the lieutenant and his men had left he told Grayle, "I'm afraid I don't know much about art, and some of these are rather odd, but some I like very much."

Grayle smiled his appreciation of the compliment. "If I may ask, is this search merely routine, or . . ." He let it dangle.

"We are hunting for a group of terrorists. Two nights ago the enemy parachuted weapons to them, up in the Luberon."

"That is a long way from here," Grayle commented.

"Yes, luckily for you and the other people of this region. Though we have now spread the hunt to more distant areas, so far it *is* purely routine. In the region of the Luberon, however, we have been forced by this collaboration between the terrorists and the enemy to take hostages. Ten from every village. People must be made to understand that it is these terrorists, and England, that cause trouble, not us. If we fail to locate the terrorists and the weapons dropped to them, in the next two days, half of all the hostages will have to be executed. If the terrorists attempt attacks against us with these weapons in that area, they will cause the remainder of the hostages to be executed."

"That is regrettable," Grayle said evenly. "But—the fortunes of war."

"I am pleased that you are intelligent enough to understand this, Monsieur Hugonnet."

The expression that accompanied Grayle's shrug was just a shade sad. "After all, if we had conquered you, it would be French soldiers who would be occupying Germany, and the situation would be reversed."

"True, true . . ."

"My wife and daughter will have lunch ready in about half an hour. If you would care to join us?"

"I appreciate your offer. Very kind of you. But I've work to get on with, elsewhere."

"A glass of wine, then? Until your men have finished?"

Brandl nodded his acceptance. He accompanied Grayle to the chateau. Nora met them in the entrance foyer, with a puzzled look at Grayle, a frozen glance at the German officer.

"Nora," Grayle told her, "this is Hauptsturmführer Brandl. Will you bring us a bottle of the best wine, and two glasses."

Nora turned without a word and stalked off to the kitchen.

Brandl looked after her with a rueful smile. "A beautiful woman. But I'm afraid your wife doesn't share your reasonable understanding of the situation."

"Do women ever understand war? They find it difficult to accept the inevitable."

Brandl laughed, and they sat down facing each other across one of the tables in the main living room. It was Pascale who brought them the wine. As Grayle poured both glasses full, she stood there studying the German officer with open curiosity.

"Your daughter?" Brandl asked Grayle. "Such a lovely girl."

"What happened to your arm?" she asked him.

"Pascale . . ."

"That is all right," Brandl assured him. "Naturally the child is curious." He proceeded to tell Pascale about Russia.

She gave his words her full attention, while the eyes that

were so much like Nora's made their precise examination
of what she found written in his face.

Grayle took out a small pad and pencil, and began a
quick sketch. When he was finished he told Pascale, "You
should be helping your mother with lunch."

There was a bit of resentment in the look she gave him.
But what she saw in his eyes erased it. She nodded, and
hurried off to the kitchen. Grayle raised his glass and
drank: "To easier times."

Brandl took a sip of the wine and asked, a bit embarrassed, "Was that a drawing of me you were doing?"

Grayle handed him the sketchpad. Brandl studied his
portrait, obviously pleased. "A bit too flattering, perhaps
. . . I would love to send this to my mother in Stuttgart. Is
it possible for me to buy this from you?" ·

Grayle took the pad from him. He removed the sketch
and handed it to Brandl. "Let it be my present—for your
mother."

"I'm most grateful."

"Then perhaps I can ask a favor of you in return? I've
been meaning to try getting in touch with the officer in
command of your depot in the quarries. You've a lot of
troops to feed up there. I have poultry and eggs, and a
truck I use to transport other produce for some of the
farmers to market. I *could* supply some of the food you
need." Grayle's smile was that of a practical businessman.
"I understand from other men who supply such services in
other areas that the German army pays a fair price under
these circumstances."

"It may be a possibility," Brandl told him, as he put the
sketch carefully in his breast pocket. "I will speak to Colonel Stadler about the matter, this evening."

"I would appreciate that," Grayle said. He was hoping
for an extra bit of cover for the work Nora was doing—
another way of protecting her. He did not consider any
possibility beyond that.

When the search of the chateau and its grounds had
been completed, and the lieutenant reported they had
found nothing of interest, Grayle walked Brandl out to the

gateway of the courtyard. While the SS troops climbed back into their trucks, the two men shook hands again.

"I am sorry it was necessary to cause you this inconvenience," Brandl told Grayle.

"You have your duty to do." Grayle watched him get back into the command car. As the vehicles rolled away Nora came out to Grayle and put her arm around him. He asked her, "Did you send Pascale down to warn the village?"

"As soon as she returned to the kitchen. She'll be there well before *they* reach the village."

He pulled her closer to him. "You weren't very friendly to our SS man."

"It is what they expect," Nora told him. "And you were too friendly. Be careful of that. It could make them suspicious."

"I don't think it did, this time. Don't worry about me."

"Why not? You worry about me, all the time. And I'm hurting the life you wanted to have."

He took her face between his hands, tipping it back gently and kissing her lips.

She drew her head back, just a bit, looking up into his eyes. "You hate all this so much, don't you? And I keep dragging you deeper into it."

He kissed her again. "I'll go down and let the men out of the tunnel."

"I'll do it. And remember, lunch in half an hour."

He watched her go off to the outside entrance to the cellars. When she had descended the steps, and he could see her no longer, Grayle went into his studio and stood for some time studying the half-finished canvas waiting on the easel.

The sketches and watercolors from which he was drawing for the painting were spread around the easel: most of them of the Camargue marshes, in various seasons. But there were also the pastels he had done, long ago it seemed, of Nora strolling around their bedroom, her nude figure touched by the light of the many candles.

The light in the painting itself was that of the Camargue

when he'd last seen it: with sunlight trying to burn through the fog and mist of winter. One of the sketches beside the easel was of the wild horse that had charged at him out of that mist. But the horse was not in the painting. In its place was Nora, wreathed in the mists from which she was emerging: wading out of the marsh water into the tall rushes and reeds growing from the ooze of a mud bank; as though about to push through those and out of the painting.

Grayle called it his *Primavera*. It was the last work he was ever to complete.

46

While Nora was away, taking the three airmen and the two men from the Guérinis to Spain, the underground struggle between the Resistance and the occupation forces of the enemy began to change into open warfare.

Failing to locate the arms that had been dropped into the Luberon, or any of the guerrillas who had picked them up, the SS carried out its promise: half of the hostages seized in the Luberon region were executed in their village squares, while the rest of the villagers were forced to watch. Since young men had long ago disappeared into the forests and mountains to hide with the guerrilla bands, most of the hostages shot were elderly men. Three were women.

Gaillard's band retaliated the next day, using its share of the new Sten guns to ambush a three-vehicle Wehrmacht convoy outside Apt, killing a lieutenant and four troopers. From that point on the alternation of hostage executions and guerrilla retaliations escalated sharply. But, for the time, the area of Grayle's chateau and the village below remained untouched by it.

Brandl obtained Colonel Stadler's signed permit for Grayle to transport food to the garrison of the fuel and ammunition depot at the quarries.

Grayle returned from his first trip there to find Victor waiting for him in the chateau.

"Did they let you drive your truck inside?"

Grayle appraised Victor's expression. "Inside the barbed wire. But not inside the quarries, if that's what you mean. Why?"

"It's interesting," Victor said, thoughtfully. He did not elaborate on that.

The next day Victor triggered simultaneous operations carried out by Trimarco, Gaillard and Dr. Cordeau against the major railroad lines through the Rhône valley. Using the explosives that had been dropped to them, they destroyed tracks and demolished railroad bridges as trains carrying German troops moved over them. They derailed other trains carrying German supplies, blasted open the sealed freight cars and took from them whatever they could carry, including heavy machine guns and ammunition. What they couldn't loot from the trains they blew up.

This time German executions of French hostages were concentrated on cities and towns along the savaged rail lines. When Nora returned to Arles, the first sight that greeted her was of twenty bullet-torn civilian corpses sprawled along the base of the station wall. An official notice on the wall explained that the executions were a punishment for the acts of terrorism, and that as a further reprisal the mayor of Arles was being deported to a concentration camp in Germany. It also warned that anyone attempting to remove any of the bodies before nightfall, or even to touch them, would be shot on the spot.

Four SS guards stood to one side, holding submachine guns in readiness to carry out this threat. French men, women and children knelt on the ground before the bodies, some crying, some praying. Others simply stared at the dead, with newly hardened faces.

Nora had the look of someone sleepwalking when Grayle gripped her arm and turned her away, leading her to the truck.

Four nights later there was another drop of supplies by a plane from England, this time into a section of the Cévennes on the other side of the Rhône, where the largest band of guerrillas in the area was concentrated: more than two hundred men. They were led by a former French army major named Jourdan-Gassin, an extraordinary tall man in his fifties, with a great beak of a nose and haughty eyes. His resemblance to de Gaulle was often remarked upon; he knew it and was proud of it. He also had the General's stiffness in dealing with others, and the same ability to get people to obey him in spite of it.

While Jourdan-Gassin saw to it that most of the parachuted supplies were distributed among his own forces, there were again certain canisters marked with the red V. Grayle and his truck were called upon to transport them to the cave in the Ventoux where Dr. Cordeau kept the others stored in waiting.

Victor rode in the truck with Grayle on that journey. They were stopped three times by German roadblocks: first outside Uzès, then at the crossing of the Rhône and lastly along the road leading from Carpentras to the Ventoux. But in addition to the papers identifying Grayle and Victor as representatives of the firm doing military construction for the German army, Victor had acquired a new piece of protection: a card obtained by Antoine Guérini from Paul Carbone, the gangster who worked for the Germans. It was a Gestapo card, with Victor's photo, classifying him as one of its confidential agents.

A show of this card was enough: the guards at the roadblocks passed them through with no further questions, and without investigating what the truck carried. The special canisters were stored with the others in Dr. Cordeau's cave. And still Victor did not explain what they were for.

Jourdan-Gassin's guerrilla force immediately began using their new weapons and explosives to strike at targets south of the Cévennes. A small dam supplying power to a military construction plant was blown up. A German station used to jam broadcasts from the BBC was demolished. Explosions went off in restaurants and in movie theaters taken over for the exclusive use of German troops in Nîmes, Montpellier and Narbonne. Twelve Nazi collaborators were murdered within the space of four days. Miles of railroad tracks being used to move enemy troops and supplies were destroyed.

Soon SS and Gestapo units were being shifted away from the eastern side of the Rhône valley to hunt down Jourdan-Gassin's guerrillas in the west. Victor's response came on the heels of this move: he unleashed the forces of

Gaillard, Trimarco and Dr. Cordeau, to strike again at enemy trains and truck convoys in their areas.

Grayle watched Nora's nerves begin to tear as the toll of German retaliations against the civilian population mounted.

In a heated confrontation with Victor, Nora told him that what he was doing was not only inhuman, but also a strategic mistake: "You're too anxious to show what you can do, so you can warm your chilled blood a bit with the thrill of violence. It is *too soon,* Victor."

"That," he replied, "is a division of opinion that at this point runs through the entire Resistance movement. Between the activists and the temporizers. You are a temporizer. I am not."

"At this point you should be confining your activism to enlarging, arming and training your Resistance groups. So they'll be ready to go into action when the right time comes. Until the Allied armies land in France, and we can actually join our efforts to theirs and defeat the enemy, open attacks are premature. All you'll accomplish is to get your fighting men wiped out by superior forces, and cause more innocent civilians to be slaughtered."

"I'm accomplishing more than that, Nora. When it comes to training, there is no substitute for actual combat. By fighting now, our men will become experienced veterans, able to operate properly when the final battles do come. As for the civilian hostages executed by the enemy, every time that happens more people volunteer to give us active support. And one other point: The enemy troops we're keeping occupied here can't be sent to help fight the Allied armies."

Grayle listened in silence. Nothing he could say, he felt, was going to change what was coming.

"It's premature," Nora repeated angrily. "The kind of pressure you are putting on the enemy around this area will soon make it impossible to operate our escape line."

"Perhaps," Victor answered quietly, "the time has come to stop escaping and fight back."

"Not yet it hasn't. If you go on this way, the Nazis will have wiped out everybody willing to fight, before the Allies get here. My escape line contributes to the ultimate goal. What you are doing is destructive."

"I haven't done anything to draw the enemy to your escape line so far," Victor pointed out. "I intend to try my best not to, for as long as possible. Fair enough?"

He kept his word. When the relative quiet of the area around the chateau and the village below came to a sudden end, it was from a source that had not been anticipated.

Grayle and others commissioned by the German army to supply its food needs were paid a reasonable price for what they delivered. But the occupation forces had other methods of feeding themselves. One was through requisition teams sent to comb the countryside. Five German troopers on motorcycles led the way up the foothills some miles above the chateau, following the course of the mountain stream. They were followed by an empty military truck. When the slope became too steep for the truck to climb any farther, the motorcycles parked beside it. The truck's driver and the sergeant in charge of the team joined the motorcycle troopers, climbing the rest of the way to Madame Lorenzi's sheep station, carrying ropes and submachine guns.

Jumeau had run away to hide when he'd heard the approaching vehicles. Madame Lorenzi stood in front of her cabin, fists clenched on her hips, facing the troopers as they advanced to her.

"What can I do for you?" she demanded.

"Your sheep," the sergeant informed her. "We are entitled to requisition a certain percentage of what you have. Thirty percent, to be exact. But this time we will take only enough to fill our truck."

"Hold on! How much are you offering to pay me?"

The sergeant laughed. "We have already paid you, by staying here in your country to protect you from the enemy." He gestured for his men to begin roping sheep and drag them down to the truck.

Madame Lorenzi abruptly turned on her heel and went inside the cabin. Later, those who survived and learned what she did cited it as further proof that shepherds were not like normal people: spending their lives alone except for their sheep and dogs, they lost the ability to comprehend what the reaction of others might be to their actions.

Going to her knees on the packed-earth floor in front of the raised fireplace, Madame Lorenzi dragged split logs out of the storage recess under it. At the back wall of the recess were several bricks which she was able to pry out with her fingertips. She pulled her double-barreled shotgun from the concealment hole behind the opening.

The sergeant stepped into the cabin doorway behind her as she was rising from her knees. When she began turning toward him he had time only to register the essential: the weapon in her hands. His trigger-squeeze was an instant, automatic response. The burst from the submachine gun tore her chest apart and spun her away from the fireplace, slamming her against the wall like a huge broken doll flung aside. She must have been dead when she fell away from the wall. The tightening of her finger across both triggers could only have been a final, meaningless spasm of the nerves in her hand. A shower of dirt struck the sergeant as the close-packed loads hammered into the earth floor between them. He leaped backward out of the doorway, frightened but untouched by any of the shotgun pellets.

From his hiding place, Jumeau heard the gunfire, but could not comprehend its significance. He remained where he was. Not until he heard the motorcycles and truck driving away, down the steep slopes, did he cautiously emerge and make his way back to the cabin.

The soldiers had taken the shotgun away with them. Madame Lorenzi's dog was huddled in a corner of the room, trembling as it kept watch over her sprawled body. Jumeau sat down on the floor beside her. It was some time before he accepted that she was dead. Tears streamed down his face as he stroked her cheek. He was still crying when he got to his feet, stumbled to the kitchen cabinet and chose the sharpest knife.

* * *

The village below the chateau was the nearest place for soldiers from the quarry depot to spend a few hours' liberty. There were two of them there when Jumeau entered the cafe. They were drinking at a table near the warmth of the fireplace. Jumeau went past them to the bar and asked for a pastis. He gulped it down, and then walked to the fireplace behind the soldiers to warm his hands.

He drew the knife out from inside his sheepskin coat before he turned from the fire. Taking careful aim, he plunged the knife into the back of the neck nearest him. He yanked the knife free as the soldier toppled forward across the table, spilling off it to the floor. The other one had leaped to his feet, his chair falling over behind him. He still had not quite grasped what was happening when Jumeau drove the knife into his stomach, low and deep, and ripped upward as though gutting an animal.

Everyone else in the cafe was frozen in position, stunned, staring at Jumeau and the two dead soldiers at his feet. Jumeau threw down the bloodied knife and ran out. He kept running until he was outside the village, heading across the valley toward the chateau.

Only Grayle and Nora were there at the time. Grayle was on watch at the top of the ancient defense tower, and he focused the binoculars on the figure that crossed the road and kept coming, alternately running and walking. By the time the figure vanished into the wooded ravine that led up to the chateau, Grayle knew it was Jumeau.

Leaving the tower, he met Jumeau as he climbed out of the ravine. Words spilled from Jumeau as he threw his arms around Grayle, clinging to him. When Grayle finally understood what Jumeau was trying to tell him, his blood ran cold.

Taking him into the chateau and quickly telling Nora what had happened, Grayle hurried back to the tower with the binoculars. People were leaving the village: two on bicycles, then several more. They took the valley road, in the direction of Arles. Two more came from the village, on foot, each carrying a suitcase. But these two did not take the road. They crossed it, and kept coming.

Nora was running from the chateau to the tower when Grayle climbed down. "What have you done with Jumeau?" he asked her.

"I put him in the tunnel with food and water for a couple days, and told him to stay there until one of us comes for him." She started to push past him toward the truck shelter beside the tower. "I have to get down there and . . ."

"They're already coming," he cut in.

Nora turned and ran to the ravine. Grayle looked at his watch and went to the truck. He drove it out to the start of the hill road. As he climbed down from it, Nora came back with her mother and Pascale.

"Most of the people are staying in the village," she told him raggedly. "Although they know what is certain to happen."

"What do you expect of people?" her mother asked tightly. "There aren't many prepared to leave the only lives they know behind, even when common sense tells them it is the only possbility for survival."

Grayle took her suitcase and Pascale's, and put them inside the truck. "Nora, there's a train from Arles to Marseilles leaving in half an hour. You've just got time to make it. The Germans won't find out what's happened here for a while, so your ordinary papers should be all you need to get through. Drive to Arles snd take the train. In Marseilles take Pascale and your mother to Meme Guérini."

She was startled. "Meme?"

"I talked to him about this possibility the last time I saw him. He'll put them with a good family. One with no connection to the Resistance. They'll be safe there."

He didn't add that it would be best if Nora stayed there, too. There was no time to argue about something that she would never accept.

Madame Cesari was looking at him in a strange way. "I want you to know," she said softly, "I have always liked you—cared for you." She reached out a hand, placing her palm flat against his heart, the gesture oddly touching. "Even that first time, when you . . ." She dropped her hand, not finishing it.

"I know," Grayle told her, and kissed her cheek before turning to Pascale.

"It may be that we won't be able to see each other again, for a long time." He took her in his arms and kissed her. "Please remember though—I love you, very much."

"I love you, too . . . ." Pascale suddenly began to cry, her arms tightening around his neck.

When they were gone in the truck, he climbed back up the tower with the binoculars.

It was almost two hours later that two motorcycle troopers rode down out of the Alpilles and turned in to the village. Grayle doubted that anyone had summoned them. It was either a routine patrol of the area, or they were going to spend a few hours of liberty at the cafe, like the two Jumeau had killed.

Less than ten minutes passed before they reappeared out of the village, racing their motorcycles back up into the Alpilles. Grayle stayed atop the tower, waiting.

Within an hour there were two military cars and three truckloads of troops down there. Some of the troops surrounded the village, setting up several heavy machine guns. The rest entered the village. A police car sped up from the south, from the gendarmerie in Arles. It was followed by a civilian Peugeot-75 that almost certainly carried members of the Gestapo.

A short time after these had entered the village, a military car left it, and took the hill road leading to the chateau. Grayle climbed down the tower, put the binoculars away and strolled to the courtyard gate as the car pulled to a halt. Four soldiers holding submachine guns ready jumped out. Grayle was relieved to see that the officer who climbed out after them was the lieutenant who had been with Brandl during the last search of the chateau. He opened the gate and advanced to meet him, holding out his hand.

"Good to see you again, Lieutenant."

The lieutenant, a bit embarrassed; shook his hand very briefly. Then, conscious of his men watching, he said stiffly, "I am sorry for the necessity, Monsieur Hugonnet, but we must search your place."

"Another routine spot check? I'm surprised. You know I have always cooperated with your commanders."

"I do know, but this is an extraordinary circumstance. Two of our men have been murdered in the village. It seems that the terrorist who committed this atrocity has worked for you here. So we cannot overlook the possibility that he would come here to hide."

Grayle looked puzzled. "A man who worked for me?"

"He is called Jumeau. Real name unknown."

Grayle had no doubt that some in the village had been pleased to implicate him in what had happened. For them, his volunteering to provide food supplies to the enemy had branded him as an active collaborator. "Yes, Jumeau did work here in the past. But he left long ago. I must say, I'm surprised to learn that he has become a terrorist. But then, I haven't seen him in over a year."

"Nevertheless, we must conduct this search." The lieutenant added, politely, "I will see to it that nothing is damaged."

"Thank you."

The lieutenant led his men into the courtyard. Grayle accompanied them to his studio. The search there was brief. When the lieutenant led his men out to search the rest of the place, Grayle remained under the abbey arcade, watching and waiting. The search of the chateau and other buildings, and of the grounds was quite thorough. But it failed to lead to the cave where Jumeau was hidden at the end of the concealed tunnel.

When it was finished, the lieutenant met Grayle in the courtyard. "Your truck is not here, I see."

"My wife drove it to Arles. She took her mother and our daughter to Marseilles by train, to visit with friends."

The lieutenant took a small notebook and pen out. "I am relieved that you have volunteered this information." He crossed out something written in the notebook. "I already knew that your daughter and mother-in-law left their house in the village. Most sensible of them, considering the situation."

"What's happening down there?"

"Hostages are being taken, of course. If the murderer is not found by tomorrow morning, some of them will certainly be executed. I suggest that you remain here, Monsieur Hugonnet. It would be much safer for you."

Grayle watched the lieutenant and his men drive away. It was dusk when he let Jumeau out of the tunnel. They took turns standing watch through the night that followed.

Nora returned late the next morning. "What is happening in the village?" she asked as soon as she saw Grayle.

He told her what the lieutenant had said. "More than that, I don't know."

She drew a harsh breath. "I have to find out."

"We had better keep away from the village, for a time."

"I'm going," Nora said flatly, and started back to the truck. Grayle sighed, and went with her.

They were stopped by one of the roadblocks just outside the village. Two SS men aimed submachine guns at them and ordered them to get out of the truck with their hands up. Luckily, the sergeant who had been present during Brandl's search of the chateau, and who knew that the commander at the quarry depot had an arrangement with Grayle, came out of a village street at that point and recognized them.

He ordered the soldiers to lower their weapons, and asked Grayle, "What do you want here?"

"What's happening?" Grayle countered quickly, before Nora could say anything.

"Two of our men were killed in the cafe." The sergeant hesitated. "I had better take you to Hauptsturmführer Brandl. Come!"

They went with him into a steep, narrow street of cobbled steps, and through a passage along the side of the church. There were troops posted at corners, but not a single civilian in sight anywhere.

Nora came to a slow halt as they entered the Place Clemenceau, staring at the great tree. Six people hung by their necks from the branches that spread over the square. Four men and two women. One of the men was Pierre-Baptiste Chabot, the mayor of the village.

Two men coming from the church diverted to intercept Grayle, Nora and the sergeant. One was a Gestapo agent, wearing the inevitable black leather coat. The other was Alain Nugon, in his uniform as adjutant of the Arles gendarmerie.

"What have we here?" the Gestapo man demanded.

"I was taking them to see the hauptsturmführer," the sergeant explained. "They . . ."

"He is busy with other matters at the moment," the Gestapo man interrupted him, "questioning the villagers inside the church, with the aid of our French agents." He examined Nora and Grayle with something akin to pleasure. "Are they of this village?"

"No, we're not," Grayle told him. "We only came to have a drink at the cafe."

"You have chosen an unfortunate time for it . . ."

Nugon spoke up for the first time: "These two are of no interest for us. Colonel Stadler himself has commissioned them to help supply his regiment. They've been most helpful to him. So much, that you'll find many of the villagers detest them."

"Ah, I see . . ." The Gestapo man had abruptly lost interest.

Nora was looking at the entrances to the streets leading off the square. "Where is everybody?" she asked Nugon softly.

It was the Gestapo man who answered her: "They are inside the church. The entire village has been made hostage."

Nora stared at him, narrow-eyed. "Everybody? What about the children?"

"Everybody," he assured her amiably. "You might pass this information on to everyone you meet. Perhaps it will eventually reach the ears of the terrorists." He gestured toward the bodies dangling from the tree. "If there is any further act of terrorism in this region, the village will be wiped out, with everyone in it."

He turned and strolled away. Nora studied Nugon. "I can't believe you would be part of this."

"I do what I have to," he said tonelessly. "It is no different from *your* cooperation with the occupation army."

Grayle said, "He meant that, about killing everyone."

Nugon nodded. "They'll be kept inside the church. The next bit of violence and the interior will be soaked with gasoline and set afire, with the doors and windows blocked so no one gets out." There was no expression in his face or inflection in his voice. "I advise you to leave now. And stay away."

Nora was looking again at the dead hung from the tree, their bodies turning slowly in the confused winds entering the square from various passageways. Her face was utterly blank; there was an emptiness in her eyes. Grayle put an arm around her waist and led her away. The sergeant conducted them back to the truck.

As Grayle drove to the chateau with Nora beside him, she began to weep, in a way that prickled the hairs at the back of his neck. There was no sound to her weeping, none at all.

47

Because the parachuting of supplies into the Cévennes had been accomplished without being detected by the enemy, Victor chose that area rather than the Luberon for the next drop. It was a wise choice. As on the previous occasion, Jourdan-Gassin's men carried out the pickup with no trouble. Again, certain of the canisters were marked with the red V. Again, Victor came for Grayle's help with the truck in shifting these canisters to the Ventoux.

But this time Grayle was not at the chateau, though the truck was. He'd taken the train to Marseilles: to ask Meme Guérini to begin negotiations with his collaborator friend, Carbone, for special papers that would allow him and Nora to leave safely by ship with Pascale and Madame Cesari—if he had to get them out quickly and the escape route was blocked. But he'd told Nora that the purpose of his trip was to obtain increased gas supplies.

"He should be back tomorrow morning," Nora told Victor.

"It can't wait until then." Victor regarded her for a moment before explaining: "I've arranged a meeting of all our key leaders in the area, for tonight."

It was Nora's turn to study Victor for a moment. "The time has come to use those special supplies of yours?"

His hesitation was brief. "Yes. I've never driven a truck before, but I suppose I can manage it if . . ."

"I'll go with you," Nora told him quietly. "I want to be present at this meeting."

They picked up Jourdan-Gassin in the Cévennes. Because it would have looked odd for a woman to be driving a truck with two men beside her, it was Jourdan-Gassin who drove them east across the Rhône. As on the last such trip, Victor's Gestapo card got them past the enemy road-blocks without the truck being searched.

The truck began the climb into the Ventoux Massif through a cold dusk with a flutter of snowflakes in the bleak light. Even Jourdan-Gassin had to acknowledge the efficiency of the security Dr. Cordeau had established for the zone around his command base. Lookouts with binoculars were posted atop the heights and patrols prowled the perimeters of the security zone, where they could give warning of an enemy encirclement attempt. If the enemy force was too large to cope with, there would be ample time for Cordeau's men to disperse before the alternative escape routes had been blocked, and join up again at a distant, predetermined rendezvous point. If the enemy was a relatively small search patrol it would be allowed to get inside the security zone: to be ambushed and wiped out by guards concealed in camouflaged outposts along the few approaches to Cordeau's base.

With so much security around it, there was no need for more at the command base itself. There was only one man on guard outside the cave that held most of Cordeau's explosives, along with the store of Victor's special canisters—and he was there merely to warn off any of Cordeau's men who became overly curious about the mysterious canisters.

The man on guard when Nora arrived with Victor and Jourdan-Gassin was Jumeau. Grayle had taken him to Cordeau to get him out of the way. Though Jumeau could not be counted on in a battle situation, he was dependable enough for routine watch duty. Happy to see a familiar face, he jumped up from the flat rock on which he'd been sitting and pumped Nora's hand while the new supply of Victor's canisters were carried inside.

The other four key Resistance leaders Victor had alerted for this meeting met them outside the cave. Nora had never met Dr. Cordeau and Anatole Gaillard before. The other two she knew well; but though Sylvio Trimarco's presence was not a surprise, the other one was: Alain Nugon, wearing his adjutant's uniform.

It took her a moment to adjust to it as she automatically

took his extended hand. "Have you been part of all this from the start?"

Nugon nodded. "And since they deported our mayor, I have had to assume charge of the Arles Resistance sector."

"You were lucky to escape suspicion when they took the mayor."

"He is not the kind they would be able to get much information out of," Nugon said simply. "I can only hope he will live through it, to see the results."

Dr. Cordeau led them to his own command post: a larger grotto, lit by kerosene lamps and a wood fire. They seated themselves on blankets close to the warmth of the fire. Victor opened a military survey map of the Alpilles and spread it out on the cave floor where they could all see it.

"This is our target area." He took out a red crayon and made a mark on the map. "And this is our objective."

"The underground quarries?" There was a shade of awe with the excitement in Dr. Cordeau's voice.

Victor nodded. "The enormous supplies of fuel and ammunition the enemy has stored inside them."

"That supply depot," Jourdan-Gassin pointed out, "has been made virtually impregnable."

"Virtually." Victor smiled. "They've sealed up all the quarry entrances except two, and those *are* impregnable. But, of course, that is not what I have in mind."

Trimarco took the crayon from him. "I know the exact location of every entrance they sealed up. And the best way to reach each of them." He made a dot on the map with the crayon. "This is the one we've picked, because it's farthest from the two they've left usable. I lead my group in, cut through the barbed wire, get to this one and blow it open."

"And while you're taking all the time to do that," Alain Nugon said, "the enemy will have detected the penetration and be all over you."

"No," Victor told him. "For two reasons. First, the enemy will be too busy elsewhere. That is the purpose of the mortars, the other explosives, all your weapons and ammunition. We are going to attack the perimeter of their defenses, at three points far from the place Trimarco will be penetrating. With everything we have."

He spoke calmly, but the set of his mouth told Nora of the intensity behind it. "And while all their forces are engaged in stopping our diversionary assaults, Trimarco will have reached the sealed entrance he's marked there. And blown it open, very quickly. One of the canisters in this last shipment is marked with a blue X, in addition to the red V. That one contains exceptionally devastating explosives. Plus a package of new delay-action detonators. They work the same as the ones you already have used: insert into the explosive, and break it. The only difference is the timing. The ones you've used so far were timed to detonate in thirty minutes to two hours, depending on their color. These are much quicker. The white ones detonate in five minutes, the red ones in ten minutes, the green ones in twenty."

Gaillard's grin had anticipation in it, but no vestige of mirth. "If Trimarco can get inside fast enough, and stick just a couple of timed explosives among the nearest boxes of ammunition or drums of gasoline . . ."

Trimarco nodded. "That whole place is a bomb. Each section that blows up will set off the next."

Dr. Cordeau said softly, "It would be the biggest fireworks display anybody ever saw."

Jourdan-Gassin had made his decision: "All right. When?"

"Four nights from now," Victor said. "February twelve. That gives Cordeau, Gaillard and Nugon time to get their men to their places in the Alpilles, and for you to bring yours over from the Cévennes."

Nora had been holding herself in until she could be sure that her voice would be controlled. "Everyone in my village is being held hostage against any further act of violence in that area. If you do this . . ."

"Your mother and daughter," Victor cut in quietly, "have already been taken to safety."

"There are all the rest, damn you!" Nora stopped herself, and reasserted control over her voice. "*Think* about it: an entire village. And all the other hostages, in St. Remy and Fontvielle and every other village around the Alpilles. They'll *all* be killed."

Jourdan-Gassin told her stiffly, "This is not a game we're playing, my dear girl. It is a war."

Alain Nugon shook his head. "Even in war one has to weigh what is gained by an action against what is lost. Until the Allies land in France, a sacrifice this great isn't justified by the results."

"But it is," Victor informed him. "London has learned that most of the fuel and ammunition in those quarries is scheduled to be shipped to help Rommel fight the Allied armies. Their convoys will be too heavily guarded to hit. The only place we can stop it is here, at the quarries. And if we can do it, we'll be saving a great many lives—among the Free French forces, as well as the British and Americans."

"This plan," Nora asked Victor, "did it originate in London? Or is it something *you* sold to them?"

"I explained what is in the quarries, and the possibility of destroying the entire supply depot, yes."

Nugon said softly: "Wars are supposed to be fought between armed men. A soldier going into battle knows his danger and his chances. *That* is fighting a war. Hostages are something else."

Nora seized on his words gratefully. "We're talking about killing children, women, helpless men . . ."

"If anyone kills them," Dr. Cordeau reminded her angrily, "it won't be us. It will be the Germans. Get that straight in your head!"

Nora felt a horrible tiredness taking possession of her. She remembered the bodies sprawled along the wall at the Arles station, the six corpses hanging from the tree in the village square. "But if you do this thing, you'll cause them to be killed."

"We're fighting a vicious enemy," Jourdan-Gassin said. "We have no hope of ever beating them, unless we fight as viciously as they do."

She looked at their faces, one after the other: Jourdan-

Gassin, Trimarco, Gaillard, Cordeau. "Even if we win," she asked wearily, "what will we have won if we've become the same as they are?"

"When the war is over," Victor told her, and his voice became surprisingly gentle, "we can all go back to being what we were before it."

"Can we? And all the people who will have died because of you, will they be able to go back to being what they were?"

Nugon rose to his feet. "I stand against it."

Victor looked up at him. "You can't stop it, Alain. You can only help, or not help."

"I won't help you with this. I won't lend any of my men to it."

"I'm sorry about that, Alain. But we still have enough men to get it done—without yours." Cold sarcasm coated Victor's voice: "That way, it will still happen, but your conscience can comfort itself with your lack of responsibility for any of it."

Nugon turned and walked out of the grotto, into the night. Nora got up to follow him. Victor stopped her with a raised hand: "Wait, just a moment. I don't expect you to take part in this, of course. But . . ." He stopped himself, because he had been about to use Grayle's name. He resumed: "But your husband can be of help with the truck. If he were to deliver food supplies to the quarries, at the proper moment—with explosives inside some of the crates and barrels, timed to go off after he'd left—that would create a bit of extra diversion for us."

She was on her feet. "No."

"I don't think that even you can make that decision for him. He does think for himself. I'll speak to him, tomorrow."

"He won't do it," she told him flatly, and hurried out.

But she stopped when she was in the open, having difficulty breathing. She opened her mouth, gulping the cold air into her lungs. More snow was falling, the fat, soft flakes melting against her face. She found herself walking to where Jumeau sat, on the flat rock outside the other cave.

"I have to get something," she said, in a voice that was not her own.

Jumeau nodded as she went past him into the cave with the explosives and special canisters. She came out minutes later, and went down the path to the place where the truck had been left.

Nugon was standing between it and his car. "What took you so long?"

"I . . . was sick."

He couldn't see her face well in the dark, but her voice *was* sick. "Can you drive?"

She nodded.

"Stick close behind my car," he told her. "In case of roadblocks."

They ran into only one, just above Apt. The guards took a look at Nugon's uniform and papers, and accepted his statement that the woman with the truck was with him. They passed her through after him, and Nugon stayed with her until she turned off below the Alpilles, taking the hill road to the chateau. He drove on alone then, to his home in Fontvielle.

Inside Dr. Cordeau's command post, Jourdan-Gassin interrupted Victor as he went through the details of the planned assault for a second time: "Let's break out those mortars, detonators and new explosives," he said as he got to his feet. "We have to begin familiarizing ourselves with them."

The others followed him outside. Attempting to rise, Victor found his bad leg had gone dead on him again. Cursing himself for a cripple, he seized the cane with both hands and slowly shoved himself upright with it. Leaning heavily on the cane, he laboriously hobbled out after the others. He was flung backward by the explosion in the other cave that seemed to shake the entire mountain.

Grayle got off the train at Arles the next morning and saw Nora waiting in the truck beside the station. She moved over to make room for him behind the steering wheel, but she didn't look at him when he climbed in beside her. He saw the way she was staring through the windshield, her eyes utterly empty.

"What's happened?" he asked her.

There was only a very slight shake of her head. Her lips were clamped.

Grayle started the truck without asking her again. Something was very wrong, and he wanted her at the chateau where he could pry it out of her with care. She remained silent through the drive, her figure pressed stiffly against the back of the seat, the empty eyes staring straight ahead.

The car Victor had gotten from Guérini was parked outside the courtyard. Nora looked at it for a moment. Then she strode past it and through the courtyard to the chateau. Grayle had to lengthen his stride to catch up with her.

Victor sat in a living room chair, facing them as they came in. One hand held the knob of his cane. His other hand rested on the arm of the chair. Grayle saw the glint of the revolver it held and stepped in front of him, blocking Nora.

She touched the back of his shoulder. "Don't do that. He came to kill me. Let him do it." In the same listless tone: "I thought you were dead, Victor, when you didn't come last night. I'm sorry you're not."

Victor laughed. Grayle had never heard him laugh like that. "My survival, Nora, doesn't matter. You've won. It can't be done now."

"Too many people would have died . . ."

"And those *you* killed—weren't they people?" Victor used the cane to help him stand. The gun in his other hand was leveled at Grayle's midsection. "Stand aside or go with her. You can choose but you can't save her this time. It has to be done."

Grayle didn't move. "Tell me about it, Victor."

"She blew up everything we had at Cordeau's base. Everything we needed—and people we needed. I'm alive. So is Gaillard, though he's hurt badly. Jourdan-Gassin is dead. Cordeau is dead. Trimarco is dead. Even Jumeau is dead."

There was an involuntary spasm in Grayle's face. "Jumeau . . ."

"*Now* you understand. She killed him. And Trimarco. And . . ."

Grayle spun away from him, his arm slashing at Nora. His open hand struck the side of her face with a sharp-edged sound that created a hard, flat echo within the room. The force of it hurled her against a chair and it crashed to the floor with her.

Victor lurched forward, startled by Grayle's attack on her, and Grayle twisted and kicked his cane away, making him stumble off-balance. One hand grabbed the revolver's barrel and turned it aside. The side of his clenched fist clubbed Victor across the temple.

Victor felt the gun pulled from his strengthless fingers as he fell. He scarcely felt anything when he struck the floor.

The room around him was darkly blurred but it seemed to him that he had never entirely lost consciousness, or only very briefly. He was aware that he was slumped into a chair with his wrists bound behind it, drawn down to its back legs. He felt rope tightening around his left ankle, fastening it to a front leg of the chair; then his right ankle.

He heard Nora, her tone hopeless: "There is no point to this. I knew when I did it that I would have to die for it. And I deserve to . . ."

And Grayle's voice, was it sometime later? ". . . boots for climbing, and heavy sweaters under your coat. Then pack a knapsack with food. Only food, nothing else."

When Victor's vision finally cleared he was alone in the room. He struggled at the ropes securing his ankles and wrists to the legs of the chair, but soon gave that up and just waited. It seemed a long time before Grayle came back into the room and placed an envelope on one of the tables.

"Something for you to read, Victor, when you get loose."

"You're a bit too efficient with knots for me to get free. If you leave me like this . . ."

"Your feet are on the floor," Grayle interrupted. "All you have to do after we've gone is to start edging across the floor, *with* the chair, until you reach the kitchen. I've left a knife on a chair there. It's the right height for you to get a hand on."

"In my condition that could take days."

"A few hours, probably." Grayle examined the ropes binding Victor. "Don't pull at them, you'll only hurt yourself."

"Where do you think you can take her where she'll be safe?" There was no anger now in Victor. His tone was merely reasonable. "Back to Algeria, perhaps?" He shook his head. "You'll never get her out of France. No chance at all, don't you know that? There is no border crossing safe for you any longer. And that emergency way out by ship you told me about will have become a trap. There is such a thing as a telephone, remember. If the Germans don't get you, *our* people will. No matter how fast you go, no matter where you go, they'll be waiting for you."

Grayle stood looking down at him. "Are you trying to persuade me to kill you, Victor?"

"What would that serve? Everyone at Cordeau's base knows she did it. *They'll* be spreading the word by now—to the safe-houses along every escape route, to the Guérinis in Marseilles, the Basques in the Pyrenees, everywhere. And even if you did reach Spain, Nora is wanted by the authorities there, and no consulate will help you—not when they've learned how she betrayed us. But you won't get that far. Nora knows that, if you don't."

"I'm going now," Grayle said, as though he hadn't heard a word. "Remember, push toward the kitchen, just a little at a time. Don't try to make it quickly. You'll only tire yourself, or fall over with the chair."

Victor tipped his head back a bit, to study Grayle's face more easily. "Why are you doing this?" he asked, with genuine curiosity. "When you know all you will accomplish is to throw your life away with hers?"

"She's my life," Grayle told Victor. He smiled down at him. "You always wanted everything explained. I told you once, words are a poor language, for explaining certain things."

Victor's answering smile was bleak. "Don't you have a feeling of having done all this before? Only this time it isn't an innocent child you are trying to take across a desert to safety. Nora knew she was condemning some of us to death when she set that detonator."

"Ahmed wasn't an innocent," Grayle told him quietly. "He knew he was condemning Bou Idriss to death, too, when he watched him kill Salah and the other two so he'd have enough water to go on. There really aren't many innocents in this world, Victor." He reached out and touched Victor's cheek with his fingertips. "You are one of the very few I know."

And then he turned away, and was gone.

48

They were last seen in the heights of the Pyrenees, four days later, by a Basque guide. He saw them at a distance above him, two figures making their way through deep snow covering an incline leading up into the peaks. It was an exceedingly dangerous route for anyone to attempt. Only a greater fear of using any of the few relatively safer routes that could still be negotiated in that part of the winter, could have driven anyone to try this way. The Basque realized who they must be, and started down the lower mountain slopes to alert the Resistance patrols that Grayle and Nora had slipped past them.

It was night before he found one of the patrols. By morning that area of the Pyrenees was struck by a violent snowstorm, making pursuit impossible.

What happened to Grayle and Nora in that storm can be reconstructed from the way they were found.

Nora fell into a crevasse, and her leg was broken. Grayle dragged her out and went on, carrying her. Until his strength gave out, and he could take her no farther. Finding a niche in a slope that would protect them from the full force of the freezing wind, he pulled her inside it with him.

Sitting there, leaning back and drawing her close to him, he cradled her in his arms, her head lying against his chest, while the numbing cold did its work.

That was how they were found eventually, frozen in that position, their joined figures encased in gleaming ice.

EPILOGUE

But even when he knew, I think, that he was going to his death, he had refused to accept that as an ending, or a defeat.

When I finally cut myself loose from the chair to which he had tied me, I went first to the envelope he had left on the table. It contained his will, naming me its executor and leaving everything to Pascale: the chateau, accounts in certain banks and his work. I left the chateau and crossed the courtyard—but I was quite sure, even before I entered his studio, what I would find.

Before he had left the chateau with Nora, he had, in his own way, at last completed what he had set out to do so long before, when he had first come to Europe in his twenties.

Each painting was signed now: *Nicholas Grayle.*

**VOLUME I
IN THE EPIC
NEW SERIES**

*The Morland
Dynasty*

The FOUNDING

by Cynthia Harrod-Eagles

THE FOUNDING, a panoramic saga rich with passion and excitement, launches Dell's most ambitious series to date—THE MORLAND DYNASTY.

From the Wars of the Roses and Tudor England to World War II, THE MORLAND DYNASTY traces the lives, loves and fortunes of a great English family.

A DELL BOOK $3.50   #12677-0
